ROUGHED UP

TROPHY DOMS NEW YORK #4

KATE HAWTHORNE

ROUGHED UP

KATE HAWTHORNE

Roughed Up
Trophy Doms New York #4
by Kate Hawthorne

Copyright © 2024
Kate Hawthorne

Edited by | Jordan Buchanan

Cover Design | Amai Designs

DEDICATION

For those who are willing to pay the price for love.

CONTENT NOTE

Roughed Up includes on page transactional encounters which are under-negotiated and dubious in nature between one main character and multiple third parties. There is also a scene where a main character is drugged by a third party, resulting in physical (not-sexual) injury.

CHAPTER 1
DYLAN

It was a slow Saturday night at Tryst, but the man who just walked in the door looked like he had the potential to make my whole night. He was tall and tanned, with tousled brown hair and thick-rimmed black glasses, both doing their best to obscure his red-rimmed eyes. He looked like he'd either been crying or not sleeping. Maybe both. Lord knew I was familiar with the look. It was one I'd been wearing myself since my parents cut me off from their financial support and I'd been struggling to keep my head above water.

New York City was expensive, even more so without the cushy monthly deposits heading my way, but losing out on their money was my choice and mine alone. I was a trust fund kid, born of wealthy parents with a well-off lineage that traced back more generations than I'd ever cared to learn about. It didn't matter, because my future was never going to be in banking and finance. I had no interest in taking over the family business. It was my parents' fault, though. If they didn't want me to fall in love with music, they shouldn't have put such an emphasis on it when I was younger.

As an adult, I understood that the years of music and art lessons had only meant to make them look like they cared about me. The real intent of tapping into my musical talent was so I could make them look good to their friends. Dylan Michael Rivers—the savant, the concert pianist, the composer.

I was never meant to be Dylan Rivers—occasional bartender and dive bar guitarist. But writing my own songs, lyrics and all, had been the only thing about my childhood and teenage years that had ever felt special, that had ever been mine. Deciding to apply to Juilliard had caused the largest fight we'd ever had, but somehow my mom convinced my dad it wouldn't hurt to entertain the idea.

"Let him study music," she'd said. "He can learn the business after he graduates."

It was an agreement my father wasn't willing to make, but I applied to Juilliard anyway. I got accepted on my own merits, but the only chance I had at covering tuition was getting my parents total buy-in. It was, after all, their money. The day I delivered my acceptance letter to my dad was the second biggest argument we'd ever had.

It was a fight I didn't win.

I had to walk away from Juilliard and into an internship with the top VP at the company. The concession was that I'd be allowed to try and make a go of music—on the side—while leaning the ins and outs of the job. If at any time it was reported back that I was slacking with what he demanded of me at work, my dad would cut me off. I had so much tied up with my parents' money...the rent, the instruments, the living expenses, the spending money, the lifestyle. I had no choice but to agree and give in.

Juilliard was a pipe dream.

I tried my best to carry on both parts of my life for as long as I could, even though finance sucked the life out of me. It was the boring monotony and the bleary finance reports day in and day out that started to wear away at me first. But I swallowed it down and persevered, committed to getting though as many gigs as I could land and then figuring out how to tell my dad I was ready to walk away from my inheritance.

It didn't take much time for the misery of the internship and the weight of that expectation to overwhelm me. Music turned from a passion to an escape to a reminder that I had no idea who I was or who I wanted to be. I realized there wasn't room in my life for me to be Dylan Rivers the musician and Dylan Rivers, doting and responsible inheritor of the Lang empire.

Then came the third biggest fight, the termination of my internship and the freezing of my bank accounts.

My roommate—and best friend—Tate Barlowe wasn't anything like me. He wasn't from money and he barely had any. He worked over forty hours a week to make ends meet, and he worked hard. There was no way I could tell him what happened with my parents. I didn't want him to lose his half of our apartment and I definitely didn't want him to worry about overpaying to make *my* ends meet. But bartending shifts weren't quite cutting it anymore and the gigs had dried up.

I was on the verge of crawling back to my parents to ask forgiveness when the answer to that month's rent walked through the front doors of the bar where I worked most weekends. Sad Eyes took a seat at the bar, setting a black matte motorcycle helmet down beside him.

Oh, so he was dangerous.

I slid my way down the bar, pushing my hand through my own tangled hair and plastering on what I hoped was a flirty enough smile to get me sufficient tips to not have to overdraft my bank account again. He barely looked up at me, and my smile faltered. Maybe this was going to be harder than I'd initially thought, but if there was anything I'd learned since going broke, it was how to use my best assets to my advantage.

"Hey there." I slid my hand toward his elbow, which caused him to look up at me, just like I'd intended.

I hadn't planned for the dark intensity of his stare to take my breath away. I choked on air, which was very *not* sexy, then did my best to recover and give him another flirty smile.

"What can I get you?" I asked.

He cocked his head to the side, giving me a onceover so thorough it felt like his fingers had actually tugged at the hem of my shirt and the cuff s of my jeans to inspect what was beneath. Heat pooled low in my stomach, which was a relief. At least flirting with him the rest of the night would be easy.

"Dirty martini," he said simply, holding my gaze and not looking away.

My breath caught again, and I gaped a little like a fish. Turning away from him was like fighting against a physical force field tying us together, but I managed it. I made his martini, dropped in a skewer of olives, and gave him another million dollar smile.

"I'm Dylan," I told him. "Let me know if you need anything else."

He poured the entire drink down his throat in one swallow, not even flinching.

"I need to get laid," he said with a self-deprecating laugh, "but I don't think you can help me there, so I'll have another martini."

I could help him there.

I *would* have helped him there, even if my boss, Marigold, wouldn't have approved of it. She had one rule at Tryst, and it was don't fuck customers. It had been an easy rule to maintain, but I'd also never had a customer look as fuckable as this one did.

"I'm sure you won't have a hard time with that one," I said.

The corner of his mouth quirked into a wry smirk that fell away as he shrugged at me, sliding the empty martini glass toward my side of the bar.

A group of young hipsters came in, blowing in the smells of smoke and smog behind them. They headed for the other side of the bar while I finished shaking up the second martini. When I set it on a napkin for him, he gave me a curt nod, but otherwise didn't move. I assumed that meant he wasn't going to drink it like a shot.

It took me fifteen minutes to get through the drink order for the new group of guests, and when I made it back to the depressed motorcycle guy, he hadn't even touched his drink. He had eaten the olives, though, and the toothpick hung out of his mouth looking far sexier than it had any right to do.

"Any of those girls suit your fancy?" I asked, coming to check in on him. We both turned toward the group I'd just served. "I'm happy to put in a good word for you."

"They're not my type," he said simply. "Can I have more olives?"

The heat in my stomach swirled up the base of my spine, and I skewered him three more olives.

"What's your type?" I asked.

"Sturdier," he said, giving me another long look. "Less feminine."

"There's men in the group." My voice cracked.

"There is," he agreed, licking his lips. Slowly, he took the empty toothpick out of his mouth and chomped down on a fresh olive, chewing it thoughtfully. He swallowed, throat working, and I tried my best not to look, but it was impossible to not.

The man was gorgeous.

"Not your type?" I asked.

"I have..." He trailed off and sighed. "Dating isn't my scene."

"Hookups only?"

He looked up at the ceiling, sliding another olive into this mouth. I followed his stare upward, even though I'd seen the painted black ceiling more times than I could count. Sometimes it was clear, sometimes it was a mess obscured by barely restrained tears when I'd had a shitty tip night.

The man took a healthy swallow of his drink and smacked his lips, leaning back on the stool like he'd just made up his mind about something.

"I think it's time to seek out a professional."

"Pardon?"

He took another drink and reached into his front pocket, pulling out an absolutely-stacked money clip. Throwing a fifty down on the table, he stood up and stretched, revealing a muscled strip of skin above his waistline. His belt was Gucci.

"Watch my helmet?" he asked. "I need to use the restroom."

"Right."

I grabbed the crisp fifty, the only imperfection was the fold down the middle from where it had bent in his money clip. Shoving the bill into my pocket, I watched quietly as he slid the helmet from the empty seat beside him to the one he'd been sitting at. He didn't even give me a second glance, taking my word as my promise or something.

He walked away and I tried to not stare at the way the muscles of his back stretched and pulled at the material of his t-shirt, but even in the dim light of the bar, it was impossible to not notice the musculature or the strength of him. I blinked slowly, giving myself five seconds to imagine him naked before I went to check on the other group at the end of the bar. But as soon as I closed my eyes and pictured him sprawled naked on a bed, one arm bent behind his head and his legs spread, other hand stroking up what I conveniently imagined to be a thick and long cock, his voice rang through my head.

"I think it's time to seek out a professional," he'd said.

Three things happened after that, almost at the same time.

The new group of customers finished their drinks and stood up. One of the girls dropped a wad of cash on the bar, and the whole lot of them walked out. Marigold hated when people did that, but she was generally a go with the flow kind of boss—and bartender—so I didn't try to stop them. I waited until they were gone, then grabbed the cash from the bar. It was dirtier and stickier than the fifty I'd just pocketed, and after I counted it out, I tallied up the drinks on the till and found they'd paid the amount to the dime.

Not a tip in sight.

I screwed my eyes shut, stabbing my fingertips against my eyelids to try and push back the tears that threatened to spill. The fifty from the hot and sad man at the other end of the bar was not going to be enough to cover my rent, and while I knew he would pay well, I still didn't trust it.

I bussed the empty glasses from the stingy group, my earlier thought stopping me in my tracks.

I knew he would pay well.

I knew he would *pay* well.

He wanted to fuck and I would have done it for free, Marigold's rules be damned at this point, but he'd also said…

"I think it's time to seek out a professional."

He was still in the restroom, so I made a split-second decision that was going to change the rest of my life. I didn't want to think too hard about it. I pulled my phone out of my pocket and reactivated the hookup app that I'd only installed to try and help Tate find hookups in the first place. He and I had spent plenty of time on the app and we'd both become familiar with the abbreviations and the codes people used to explain what they wanted and what they were looking for.

I'd been hours away from crawling back to my parents and telling them they were right, that I couldn't cut it as a musician after all. But instead, with shaking fingers, I typed out a new bio and slid my phone back into my pocket.

The rich man I'd been waiting on returned to his seat, sliding the helmet back to the side so he could sit down. His ass had barely hit the stool when his phone pinged with a recognizable alert tone.

I dropped my phone by the cash register, glancing at him in time to see his eyes go wide at the sound. He must not have realized the ringer had been on, which made me laugh, so I turned away from him, not able to bear the sight of his face when he saw my profile come up in his radius. I hadn't thought my plan through at all, but I was in need of money and if he was willing to pay, sleeping with him wouldn't be a hardship. I could get my rent paid and hopefully I'd get an orgasm out of it.

He looked like he knew how to fuck.

Minutes passed, and I finally had to head down toward his end of the bar. His second martini was empty and his money clip was sitting on the bar top. He drummed his fingertips against the monogrammed silver metal, head cocked to the side as I approached.

"Did you want another drink?" I asked, voice hoarse.

He pulled six bills out of the stack, all of them hundreds.

"I'm good," he said, standing up and collecting his things. "Keep the change."

I pocketed the money, disappointed that he hadn't taken me up on the offer, but not let down that he'd paid me over six hundred dollars for less than forty dollars' worth of drinks. I took everything to the cash register to ring the tab in just in time to see my phone screen flash and go dark.

I swiped the screen open, an unread message alert in the corner of my screen. His profile picture was a zoomed-in crop, showing not much more besides his hand around a glass of whiskey and a muscular forearm that I'd already spent half the night drooling over. I turned quickly, looking back at the door, but he was long gone. Outside, I heard a motorcycle engine roar to life, and I tapped his avatar, loading the message on my screen.

It was two simple words that were enough to change everything.

"I'll host."

CHAPTER 2
ALEX

DYLAN THE BARTENDER SHOWED UP ON MY FRONT PORCH AT TWO-forty-five in the morning. His hair was still a tangled mess, dark roots fading into bleached ends around his ears, and his eyes were green as a chunk of polished jade. He chewed nervously on the corner of his lip, and I leaned against the doorframe staring down at him, wondering if I was making a terrible mistake.

Paying a stranger for sex couldn't be any worse of a decision than sleeping with one of my best friends, which I'd already done to disastrous results, so I shoved that worry as far out of my head as I could manage. It had been months since my friend Carter Royce IV—affectionately called Beamer—and I had accidentally fallen into bed together. He was an attractive man, but I'd known him for years and never once thought of him as more than one of my dearest friends.

We'd been up late drinking one night, partying long after the party should have stopped and he'd confided in me how miserable he was without someone to *play* with. I was a dominant, I always had been, and I knew Beamer absolutely was not. I'd never had difficulty finding people to play with—or to fuck—so I found it hard to believe that he was struggling to find a dominant man himself. Maybe it was the whiskey, but that night was the first time he told me, in detail, the ways he liked to play...the ways he wanted to fuck, and it so closely aligned with my own interests, I could have choked on my tongue.

Instead, I grabbed him around the throat, hauled him onto my lap, and I kissed him. I kissed him until we were both hard and naked and he was on his back and I couldn't bring myself to call him by his nickname any longer. In my bedroom, on his knees for me, he was Carter, and he was so much more than I'd expected. We'd barely had a chance to get started when everything ended, when we all found out he was married, when he fell in love with his husband, when he moved to California...

The taste of pleasure I'd found with him had been enough to ensure I never settled again. But finding people who were down for my flavor of sex and kink was easier said than done. Even though there'd never been a shortage of willing subs wandering around The Black Door, it was always a fleeting kind of hookup. I could find someone who wanted the impact play I craved, but they didn't have any interest in actual submission. Or if I found someone who wanted to submit, they were scared of the pain.

I wanted both.

And after having it with Carter...with Beamer...I needed it.

His move to California had sent me into a depression spiral so deep I didn't see any of my friends for weeks. I couldn't bring myself to justify what he and I had done together, nor did I want to. I didn't expect them to understand

and I didn't have the energy to try and explain. It was easier to isolate and to mourn.

So I did.

My comment about paying for sex had been in passing, and Dylan was far from my usual type. I'd had a long week at work, and my friends were starting to get annoying about the fact I wasn't hanging out anymore. I needed to blow off some steam and my right hand hadn't been cutting it for weeks.

"Dylan." I stared down at him, again wondering if this was all one mistake in a long line of them.

"I don't think you ever told me your name," he said, voice sounding as quiet as it had in the noisy bar.

"Alex Burke."

The corner of his mouth quirked up. "Should I text that to someone so they can find my body after you dig out my kidneys and leave me for dead in your bathtub?"

"Last I checked, I wasn't in need of an organ transplant."

"You could sell it," he said, letting out a low laugh that vibrated straight through the base of my spine.

"I don't need the money," I told him.

Dylan's smile fell away and he tilted his head back, checking out how many stories my house had. The answer was three, which must have been acceptable because he dropped his chin back toward his chest, his expression steely.

"I do," he said.

I nodded and stepped out of the doorway to let him inside.

He was still in his work attire—a tight pair of black jeans with rips at the knees, a worn-down pair of black Vans, and a tight black t-shirt. He was slender, but strong, with tight muscles that wrapped around his arms and his thighs, testing the durability of his too-small clothes.

"Do you want a drink?" I asked.

Dylan bent down and untied his shoes, using his toes to push them toward the shoe rack just inside the door. We both looked down at our feet, his socked and mine bare.

"I don't think so," he mumbled.

I'd never paid for sex before, so I had no frame of reference about what to expect, but I was quickly getting the impression that Dylan had never been paid for sex either, which left us both at more of a disadvantage than I would have liked.

"Can we talk about limits?" I asked next, leading him to the couch and taking a seat. He followed after me, more nervous than not, but he was definitely trying to hold it together. I threaded my fingers together in my lap, hoping he wouldn't see my hands shaking.

"I want to use condoms," he blurted.

I chuckled. "That's a given, I meant..."

Realization dawned, and Dylan's eyes went wide. "Oh, you meant like...kinky limits?"

"Kinky limits," I agreed.

"I don't have a lot of experience with kink."

I cursed under my breath and reached into my pocket, ready to pay Dylan for his time and send him on his way. We were both in over our heads and the last thing I wanted was to traumatize or hurt someone who didn't understand the entirety of what I was asking for in the bedroom.

"My best friend does," he blurted, holding up both of his hands like he was ready to reach out and stop me.

"You aren't him."

"He's talked to me about it. He likes to...do it really rough. Sometimes he comes home with bruises."

I dragged my tongue across the front of my teeth. "Does he like that?"

"He's had better."

"Does the idea of getting hurt during sex make you hard?" I asked.

Dylan gave a small shrug.

"What about submitting?"

He snorted, rolling his eyes. "You mean like doing what I'm told? I've spent my whole life doing that."

I opened my mouth and closed it again, pulling my lips in between my teeth to think. My hand was still in my pocket, curled around the money clip. When I'd told him at the bar I was ready to pay for it, I hadn't meant I was in the market to walk a beginner through the ABC's of BDSM.

"There's safe words, right?" he asked, green eyes wide and half-filled with tears.

"Yes."

"Give me one, then. And if it's too much, I'll use it. And is there like, I don't know, a reverse safe word?"

I pulled my hand out of my pocket, and his shoulders noticeably relaxed. "What is a reverse safe word?"

"I don't know," he said with half a grin. "This is your scene, not mine. But I meant like... there's one to stop, right? There should be one for more."

Licking my lips, I swallowed nervously. My palms had started to sweat, which was entirely unlike me and far from the energy that I ever wanted to take into the bedroom. If I wasn't steady and sure, how could a partner rely on me to handle them in the ways we were both after? Even though, in this case, it was more the ways that I was after. Dylan was in it for the cash, which needed to be fine for me.

"Green for more," I told him, trying not to think about how many times Carter had cried out the color our first time together, constantly pushing me toward my own limits in his quest for more.

"And Juilliard to stop," he said.

"Okay."

This was still a mistake.

I pulled my money clip out of my pocket and pulled all the cash out of it, which had to be near a thousand dollars after what I'd left him at the bar. The bills were new and crisp, and I held them out to him. At the sight of the money, Dylan's cheeks burned the most beautiful shade of crimson. He took the money, not even counting it, and shoved it into his pocket.

"What now?" he asked.

"You had said you wanted me to use condoms," I said, looping us back to the basic part of the limits conversation we'd started with.

"For penetration."

"Even in your mouth?"

His jaw went slack, giving me a peek at the tip of his tongue behind the backs of his teeth.

"Just don't come in my mouth," he said.

"My tests are clear, Dylan. I get checked monthly."

He nodded.

"Better safe than sorry," I said, matching his nod. "And I take PrEP."

"So am I," he rasped.

"Good boy."

The red on his cheeks rushed down his throat.

Maybe it wasn't such a horrible idea after all.

"Did you like that?" I asked. "When I just called you a good boy?"

Dylan shifted his weight on the couch, folding his hands in his lap. He was trying to hide his erection, which was adorable but entirely unnecessary considering what we were both there to do.

"Yes," he whispered.

"How does it feel if I call you a whore?" I asked.

"Aren't I?"

My lips twisted into a frown, and I shook my head. "That's a backward way of thinking. There's nothing wrong with sex work."

He licked his lips. "You didn't call me a whore. At least, not the way you'd called me a good boy."

Dylan was cheeky, that was for sure. Even without his experience, he'd be a handful when it came to submission. And up until that moment, I hadn't thought I wanted a challenge, but suddenly the potential that existed with breaking that attitude right out of him and molding him into the kind of partner I'd lost...

It felt like a reachable goal.

"You're a whore, Dylan," I said next, my own cock pressing insistently at the fly of my jeans. "Sitting on my couch, ready to take your clothes off and let me fuck you."

His chest swelled as he sucked in a breath.

"You want it," I went on. "I can see how hard your cock gets."

"I like good boy better," he whispered, blinking quickly and starting down at the erection I'd just teased him about.

"That's good, Dylan." I reached forward and touched him for the first time, cradling his cheek in my palm. He leaned into me like we'd been doing it for years. The relief that coursed through him was so palpable I felt it in my own bones, forcing me to let out a breath I'd been holding since my app pinged him at the bar. "I like good boys better too. I like when they listen and do what they're told so I can come. You can listen, can't you?"

"I can make you come too," he said, lashes already damp, but he looked up at me, all earnest want and drive.

"I believe you," I told him. "Now let's go into the other room so you can prove it."

CHAPTER 3

DYLAN

I was terrified, but my cock had never been harder. My legs managed to carry me after Alex, up the stairs to a room the definitely wasn't a bedroom. Tate had told me about men like this, men who fucked for sport, but my brain hadn't been able to grasp the meaning of it.

Alex was a man who fucked for sport and won trophies for it.

He had a whole room dedicated to sex. Instead of mounted animal heads on the walls, he had a giant wooden X in a corner, a leather covered bench that looked like it was meant to be used for fucking, an armoire tucked against a wall with the doors open and an array of paddles, sex toys, and God knew what else hidden in the drawers.

The money he gave me burned a hole in my pocket, and even though I was scared of taking off my clothes for him, I needed to be naked. The bills were heavy against my thigh, a reminder of how quickly my life had changed. He'd said earlier there wasn't anything wrong with sex work, and he was right. But I hadn't given myself time to wrap my head around the idea yet. I'd acted out of reflex, like a basic hierarchy of needs designed to keep a roof over my head and food in my belly.

"Green?" he asked, reaching into the armoire and pulling out a pair of black leather cuffs.

"Green."

"Strip," he said. "Fold your clothes and leave them in the corner."

I flew out of my clothes, desperate to be free of the burden that came with his money, but I quickly learned that being naked was worse. The appraisal he'd given me in the bar was nothing compared to the way he studied me then, like he was cataloging every muscle and bone in my body. My cock loved the attention, swelling and jutting toward him like it wanted to be known as the best part of me.

Alex was still dressed in jeans and a t-shirt, his feet bare and his glasses on. He closed the space between us with the cuffs in hand. Without being told, I held my wrists out for him. He made a pleased sound when I presented myself to him like that, and then he made quick work of looping the unlined leather around my wrists and latching them closed.

"Green?" he asked again.

"Green." I swallowed, blinking hard.

"You look like you're about to cry," he said, taking my face back into his hand the way he had on the couch. His touch was too soft, too tender. It didn't align with any of the things we talked about—or any of the things I deserved.

"Is that a problem?" I asked. "It looks like this room is designed for tears."

Alex cocked his head to the side, studying me again like

he'd peel my skin off and sketch the sinew of my muscles if given the opportunity.

"It's designed for pleasure, Dylan," he said softly, tracing his finger along my wrist where skin met leather. "Sometimes that comes with pain and sometimes it comes with tears."

"Green," I rasped. "If I cry, don't stop."

"I'll only stop if you say Juilliard," he promised, letting go of my wrist. "Take off my clothes, Dylan. I'm ready."

He was ready, but was I?

Thankfully, my body knew what to do, fingers working independently of my brain as they reached for the hem of his t-shirt. The material was thicker and softer than any t-shirt I'd ever owned, and I was from money. His bank account would have dwarfed mine on a good day, probably even bigger than my parents'. Alex was taller than me, and I fought to get the shirt off his arms and over his shoulders. He didn't bend or angle himself down to make it easy for me, which frustrated me.

In that moment, he reminded me of all the men in my life I hated, but I wasn't ever going to back down from the challenges they presented, and I wouldn't back down from Alex's either. Letting go of his shirt, I grabbed the bench and dragged it across the floor so I could use it as a step stool. The bottom piece gave me enough leverage to get his shirt over his head.

I muttered a curse under my breath and pushed the bench back to its original location. His pants were easier, even though he made me lift his feet from the ground to get them off all the way. His underwear followed next, the same brand as mine. I folded everything and without being told, set his pile beside mine. Turning back toward him, my stare dropped between his legs.

When I'd met him at the bar, I imagined Alex with a cock as long as his height would have implied, but it was shorter than I'd expected. Still a decent length, but the girth of his shaft was one of the thickest I'd ever seen. Definitely wider than anyone I'd ever fucked before. I hadn't had sex in almost a year, and I was glad he didn't care if I cried because there was no way I could take him without it.

"You good?" he asked.

"Green."

"Get on the bench," Alex said, "but on your back with your head hanging over the side."

This was it.

There was no going back.

Carefully, I climbed onto the bench I'd used as a stool, sitting on it before arranging myself onto my back with my head over the edge. The top part of the bench was probably six inches across, enough to hold my spine steady and secure. The lower parts of the bench were at the right level for my feet, so I bent my legs and situated myself as comfortably as I could.

I didn't know what to do with my hands, but Alex took that problem out of the equation by stretching them down to the floor and clipping them into O-rings at the bottom of the bench that I hadn't noticed.

"Test it," he said, voice lower and darker than it had been earlier.

I did as he'd told me, trying to move my arms. The clips around the cuffs rattled, and there was nowhere for me to go. Fear raced through me, and my cock twitched against my stomach. I was terrified, but my dick hadn't gotten the message. It leaked against my abs, throbbing in time with my heartbeat.

"Do you want me to bind your legs?" he asked.

I exhaled, sinking into the bench and trying to process the flurry of emotions the pose and the binding had brought up for me. I'd never been more in control, even though I was at his mercy. It was terrifying and powerful in the same breath. Adrenaline spiked through me, and I knew I could have broken free of his little clips if I had to, but I didn't want to. I wanted to let him restrict me down to the silly little leather and wood bench and then do whatever he wanted. The money didn't even matter—I just wanted to give my whole being up to him, even though I didn't understand what that meant.

"I thought the dominant one made those decisions," I managed to answer, my voice shaking.

Blood was already rushing to my head, making me feel drunk and high simultaneously. Alex walked around to the front of me and rested his palm against my throat, just like he had earlier against my cheek. The touch was the same, but decidedly different. He didn't say a word, just pressed his palm against my Adam's apple, then he went to the armoire.

On my back on the bench, I didn't have a clear view of the whole room, but I heard him rustling around, and then he was back, yanking my feet roughly off their perch. My toes grazed the floor as he cuffed my ankles and bound them to the bench, just like he had done with my wrists. I was drawn apart and open for him, on display like something for sale, which...

I supposed I was.

"Green?" he asked me again.

"Green."

He drew his fingers up my calf, around my knee and over my thigh. When he reached my stomach, he swirled his finger through the precum I'd leaked there. I couldn't see him, but he groaned when he touched the wetness, and I worried I was going to come entirely untouched on the spot.

I'd never been hornier than I was on that bench in his sex room with his money burning a hole in my pocket, tucked away safely in the corner.

Alex worked his way up the rest of my body, coming to stand in front of my upside-down face. I could see his thighs and his heavy balls...he had his shaft in his hand... until he dropped it on my chin like a weight.

"What do you think happens now?" he asked, dragging his tip across my chin. He was wet too, smearing precum over my face with every swipe.

"I suck your cock," I said.

"Good boy, Dylan." He fed his cock into my mouth, growling as my lips sealed around his crown. "Fuck, that's a good boy."

Sucking Alex's cock on a good day would have been hard, and that day was far from one of my best, but with my head upside down on the bench, it gave him a straight line to my throat. All I had to do was relax my jaw enough to get the thick middle of him past my teeth. He didn't fuck my face like he was in a rush, though. Alex groaned low and deep as I swirled my tongue through the salty slit on the top of his dick, trying to will my jaw to open up for him. He settled his hand back on my throat, just a weight, not a pressure.

"Calm down, Dylan," he whispered, stroking his hand down my throat. "It's a marathon, not a sprint."

I hummed, closing my eyes and trying to focus on how much I enjoyed sucking his cock. And it wasn't a lie. I loved sucking cock—I always had—and Alex's thick shaft was no exception to the rule. I was just impatient and I wanted more of it. I also didn't want him to feel like he'd wasted his money by bringing me home. Picking up a bartender with the right flags in his bio who couldn't even get a dick in his mouth. How laughable. He pulled out of my mouth and stepped back, using his hand to smear my spit around the top inches of his shaft.

"You're stressed out about this, Dylan, and that's all wrong," he said softly. "This is supposed to be foreplay before we get going, but if we have to spend all night getting my cock in your throat, that's what we'll do."

"You're massive," I told him, like there was no way he didn't already know.

He scoffed, pointing his dick at my forehead.

"Plenty of men have sucked me off before," he said, before adding, "for free."

"Your mistake, then."

"Green, Dylan?"

"Green," I bit out.

He stepped back up to the bench and lodged his cock into my mouth with much more force than he'd used on the first go around. He was in there alright, and it was hard to breathe, hard to focus, hard to do anything else besides be aware of his dick in my throat.

"See?" he said calmly, using his hips to get another inch of his shaft past my teeth. His shaft pressed against my tongue, the roof of my mouth, every possible surface. "That wasn't hard, was it?"

Frustrated tears leaked from the corners of my eyes, racing around my eyebrows and over my forehead before dripping down into my hair. He pumped another inch into me, and I desperately tried to breathe through my nose, but it was hard to get a breath. Another inch and my nose was buried in his balls. He smelled like soap and sweat, and my own cock spasmed in response.

"There you go," he said. "Keep your mouth just like that, Dylan."

He cradled my head in both of his hands, pulling all the way out of my mouth. Spit trailed from my lips to his cock and before I could even draw in a full breath, he pushed his whole shaft back inside of my mouth. He stole my air, quieted my gags and my tears, even though both were still very much happening.

"Your mouth is the hottest thing I've ever fucked." Alex grunted, angling himself deeper toward my throat. His balls made it impossible to breathe through my nose, the short hairs tickling my nostrils. "Now use that perfect tongue to get me off. I'm ready to let loose on you for real."

It took all my willpower not to come straight into Dylan's perfect, tight throat, but we'd agreed that was off-limits, so I wrestled my way out of his mouth and shot my load in the middle of his chest.

With his mouth free of my cock, he sucked in breath after breath, his chest heaving on every inhale. Spit smeared down his chin and cheeks, running into his eyes and mixing with the tears he was helpless to not shed. Upside down like that on the spanking bench, he was the dictionary definition of debauched. My only regret that I hadn't shoved a vibrating plug up his ass before we started to stretch him out.

My legs trembled from the force of my orgasm, and I knew I needed to check in with him, but I also needed to make sure I was still capable of basic speech patterns. Dylan's eyes were closed, and I took the opportunity to brush my hair back out of my face and adjust my glasses.

"Green," he said softly, eyes still slammed shut.

I hadn't even had a chance to ask.

"Do you need a minute?"

"I said green," he repeated, yanking his wrists around so the metal chips clanked against the O-rings.

"Green it is," I said, making my way around the bench and undoing all the restraints. Without warning, I fisted his hair and hauled him up. His limbs splayed out like he was an awkward baby deer trying and failing to walk for the first time.

Dylan's ass hit the ground hard enough to mark, but before I could check in, he reached up and wiped the spit out of his eyes and said again, "Green."

My cock pulsed back to life, still hard even though I'd already gotten off, thickening even further as I slammed him up against the cross and bound him back into place. With his shoulder blades against the leather, I had to step back to catch my breath again, the sight of him enough to bowl me over. My cum was stuck to his chest in some places, running down the deep cut lines of his stomach in others. His cock looked hard enough to burst, violently red and purple, the head swollen and leaking.

I'd been rough with him and everything about Dylan, from his posture to his facial expressions, told me that he liked it. His muscles were loose and relaxed, his features slack, his eyes hooded and drunk with lust. He'd just choked on my cock and he was far more than ready to impale himself on it given the chance. Dylan didn't know what he was asking for, yet he asked at the top of his lungs just the same.

"Alex."

It was so uncommon to hear my name uttered inside the walls of my playroom, the sound of it caught me off-guard.

But Dylan and I hadn't talked about honorifics or endearments, and none of them would have sounded anywhere near as right coming out of his mouth as the soft whisper of my name had.

"Yes?"

His head lolled forward, and he opened his eyes, searching me out. It was hard for him to support himself, his muscles jelly as his wrists tugged against the pinch points at the top of the cross.

"Will you spank me?"

"Have you been spanked before?" I asked.

"Not the way I think you'd spank me."

I swallowed, rubbing at my thumbnails with the pads of my middle fingers. "How do you think I'd spank you?"

"Hard," he answered. "Hard enough to make me cry."

"Do you want to cry?"

Dylan clenched his jaw together and shook his head no.

My follow-up question came softer, "Do you need to cry?"

He gave me one short jerk of his head. The answer wouldn't have even registered to someone who hadn't been watching him as closely as I had been.

"Okay," I said, unclipping him from the cross. I'd have to save those ideas for another day. "Get back on the bench, hands and knees."

Dylan was bent over before I made it to the armoire, his ass on display in the way I liked the most.

"There's handles at the bottom," I told him, waiting for him to reach further down and curl his hands around them. "Consider yourself restrained, Dylan."

"Alright," he rasped.

"I'm going to put a plug inside of you first," I said, pulling a mid-size steel plug out of a drawer and slathering it with lube. Dylan wasn't the only one primed and ready, and once it was time for me to get inside of him, I didn't want anything to stop me. No time for prep or easiness with him, but I could tell he didn't want it. And neither did I.

"Thank you."

It was impossible, I thought as I flattened one hand against the small of his back and teased the tip of the toy against his hole with the other. Impossible that he was so naturally tuned in to the right things to say and the right way to act. The only thing that would have made the statement better was a breathy little *Sir* at the end, but this was a just-for-tonight thing, not a long-term thing.

There was no need to take things that far. It would just break my own heart again.

I pressed the plug against his tight hole, and Dylan arched his back, gasping.

"Bear down, Dylan," I said soothingly, flexing my fingers against his skin. "You can take this. It's nothing compared to what I'm going to give you later."

He cursed under his breath and relaxed his muscles, swallowing the top half of the plug, and then the rest. I covered the base with the palm of my hand, closing my eyes and groaning at how his skin burned my palm and contrasted with the cool metal feel of the plug.

"I can't wait to fuck you," I whispered, using the heel of my hand to push the toy deeper inside of him.

"Will it get you off?" he croaked, turning his face to the side and resting it on the bench. "To fuck me when I cry?"

"You doing what you're told will get me off," I said. "You submitting and *taking*..."

"Taking what?" he asked.

Everything.

"Whatever I want to give you."

He sighed, content.

"I'm going to use my hand on you," I warned him, stepping to the side of the bench so I could get the right angle to spank him.

"That's all?"

"You'll get your release," I said. "I could make you cry without even touching you, Dylan. Consider my hand a fucking mercy."

A shiver tore through his whole body, and I delivered the first strike when he was right in the middle of it. He sucked in a startled breath and I spanked him in the same spot, but harder. I should have offered him a warm-up, some teasing pulls against his ass and some soft taps to test the waters before going in hard, but Dylan had been pushing my buttons from the moment he stepped foot into my house.

He was a brat by definition, even if he didn't know what that meant in my world. And even if he was only part of my world for a night, I wanted to show him the appeal of walking on the rough and tumble side of things. Because while I would absolutely fuck him into oblivion before the night was through—I wanted my money's worth, after all—I would give him everything he needed on the way there in case he ever decided to come back.

"Check in," I said, hand hovering inches away from his already pebbling skin.

"Green," he said, not even getting the whole word out before I started in on him again.

I spanked Dylan until my hand hurt and my arm ached, until he was halfway off the other end of the bench and his ass and the backs of his thighs were decorated with green and purple fingerprints. My palm stung, but I kept up my end of the bargain. Dylan had been crying for what felt like hours, but couldn't have been more than five minutes.

The first time I slapped him in that tender spot where the back of his thigh met his ass, he burst into tears, screaming out so loud I thought for sure his safe word was soon to follow. I paused long enough for him to get through the initial cry and gather himself, and as soon as he let out another garbled color instead of his safe word, I went to town.

Undoubtedly, there would be pools of tears on the floor below his face, but I was far more concerned with the copious streams of precum that had made their way out of my cock. Every flinch and cry and moan that fell out of Dylan's mouth was like a drug to me. He had no idea what he'd walked into with me, but it was clear with him bent over my bench and my handprints all over his ass, it was exactly what the both of us needed.

I spanked him through the rise and crescendo of his tears, and I kept it up through the cooldown. His cries turned to pained whimpers, and he sounded absolutely exhausted, which was a relief for my hand. I spanked him one last time, hard as my quivering muscles could manage, then I left him alone and went to the armoire. Grabbing more lube and a condom, I sat on the ground beside the cross and spread my legs in front of me.

"Dylan," I said his name like a warning before biting open

the condom packet with my teeth. "Get off the bench and come here."

He moved slowly, unfolding himself from the bench and wincing as the bruising on his ass shifted in new ways. Bracing himself against the bench before he straightened his spine, I stopped him with a warning click of my tongue.

"Be a good boy and crawl, though."

Heat flashed across his face and when his hands and knees hit the floor, I rolled the condom down my erection and covered it with as much lube as I could squeeze out.

"You listen so well," I said approvingly as he made his way across the room. With my head resting against the wall, I stared at him down the length of my nose, watching his approach and the sultry way he swung his bruised ass and narrows hips in the air. "The best student, Dylan. A practical teacher's pet, aren't you?"

He reached me, and I expected him to stop at my feet, but he didn't. Dylan crawled the rest of the way toward me, between my legs with his tear-stained and red-splotched face inches away from me when he finally came to a stop.

"What's my next instruction then?" he asked, voice cracking.

"Turn around and ride me," I said. "I want to see your bruised ass bouncing up and down my cock when I'm coming."

Dylan turned his back to me and reached around behind himself to pull the plug out of his ass. I held out my palm and he dropped it into my waiting hand, and before I could set it aside, he had his fingers wrapped around my cock like a vise and he was angling himself down around me.

"Slow down so you don't hurt yourself," I warned.

He barely listened, taking my shaft into his ass much faster than he'd managed to with his mouth. But the heat of him swallowed me so quickly that it punched the breath out of my lungs. I grabbed him around the waist and held him still on my lap. For one reason so he didn't hurt himself, another so that I didn't come before things had a chance to get started.

"I love the way your ass swallows my cock," I whispered, tilting him forward so I could see the place where I disappeared into his body.

"Let me ride you," he begged, circling his hips as much as my grip on him would allow.

"Short thrusts, pet," I instructed, slipping one hand around to his dick so I could hold him like it was a leash. "Fuck yourself on my cock and fuck my fist with your dick."

Every muscle in Dylan's legs quaked, and when he landed too hard on my thighs with his bruised backside, he let out a watery sniffle. He was clearly in that delicate stage of play when the pain was starting to feel more like pain again. He'd flirted with the edge of subspace, but hadn't quite fallen over the edge. After ten minutes of shallow and measured thrusts, Dylan became frustrated. The slow pace had given me enough time to get my own strength back and before he could protest, I shoved him forward onto his hands and knees.

"Green?" I asked, cock still deep inside of him.

"Green."

There were so many things I wanted to do to Dylan, to do with him, but our time together was a once-off, a transaction. Another man would have tried to fit as much into the night as he could manage, but I wasn't that greedy. Dylan had gotten his release, gotten his money, and I'd gotten to spank someone hard enough to make their cock leak. It was as close to a win as I could have hoped for and I knew better than to ask for more.

I slammed into him so hard my glasses knocked loose from my face, clattering onto the ground, but I didn't need the prescription lenses to see the bruises mottled on his ass and the backs of his thighs. I didn't need focused vision to see how he shifted onto his forearm and reached between his legs with his other hand, pausing before he touched himself.

"Can I?" he asked, the question pushed out of him with every thrust I made into him.

"If you come on my floor, you're cleaning it up," I warned.

He stroked his cock fast, and I wondered how he liked to jerk off when he was alone. If he went at himself hard and fast or slow and loose. If he took his time and dragged it out. I knew if it was any other scenario, I would have asked, I would have taken my own time with him, but my orgasm was loud as a freight train ringing in my ears.

Dylan's entire body seized, and he came seconds before me. Jets of cum shooting out of his dick and bypassing his hand, painting white stripes across my original wood floors. The muscles in his ass gripped my cock and milked me of my own release, which I spilled forcefully into the condom. I collapsed on top of him, taking us both down to the ground as I fucked through the rest of my orgasm.

My vision went black as I emptied into the condom, and I pulled us both back up to our knees. Fisting the back of Dylan's hair, I rocked him up onto my lap, wishing I could see the way my cum from earlier and his recent release had mixed together in the middle of his chest.

"Green?" I asked, lips moving against his ear.

"Green," he answered, falling back against my chest. My

cock slipped out of him, the saggy condom warm against the inside of my thigh, his body burning hot on top of me.

"Good." I realized I hadn't kissed him yet. I also understood I *shouldn't*. "The cleaning supplies are in the kitchen under the sink. Clean your mess off the floor then I'll deal with getting my mess off of you."

Two days later, I was back at my apartment in Chelsea. Tate was at work, the rent was paid, and I'd been cleaning the same spot on the floor of the shower for an hour. It was clean, it had been clean for a while, but something about the position of being on my hands and knees, of cleaning the floor, of my ass being in the air and still sore from how thoroughly Alex had fucked me...all of it had my cock half-hard and my balls heavy. I wondered if I kept scrubbing the sponge over the now invisible stain on the tile for long enough, the erection would go away, but it hadn't.

Tate wasn't due home for another hour at best, so I made a quick decision. Rocking back on my heels, I tore open the fly of my jeans and curled my hand around my shaft. The release was almost immediate, my body responding to some stimuli I wasn't even aware of. With the smell of bleach in my nose and my fingers pruned from being wet so long, I shot my load right onto the spot I'd spent the last hour cleaning. I didn't bother giving myself time to enjoy the release. I was immediately back at it with the sponge and the bleach, scrubbing the tub until my cum was gone.

"What the fuck, dude?" I muttered under my breath, slumping against the wall and screwing my eyes shut.

After I finished cleaning up the mess I'd made on Alex's floor, I'd made quick work of getting my clothes on. I was still horny, but I was embarrassed, the heat of shame racing through my veins and threatening to combust if I didn't get out of his house quickly. The air smelled like leather and sex, and I could still taste the salt of my tears on my lips.

I'd taken money for sex, but that wasn't what had made me cry.

I wasn't embarrassed about that, no.

I was embarrassed about how hard my cock got when Alex had spanked me. He'd set out with the intent to hurt me, and I'd not only consented, I'd welcomed it with open arms. Before Alex, the extent of my kinky experience had been a couple soft slaps on the ass while taking it from behind. Maybe once there had been a blindfold; I couldn't remember now. A blindfold was nothing compared to what he'd done to me, and some-how…I knew what he'd done to me was nothing compared to what he'd wanted to do.

With a simple exchange of cash for skin, Alex had inadvertently cracked my entire understanding of the world open. I wanted to hate him for it. Tate was already on a hellbent chase for the high from the best sex of his life. There was no way I could follow suit. If I let myself chase after Alex—or men like him—I'd lose sight of the most important thing in my life.

Which, at this point, was making enough money to pay my rent.

I could jerk off and clean the floors for a few months and

wait the feeling out. I didn't need it again. I wasn't even sure I wanted it, because getting hard at the thought of cleaning the floor sounded like a problem for a therapist, not a John. I could get through this. I had to. It was just like all the other curveballs life had thrown at me.

Tucking myself back into my pants, I shoved the cleaning supplies under the sink and forced myself up off the floor. Maybe the shitty ventilation in our tiny apartment had finally gotten to me. The bleach must be making me crazy. Desperate to clear my head, I grabbed my guitar and a beer, then shoved open the window to the fire escape. Sitting down on the floor beside the window, I stretched my legs in front of me, strumming some chords while I tried to settle my brain. That mindless relaxation that normally came from having the guitar in hand was lost on me, the pain in my ass and the backs of my thighs far too noticeable to let me fall into the familiar comfort.

I'd left Alex's house with purple bruises scattered across my ass, and I'd woken up the next day looking like I'd been thrown into a brick wall by a catapult ass first. If I got close enough to the stand-up mirror in my bedroom, I could see the shape of his fingers curling around my thighs. if I pressed my own fingers into them, my cock thickened. It was some new and unwanted Pavlovian response, between the near-constant pain and the act of cleaning, I was an aroused mess pretty much all the time.

It was going to ruin my life.

The easy solution would be to tell Tate that I didn't have the money to keep the apartment. We could sit down together and figure out what to do, how to balance things so neither of us got underwater. He'd started out years ago as my roommate, but he was my best friend now. He'd understand.

But Tate was one of those good-hearted people, and I was sure if he knew about my finances, he'd take all the overtime his work offered. I'd never see him, and he'd work himself into a state of exhaustion to cover the loss on my end of the rent. Chelsea wasn't as expensive as Manhattan, but it was far from cheap. I'd picked it because it was distant enough from my dad's office that I'd be able to escape at the end of the day, but the price tag of the rent hadn't had any bearing on my choice at all.

I should have paid better attention.

Or something.

I chugged the beer and tossed the empty bottle into the sink, then closed my eyes and forced my fingers to do their job. Strumming through a progression of chords, my brain went soft enough for me to get lost in one of the only comforts I'd ever known. I was able to ignore the ping of my cell phone, which had been going off near constantly since I'd changed my bio at the bar. I had at least a dozen men in my inbox wanting to pay me for sex, and I'd left them all unread.

It was one thing to do it with Alex. He was a stranger, but I'd had a decent amount of time at work to watch him, to pick up his vibe before agreeing to go home with him. I had clocked him long before I made the decision to fuck him for money, which I could tell he had plenty of. These other men in my inbox? I didn't know anything about them. It was risky, and there was something arousing about that fear, but not enough to overwhelm the arousal that had become a near constant state for me since Alex had spanked me for the first time.

I must have lost track of time because the next thing I

knew, Tate was home, loosening the top button on his shirt and flinging himself onto the couch. He propped his feet up on the table and crossed his legs at the ankle, awkwardly trying to toe off his too tightly-laced dress shoes.

"How was work?" I asked, forcing my eyes open.

The sun had sunk below one of the buildings, and the room was cast in a gray and orange glow. It was a color that felt specific to New York. I imagined, with as much concrete as there was, everywhere just always looked some degree of gray.

"The usual," he said, waving a dismissive hand. "I've been trying to see if the guys from the tenth floor are going back to that club again anytime soon—"

"You're obsessed," I told him, knowing I wasn't much better off. I'd just committed myself to wiping my memory instead of trying to replicate.

"It was the best sex of my life!" Tate exclaimed. "Of course I'm obsessed."

"How many men are you up to after him?"

"Ten," he answered, frowning.

"And?"

"No one even comes close."

I set my guitar down and leaned toward the fridge, opening it up to get a second beer. I had to work later, but two beers weren't enough to get me anywhere close to buzzed. Besides, the conversation with Tate was enough of a downer to make sure the alcohol didn't do anything to my head space.

He'd lost his virginity to a rando at a sex club, and he'd spent the past handful of months trying to find someone else to fuck him as well as the Upper East Side stranger had. He'd come up short, but he'd added nearly a dozen notches to his bedpost, which felt commendable. There wasn't anything wrong with it, but I wasn't ready to try and catch up to his tally, even if it would have kept the lights on for another month.

"The true loss of our generation," I told him, taking a swallow of beer.

The only reason we could afford beer was because Marigold let me take home the bottles that she couldn't sell. It was almost always some weird flavored IPA from California that no one in New York cared about, but I admired her optimism.

"Do you work tonight?" he asked, falling sideways on the couch. His hair fell over his eyes, and he looked so sweet.

There was no way I could ever tell him.

About any of it.

"Yeah. Did you want to come get a drink?"

"Are you playing or…"

"No gig tonight," I said, feigning a smile when he opened his eyes. "Just bartending at Tryst."

Tate hummed, rolling onto his back and flinging his arm over his eyes. "Maybe I'll come by in a bit, but I'm pretty wiped out from work."

"What happened?" I asked, finishing the rest of my beer and pushing myself to my feet.

I listened to Tate tell me all about the intern at his office who wasn't pulling her weight, which forced him—an administrative assistant—and a paralegal from the tenth floor to pick up the slack. While he talked, I dumped the two empty bottles into the trash and frowned at the small puddles of beer left pooling in the sink. Turning the water on, I rinsed the basin, ignoring the way the extremely mundane and basic task made my cock twitch against my thigh.

I'd *just* gotten off. There was no way cleaning beer out of the sink was going to be a new trigger for me because, if so, I'd have to quit the only paying job I had left. Music sure wasn't cutting it, but bartending at least helped me get close to the total owed to our landlord at the end of the month.

"That sounds frustrating," I said to him, drying the sink and tossing the soiled paper towel into the trash can.

"It's just part of the gig, I guess." He sat up and shrugged. "The intern's mom is some SVP or partner or something like that. It's just a checkmark on her resume that she doesn't even need. She'll have a job when she's ready to stop bottle bleaching her hair."

"You sound bitter," I said, scratching my ear.

Tate knew my parents were rich. He *thought* they funded my bank account so I could pursue music. He didn't know I'd turned down the same kind of internship he was currently bitching to me about.

"I just think it's stupid to pretend she needs the work experience," he said. "She doesn't need a job; it's just trying to satisfy her parents."

"Parents are the worst."

"Except yours." He grinned at me so earnestly, I thought my heart was going to shatter. But as a bonus, at least my erection had gone away.

"Yeah." I cleared my throat and pasted on a fake smile. "Except mine."

CHAPTER 6
ALEX

I made it a week before I caved in and sent Dylan another message.

A week of staring at the spot on my floor that he'd scrubbed so diligently that it almost shined under the light. I hadn't even realized my floor was dirty in the first place until he'd cleaned that single spot so well. And all I could think about was having him naked with a plug up his ass, making the rest of the surface match. Getting through work had been a fucking struggle, the only saving grace was that my friends were used to my reclusive tendencies so, for the most part, they left me alone.

I didn't have to pretend I wasn't preoccupied. That I wasn't thinking about how a too-skinny bartender from a little dive bar in the city had flipped my life upside down. I didn't have his phone number, didn't know a thing about him besides where he worked and how his asshole grabbed my dick for dear life when he came. I messaged him on the app and he didn't even bother to read it, which wounded my ego more than I wanted to admit. But he was probably embarrassed, I told myself. It had been obvious he was new to sex work and maybe he'd spent the whole week regretting what we'd done.

I should have left it alone, but I was a man obsessed. It wasn't healthy to replace Carter with Dylan...I knew that. But my cock didn't care. Ignoring a dinner invitation from one of my closest friends, Ford, I made the decision to go to Tryst and see if Dylan was working. I spent ten minutes debating if I wanted to take the motorcycle, deciding against it and opting for a walk instead. The fresh air would do me good, I hoped. Clear my head enough that I didn't make a fool of myself when I got to the bar.

What was I supposed to say even if he was working? Was I supposed to pretend that the sex had never happened? Buy a drink or two and then head home for the night? I didn't think the last scenario was possible, but if that was what the situation called for, I would manage it.

It took just under half an hour to reach Tryst, and Dylan was behind the bar when I got there. He saw me almost immediately, eyebrows racing toward his hairline and his cheeks turning pink. He swallowed and turned away from me, busying himself with a mixed cocktail for someone at the far end of the bar. Tryst was busier than normal, but I found a single seat at the bar near the hallway that led to the bathrooms, and I waited for Dylan to make his way over to me.

"Dirty martini?" he asked, body swaying behind the bar.

"To start with."

His lips parted on a breath, and then Dylan made me the best martini of my life. I sipped it slowly, studying him while he worked, making note of the way his body leaned back toward me even when he was helping someone at another part of the bar. Even though he wasn't close, and hardly paid me any attention, his body was screaming for me...betraying him.

I finished my drink and slipped a fifty under the bottom of my martini glass. I'd gotten the answers I'd come looking for, and that felt like enough. But as I moved to climb off the bar, Dylan turned toward me, his whole face falling at the sight of my pending departure. He was quick to try and school it, but he was so easy to read. Making another rash decision, I pulled one of my business cards out of my money clip and beckoned him closer.

"Are you working until four?" I asked.

"Off at two tonight."

"Pen," I told him.

He pulled one out of his back pocket and I scrawled the address for The Black Door on the back of the card, setting it down on top of the fifty. I set the pen down on the bar and looked up at him, studying the way his brow furrowed so softly in the center while he stared at the bar top.

"What's your last name, Dylan?"

"Rivers," he croaked.

"Meet me there." I tapped the back of my business card.

"Alright."

I didn't think there was anything else to say, so I gave him a jerky nod and walked out of the bar. The fresh night air was sharp against my burning hot cheeks, and I prayed none of my friends had ventured out to The Black Door because running into any of them was the absolute last thing I wanted to do. Even though I rarely said yes, they'd kept inviting me places, and tonight's message had been about dinner, not about play.

Once I reached The Black Door, I told the man at the door I

was expecting a guest and gave them Dylan's name and where I planned to be. I ordered another martini at the bar, even though it was lackluster compared to the dirty drinks Dylan had made me, and headed to a small table for one in the back of the main room that everyone seemed to overlook. It had never not been available when I wanted it and, in my opinion, it gave the best view of the club...and it was a straight shot to the private rooms down the back hallway.

I'd never considered myself to be a voyeur, but I was always curious about the ways people fucked. Maybe that came from the transparency all my friends shared when it came to the bedroom and the playroom. The guests at The Black Door rarely escaped my attention, and I considered it to be the most entertaining form of people-watching. You could learn so much about a person by what their kinks were, by the way they liked to fuck or be fucked.

Dylan, for example, was obviously desperate for some semblance of control in his life. Barely hanging on by a thread, the way he'd cried on my spanking bench had sounded like a release I'd be jealous of for the rest of my days. I hadn't cried after Carter left for California, but the pressure of that loss had lived in my chest just the same. Rubbing my sternum, I tried to turn the same sort of speculation onto myself. What must Dylan—or anyone, for that matter—think of me based off the way I wanted to fuck?

If they pinned me as a dominating control freak who held on far too tight because he was terrified of losing his grip, they'd be right. If they called me a man with unattainable standards, who set everyone in his life up to fail, they'd also be right. That wasn't by design, though. I didn't *want* people to fail—I just wanted them to try. I wanted to be worth the work.

That was probably something to talk to a therapist about, but my parents had sent me to one after they caught me kissing our private chef's son in the pool house my freshman year of high school and that hadn't ended well for any of us.

He told me he loved me, and I believed him. But all I got out of that whole thing was a prescription I refused to swallow and a one-way ticket for a boarding school in Connecticut. I had no idea what happened to Brandon, but I knew better than to ask. When I came home for holiday visits, there was a new chef in the kitchen, and the pool house was padlocked closed. It had been a cutting lesson in chasing after my own pleasure, the pain of the judgement and isolation so acute that I never even thought about kissing another boy again until I was in college.

I kissed plenty of boys in college, plenty of men. Plenty of women too, but my preferences quickly became clear. It was easier to be rough with men, and I don't think I wanted to hurt them the way I'd been hurt. The emotional betrayal of my teenage years could never be matched with physical bruises. Brandon had said he loved me, but after I was sent away to school, he never answered my emails, lost to history. It had been so easy for him to let me be taken away from him. I wanted someone to fight for me.

Maybe I was selfish or unfair, but...

I wasn't going to stop.

I tossed back the rest of my martini, no idea what time it was, but when I pushed up from my seat to go get a new drink, there was an already familiar pair of dirty sneakers situated between my feet.

"Did you want another?" Dylan asked, reaching out for my glass.

"Is it two already?"

The corner of his mouth twitched. "It's two-thirty."

"Put it on my tab, then. Get yourself one."

"What's your last name, Alex?" he asked, head cocked to the side. "For the bar tab."

"Don't pretend you didn't already commit my business card to memory, Dylan. I don't like men who play coy with me."

Dylan hummed, not even bothering to look ashamed. "Alex Burke. Financial Advisor."

"You didn't memorize my phone number too?"

The quick flush on his throat confirmed for me that even if he didn't memorize the number, it had already been saved into his phone.

"Drinks," I said, clearing my throat and letting us both off the hook.

I watched Dylan the whole time he was at the bar, and I wondered if he was still bruised beneath his clothes. It had only been a week. There still had to be some proof of our time together on his skin. I let myself think about stripping him naked somewhere, a private room here, the alley, the back seat of a town car, and pressing my fingers one by one into every bruise of mine he'd worn for the past week. Blood rushed to my cock, and I palmed the base of my shaft, pushing it back down into submission.

When Dylan turned away from the bar and headed back toward my table, I forced my attention up his face, ignoring the fact there was the slightest tease of a shadow between his legs where his cock had thickened and started to tent the material. How was it possible he was hard after ordering me a drink? I didn't have time to think about it because he was back and handing me one of the drinks, keeping the other held tight between his white-knuckled fingers.

"Table for one?" he asked, hint of amusement in his voice.

"There's room for two," I said, tipping my chin toward the floor.

His nostrils flared, but he didn't look annoyed. He looked like I'd offered him a gift.

Taking a sip off the top of my drink, I eyed him over the rim of my glass. "On your knees, Dylan."

His drink sloshed over his fingers as he moved to his knees, clearly not familiar with the positioning and far from graceful about it, but there was something obscenely sexy about that. He'd never done this for anyone besides me, and that made it feel special enough to tamp down some of that other emotion that took up so much space in my chest.

He dragged his tongue over the spilled alcohol on his hand, and I shifted my weight.

"This is a shitty martini," he grumbled.

"Maybe you should work here."

"Get me a job then," he said.

I arched a brow and gave him a quick onceover. "Didn't I?"

"Are you paying me *now*?"

The counter question was well deserved, but still felt like a slap in the face. I understood the basis of our relationship—or whatever it was—had been built as a transaction, but maybe there was part of me that foolishly hoped this second interlude could be more personal. Always quick to recover, I made sure to wipe my face of any indication that I'd hoped for a different outcome in the night.

"Most men generally get on their knees for free if I ask," I said.

He blinked at me slowly, throat working as he swallowed down a mouthful of his shitty martini. "I'm not most men."

"No," I said quietly, "you most certainly aren't."

"Is that a yes?"

"I'll pay," I promised. And I would, but I was going to get my money's worth.

"Good."

"Finish your drink, Dylan. It's getting late."

Alex walked me down a long and dark hallway, stopping in front of the last door on the right.

"Do you remember how this went last time?" he asked, hand on the knob.

"Clothes in the corner," I said, cock already halfway to hard.

I was so far beyond exhausted, tired from work and worn down from the week spent thinking about him incessantly. I wanted to go home and crawl into my bed, but if I didn't get the rent for the following month paid, there wouldn't be a bed to crawl into.

"And then?" he prompted.

I swallowed. "Then yours."

"Good listening, pet."

Heat burned at the base of my spine, my brain still unable to determine if I liked the endearment or if it was embarrassing. The heat of shame and arousal felt the same these days, and then Alex opened the door and I stepped into the room.

Even though the club was beyond posh, I didn't have high

expectations for the private room. It was dark and simply decorated with what I imagined to be the essentials—including a bed—but everything *looked* rich. After all, I wasn't poor by birth. I knew how to spot luxury materials and it was clear that in here, just like Alex's home, no expense had been spared.

"I'm waiting," Alex said, the door lock sounding loud as a gunshot.

I smelled like spilled vodka and lemons from work, the scent whooshing up around me as I stripped out of my dirty work clothes and folded them into a neat pile by the door. Once I was naked, I turned to find Alex standing in the middle of the room, his legs spread and his arms crossed in front of his chest. He had on another expensive pair of jeans and a white V-neck shirt that looked like it must have just come out of the package. Heading toward him, I realized he was also wearing a Rolex, which shouldn't have surprised me, but I'd never seen that style of Submariner in person before.

I hesitated when I reached him, debating what I wanted to take off of him first. I knew, somewhere in my gut, that taking his clothes off should have been demoralizing or demeaning in some way, but the first time he'd asked it of me, it very much felt like a privilege. This second chance was no different, sensation pricking the tips of my fingers when I lifted the hem of his shirt over his head.

Like last time, he didn't help me at all, which made it difficult by the time I got to his shoes and socks, but I fought through it, leaving us both naked in the end. I set his clothes in a pile beside mine and met him once again in the center of the room that somehow felt so much larger without my clothes on.

"Turn around and let me see your ass," he said.

I did.

Alex dropped into a squat behind me, kneading and pressing his way around the remnants of the bruises on my ass and the backs of my thighs. Some were worse than others, and some had faded entirely. I didn't want to admit I'd secretly been dreading the day the last of them healed back to healthy skin. Hopefully, he'd leave me with more so I could think of him for longer this time.

"How many times have you jerked yourself off since I saw you last?" he asked.

I snorted, tilting my head back to stare at the black painted ceiling. "I lost count."

"More than five?"

"Yes."

I'd managed five times in the first two days.

"Ten?" he asked next.

"More."

He stood and stepped closer to me, pressing his chest against my back, his hard cock against my bruised ass. Wrapping one arm around the front of my chest, he hauled us close as our bodies could get, throwing me enough off-balance that I reached for his forearm with both hands to steady myself.

"I haven't touched myself once," he whispered in my ear, lips warm against my lobe. "Though I haven't been able to stop thinking about you."

"Why not?"

"Why didn't I touch myself?" he repeated.

I nodded.

His fingers dug into my forearm and, in one quick motion, he spun me and shoved me down to my knees. Alex fisted my hair, angled my head back and teased his wet dick against my mouth, which I quickly opened for him.

"Because the real thing is better."

"You didn't reach out," I said, but as I opened my mouth he took it as an invitation and pushed his cock past my teeth and onto my tongue, silencing me.

"I reached out when I wanted to," he said, pushing his thick shaft into my mouth with far less patience than he'd used the first time. "When I was ready for your throat again."

I should have been offended at the comment. I *knew* it. An entire lifetime of social conditioning and expectation dictated that his reduction of me to nothing more than a body to use and fuck should have been humiliating. Instead, my cock leaked a stream of precum against my thigh and I breathed through my nose so I could open my mouth wider for him.

What I felt instead of shame was an overwhelming sense of pride and longing. He'd waited for me, for this. I'd been so good to him, so good for him, he'd wanted more. Considering how many things I'd recently failed at, all the circumstances that had come together in my life to send me to the brink of mental and financial collapse, Alex wanting me, waiting for me…it was the biggest win I could have ever asked for.

He tested his entry into the back of my throat and I gagged around him, back bowing even though his tight grip in my hair didn't allow me to get away from him. The gasping breath I tried to manage allowed me enough of a reminder that be the rest of it as it may, Alex was still a stranger who was paying me for sex. While the end result might have been a win, the relationship itself was the same as the rest of the ones in my life.

It was transactional.

Cost of goods sold.

"Green?" he asked, jaw clenched.

I answered with a jerky nod.

"I want to fuck your throat." He licked his lips and I wanted to melt into the floor. "Can you handle that?"

Probably not.

I nodded again.

Alex grabbed my head, one hand on either side, and then he delivered on his promise, shoving his fat cock so deep into my throat I didn't think I'd ever be able to breathe again. My body didn't care, responding by breaking out in gooseflesh down my arms and legs, my cock twitching its way toward my stomach with every pump of his hips.

I closed my eyes, tears streaking past my lashes as he set a punishing pace that had my jaw quaking for how much work it was to hold it open. I finally had to reach between my legs and press the heel of my palm against my cock so I didn't shoot a load onto the floor.

"You're so good at this, pet," Alex whispered, fingernails biting into my scalp. "So good at being used."

I whimpered, spit sputtering out of my mouth, and as fast as Alex put me on my knees, he had me on my back. With one of his knees on the floor and the other digging into my forearm, he covered my eyes with one hand and took his dick into the other. Before I could even register or ask why, hot bursts of cum landed on my swollen mouth and my tear-slicked cheeks.

Alex grunted and groaned, his knee boring into my muscle with such an acute pressure, something in my body misfired. That had to be what happened because I cried out beneath him, my own cock emptying untouched onto my stomach. If he noticed, I couldn't tell. His fingers were still clamped down hard across my eyes, and I sucked in a breath, choking out another strangled cry as my cock spasmed and spurted.

After what felt like an eternity, he peeled his hand off my face and took his knee off my arm. Blood rushed to the pressure point, another searing burst of pain—an unwanted awareness of my body—and the last bits of cum trickled out of my slit. He sat on his ass and smeared his fingers through the mess on my stomach, tracing his way up to my mouth and tapping at my lower lip.

"Green?" he asked softly.

"Green."

He shoved his fingers into my mouth, depressing my tongue and pushing my cum straight into the back of my throat. I gagged around him, arching up off the floor and practically flying into his arms. He kept his fingers deep in my mouth, pushing further until the need to throw up all over him passed.

"That's how deep inside your mouth I was," he said, pulling his hand free.

The rush of air caught me off-guard and I choked at the same time I tried to breathe, coughing so hard it hurt my ribs. Alex waited silently beside me on the floor while I tried to compose myself and staying silent long after I had pulled myself together. His cum dried on my face, cracking around my mouth and mine had pooled in my navel, tugging at the thin trail of hair that ran down my stomach to my still-hard cock.

"There's a cabinet in the back of the room," he finally said. "Go find something in there that interests you."

"I don't know about any of this." My voice broke, hoarse and tired.

"Use your imagination."

I was halfway to the cabinet when his voice rang out again, "And get condoms and lube."

I swallowed, pulling open the cabinet doors and doing my best to swallow down the overwhelm I felt at the sight in front of me. There was plenty in the cabinet I knew about—cuffs and gags and paddles and blindfolds. I'd seen enough porn in my life to understand the basics of that kind of kink, but there were other things… whips and chains, and implements that looked far more severe than the rest of it.

The only thing I knew was I wanted Alex to hurt me.

I wanted him to leave fresh marks on me that I could sit on and poke at for days after we parted, so I pulled a wooden paddle off one of the hooks. It looked like it was oak, polished and heavy, the threat of it enough to make my cock twitch back to life after my earlier unplanned release.

I took the paddle, lube, and a strip of condoms back to where Alex still sat in the middle of the room. He squinted up at my selection, mouth pulling into what almost looked like a frown.

"Green?" I asked *him* for the first time.

He huffed, the frown quickly shifting into half of a smile.

"Green," he said, pushing onto his feet and taking the supplies out of my hands. "Go bend over the bed, stretch your arms toward the wall and spread your legs as far as you can."

I did, tucking my cock up against my stomach as I situated myself the way he'd instructed.

"You're still marked from my hand," he said, sounding almost proud. I wished I could see his face to confirm. "This paddle is going to make it worse."

"I like the bruises."

"There's cream to help heal them," he said.

"I like the bruises," I repeated.

"I imagine you do, pet." Alex tossed the lube and the condoms beside my face on the bed. "Tell me how many times you got yourself off this week."

"Twelve," I admitted, closing my eyes.

Fuck, I was tired.

Alex rubbed the wood against my ass. The surface didn't feel so smooth as it pulled against my sweaty skin. "Twelve strikes, then. A hundred dollars each sound fair, pet?"

I wanted to scream.

I would have done it for free, but I needed the money more than I needed the orgasms.

Tears pricked at the backs of my eyelids again, a salty reminder that no matter how kind the words out of his mouth sounded to my ears, this wasn't anything more than an exchange of services for payment. Sex for money. That was what he'd offered and what we'd agreed on. That was the reason I was here, bent over a bed with my ass on display and my cock ready to burst.

"More than," I said through gritted teeth.

"I hope you think that when I'm finished."

Before I could reply, he brought the paddle down on my ass hard enough to lift my feet off the floor. I screamed, clawing for the wall, my cock pushing another pulse of precum onto the sheets.

"Green?" he asked.

I fucking sobbed, gasping for breath. "Green."

As quickly as I'd thought about the money, I forgot it, unable to focus on anything besides the sound of that handcrafted wood paddle landing down against my bruised ass with all the force Alex had in him.

"Fuck, Dylan," he cursed under his breath, and I didn't dare open my eyes to find out why. "Just...fuck."

He spanked me a third time, fourth time, fifth.

The walls fell away and I sucked in the cleanest breath of air I'd ever breathed in my life. The pain twisted and morphed, shapeshifting into sensations I'd never have words for. I understood why Tate was chasing after sex, if what he wanted to replicate was *anything* like this.

Six.

Seven.

Nothing fucking mattered anymore. Nothing beyond me bending over the bed and taking this blunt force against my ass and my thighs, but every strike of the paddle felt like a caress, a promise.

Eight.

Nine.

Ten.

I was coming again, my whole body burning from the inside out as I spilled onto the sheets, my cock so hot there was no way it wasn't branding itself into my stomach with every pulse. I needed to crawl away. I needed to push back. I needed less and more and everything all at the same time.

Eleven.

Twelve.

The paddle dropped onto the floor and Alex tore open the condom wrapper with his teeth. Time was fast and slow, and the lube was cold between my cheeks. He pushed two fingers into me and I didn't even have the words to tell him I'd already gotten off, that my body was already loose and pliant for him.

He replaced his finger with that perfect, thick cock of his, pushing into me with one forceful thrust. His coarse thigh hair abraded the backs of my thighs like razor blades, and I welcomed it. The pain wrapped around me like a blanket, tighter and tighter until I found security in the weight of it.

It was so confusing, but it was also the only thing I'd understood for months.

Alex fucked me onto the bed, using his body to push my knees onto the edge of the mattress. He hauled me onto all fours and slammed into me, cock splitting my ass open just like he'd finished doing to my mouth. He rutted into me, chest rumbling with a low growl when his cock impossibly thickened inside of me. There was no protest in me, only compliance and greed for more. My body was bruised and battered for him, at his pleasure, and I bore down, swallowing the last centimeter of his cock into my body as he filled the condom.

"Jesus, you're the best hole I've ever fucked."

I knew it was a compliment; I told myself over and over as he bowed over me, body shaking from the force of his orgasm. I was still a wet and trembling mess myself, but the reality began to trickle in.

The only things I'd get to go home with were twelve hundred dollars and the need for a shower.

Not him.

Sex for money was fine, but I couldn't have sex with Alex Burke ever again.

I wanted him too much.

I wanted him for real.

AFTER THE NIGHT AT THE BLACK DOOR, DYLAN STOPPED ANSWERING my messages. He read them, but never replied, leaving me at a loss for what to do next. I wanted to see him again, but I didn't want to chase him down at Tryst for a second time. In a much more reasonable response to being ignored, I pulled some strings and got him a job at The Black Door. I put in his name with the owner and if fate called for one of his shifts to overlap on a day I happened to be there, I wasn't going to look that gift horse in the mouth.

He didn't have to take the job, but...I hoped he would.

I lost count of the days, but on a Friday night my app pinged with an incoming message. My heart caught in my throat when I realized it was from Dylan. I'd subconsciously known that my body had been primed and waiting for him to get back to me, but there was also part of me that hadn't ever expected it to happen. Instead of a message asking to hook up or meet, it was two simple words.

Thank you.

I was certain he didn't intend it as an opening, but I took it as one just the same.

I could have messaged my friends, talked to Brooks or Ford or even Kale. They were all worried about me, but I didn't want their sympathy looks or their pity drinks. It was easier to pretend I hadn't lost *anything* when Carter left than to try and minimize the loss of him in their company. I'd seen Ford for drinks at Tryst before Dylan ghosted me, and I'd had lunch with Brooks on more than one occasion. They weren't being deprived, and besides, I knew I wasn't the best company.

I silenced my phone, got dressed, and headed to The Black Door.

It was a decent crowd for how early in the night it was, and it was easy to find Dylan behind the bar in the back of the main room. He was feet away from the room I'd spanked him senseless in the last time we were together, and seeing him there...I could feel the pull. I wanted to take him in the bathroom, rough fuck him against a wall just to remind myself how good it felt to be inside of him, but things were different.

This was his job now.

And I didn't know much about what had led to the circumstances that pushed him into my bed, but I knew he needed the money. If he wouldn't take mine, I wasn't going to interfere with the ways he chose to find it. I had a membership to The Black Door and it wasn't a mystery that I had a hand in getting him hired. He had to have taken the job expecting to run into me sooner or later. If the look on his face when I stepped up to the bar was any indication, he was just as relieved to be back in my company as I was to have him in mine.

"Thank you," he said to me instead of hello.

"I just put your name on their radar," I said. "You got yourself the job."

"You know what I mean." He worked his jaw back and forth like he was chewing on his cheek. "Can I get you a drink? It's on me."

"I can pay," I reminded.

He rolled his eyes. "Martini?"

"Yes, Dylan. Thank you."

His nostrils flared, but he turned and grabbed the gin from the top shelf and set to work mixing me the dirtiest martini I'd ever seen.

"I haven't been able to stop thinking about you," he said softly when he delivered me my drink.

"You could have called."

"I didn't think it was appropriate."

This felt like a gray area, and it seemed we both knew it. Every time we'd been together, it had been a transaction. Money for sex. But the interest I felt for him and the desire that burned in my chest every time I thought about him was far beyond reasonable for the unspoken limits of our relationship. It was the main reason I hadn't reached out to him either.

"I still have marks," he said, seeming to change the subject.

"This long?"

His mouth twitched in the corner. "I keep poking at them."

"Did you want more?"

"I don't know if that's a good idea," he said, glancing sideways as a man I recognized and knew far too well made his way to the bar. "But are you—"

"You look like you're in a good mood," Brooks said, stepping up beside me at the bar.

"My favorite bartender from my favorite bar just got a job here," I said, and just like that, a mask slipped over Dylan's face and he was back in bartender mode, the same way I'd met him. He made easy conversation with Brooks, made him a martini almost as filthy as mine, and paid him no mind when Brooks ushered me away from the bar and out toward the elevator.

On the rooftop, I entertained his twenty questions about Dylan, making it clear we had history together without going into the sordid details he was trying to get out of me. The night turned far more interesting when Dylan's best friend showed up, and we all learned Brooks had been a scoundrel, stealing the man's virginity without so much as a call the next day. It was far too much excitement for me, considering I hadn't even wanted to see anyone besides Dylan that night, so I left Brooks to clean up his mess with Tate. I'd get hell for it later, but I'd manage.

I didn't bother saying goodbye to Dylan, which felt shitty of me, but his voice hadn't quit echoing in my head.

I don't know if that's a good idea, but are you...

Brooks had cut him off before he could finish his sentence, and if the final word had been paying, I would have thrown myself off the roof. Because yes, I would gladly pay for a chance to get him into my bed again, but I didn't want to pay. I wanted him to want more from me, to see me for the man I was or could be for him and more than just a way to get his rent paid easily.

I went home, put on a pair of lounge pants, and collapsed on my couch with a bottle of red wine. I fell asleep halfway through, the half-drank glass falling out of my hand and shattering on the floor. The wine spread out like a pool of blood, my own personal crime scene. In a way, it was—or it should have been—because I needed to cut Dylan out of me once and for all or it would kill me.

I could not handle another loss if it wasn't on my own terms.

I stared at the wine spreading across my floor, every part of my tired and buzzed brain so focused on the stain that I almost missed the way my phone screen flashed to life on the arm of the couch. I'd silenced it before heading to the club, which meant I had a dozen text messages from Brooks that I'd ignored, and one unread message from Dylan.

"Can I come over?" he asked.

No.

"Yes," I told him.

I confirmed he had my address, understanding it was going to be impossible to be rid of him unless the feeling was mutual. I didn't want to hurt him, but I lost my head around him. If I told him I wanted to fuck him for free, would it scare him off? Would it bring him closer? I didn't know which one I wanted...which outcome was better. My mind raced, palms sweating as I ran through every possible scenario and ending, and by the time Dylan arrived on my porch, I wasn't myself.

I mean...I *was*, but far from the best version of myself.

I had five hundred dollars cash upstairs on my dresser, and if all Dylan wanted me for was my money, I was going to make him earn it.

"Thank you for the job," he said again, and I didn't know if he was talking about The Black Door or about fucking me.

I sniffed, scrunching my nose and stepping out of the way

to let him inside. He toed his shoes off just inside the door, his stare raking over my bare feet, up my legs, and across my naked torso and chest before landing on my face. He looked tired and halfway hopeful.

I didn't even know what time it was.

"Strip," I said, stepping out of the way so he had space to get out of his clothes. Why did he smell so good all the time? Like lemons and limes and sweat, all of it living just beneath the surface of his skin.

Dylan smelled like spring.

He'd only done it for me twice, but he folded his clothes so neatly in a pile, like he didn't want to exist in my home without explicit permission. It made me want to cry and scream and slam him against a wall. He was so perfect for me, it was unfair. Everything I wanted in a person, and he didn't even know it. He didn't understand.

I'd make him understand.

"I spilled my wine by the couch," I said. "Go clean it up."

He opened his mouth to argue. I saw the fight flash across his face, but he snapped his mouth closed and shuffled past me. Upstairs into the kitchen and down the hallway into the living room. I didn't follow after him, but the house was deathly quiet and I listened to the broken glass clink together as he dropped it into a pile, heard him spray cleaner onto the floor, his bare feet padding back into the kitchen and putting everything away...

His hesitation as to what came next.

So he waited.

I climbed the stairs, using the banister to haul myself up because my feet felt like lead. Knowing I would find Dylan naked in my kitchen, it was unfair. The biggest cruelty of my life, short of losing Carter to Dalton Fox. At least it had been, until I found Dylan in my kitchen, just as I'd expected, except his cock was hard.

Maybe losing Carter hadn't been such an injustice after all.

"What now?" he asked, and I wished I had an answer.

"Show me your ass," I said. "You told me you were still bruised and I want to see it."

Dylan turned around slowly and bent a little at the hips, jutting his ass out toward me. I leaned against the wall and folded my arms in front of my chest so I didn't touch him.

"I don't see anything," I said.

He reached behind himself and pressed his finger into the fold between his thigh and his ass. He knew exactly where the bruise remained, and I imagined it was only there because he'd been fucking with it the longest.

"Go to the playroom. Get on the bench and wait for me."

Dylan sucked in a sharp breath and disappeared toward the playroom. I took the time to compose myself, my earlier buzz from the bar long gone. It was nearly five in the morning, and I should have been in bed. Nothing good had ever come from being awake with a man an hour before sunrise.

Just the same, I got my cash from my bedroom and went back to the front door, tucking it in a pocket of Dylan's jeans before heading into the playroom. I was never prepared for the sight of him, bent over furniture he didn't have names for, fighting against arousal he didn't understand. He looked like an angel, tense and pale on the back of my black spanking bench, ass in the air.

"Use the handles," I said, stepping into the room.

He stretched his arms down and curled his fingers around

the handles I'd had installed above the O-rings. I appreciated the psychology of kink as much as the physicality, and sometimes it was fun to restrain partners, sometimes it was better to make them do it themselves.

I picked a thin leather riding crop out of my armoire and joined Dylan at the bench. I didn't get condoms or lube because I had no plans on fucking him again. If I dared to put my cock back into him, there was not going to be any coming back for me. Head over heels, ass up, whatever you wanted to call it. I would have been done. Instead, I stood behind him and pulled my dick over the waistband of my pants, giving a slow stroke up my hardness.

"Green?" I asked.

"Green."

Tucking the crop under my arm, I braced myself with one hand against the small of his back and began to stroke my cock, not bothering to hold back my moans or sighs.

"You're trouble, pet," I whispered, lining the tip of my cock up with the bruise he'd poked in the kitchen. "You're no good for me."

"Yes, I am," he argued.

"I wasn't asking for your opinion."

I came on the back of his leg, jets of cum streaking over the barely visible bruise, the only evidence that we'd ever been together. Dylan's whole body went rigid, his head jerking to the side. It didn't give him an angle to see me, though, and the fact he kept his hands on the bench was enough to push another stream of cum out of my dick.

He really was the best listener.

The tightest hole.

The most willing submissive.

After my orgasm settled, I tested the crop in my shaking hand, then cracked it down onto his skin. I focused on the spot he'd shown me, the place I'd just marked him with my cum. Over and over, I spanked the same spot with the biting leather tip of the crop, hitting him until there was definitely a fresh bruise and my release had been pushed straight into his pores. Dylan humped himself against the bench, undoubtedly chasing after an orgasm he didn't have permission for.

"Stop it," I warned, finding the last bits of strength in my arm to hit him six more times before letting the crop fall onto the floor.

"Green?"

He whimpered, "Green."

I helped him up off the bench, rubbing my fingers over his white knuckles, trying to work blood back into them. There was precum smeared across the bench and over his stomach, his cock impossibly hard and angry between his legs. Once he was on steady feet, I gave him a onceover and stepped away.

"Can you walk?" I asked.

"Yes," he rasped, flexing his hands at his sides.

"Good." I nodded, tucking my cock back into my pants. "I'll call you a car."

CHAPTER 9
DYLAN

Honestly, fuck Alex.

That's what I said to myself over and over when I scrolled through the dozens of unread messages from other men who wanted to pay me for sex.

Fuck Alex, and I would call my own fucking cars.

I picked a random message from the list. His picture wasn't anything more than a muscular torso with some strong arms in the frame. He had pictures of his cock, carefully hidden behind a pair of tight white briefs that left little to the imagination. Judging by the outline, he wasn't thick as Alex, which would be a relief. I hadn't fucked anyone since him, and the bruises he'd spanked into my skin had long since faded. He hadn't messaged me, and I was thankful because I didn't know if I'd be able to say no to him if he did.

I hated the way my body reacted when I thought about him. Hated that I still jerked off thinking about cleaning his stupid floors, folding his clothes. All of those things shouldn't turn a person on, shouldn't turn *me* on. But every time...

Every fucking time.

The torso on the app told me his name was John, which I didn't believe, but it didn't matter. I went to his studio apartment in Manhattan and he fucked me for six minutes before he came.

He paid me a hundred dollars.

I didn't get off, but it didn't really matter. The money was better than the orgasm, so I answered another message the next night, and another the night after that. Keeping my bank account in the black was suddenly a possibility, and the best part...Tate was none the wiser. He was falling more in love with Alex's friend every day, and I was absolutely not going to ruin that for him with my bad decisions.

I was halfway through a shift at Tryst when my phone vibrated in my pocket, another message on my app. My heart skittered around my chest, part nerves and part excitement. I couldn't lie, the edge of fear that came with all the random hookups definitely helped get me hard most of the time. Even though it was all transactional, it was a huge boost for my ego. My parents had told me I was worthless, yet here were all these men who proved otherwise.

They saw me and they *wanted* me.

Some of them even wanted me more than once, but I said no. I learned that lesson with Alex, and I wasn't going to fall into the trap of repeating that confusion all over again.

I checked the message and found it from a generic profile that didn't even have a profile picture. The message had the content, though, a picture of a long cock hanging half-hard below a soft belly, a thick hand wrapped around the shaft. I would have judged him to be a construction worker based off the size of his fingers and the callouses around his knuckles.

He sent me an address and a dollar amount, and I answered him back with a time.

I finished up my shift at work and plugged the address into my phone. It was a seven minute walk from the bar so I enjoyed the fresh air up until the moment I buzzed for entry into the building. That was when the nerves started to take over, my palms started to sweat, my heart rate spiking.

He'd also said his name was John, and his apartment door was cracked open when I got there. It was a nice enough looking place, even if it appeared the furnishings came straight out of a college dorm dumpster. Alarms blared in the back of my head, a feeling I hadn't had any of the other times I'd hooked up with men on the app, but then he was in front of me, impossibly tall and broad.

"Never—" I started to call the whole thing off, and he shoved a handful of crumpled bills toward me.

"It's double what you asked for."

"Why?" I asked, voice shaking. I jammed the bills into my pocket, not bothering to check.

"Because I like it rough."

I swallowed, blinking slowly and mentally working through the options available to me. I could try and run, bolt out the door with or without the cash. Or I could make the best of the situation. Alex liked rough sex. I liked rough sex. Maybe getting tossed around by the wall of a man in front of me would be enough to shake Alex out of my head forever. If not...there would always be another one.

And anything was better than crawling back to my parents.

I shrugged my consent and he pushed me down to my knees.

His cock was as big as I'd imagined it, and in the back of my throat he tasted like soap and skin. It was far from the worst cock I'd ever sucked, and he fucked my mouth so aggressively, I started to cry. Tears streaked down my cheeks, mixing with the spit that he'd fucked out of my mouth with the force of his thrusts.

This was fine.

Honestly, better than fine.

But it wasn't long until the look of hooded arousal on his face shifted to something darker and far more menacing. He pulled his cock out of my mouth, spit on my face, and yanked me up by my hair. It happened so fast, the biting pain in my scalp didn't even have time to register before he turned me and shoved me against the door.

"Only pussies cry during sex," he growled.

Ah. I understood what was happening now.

He changed hands, holding me against the door by my throat so he could get my pants down. Somehow, he managed to get a condom on, which was the only saving grace of the whole thing, and then he pushed his entire erection into me with one sharp pump of his hips. There was so much force behind it, it lifted me onto my toes, my fingers scrabbling at the his around my throat, but he was steadfast.

He came in less than a minute, pulling out of me and letting go of my throat at the same time. I slumped down to the floor, mind racing and somehow blank at the same time.

"You're disgusting," he said, stroking his cock over the condom. He was still hard, still angry.

I scrambled to my feet and ran out of his apartment, doing up my pants on the stairs. I waited until I was halfway home to pull the wadded up bills out of my pocket. He'd made good on his word at least, paying me double what I'd asked for. I couldn't even be mad about it. He told me he wanted it rough, and he took it rough. He paid more than what I'd agreed on and I was in and out in under ten minutes.

I was still shaking when I got home, thankful that Tate was at his boyfriend's house so I didn't have to explain. Sitting down on the couch, I smoothed the hundred dollar bills out with shaky hands, lining them up on the coffee table and tracing the edges with the tip of my finger until they laid flat.

"You're fine," I said to myself, frowning at the money and reaching for my guitar.

The sound that came after the first strum of the strings sounded as off key as it had the first time I'd played. Taking two deep breaths, I twisted the keys, checking the result until everything sounded closer to normal. By the time I'd finished, my heart had stopped playing an accompaniment, and I softly hummed my way through the beginnings of a new song.

Three hours later, the bills on the table had curled up again at the edges, but I had a chorus and two verses, scribbling the words down onto the back of our water bill. Another hour after that, I'd forgotten John entirely, the lyrics and the crescendo of the bridge enough to sweep me out of my life and into a better one. A life where I didn't have to rely on my parents for anything, where my music was good enough to pay the bills, where I could go to Juilliard and stay living with Tate and have the life I wanted.

It was nearly eight in the morning, and I needed to go to sleep, but I was so close to being done with the song. With a yawn, I set the guitar down, my body protesting as soon as I stretched my legs out. I was sore from sitting so long, sore from being fucked against a wall without any prep and barely any lube. I stood and shuffled into the bathroom to piss and shower, hoping the blast of tepid water would be enough to keep me going until the afternoon.

Flipping on the lights, I reached behind me and grabbed my shirt. Rucking it up over my head, I tossed it onto the floor and then blearily blinked at my reflection. The man who stared back at me had my blood running cold. There was no way that was me.

That...

Slowly, I lifted my fingertips to my throat and craned over the sink to get closer to the mirror. My neck was bruised, my throat...those calloused, thick fingers having done more to me than his cock had managed in either of my holes.

"Shit."

The bands of purple wrapped around the side of my neck, and there was no way to pretend they were anything other than exactly what they were. I had work at The Black Door later, a gig in a couple of days...I couldn't do any of those things with a handprint around my neck, but I didn't have much of a choice.

What if Tate came home?

What would I tell him?

"Just rough sex," I said to my reflection. It was a lie, but it was also the truth and it would have to do. But the dichotomy of the situation wasn't enough to stop me from pulling my phone out of my pocket and scrolling through my contacts. My finger hovered over my dad's number. All I had to do was call him and apologize. Tell him he was right and I was wrong and ask for a job. He'd probably make me sell my guitar, which would be more of a punishment than anything Alex had ever done to me.

More than anything I'd done to myself.

Before I made a mistake, I threw my phone into the sink and climbed into the shower. It wasn't until the water was burning the top of my head that I realized I hadn't taken off my pants.

I should have called my dad.

Getting out of wet work pants with an asshole that felt like I'd ridden a two-by-four was the hardest thing I'd done in weeks, but maybe that was just the exhaustion setting in. I finally kicked free of them and my underwear, and I washed myself as gingerly as I deserved, then I curled up on top of my soaking wet clothes and cried until the water ran cold above me.

Then I dried off, wrung out my clothes, tucked the money into my wallet, and finished writing the song.

Life kept going, and I needed to do the same.

CHAPTER 10
ALEX

FORD AND I HAD BEEN IN MY BACK YARD FOR HOURS, FEET BARE AND legs stretched out across the bricks, bottle of gin half-empty between us. If I closed my eyes, I was almost myself again. Almost the man I'd been before Dylan ruined my life, before Carter ruined my life...before *I* ruined my life.

"Is Boston going to be waiting up for you?" I asked, dropping my head back and opening my eyes. The lights were off, but New York was nothing except light pollution. There wasn't a star in sight, even though it was well after midnight.

Ford hummed, pouring himself another drink. "I'd rather talk about you."

I huffed. "I'm sure you would."

"I'm boring," he said with a sloppy shrug. "I'm in love with my best friend's brother. I just bought him a farm. My other best friend bought a goddamn motorcycle and is turning into a recluse. There's absolutely no chaos in my life at all."

"Me, on the other hand?" I prompted.

"You." He clinked his glass against mine and I closed my

eyes on a weary exhale. "You are pretending you're not in love and hoping none of us notice."

"I don't love Beamer," I said simply.

Ford sniffed. "I didn't mean him."

There was no practical way Ford could have known about Dylan, known anything that had been going on with me besides the things I'd told him, which were few and far between. And I definitely hadn't given enough away with Brooks for him to have pieced anything together. Ford was doing what he did best, I guessed. He was fishing, which was the same way he'd talked Kale's younger brother into bed and gotten him into the very un-chaotic mess he'd just been referencing.

"I'm not in love," I said.

"Lust."

"A stretch."

Ford took a swallow of gin. "I know the look of a man who's had a taste of the one thing in life he never even realized he needed."

"You're drunk, Ford."

"I'm drunk and you're in love."

I was not in love with Dylan Rivers.

I enjoyed the time we'd spent together, enjoyed the way he let me play, the way he sucked and fucked, but that didn't mean I had feelings for him. Avoiding an emotional attachment was the exact reason I'd sent him home the last time he'd come over. It was a dick move—I knew that when it was happening—but Dylan...he was broken in ways I wasn't ready to fix. Wasn't *able* to fix. It was too easy for me to still see Carter tied down in my playroom when it was Dylan's body before mine, and that was reason enough to keep my hands off of him. He was young, attractive, and great in bed. He wouldn't have a hard time finding someone better than me to scratch all of his itches and then some.

"I slept with someone a couple of times," I finally admitted, knowing Ford well enough to know he wouldn't leave it alone without at least some morsel of information. "After Beamer moved away."

"Recently."

"Very."

"And then you fell in love with him?" he asked, chuckling under his breath. "That's how Boston got me too."

"I'm not in love with him," I snapped. "It's over. It...it didn't even start. He was just a body."

"Okay, Alex." The sarcasm in Ford's tone was thick enough to cut with a dull butter knife.

"I can't believe you came over here, drank my best gin, and then had the audacity to talk to me this way."

"Brooks called me out about Boston, and I'm repaying the favor to you." Ford shrugged, head lolling to the side so I could see the smug and shit-eating grin on his face. "What's his name?"

"It doesn't matter."

"What's his name?" Ford asked again.

"Dylan."

Stressing his name was near enough to a spell, dangerously close to willing the scent of him back into existence. Thankfully, the wind kicked up, whipping through the green shrubs that lined the perimeter of my back yard. Every time of year the garden was one of my favorite luxuries at the house. Most places in the city didn't have much outdoor space, let alone the manicured slice of heaven that had been in my family for generations.

"Dylan," Ford repeated. "Tell me about him."

"Nothing to tell. I told you it's over."

"Tell me anyway."

"You're such a prick."

Ford grinned at me, expression full of that deviant charm that had always made him so irresistible to everyone else.

"I met him at Tryst—"

"I like that place," Ford interrupted.

"Met him there, brought him home, spanked him, fucked him, made him kneel, a lot of the usual."

"That's hardly usual for you," he said softly, squinting one eye at me while he sipped at his drink some more.

"What is usual for me?"

"Meeting a man at The Black Door and pretending you're getting enough satisfaction from throwing him over your lap and making him come before his ass even turns pink, for starters."

I licked my lips, cheeks burning. "I'm apparently just too good with my hands."

"That's the rumor." Ford set his glass down. "Tell me more about the kneeling?"

I cleared my throat, pushing out of my chair and onto my feet. "I don't want to talk about that part."

"Because it has to do with Beamer?" he asked.

"I liked you better when you were drunker." I gestured to the bottle on the table beside him. "Have some more gin."

"There's no harm in learning you like a man at your feet, Alex."

"I've always known what I like." I walked across the yard, putting as much space between us as I could. Resting my back against the cool bricks, I folded my arms in front of my chest. "Beamer was just the thing that made all of you find out about it."

"Rough enough to leave marks?" he asked, knowing damn well that was true. It was bruises around Carter's wrists that had given us away in the first place. Well, bruises around his wrists and an eagle-eyed Kale Sheffield.

"Yes," I said.

"And Beamer liked that."

I didn't say anything because he knew the answer.

"Your Dylan," he half slurred, licking his lips, "he likes it?"

"He liked it."

"Past tense?"

"That's what I told you." I pushed off the wall and headed back to my chair, throwing myself down in it with a sigh. There was no escaping Ford. "Things didn't work out and that's the end of it."

Ford finished the last of my gin and made a show of smacking his lips in satisfaction. "You should call him."

"You should call Kale," I said, rolling my eyes. "Clear the air over all the brother fucking you're doing."

"You're comparing apples and potatoes," he said, fishing his phone out of his pocket and stabbing a bleary finger at the screen. "I'm going to tell Boston I'm staying here tonight."

"I'll call you a car, Ford," I offered, hauling him up to his feet. He was a tall son of a bitch, and his weight knocked us both sideways into the door.

"I don't want a car," he pouted, pushing his phone back into his pocket. "I want to stay here."

Something barbed and hot twisted in the middle of my chest, making it far too hard to breathe.

"I already told Boston," he went on, unfazed by my unease. "He knows I'm safe here."

I clenched my jaw together so tight, I wondered if it would crack my molars. As I walked Ford into the house, his words bouncing around all the places in my brain I'd tried to evict Dylan from, I found myself feeling like more of an asshole than Kale ever had. I *knew* Dylan had some serious shit going on, but I'd brushed it aside to make it easier for me. Paying him for sex was nothing for me and everything for him, and maybe I'd taken advantage by how I'd let things play out the last time he'd come over.

The abrupt cutoff had been an act of self-preservation because I'd done so much work to heal from the way my heart ached after things with Carter went away, and I didn't want to slide right back into the same headspace all over again. I didn't want to have to pretend or lie to my friends anymore. I wanted my life back, and Dylan could have been enough to sweep more than just the rug out from under me.

Whether he felt safe underfoot was another story entirely, but I had a sneaking suspicion he did. If not, there would have been no reason—short of a quick fix—for him to answer any of my messages and come back to me. Money made some people do crazy things. I'd seen it enough with the men my friends had made habits of bringing home in the past.

With all those distractions in mind, I walked Ford into the guest room and gave him a little harder of a push than he deserved down onto the bed. He landed with a dramatic *oomph* noise, which turned into a laugh.

"You're in love with Dylan," he said.

I yanked the blankets down and shoved Ford's legs beneath the sheets.

"I'm not undressing you for bed," I said, turning on the bedside lamp and heading for the door.

"But you'll get me water." Ford rolled onto his side and tucked his hands together under his head, arms aligned from his fingers down to his elbows. "And something for my head."

I'd already been planning on doing just that, but the awareness he knew that was almost enough to make me take it all back.

"Anything else?" I asked, hand braced on the door frame.

"No, Alex. I have everything I need."

I turned off the overhead light and stalked down to my kitchen, where I angrily filled a glass with water. Slamming the faucet off with a rough slap, I detoured to the bathroom for the Advil and found Ford dead to the world by the time I returned to the guest room.

"I hate you," I told his sleeping body, leaving both the water and the pills on the nightstand.

He'd fallen asleep with that cocky grin on his face, so I turned off the bedside lamp and closed the door behind me on the way out.

I didn't know if an easy slumber was in the cards for me. It so rarely was, but I went to my room anyway, willing to try.

———

The gin must have done the trick because I slept through Ford making himself a continental breakfast in my kitchen. There were dirty pans everywhere, a dried coffee ring beside the stove where he'd set his mug down, and the mug itself in the sink, half finished. He'd brought my paper in, at least, scrawling a *thank you* note across the top of the crossword page because he knew it would be my first stop after sitting down in the morning. Even with the glaring headache that came from too much gin, I set to work with coffee, hoping the caffeine would be enough to kick start my brain. I had no idea where my cell phone ended up after I'd gotten Ford into bed, and judging by the incessant knocking at my door, I wasn't anywhere closer to finding out.

I set the pen on top of the folded newspaper then went to the door, less than pleased for find Brooks on my stoop, dressed for work and primed for an argument.

"To what do I owe the pleasure, Brooks?" I sighed, leaning against the door frame.

"That's what Kale said when I called him this morning. I'm starting to feel like none of my friends like my company anymore."

"I enjoy sleeping," I told him, stepping out of the way to let him in. Brooks followed me into the kitchen, back to my crossword and my coffee and the leftover breakfast Ford had left behind.

When I didn't offer, Brooks asked, "Can I have some coffee?"

"You know where to get it."

I turned my attention back to the crossword puzzle, but the heat of Brooks' stare was searing against the top of my head. I finished two more clues and returned my pen to the table. "What do you want, Brooks?"

"I want to talk to you about Dylan Rivers," he said.

I swallowed down bile, heart exploding in the middle of my chest. "What about him?"

"I just want to know your history with him. He's not just a bartender."

"I know he's not."

"You hired him?" Brooks prompted. "For sex?"

My cheeks flamed, somehow hot and cold all at the same time. Was this embarrassment? Shame? Guilt?

"It's not a secret, Brooks."

"I know it's not. I'm not here to accuse you of anything. I just…"

"What, Brooks?" I picked up a half-eaten slice of toast and bit into it, trying to wait for Brooks to explain what he wanted with Dylan instead of jumping to conclusions.

"He needs…help. I picked him and Tate up from Tryst last night."

"Drinking on a Sunday isn't a red flag."

I should know. I'd done more than my fair share.

Brooks narrowed his eyes at me, lips pursed. "Is it a red flag to have to pull him up from his knees on the bathroom floor and make sure he doesn't choke on the cum a stranger just shot down his throat?"

I couldn't look up from the plate in front of me, form the unfinished crossword, the unfinished *business*. If Dylan wanted to get drunk and suck a stranger off in a bar bathroom, I wasn't anyone to stop him. He wasn't anything to me. *We* weren't…anything

"He's not anything to me."

"I didn't say he was."

"He can suck whoever's cock he wants," I bit out.

"I asked if I could touch him last night and he thought I meant sexually."

"Is that what you meant?" I'd never wanted to hit any of

my friends before, save for Kale, but with the question out of Brooks' mouth, he was very close to making the top of the list. It shouldn't have bothered me at all. If Brooks wanted to fuck Dylan, he could. Dylan wasn't my property. He didn't belong to me.

"I'm in love with Tate, Alex. I assure you it was the last thing I meant. I wanted to console him, rub his back so he didn't throw up all over my stairs." Brooks paused. "He needs someone to be easy with him."

"That's the last thing he wanted when we were together."

"Be that as it may, Alex, I think it's what he needs now."

"I'm not the one for that." I recognized a crossword clue I knew the answer to. Synonym for unharmed, starts with a P. Protected. "That's never been me, and it won't ever be me."

"You can do both, you know," Brooks said gently. "I do."

"That's not...Dylan, he...Have you ever ran the Boston marathon?" It wasn't that I wasn't paying attention, wasn't that Dylan didn't deserve it even though he wasn't here. I just wasn't ready to face the weight of what Brooks was asking of me.

What Dylan was in such a desperate need of.

"Twice."

"What is the town at the eighth mile of the marathon? Six letters, second to last one is a C."

"It's Natick." Brooks took a swallow of coffee, then set the empty mug in the sink beside all of Ford's soiled pans. "Thanks for the coffee. We're taking a trip to Ford and Boston's farm in two weeks, don't think you're getting out of it."

I didn't want to ask why Ford hadn't bothered to bring it up while he was half-conscious in my guest room the night before, but like all things, I was sure there had to be a reason for it.

"Is Kale going?" I asked.

Brooks was already at my front door when he said, "All of us."

I spelled Natick out into the small boxes and closed my eyes with a weary sigh. It was time to face the things I wanted, the truth I'd been hiding from. Before Brooks could close the door, I hollered after him, "I'll call Dylan."

He didn't say a word, but he didn't have to.

The silence was loud enough.

CHAPTER 11

DYLAN

LYING ON MY BED AND STARING UP AT THE CEILING, I WAS THANKFUL I'd drank enough gin the night before to blur most of the memories. I remembered having drinks with Tate at Tryst. The beefy dude who'd left his fingerprints on my neck the night before was there, talking sweet to me and offering me money again. I'd had too much to drink, far too much, and then I'd been on my knees and Tate knew.

Tate knew.

Brooks knew.

Marigold knew.

Everyone knew.

In the comfort of Tate's boyfriend's penthouse, the confession had poured out of me, spilling down the stairs like every word was a drop of blood. Neither of them had judged me, which somehow made me feel worse. Sleep came quick for me that night, and the next morning, Brooks had made sure I found my way home safe and sound. No dicks sucked on the way to Chelsea. Tate came home after lunch and slipped me a chocolate bar beneath the door, and I'd promised him a conversation, just...later.

I'd spent the day playing guitar and trying to decide if Alex had been the catalyst that sent my life into a spiral, but even as my hungover mind tried to put the blame on him, I knew it wasn't true. I was an adult, a spoiled one at that, and I'd made all my own decisions. Every choice had been mine, from the first time I picked up a guitar to the last time I'd told my parents no.

Sometime after the sun sank down below the skyline, there was a loud and demanding knock at my door. I definitely wasn't expecting company and Tate had a key. Slowly, I set my guitar down on the bed and shuffled to the front door, finding Alex's scowling face on the other side of the peephole. I fussed with the deadbolts and pulled the door open, glaring at him.

"What?" I asked, voice sounding far more tired than I would have liked.

"What," he repeated, giving me a slow onceover from my bare feet to my tangled hair. I sighed, wondering if he could see the broken heart in my chest, the twisted knot of misery in the pit of my stomach.

"Why are you here?"

"Brooks called me last night, tracked me down today."

I cracked my neck, staring at the brick on my entryway hall, then I stepped to the side to let him inside.

I tapped my fingers against the bruises on the base of my throat. "I told Brooks this wasn't you."

Alex almost growled, taking the door out of my grip and shoving it closed.

"I don't want to talk about that," he said.

"Then why are you here?"

"I don't know."

Dropping my chin to my chest, I managed half of a nod. It was weird to have him in my apartment, my space...with his clothes on and his arrogance so fucking self-righteous, sucking out all the air. There was no money between us, no skin, just us and the mess we both were.

"Do you want a beer?" I asked, heading to the living room.

"No," he said.

I opened the fridge and his next words stopped me in my tracks. "And you don't need one either."

"You're not my boss, Alex."

I closed the fridge anyway and sat on the couch in the comfortable corner spot that Tate had long ago claimed as his own. Alex sat down without asking, turning his body so he faced me head on.

"Why did you pay me for sex the first time?" I asked.

His eyebrows lifted toward his hairline. "Because I wanted to fuck you."

"Why, though?" I pressed. "It could have been anyone. Why me?"

"Bad idea," he muttered.

I pushed out my lower lip and nodded, wishing I'd gotten a beer when he told me no because the thought of hauling my body up off the couch now was too much for me to even begin to entertain.

"Not many people like things the way I do," he said after a couple of silent minutes had passed.

"People will do anything for money," I told him, "and I'm sure there's plenty of people at The Black Door who have the same kinks as you."

"And what are my kinks, Dylan?"

Even if I had a hundred years, I didn't think I'd be able to unpack Alex's kinks. I didn't even know what my own were, but thanks to him—or not—I had a starting place.

"It doesn't matter," I said.

"I'm a dominant man," he said, words softer but tone somehow harder, more demanding.

"I know," I whispered, tangling my fingers together in my lap. My palms had already started to sweat and I was eighty percent confident it didn't have anything to do with my hangover.

"It's not a kink. It's who I am."

"And what does that mean?" I cracked my thumbs, then my pointer fingers. "Telling people what to do makes you hard?"

"You got hard being told what to do, Dylan. Don't sound so disgusted with it."

I huffed, rolling my eyes. "And that's why Brooks called you?"

"He called me because he loves Tate and wants all of Tate's attention," Alex answered with a half-shrug.

"And he can't have that if Tate is worried about me."

"Correct."

I swallowed, managing a shaky nod. I'd spent so much time worrying about shielding Tate from the mess my life had become that I hadn't even thought about how it would impact him if and when he found out what had been going on with me. He'd become my best friend, and I'd been beyond unfair to him. But that was one more thing for me to add to the list of shit I'd have to apologize for, one more person I owed something to.

Another exchange to make things right.

"I don't need a keeper," I said, pushing myself off the couch. "I need a beer."

"No, you don't," Alex said, not moving, even as I went to the fridge and pulled it open. The apartment was dark, save for the fridge light that washed out in a white fan over my toes.

"You don't know anything about me," I told him, not looking back.

I knew I was playing with fire, and I had no idea what the outcome was going to be. Was he going to offer me more money? Was he going to walk out? Was he going to spank me again?

The thought of Alex taking me over his knee on my couch, tearing down my pants and spanking my ass raw was enough to make my tired cock twitch to life between my legs. I reached into the fridge, hooking my finger around the neck of a beer bottle. It was some crappy IPA Marigold had sent me home with the week before. I didn't even want it. I didn't like IPAs, I just wanted to see what would happen if I pushed Alex too far. It couldn't be any worse than the things that I'd already brought onto myself.

I took the bottle out of the fridge and he still didn't move.

Took the top off...nothing.

Raised the rim to my mouth, smelled the overdone hops.

Alex watched me without a word, arm casually propped on the back of my couch, mouth twitching up in the corner because he already knew I wasn't going to drink it. I tried, willing my elbow to bend, forcing my arm to tip the bottle back. The beer washed across my upper lip and Alex still hadn't said a word to me.

"Fuck," I cursed, throwing the bottle into the sink. It

smashed into pieces against the steel basin, contents glugging down the drain. Spinning away from him, I shoved my hands into my hair, pulling at the roots, desperate for *something* to ground me, to make sense of my life.

"Get on your knees, Dylan," Alex said from the couch.

The command was soft and simple, and my body responded like I didn't have any choice except to obey. Taking the drink out of the fridge—against his wishes—had hurt me, but my knees landing against the wood floor of my apartment felt easy as breathing. My shoulders sagged and before I could even catch a breath, I burst into tears. Covering my face with my hands, I bent forward, pressing my forehead against the edge of a rug we'd picked up off the street a year earlier, and I cried.

I cried, and cried, and Alex didn't move from his throne on my couch. He offered me no kind words, no consolation, but I felt the weight of his stare on me sure as I would if it had been his hand against my back, pressing me down into a ball until I'd soaked the carpet with the last of my tears.

"Why did you let me pay you for sex?" he asked.

My face was covered in snot and tears, my lips wet with spit and my chin still quivering. I felt better and worse in the same breath, relieved and more scared than I'd ever been. I let go of my hair and spread my hands out on the floor in front of me, bowing my back, but keeping my face down.

"Because I needed the money."

"Why *me*?" he asked.

"You looked like you could afford it," I said, sucking as much snot back into my nose as I could manage. "You looked sad."

"Sad people are the dangerous ones, Dylan. They have less to lose."

I rocked back onto my heels, using my head to toss my hair back. My hands fell open on my thighs, palms up. "Like me?"

"I think you've lost enough," he said, tracing his tongue across his lower lip. Back and forth and back and forth, like a metronome.

He was hypnotic, and I wanted him to take me under.

"Why did you let me pay you for sex?" he asked again.

"My parents cut me off."

"Why?"

"Because I wanted to play music and they wanted me to fall into line." I pressed my fingers against the swollen pockets beneath my eyes, swiping the tears away.

"Is your family wealthy?"

"My father is Russell Lang," I answered, his name well enough known in the city that I didn't need more of an explanation than that. "Rivers was my mother's maiden name. She never took his when they got married."

"Surprised he allowed that."

I shrugged. "He wanted her."

"And you?" Alex asked.

"He wanted me to do what he told me to do," I said.

"You do what I tell you to do." He moved for the first time, leaning forward and resting his elbows on his knees, coming closer to my level down on the floor. The apartment was bigger than a shoebox, but it was nowhere near as big as Brooks' penthouse, as Alex's townhome.

I didn't know how to explain the difference to him, that my father told me what to do because he liked the control and the power. He didn't care how I felt about the things he wanted. The only thing that mattered to him was everyone around him toeing the line. The only interest he was worried about was his own. Alex, sitting there on my couch, worry knit between his brows even though he tried to hide it—he cared about much more than *just* himself.

"It's different," I finally said, because if he didn't know the truth, I didn't want to tell him.

Alex hummed out a curious breath, straightening his back and shifting to get more comfortable on the couch. He wasn't going anywhere, and the sense of relief that gave me was better than any orgasm he'd ever given me or ever would.

"Music, then?" He tilted his head to the side in time with the ask.

"Guitar mostly," I answered.

"It means a lot to you?"

No.

Maybe.

It's cost me everything.

"Yes." The answer would never change.

I was on my knees in the middle of an apartment I couldn't afford, with bruises around my neck from a man who didn't even know my name. If this wasn't bottom, I didn't want to know how it could get worse.

"Go get it," he said, jerking his chin toward my bedroom. "Show me what makes this worth it for you."

I squeezed my eyes closed, digging the heels of my hands into my eyes and propelling myself to my feet. The room spun, the gin from the night before still too fresh in my mind. I swallowed down bile, bracing myself on the edge of the kitchen counter. And Alex still didn't move. He offered me no help.

Just like everyone else.

But for some reason... to him, I listened.

I got my guitar, sat down on the couch, and waited for whatever came next.

Dylan was so close and so nervous I could hear his heart beat. Or maybe that was mine, battering a terrified rhythm against my sternum. I knew exactly what to do with Dylan, but I hadn't expected it. I'd spent the past two weeks making peace with walking away from him entirely, then Brooks had thrown me back into his life without even understanding. Ever the philanthropist at heart, and now he trusted me to make the right decisions not just for Dylan or myself, but also for Tate, and by connection—him.

"What do you want me to play?" Dylan asked softly, strumming his fingers up the strings. He winced a bit when he hit the deep reverberation of the E, and I imagined his head was killing him after the night he'd had.

I didn't care, though.

Dylan needed to learn to live with the repercussions of his decisions, good and bad.

"Your choice."

He cleared his throat and opened his mouth like he was

either about to speak or sing, then he snapped it closed just as quick.

"This one doesn't have words," he said.

He lied.

"I don't care," I responded.

"I just wrote the music for it recently."

"And no words?"

He glanced at me from the corner of his eye, confirming we both knew there were lyrics. He just didn't want me to hear them.

"They're not finished."

"And the chords are?" I asked.

He nodded.

"No lyrics then," I agreed.

Dylan sniffed and strummed a couple chords before tapping out a one-two-three-four for himself and launching into one of the saddest melodies I'd ever heard in my life. To call Dylan a talented musician wouldn't have been fair. He was nearer a prodigy, the way his fingers moved up the board, the combination of chords...the song was beautiful. Haunting.

Heartbreaking.

"And you just wrote this?" I asked after he finished.

Dylan tucked the pick behind the strings on the trop fret of his guitar. "A couple weeks ago."

"It's really good."

He shrugged and leaned forward, setting the guitar down on the table. "What now?"

"Did it make you uncomfortable to play it for me?"

He scrunched his nose and gave another shrug. I hated the indecision and weariness every time he raised his shoulders up instead of giving me a real and honest answer.

"Use words," I said, tone more severe than before.

"I'm used to playing in front of people. It's the compliments."

"What about them?"

"I don't believe them." Dylan folded his arms in front of his chest and sank down against the back of the couch. I wondered if he hoped it would swallow him whole.

"Why not?"

"You're only here because Brooks called you."

He wasn't wrong, but it wasn't the whole truth either. I was here because I wanted to be. Brooks had kicked me in the ass, and that was what had physically brought me to Chelsea, but in my heart, I did *want* to be here. Even if that was horrible news for all of us in the long run.

"Do I look like the kind of man who does things he doesn't want to do?" I asked.

Dylan exhaled half a laugh out of his nose and turned toward me, moving so fast at me I didn't realize he was coming for my glasses until he had them off my face. I wasn't blind, but the shape of him was blurred around the edges the closer he sat to me.

"That's bold, Dylan," I warned, and he ignored me, folding my glasses and tucking them into the palm of his hand.

His fingertips grazed over my cheek, down over the two days of stubble that had sprouted along my jawline. He came dangerously close to my mouth, tracing over my cupid's bow before he returned my glasses to their perch on my face.

"No," he said after dropping both hands into his lap. "You don't."

I was so hard for him it took every ounce of willpower I'd

ever had in my entire life to not throw him onto his back and make a home for myself between his legs.

"Why did you send me away last time?" he asked.

"The way I am, Dylan, the things I like..." I trailed off, searching for words to explain a part of myself I'd never had to before. "It doesn't always end happily."

He let out a miserable-sounding snort that died halfway out of his throat. "Sounds like life."

"Happy eventually," I corrected. "But sometimes scenes will leave you unfulfilled."

"Like life," he repeated, rolling his eyes.

"I didn't want you to expect a certain thing from me." I closed my eyes and rubbed the bridge of my nose, Ford's drunken slurs about knowing he was safe, knowing I'd take care of him bouncing around my head like a pinball machine.

"This didn't even hurt," Dylan said next, tapping his fingers against the bruising around his throat.

"Who did that to you?"

I didn't want to talk about the marks because they made me feel too close to unhinged. Balling my hands into fists, I tried to ask the question casually, but I knew the marks had come from carelessness, not informed consent.

"It doesn't matter." Another one of those goddamn shrugs.

I surged forward and grabbed him by the throat, covering the bruises with my hand and using my body to shove him against the wall. His nostrils flared, eyes falling half closed like he had an erection between his legs. I didn't need to check to know he did. I had one too.

"Who?" I asked again.

"I don't even know his name." Dylan let his head fall back

against the exposed brick, and I flexed my hand against the sides of his neck, his rapid heartbeat fluttering beneath my fingertips. "It didn't even count."

"How does it *not count*?"

He lifted his hips off the couch. "It didn't hurt. I didn't even feel it."

I had to let go of him, reel back, thread my fingers together so I didn't reach for him in a different way entirely.

"Is that what you were looking for?"

"No, I just...the money. I didn't expect *that* part of it."

"That was assault, Dylan," I told him.

He scrambled up into a more upright position, eyes narrowed and angry. "No, it wasn't."

"Almost by definition."

"You're wrong," he protested.

"And whatever happened in the bathroom—"

"I was drunk!"

"Exactly." I unfurled my fingers, nails having gouged eight perfect crescent moons into my palms. "You can't consent if you're drunk."

"You don't know what you're talking about." Dylan jumped up from the couch, red-faced and trembling. He pointed to the door. "You can go, Alex. Thanks for coming."

I stood, tucking my half-hard cock down so it wasn't evident how turned on he made me. "Is that really what you want?"

"I don't want you to come in here acting like you know more about my life than I do," he snapped, arm falling to his side. "You don't know what happened."

God, this man was twice as stubborn as Kale, but with half the common sense. He was going to be the death of me and all of my friends would laugh me right into my grave.

"Do you need a demonstration, Dylan? Do you want me to show you what consent looks like?"

"You already have."

"And still." I held up a hand to stave off any other protest that he thought about trying to throw into the conversation. "And still you try to tell me otherwise."

Dylan cleared his throat, turning his attention toward the floor, voice soft when he asked, "Why are you here, Alex?"

I almost told him I didn't know, but at this point, it would have been a lie. I sucked in a breath, studying the slope of his shoulders and the sorrowful hang of his head, the way he tapped his fingers against his thigh while he waited for my answer. I took stock of him, then myself. The unsteady pulse that strummed in my neck, the sweaty palms, the tightness at the base of my spine. Dylan pushed all of my buttons, and I liked it. My whole adult life I'd wanted someone obedient, someone unquestioning, someone like Carter, but then...

"I'm here because I want to be," I finally told him.

He frowned.

"I'm not an easy man, Dylan."

"I don't think I am either," he mumbled.

"Why am I here?" I turned his question back on him, raising a brow when he blinked up at me with confused eyes. "What do *you* want?"

He answered with another one of those miserable shrugs. There had to be some sort of predicament bondage I could put him in where his shoulders couldn't answer for him.

"Think harder," I told him.

I had to know if we were on the same page before going

any further. My damned emotions were pushing too hard at the edges of my common sense, and I was too wounded from Carter to risk another fall.

"I don't know how to pay my rent," he finally said, and all the hope that had begun to bloom in my chest wilted.

"So you want my money?"

"I don't want *your* money. I want *my* money." Dylan shifted his weight, his hands on his hips in the weakest show of defiance I'd ever seen. It was enough to soften some of the ice that had blanketed my own emotions with his original answer.

"Do you only bartend?" I asked.

"I play gigs when I can, but they don't pay well."

"So you need better gigs," I said.

"Easier said than done."

There had to be a string I could pull for this one, a call I could make. I made a mental note and moved on.

"What else do you want?"

"I want Tate to not worry about me." His bottom lip quivered, a stray tear racing out from the corner of his left eye. He swiped it quickly, but there was no hiding it from me.

"You love him."

"He's my best friend. My only friend."

"Music and money," I summarized. "Your friend. What else?"

"I want you to stop looking at me like you feel sorry for me." Dylan snatched his guitar off the coffee table and stalked past me into his bedroom. He kicked the door behind him, but not hard enough to close it and that was as much of an invitation as the situation called for.

I followed after him, leaning against the door frame while

he settled his guitar onto a stand in the corner of his room. He turned toward me when he was finished, not surprised in the slightest that I'd come after him.

"I don't feel sorry for you."

"What then?"

"I want you, Dylan. That's how I look at you."

Ignoring my answer, he threw himself down onto the foot of his bed. There was a full length mirror propped up in the corner, and even though Dylan's back was to me, I could see half of the tired melancholy on his face.

"Why did Tate's boyfriend call you?" he asked.

"Brooks called me because he knew we have a history."

"We had sex," he bit off. "Which you paid for."

I ignored the sting he'd intended for his comments to land with. It was enough of a response to my earlier answer about wanting him. He either didn't care, or he didn't believe me. "He called because he knows who I am. He knows my tastes."

Dylan licked his lips. "He thinks you could get my act together for me."

It wasn't a question.

"He thinks you could do it yourself," I countered, "with some help."

"And he thinks you can help me?"

I turned the question around on him. "What do *you* think?"

Dylan covered his face with his hands, letting out a desperate sound that might have been a cry for help. He dug his elbows into his knees, fingertips gripping his hair. I ventured into the room, sitting down beside him and peeling his fingers loose, one by one. Eventually, he sagged against me, half in my lap and half in my arms. I held him, stroking my fingers down the top of his arm and across his ribs.

"I don't want a handout," he mumbled into my chest. "That's why I didn't tell Tate."

I had a split-second to make the right decision.

Help myself or help him.

Time slowed. It stopped. I buried my nose into his hair, breathed him in, and relished the way he shivered in my arms. I wanted him so much that I'd break my own heart in the process of having him.

I took too long to answer, a breath, a beat, the words were still on my tongue when Dylan worked his arms around my shoulders, when he flung his leg over my lap.

"What are you doing?" I asked, bracketing my hands against his hips.

He felt so fucking good on top of me like this. Even with the weight of his unhappiness bearing down on us both, I wanted to carry it for him.

I *wanted*.

"You said you want me," he whispered.

At least my answer hadn't gone ignored. "I do."

"Then have me."

And he tilted his head to the side, slanted our mouths together, and he kissed me.

I was making a fool of myself, covered in tears with last night's gin oozing out of my pores, but Alex spread his fingers against the small of my back and hitched my body closer to his anyway. He licked his way into my mouth, only kissing me for a second before working his way down my chin to my throat. I arched into him and the firm press of his hand on my back was strong enough to hold me up while I melted beneath his touch.

"You infuriate me," he murmured against my throat.

Then I was on my back and Alex was on top of me, his body heavy and warm. I wrapped my legs around his waist, desperate for a distraction from the indents left in my fingers from my guitar strings and the chaos in my mind.

"I'm sorry," I rasped, screwing my eyes shut.

"You're not," he said, biting my ear lobe. "You can't help it."

He bit harder and I whimpered, arching up against him. My dick hurt for how hard I was, how hard I'd been the whole time. Just breathing the same air as Alex gave me an erection and the studious way he always looked at me didn't help matters at all. He was like an eraser for every shitty decision I'd ever made, and with his dick burning like a hot iron against my hip, I thought—for the first time—it just might work for good this time. Maybe with his mouth, he could take all of this away.

Alex propped himself up with one hand beside my head and he moved the other between my legs. His fingers were quick to get my pants off, shoved down to my ankles. I kicked free of them and spread my legs wider for when he leaned to the side to wrestle with the fly of his own jeans. He yanked them down enough to get his cock out, then reached into his pocket and pulled out a condom. He rocked back and rolled the condom down his length, stroking himself as he went.

"You have two seconds to give me lube," he said, frowning at my empty bedside table.

"The drawer." I couldn't get out from under him, didn't want to. I rucked my shirt up to my chin and grabbed both of my nipples, twisting and tugging them while he slicked his cock and his hand.

"Tighter," he growled, shoving his slippery fingers into the crack of my ass. He pushed one finger into me, then another, scissoring them apart on every backward stroke.

I pinched my nipples with more force, my neck going tense from the bite of pain. No sound came out of my mouth. It was like my body refused to comply, wouldn't let me dig down hard enough to make myself scream the way I would if it had been *his* hands on me.

"That's enough," I begged, pushing back onto his fingers. "Please, I want you."

He pulled his fingers out and lined the tip of his cock up with my hole. "Just want?"

My teeth chattered, I was so desperate for him, for the things I knew he was able to give me. More than anything, I needed that release, that reset.

"Need," I rasped, reaching for his hips.

Alex batted my hands away, grabbing both of my wrists in one of his hands and pinning them down over my head. My knuckles scraped against the wall and still...he wasn't inside of me.

"Alex, please." I licked my lips, thrashing beneath him, trying to get his cock into me. But he was taller, broader, stronger. He wasn't going to go anywhere or do anything he didn't want to do.

"I'd almost forgotten how much I like it when you beg," he whispered, dipping down and brushing his lips across mine.

"I'll beg more."

He smiled against my mouth, pressing the tip of his dick against my hole with no intention of going any deeper.

"Okay," he agreed, licking my bottom lip. "Do it."

Shivering, I tested the hold he had on my wrists. It was tight and strong, and that only made my cock leak against my stomach. My hole clenched down on nothing, the promise of being filled less than an inch away.

"Please. Please. Oh, God. Fuck. Alex, I'm desperate. I need you so much."

"Need me where?" he asked.

"Everywhere." I cleared my throat. "Inside of me."

"I like the first one," he said, kissing the corner of my mouth. He notched his tip against my hole and pushed in slower than anyone ever had before.

"Oh, God," I whined, trying to cant my hips down to get more of him inside of me. How was this not killing him? He'd barely given me an inch and there was so much more ground to cover before our chests would press together again. Until his balls would rest heavy against mine.

"Try again."

"Alex."

He rewarded that with another inch of his cock.

Sweat beaded on my temples, my palms, the base of my spine. I needed more from him, either needed him to fuck me or hurt me. Maybe both. I didn't know for sure how to separate the two when it came to him.

Didn't know if I wanted to.

"I can wait all night," he said, pulling out entirely. "I don't care if or when I come, pet. And I care even less about if you do."

"Oh, shit. *Shit.* Fuck."

Something about the nickname really did it for me, and for all the hours I'd spent on my hands and knees scrubbing at the floor of my shower thinking about Alex and the things he did to me, I hadn't tried to unpack the name and the way it made my cock throb.

Alex hummed, leveraging himself back onto his heels and letting go of my wrists. Immediately, I mourned the absence of his body, the press of his hands, his mouth...his cock.

"I told you I'm not an easy man," he said, stroking himself from root to tip, fingers curled around the shiny latex of the condom.

"I heard you."

"I have high expectations."

"Tell me," I whimpered, reaching for his thighs, still covered by expensive and soft, dark denim.

"You have to listen."

"I am."

Alex grabbed my hand and took two of my fingers into his mouth, sucking them and swirling his tongue around the length of each digit. I covered my eyes with my other hand, the indecent and wet sounds from his mouth almost enough to make me come on the spot.

He pulled my hand off my eyes, then pushed my fingers deep enough into this mouth that had it been mine, I would have choked. His stare was impossible to look away from, focused and punishing in its intensity. Unwavering, even when he fucked his mouth with my fingers, making soft gagging noises around my knuckles.

When I was about to verbally safeword so I didn't come all over us both, he pulled my hand free, kissing the two pruned fingertips that I was fairly certain had just touched his uvula.

"You have to listen to me when we aren't having sex," he said, lowering my hand between us. He pressed my fingers against my asshole, and then into it.

"I'll listen," I promised.

I swore it.

"Even if you don't like it," he warned.

Alex pushed my fingers all the way inside of me, and I spread my legs and moaned for him.

"Even if I don't like it."

"I'm not going to fuck you until you get tested," Alex said softly. He pulled the condom off and tossed it onto the floor. His mouth angled into a tight frown, and I wanted to burst into tears.

"I'm sorry."

"No, you're not," he said, mouth softening. "And if you are, you shouldn't be. You did what you had to."

He pulled my fingers out and slowly pressed them back in. His hold on my wrist was punishing, and I loved it.

"But you don't have to do it anymore."

I tried to take my hand away, but he tightened his hold and pushed my fingers all the way inside of me. He leveraged himself on my wrist, letting his body fall over mine, effectively trapping our hands between my legs. I wasn't getting my fingers out of my asshole unless he wanted them out.

"Get off of me," I grunted.

"Do you want to use your safe word?"

I huffed, turning my head to the side so I didn't have to look at him. "No."

"Tell me, then," he said.

I was so angry, but not at him. Alex was giving me exactly what I hadn't had the balls to ask for. That pain, that control. It was everything I liked the most about being with him, but was too scared to ask for. Even with the tension and the unease at being seen floating so beneath the surface of my skin, I forced the word out anyway, swallowing down bile.

"Green."

I would have cried if he stopped.

I'd probably cry even if he didn't.

"But you don't have to do it anymore," Alex repeated.

"I don't want your money."

He shifted enough to pull my fingers out of my asshole. "It's not up to you to tell me what to do with my own money, Dylan."

"I don't want it."

"I know." He maneuvered my wrist, swirling my fingers around my barely teased hole until I bore down and got one back inside. Alex huffed, pushing the digit all the way into me.

It wasn't enough.

It was hell.

"But I want you for myself and I want to fuck you when I want and where I want." Alex directed two more of my fingers into my body. "Isn't that what you want, Dylan? Isn't that better than this?"

"Yes," I answered quickly, the burning between my legs from the third finger almost enough to get me off.

Alex moved between my legs, pumping his hips against both of our hands, fucking my fingers deeper into me. Somehow he managed to pull out when he drew back, push in when he went forward. The friction and the slide was what I needed, and when I grazed my prostate, I threw my head back and cried out.

"Get tested," Alex growled into my ear.

"Yes."

"Music and bartending only," he said next.

I grunted, eyes rolling back.

He went still, my fingers half out of me, his cock hard and going to waste against my thigh.

"There's not one without the other," he warned. "This is a limit for me, Dylan. I don't fucking share."

"You didn't care when you were paying me for it."

He huffed again, pressing his forehead against mine...*hard*.

"I'm not a stupid man. I knew I was the only one then and I know I'm not now." He pumped forward and buried my fingers back into my hole. "But I'm a miserable man, Dylan.

I'm sad and I'm jealous and I *want*, so if you want more of me...
If you want more of *this*..."

He didn't need to finish his thought. I was stubborn, but I understood the point. And if I was being honest, which I hadn't been, I didn't want to keep doing sex work. I just didn't want to get evicted from Tate's and my apartment. The only thing worse than sex work was a handout, though, and Alex was asking me to walk away from one and into the other.

"Okay," I breathed out, nodding against him. "Okay, yes. Green."

Relief rolled out of him, so tangible I felt it settle over my bones when he slanted our mouths back together. What Alex did next couldn't be described as a kiss. He devoured me, sucking and licking and biting his way around my mouth, using his hips to fuck me.

"Good boy," he whispered, breath burning against my kiss-swollen lips. "Good fucking boy, Dylan."

Alex went still, cum spurting against my thigh as he spilled all over my bare leg. God, I fucking wanted him inside of me, wanted him to bury himself so fully inside of me that I couldn't make sense of where my mess stopped and his perfection started. I was angry in that moment, filled with rage that his cum had been wasted against my leg when my mouth was right there, when even though I'd fought him, I was so ready.

"I have half a mind to leave you like this," he said, pulling back enough so he could see my finger stuffed up my own asshole. He let go of my wrist and drifted his hand up to trace his finger across the place where I was stretched and slick with lube. "Incentivize you a little bit."

"Please don't," I begged, grabbing for him with the hand

that wasn't busy. He was just out of reach, inches too far away. "Please don't stop. I'll be good, I promise."

He puffed a short exhale out of his nose, his earlier frown shifting into half of a sad-looking smile.

"I hope you're a man of your word, Dylan, because I am." He wrapped his fist around my cock and stroked me once. Cum shot out of my cock, the orgasm so treacherously close, there was no stopping it.

It hurt.

It hurt.

My hole clamped around my knuckles and cum sprayed out of my dick, coating my stomach and feeling as wasted as Alex's release had been. I burst into tears, body seizing as the aftershocks of my release rolled through me. Alex pulled me up by my arms, propping me against the wall and regarding me—again with that frown.

"Thank you," I choked out, lashes fluttering closed with relief.

"Don't thank me yet, pet." Alex sighed and climbed off my bed. "Get up, because we need to talk."

CHAPTER 14

ALEX

I made Dylan take a shower and get dressed. Made him drink a glass of water and eat a piece of leftover pizza because it was all they had in the fridge. I ordered Chinese takeout and sat him down on the couch, hoping and praying I hadn't made the biggest mistake of my life since Carter.

"I want to be very clear with you," I said, tracing the sharp tip of my canine tooth with my tongue while I tried to find the right words.

"No more sex work," he said, lips pursed.

His hair was wet, flopping a bit in his face and dripping down his forehead. He had bags under his eyes, but he looked more relaxed than he had when I'd shown up. That was probably on account of the orgasm, not anything I'd said or done. But it didn't matter. At least, not really.

"I don't care about sex work," I clarified. "What I care about is exclusivity. I don't share my toys, Dylan, and I won't share you."

He swallowed audibly.

"So if you want to be with me, then you're with me."

He dipped his chin toward his chest and looked up at me from beneath the lush fan of his dark lashes. I didn't know if he intended to look the part of a coy submissive, but he was hitting all his marks just the same.

"I understand."

"And I have rules."

He nodded.

"For you." I tilted my head to the side, appraising his expression before I gave him the first one. "No drinking."

"I don't have a drinking problem," he interrupted.

"I didn't say that you did. I simply said that if you're with me...for *now*...you won't be drinking."

"Why?"

"Because I don't want you to." I held my hands out, palms turned halfway toward the ceiling. "Because what I say in this relationship goes."

"Sounds like a *dic*tatorship."

I caught his emphasis on the first syllable, and I leaned over to pick my cell phone and money clip up from the table. I pulled a hundred dollar bill out and let it fall, willing to at least pay for the dinner I wasn't going to get to eat.

Dylan scrambled onto his knees, crawling to my side of the couch and grabbing my hand before I could get any of my belongings into my pocket. His face was frantic, wide eyes and heaving breaths. "Where are you going?"

"My second rule is that you aren't a fucking asshole to me."

"You hadn't said that one yet," he grumbled, folding his arms over his chest and collapsing back onto the couch.

My phone was heavy in my hand, my palm sweaty. "It should go without saying."

"I've never done this kind of thing before," he said.

"Well, I have." I set my things back down on the table and sat down next to Dylan, closer than before. His knee pushed into the side of my thigh, his fingers drumming nervously in his lap. "And I know what works for me and what doesn't."

"What if it doesn't work for *me*?" he asked.

"Then we go our separate ways."

Dylan let out a long breath, slowly walking one of his hands to the point on my leg where his knee dug into my muscle. He didn't quite rest his hand on my thigh, but he definitely touched me. I went ahead and pulled his hand up over the hump of my leg, and his fingers splayed out overtop of my thigh, almost like his hand was dissolving into my skin.

"Why do you want this?" I asked him the question I'd been avoiding since I showed up at his apartment earlier in the night.

"I would have fucked you for free," he said quietly, "the first time."

"You didn't fuck me at all."

"You know what I mean."

"Go on," I prompted.

"You were sad and handsome and I wanted you, but you made the comment about paying for sex..." Dylan trailed off and he tried to take his hand away from my leg, but I covered it quickly, pressing his palm down flat.

"And you needed money."

"I took advantage," he offered.

"I paid far less than you're worth, Dylan."

That seemed to take the fight right out of him, his fingers digging into the inside of my thigh.

"I...after we...." His cheeks burned a dark red and he looked at the wall, the couch, his feet, anywhere but me. "The first time...I didn't think I would like some of those things."

"But you did?"

"Yes," Dylan whispered, nodding. "Very much."

"Then why didn't you answer my messages?"

"I didn't want to make a habit of trading my body for money," he muttered.

"But you needed more?"

"You know about my dad." Dylan's body reeled back, like he wanted to physically get as far away from the conversation as he could without actually moving away from it.

"I'm not trying to rehash the same conversations over and over," I assured him. "I just want to make sure you and I are on the same page going forward."

"No more sex work, no more drinking."

"No more being an asshole when your feelings get hurt," I added.

Dylan scrunched his nose, startling when the building buzzer rattled through the shoebox of an apartment.

"The food," I reminded him, plucking the loose hundred dollar bill off the table and handing it to him. "Go get it."

It wasn't a test. At least I hadn't meant for it to be one. Dylan getting the delivery from the door was probably the smallest thing I'd ever ask of him over the course of our relationship, and I needed to make sure he really understood what it meant to be with me. I was already far too invested in him and I didn't want to dig myself in deeper if the novelty of this dynamic was going to wear off on him.

I'd spent so many years not understanding my own needs, living a half-life until things with Carter had crossed that line. Some nights, I stayed up later than I should, wondering what my future would have been like if not for Dalton Fox, if not for Kale being a pushy piece of shit in the first place. But all the cards for Carter and me had fallen at the same time, so one scenario didn't exist without the other.

Dylan returned with the food and my change, which I had no intention of taking back from him. He set it on the table and, without being told, opened up the food and served helpings of each entree onto the Styrofoam plates the restaurant had provided. I wasn't hungry—it was all for him—but I didn't stop him from the dual servings.

I also didn't have to tell him to eat, which was a relief.

He sat down on the couch, just as close as he'd been before with his knee pressing into the outside of my thigh, plate balanced on his lap. I scratched an annoying itch on my ribs, and Dylan dug in, shoveling chow mein and spicy chicken into his mouth like it was the first hot meal he'd had in weeks. My own food sat untouched on the table, and if he noticed, he didn't say anything.

Watching him eat made me hard because, for what might have been the first time since I'd met him, he was doing what he needed to do without being told. Maybe there was hope for the two of us after all.

I waited until his pace had slowed, more than half his plate cleared when I said to him, "Ask me the question now."

He looked up, confused, but he must have seen the explanation in my face.

"Why did you want to pay for sex?"

"I fell in love with one of my closest friends." Saying the confession out loud for the first time gave my feelings for Carter an unexpected weight, and as soon as the words were between us, it was like I could breathe. My lungs didn't burn the way they always did on the inhale, my ribs didn't feel like they were going to shatter. "His name was Carter...everyone else called him Beamer, uhm, I...we...he ended up marrying someone else."

At that, Dylan surged forward so fast the plate tumbled off his lap and straight onto the floor, spilling sweet and sour sauce all over my left foot. He cursed, jumping up from the couch and running the few feet to the kitchen for a sponge and a towel and then he was back, on his knees at my feet, picking up noodles with his bare hands and wiping up the sauce.

It was one more thing he did without being told, and when he stood to carry the mess into the kitchen, the front of his basketball shorts sported an obvious tent from the growing erection between his legs. He turned after dropping everything in the sink, shifting his weight nervously.

"Why does this happen?" he asked.

"I can't answer that for you."

He sat back down, noticing for the first time I hadn't touched my food. He took my plate and set it on my lap, waiting with a fork in hand until I took it from him. Something twisted around the middle of my chest, a thorny and dangerous kind of pleasure that I hadn't felt in months.

"Why did he marry someone else?" Dylan asked.

"They were better suited."

"But you loved him."

"Dalton loved him more," I said, stabbing my fork into a piece of the sauce-covered chicken. "Loved him better."

Dylan made a thoughtful sound after I put the chicken into my mouth, leaning back against the couch with a groan that sounded a lot like disagreement. His knee was still boring into my thigh, burning hot.

"Back to us," he said.

"Please."

"Everything you're saying sounds very imbalanced."

I twisted my mouth up at the corner, expression wary.

"You're doing so much for me," he whispered. "Who does anything for you?"

I lifted the plate a few inches off my lap before setting it down and taking another bite of the savory chicken. "Looks like you are."

"But you're still in charge."

I exhaled, taking one more bite before setting the plate back down on the table beside the still very full paper takeout boxes. "That's complicated."

"I know I make dumb choices, but I'm not stupid."

"None of this exists with you," I told him. "If you change your mind, if you use your safe word, that's when everything stops. So, it sounds like you're the one with all the control."

"But you're in charge?"

"Yes." I nodded slowly. "You have to choose that, though."

Dylan's lower lip quivered and he scratched the shell of his ear, again diverting his attention away from me. He stood up slowly, smoothing his hands down the still visible bulge between his legs.

"I need to piss," he said, stepping over me instead of going around me.

The bathroom was close. Everything in the apartment was close, but it was toward the front near his bedroom and I watched him go, not relaxing until the door locked and the water turned on.

I dropped my head back and stared up at the ceiling, praying that I wasn't making the second biggest mistake of my life with Dylan. Not only did he not fully understand this lifestyle, let alone the dynamic, he was hard up for money which put us at a massive disadvantage.

Even though he wasn't even making it paycheck to paycheck, I recognized his father's name and knew he'd grown up with not just one, but probably a dozen silver spoons in his mouth. With me, he'd be adjusting not just to being poor, but also to being submissive. I worried it was too much for him to take on all at once, but that kind of stubborn resilience that oozed out of his pores wasn't something that men like Dylan and I could shake.

The bathroom door opened and he headed back to me, shoulders squared, eyes hooded. He was horny and he was certain, a dangerous combination. I knew from experience. But Dylan was willing to lose everything he'd ever known for the one thing he loved, and selfishly, I thought...maybe one day I could be the second thing.

CHAPTER 15
DYLAN

True to his word, Alex didn't sleep with me that night. I went the next day to get tested and met him that afternoon with results in hand, but he simply put them in his pocket and kissed the top of my head. I had to work at Tryst Monday night and Alex left me to my own devices, showing up at my apartment at four-thirty in the morning, barely two minutes behind my arrival. He didn't fuck me then either. He undressed me, settled me into bed, and tucked himself behind me, arms tight around my chest and breath hot against my neck.

It was the best sleep I'd had in months.

I woke up just before lunch, the other side of my bed cold. I assumed Alex had left, but after a quick stop in the bathroom, I found him on my couch, his feet propped up on the coffee table and a half-finished crossword puzzle in his lap.

"Don't you work?" I asked.

"Well enough that I don't have to be there," he said, setting the paper and pen down beside him. "Get a cup of coffee and your guitar. You have a gig on Thursday."

"I what?" My feet were on autopilot, taking me into my room and then to the counter so I could do what I'd been told. I took the coffee and guitar to the couch, where I sat down beside him, similar to the position we'd been in the night before.

"I got you a gig," he said, "so play me some songs. Get your practice in."

Alex made me play until lunch, when he took my guitar out of my hands, told me to get dressed, and then took me to lunch. He ordered for me, barely picking at his own food until I was halfway done with my sandwich. After we finished eating, he took me home, walked me upstairs, and told me goodbye.

Wednesday night, I worked at The Black Door, and I expected to be unsupervised like I'd been the night before, but Alex showed up just before midnight, taking a seat at the bar and ordering a martini. For the most part, he let me work, ignoring the way I tried to flirt with him, but when I went on break, he cornered me in the bathroom and pushed me up against the wall. Alex shoved his hand down my pants, crashed our mouths together, and jerked me off until I came all over his fingers. He made me lick them clean, watched as I washed my hands, then told me he'd see me Thursday for my gig.

By the time Thursday night rolled around, I was an absolute livewire. The only physical touch Alex had given me since we decided to be together was the snuggles on Monday night and the hand job on Wednesday. He was about as forthcoming as a puzzle box, and I hated it. I texted him when I got out of the shower on Thursday to tell him as much.

> This isn't what I signed up for.

ALEX

What part? The show so you can play music, which is the one thing you've been willing to ruin your life over? Or was there something else?

> The way you're treating me

How am I treating you?

> Worse than you did when you paid me.

It was a low blow, but I was horny and angry. I was confused and thankful and needy, and it was all too much after so long of going without. Alex had promised me a lot, but so far all he'd given me was an in at a venue and one orgasm. At least when he was paying me for sex, I was getting off and getting hurt. This almost felt like being ignored, and I hated it.

I glared at my phone, watching the three dots indicating he was typing out a reply disappear and reappear over and over until I finally got a short message, which definitely didn't take that long to type out.

> I'll see you shortly, Dylan.

Fuck him.

Fuck him.

I threw my guitar case onto the couch and propped the lid open. He could be an asshole all he wanted, but that wasn't enough to make me not take the stupid gig he'd arranged for me. It paid almost as much as he had, and I would take advantage. Angry as I was, I was always careful with my guitar, setting her in the case just as the front door pushed open.

Even though he didn't have a key, I still expected to see Alex there somehow. Instead, it was Tate, a broad and well-fucked smile on his face. I'd barely seen him since he started dating Brooks, and I missed him. But in light of the weekend's events and the developments with Alex, I wasn't overeager to see him now.

"Hey," I said.

Tate's happy expression fell when he saw me dressed with my bag and my guitar case ready to go.

"Are you leaving?"

"I got a last-minute gig," I lied. "I know I haven't seen you in a few days, but I need the money."

Before Alex, before Brooks, Tate was my biggest cheerleader. There wasn't a show I'd played in the city that he hadn't been front row at.

"Right. That's fine. Of course."

"Did you want to come?" I asked.

Tate was still dressed for work, and he pulled his dress shirt out to untuck it. "Of course. Just let me change and we can head out."

I fidgeted with the strap of my messenger bag while Tate got ready, trying to figure out what to tell him about Alex before we got to the show. I settled on next to nothing, which seemed fine enough for Tate until we got across town to the venue.

It pained me to admit Alex had done good. The place was an actual music venue, way bigger than a coffee shop with a full bar in the back and an actual stage in the front. When we got there, I was shocked to find Brooks *with* Alex, leaning up against the bar with drinks in hand. They whispered to each other, a thousand secrets between them, I was sure.

Alex hadn't seen me, so I ignored him, heading through the venue until I found the small dressing room behind the stage.

"I want you to tell me about Alex," Tate finally said after following me in.

"What about him?"

"Brooks said Alex had called you. That he was…"

Tate trailed off, which was a blessing. I took my guitar out of the case and checked the tuning. "I don't want to talk about Alex with you, but I promise I'm fine. We can talk about the rest of it if you want to after the gig."

"We don't have to," he said. "I don't want to press."

"I'm not ashamed of it."

"I know." Tate closed my guitar case for me and propped it against the wall so he could sit across from me on the small stool I'd used to open it up. "I don't want you to be defensive with me. You're my friend and I love you. That's all."

"I made some bad decisions, but I'm not going to do that anymore." It was as much the truth as anything else was. My stomach growled, but Tate looked satisfied with the answer. I thought about Alex out there with his friend, both of them drinking and having a great time. I thought about the shitty way he'd been treating me since Sunday and it was enough to make my blood boil.

Clearing my throat, I stood up and said to Tate, "We have time for a drink before I have to play."

It was against the rules, but if he didn't care about me, I didn't care about him.

"I'll get water," Tate said with a laugh, moments before his tone dipped down and his expression turned serious. "Did you know Alex was going to be here tonight?"

We left the dressing room and I dropped my guitar off on the stage, hooking my arm through Tate's and hoping a drink would distract him from the answer.

"Alex got me the gig."

"Oh?"

Tate and I made it to the bar, finally spotted by Alex and Brooks, who looked like Tate was a waterfall in the middle of the desert. I ignored Alex and leaned over the bar to order a water for Tate and a whiskey sour for myself. I knew Alex heard the order, but there was no way I could stop myself from placing it. Even as he pushed his body against mine so hard it shoved my ribs against the rounded corner of the bar, stealing my breath, I couldn't take it back.

I didn't want to.

"Rules two and three," he whispered into my ear.

Don't drink and don't be an asshole—I remembered them well.

"Rule number four," I hissed, "*You* don't be an asshole."

The bartender set both drinks in front of me and Alex dug his fingers into my waist.

"If you drink that whiskey, you'll find out just how much of an asshole I can be, *pet*, and I promise you that you won't like it."

The emphasis on pet had me convinced Alex hated me, regretted our arrangement entirely. Tears pricked the corners of my eyes and I closed them tight, hopefully able to push them back so Tate didn't see them slip free. Alex brushed his lips across my cheek, bringing his face so close to my mouth and nose I could smell the gin on him.

"Why can you drink, but I can't?" I asked.

"Because I'm in charge."

"I thought you said that was me."

"Do you want to use your safe word?" His lips moved against the corner of my mouth and I turned enough to taste the threat in his words.

To taste the way he wanted me.

"No," I rasped.

I didn't even have to think about the answer, which was frustrating. I didn't want to safeword, but I didn't want things to go on the way they had been for the past few days. I didn't want to be ignored, to be tortured, to be so fucking aware of how desperate I was for his attention and how miserable I felt without it.

Alex uncurled his fingers from their perch on my waist. He reached around me for the drink I'd ordered, and he downed it in one swallow.

"I hate you," I hissed.

"You know how to end this," he said simply, and the corner of his left eye twitched.

I answered him with a nod and stalked off toward the stage to warm up.

Playing guitar was like coming home for me. Even as a kid, it had always been my favorite instrument, the one that came most naturally to me. My guitar was an escape, a release, an hour-long lesson where I could forget all the pressure that came with having parents like mine. My father was an absolutely ruthless businessman and his skills as a parent weren't much softer. I would never understand what my mom saw in him.

Alex held much of the same appeal. He was like a drug,

intoxicating in his newness, but capable of taking me out entirely. My love of music had sent my life down the road that brought me to him, and I had no idea where he would take me next. The uncertainty of things with Alex was what had me the most up in arms. He was mercurial, except when he was with me, I had no doubt of his interest, his passion. It was the times we were apart that I wondered. When there was space between us, it was almost like I didn't exist to him. Those were the two extremes I couldn't find balance in, the place my anger toward him festered.

Licking my lips, I could still taste him on my tongue, and it made me hard.

I wanted to tear my hair out at the roots and fall on my knees at his feet. Wanted to beg him to make sense of all the feelings inside of me so I could understand why home used to feel like a guitar with six strings, but not anymore. The stage lights came up and I blinked quickly, the audience going darker under the glow.

The manager of the venue came out and told me it was time, and I tapped my mic to make sure it was on. I tried to ignore Alex through the rest of the gig, but it was impossible to pretend I didn't see him there beside the bar. Tall, broad, imposing, immoveable, and singing along to every single one of my lyrics until the house lights came back up.

Dylan was in a miserable mood by the time we got back to my house, but if he thought I was going to fuck his salty little attitude out of him, he had another thing coming entirely.

Earlier in the week, he'd gotten tested and provided me with clear test results. I'd given him the same in return, but I'd yet to fuck him again. Even if I jerked off thinking about how good it would be to take him again, I wanted to make sure we were on the same page with everything else before I let myself take that step again. Maybe I was too soft of a man at heart.

To say the few days since we'd agreed to be together were tense would have been the same as calling a hurricane a rainstorm. Dylan came inside with the force of the former, slamming my front door behind him and dropping his guitar case near the door. I scratched my cheek, content to watch him tantrum himself further away from the one thing he thought would fix it all.

"You were really good tonight," I said after he'd licked his shoes off, both of them thumping against the wall before landing in a pile beside my shoe rack.

"Was I?"

"I'm not a liar."

He grunted, ready to stalk past me, but I reached out and grabbed the back of his shirt in my fist. Dragging him to a stop, I yanked him against me, my lips pressed against his jaw. "What is your problem, pet?"

Dylan scoffed, fighting against my grip on his shirt. I tightened my fingers into the cotton. The only way I was going to let go was if he used his safe word and he knew that. I think part of him liked that he could argue and fight me, knowing I wouldn't leave.

"This isn't what I signed up for," he said, repeating his earlier complaint.

I let go of his shirt and moved him in front of me, his back to my chest. He still struggled against me, but went slack when I banded one arm around the front of his chest and undid his zipper with the other.

"What did you sign up for?"

"More than this."

"I can't do much with you if you're not alive, Dylan. If you're not whole."

His heart hammered against my forearm, and I kicked the back of his ankles one at a time so I could walk us into the kitchen. Once there, I let go of him and shoved him down into one of the chairs. Leaning back against the counter, I crossed my arms in front of my chest and stared down at him. The petulance leaked out of his pores and I had to fight every urge to take him into the playroom and spank him senseless. I needed it, and he probably did too, but I couldn't reward his bad behavior.

"All you've done is tell me to not drink and to eat," he

grumbled.

"The absolute basics that shouldn't even need my involvement."

"I thought the point of this was *you* taking—" Dylan snapped his mouth closed, swallowing back whatever he'd been about to say.

"Taking what?"

"Being in control," he said, abandoning whatever statement he'd been ready to make.

"I told you before, Dylan, I'm not an easy man. You're not *meant* to like all of this."

Maybe I'd been wrong about him, about what he needed. I'd misjudged him...somehow. Misjudged myself and what I was capable of.

"Do *you* like this?" he shot back, glaring up at me with nothing but defiance in his eyes.

"Not especially." I palmed my flaccid cock, the hard press of my hand doing enough to make it twitch to life. "But I can make myself like it if I want to."

Dylan's mouth contorted into a grimace, his cheeks burning red.

"You do like it, though," I said softly.

"I hate it."

"Take your cock out of your pants and prove it."

"No," he choked out.

I arched a brow. "Are we green?"

Dylan cursed under his breath, lifting up enough from the seat to undo his pants and take his nearly fully erect cock out of his pants. Even in the dim light of the kitchen, it was easy to make out the shine of precum against his tip, the uncomfortable stretch of skin for how hard he was.

"Happy now?" he snapped.

"I knew what we'd find there," I told him, my own cock quickly plumping up against my thigh. "You're the one trying to pretend you don't like it."

"I didn't say I don't like it." He jumped up and threw his arms in the air. "I said it's not what I wanted."

"What *do* you want?"

"I want you to do what you said!" Dylan stepped forward like he was going to push me, but thought better of it before his palms connected with my chest. "I want you to take care of me!"

"Aren't I?"

"No! You're making *me* do it all."

I sighed, cheeks puffing out on the exhale. Pushing my weight off the counter, I closed the space between us and gave Dylan a shove back down into his seat. He landed and stayed put, glowering up at me like he wanted me dead. I didn't blame him. Trying to make sense of the things he wanted and needed compared to what made him hard had to be a lot. All of that on top of the situation with his finances and his parents...and his passions.

"I'm not making you do anything," I reminded him. "Did you want to talk about Juilliard?"

"I'm not going to safeword," he told me.

"I'm not going to fight you forever," I countered, notching myself between his spread legs so I towered over him. I was so close I had to look straight down to see him, and he had to crane his neck toward the ceiling to keep glaring at me. Which he did. "It's fine and it's fun in moderation, like all things, but you have to want this."

"I do, but you're being mean."

"Dylan." I scrubbed a hand down my face, sucking in a much needed lungful of air. He was going to give me gray hairs and send me to an early grave.

"I thought it would be different."

"I see that." I reached down and brushed his hair back from his forehead. As soon as my fingers touched his skin, he went soft. His eyes closed and he swayed forward, pressing his cheek against my stomach and wrapping his arms around the backs of my thighs. I sighed and continued to stroke my fingers through his hair. "And it will be different, when I can trust you to keep it together on your own."

"Maybe my dad was right," he mumbled into my shirt. "Maybe I am useless."

"You're far from useless," I assumed him. "But I'm going out of town in two weeks and I need to trust that you can manage on your own for two days while I'm gone. I don't mind dictating the basics to you, Dylan, but I'm not going to reward you for doing the bare minimum."

"Are you trying to say we're only going to fuck if I do something good?" He wiggled his shoulders and dug his feet into the ground, pushing himself away from me.

"There's plenty of ways to reward you."

"But you haven't fucked me," he said. "I got tested like you wanted, and you still haven't."

"I asked you to quit drinking and you still haven't," I shot back at him.

He narrowed his eyes, working his jaw back and forth. His hands were fisted in his lap, and I wondered how close he was to springing up out of his seat and punching me in the mouth. I'd take it if that was truly what I had coming, but I didn't think it would come to that. At least, I hoped.

"Put your dick away, Dylan." I sidestepped out of our standoff to get a bottle of water from my fridge. I drank half of it in one go, then grabbed a second bottle for Dylan, who cursed my name behind me while he put himself back together. "You can say whatever you want about me, but the punishment you want is not the one you're going to get."

"Whatever." He threw himself back into the chair, and I questioned every decision I'd ever made in my whole life.

Subconsciously, I understood why he was pushing the way he did. He needed to know that I wasn't going to give up and walk away, that I wasn't going to go back on my part of the deal. But damn if I didn't miss the easy submission that came from my days with Carter, or even the times when I was paying Dylan to keep his mouth closed and do what he was told.

"You're acting like a child."

"No wonder you had to pay for sex," he said next, words so quiet I almost missed them.

I set both bottles of water down on the counter and shoved my hands into my pockets so I didn't go back on my promise of the right kind of punishment. "Excuse me?"

"No wonder your ex married someone else."

His comment was designed to hurt, and hurt it did. The sentiment landed like a barbed baseball bat against my sternum, and I looked down as if the words on their own should have been enough to draw blood. I found myself physically unscathed. The wounds were all invisible, but still fatal.

"Red," I said calmly, holding my hands up in surrender.

"What?"

"Red, Dylan." I blinked rapidly, my glasses starting to fog

from the wall of tears that were building in my eyes. "You win."

"What does that mean?"

"This isn't going to work."

I hated myself as much as I hated him in that moment, as close as I was to falling in love with him. It pained me to be another self-fulfilling prophecy for him, but there had to be a boundary. I would take his arguing and his complaining, but the low blows were far out of bounds and I'd already told him not to be an asshole. It was my only limit, and he'd doubled down with the intent to take me out at the knees.

It was one thing to prove your reliability to a person. I'd put up with his protests and his whining—none of that was enough to scare me off. But I drew the line at deliberate maliciousness, which was where his comment came from. I knew it, and when his face crumpled, I was certain he knew it as well.

"I'm sorry," he said quickly, tears already slicking down his cheeks.

Grimacing, I shook my head, walking away from him so I didn't also say something I'd regret. I headed for the door, where he'd left his shoes and his guitar. Dylan pushed the chair back and the feet dug against the wood. He chased after me, again falling short of physically grabbing me. I stopped, my hand on the doorknob, my chin seconds away from giving up how upset his comment had truly made me.

"I asked you to quit drinking and quit being an asshole," I reminded him. "I would have given you anything, everything, if you'd kept up your end of the transaction."

"I thought this was a relationship."

"It's a figure of speech." The doorknob slipped against my palm.

"No." He frowned, shaking his head. "You had it right. It was a transaction, but I was stupid enough to sign up for it again without getting paid."

I pushed my fingers against the bridge of my nose, rubbing away the weight of my glasses before letting them fall back into place.

"You're being deliberately cruel, Dylan."

"And you're not?"

"I told you I'm n—"

He cut me off, "Not easy. Sounds like an excuse to be a prick."

I wiped the corner of my eye with my knuckle, not caring if he saw my tears or not.

I opened the door.

"Good luck with life, Dylan," I said, staring at the street while he shoved his feet into his shoes and grabbed his guitar from the floor. "You're going to need it."

I couldn't figure out how Alex could be two different people. One version of him, so singularly focused on pain and pleasure at the same time, the other...I didn't even know. It was like once we'd agreed to be in a relationship—or whatever—with each other, he'd completely forgotten the version of him that I'd met. And it didn't have anything to do with me being ignorant or me not understanding. I'd worked enough shifts at The Black Door already to see the difference between what Alex did to me compared to how the other people there played together.

He'd told me he wasn't easy, but he'd never said anything about not being fun.

Alex was miserable, clearly still reeling over his breakup with that other man. Whenever I thought about what things had been like for the two of them, my blood burned beneath my skin at a low simmer, threatening to cook me from the inside out. It tasted like jealousy, but that was an emotion that had no place between the two of us. There hadn't been enough time for me to even care. If anything, it was jealousy—

envy—over the parts of him that Alex had given to his ex and refused to give to me.

I didn't want to be ordered around for *nothing*. My parents did that just fine.

It didn't matter that things between me and Alex were over.

It didn't matter that I still jerked off thinking about him, and it definitely didn't matter I got hard when I cleaned, when I played guitar...pretty much all the time. Even when I was angry, on the verge of tears, my body wanted to go back to before he'd used his safe word with me. Me and my brain hated whatever game Alex had been on, but my body...my body had been fighting a losing battle.

In the days that passed since Alex sent me away, I'd managed to not text him, but I had done some things differently. I'd quit drinking, for one. It seemed like such a stupid ask at that time, but I'd gotten home after our fight and pulled a beer out of the fridge... and I hadn't been able to bring myself to drink it. I could see him sitting on my couch, watching me with that guarded and expectant expression. It was enough to stop me in my tracks, and I dumped every beer down the drain. Even at work, I'd taken to drinking water or soda on my breaks, turning down shots from my regulars.

I wouldn't go as far to say I felt better about myself over it, but it was a choice I made on my own, not at someone else's demand. A voice in the back of my head tried to remind me that giving Alex control had also been a choice, maybe the most important one of all, but I shut it down as quick as it popped up. I didn't want to hear anything about that.

It didn't matter anymore, anyway.

So, no drinking. I'd started actively trying to seek out more gigs for myself. The manager of the venue Alex had gotten me the show at loved my music and offered me another show the following month. The money was great, the crowd had been fun, so I immediately told him yes. I wanted to play guitar more, until my fingers bled if need be. I'd given up everything for music, and I needed to stop hating it for changing my life.

I'd also deleted my hookup app entirely.

Changing the bio on my profile wasn't enough.

That was another choice I'd made on my own. Alex didn't want to share me, but I wasn't his to meddle with anymore. The money had been great while it lasted, but I didn't want to risk another encounter like the rough prick who couldn't seem to get enough of me. Even though I wasn't scared either time I'd been with him, it was a slippery slope, and Tate had been so upset when he found out.

Tate.

That was another thing entirely that I'd had to make peace with in the days following my assault and my breakup with Alex. Tate didn't look at me any differently, but he treated me differently, almost like he was wearing kid gloves around me. I kept apologizing for what I'd done, for keeping it from him, for not being a better friend, and he kept shrugging all of it off. He was so willing to look past every single one of my short-comings... and for what?

He was too deliriously in love with Brooks to really care.

And I didn't blame him.

I was on the precipice of another cliff in my life, seeing how in love the two of them were and knowing it was only a matter of time until Tate was ready to leave our apartment and move in with Brooks. I could barely afford my half of the rent—there was no way I could afford all of it. I'd have to get another roommate, which sounded necessary but miserable. I hoped Tate would at least give me enough time to find someone else before packing it up.

Find someone else, or give up entirely and call my dad.

There'd been enough nights on the couch with my finger hovering over his name on my contact list. Enough nights where I'd shoved my phone between the cushions of the couch and sat on my hands to stop myself from calling and begging for another chance. Before promising to fall in line.

Tonight was one of those nights, with Tate upstate at Brooks' friend's farm and Alex with them. I'd gotten ready for an early shift at Tryst, hyping myself up for another day of the same shit. After the blow job in the bathroom incident, I'd been lucky to keep my job. Thankfully, Marigold hadn't learned all the sordid details of what I'd been doing. She thought I'd just drank too much and flirted a little too hard. I'd let her believe that because it was what I needed. After that, she'd been great about letting me pick up earlier shifts so I could play shows, and I had a four-hour shift at Tryst, then a small restaurant in Brooklyn to get to before one in the morning. Sometimes, I felt like I was taking advantage of her, but...

I was only trying to survive. One day I would make it all right.

On my way out the door, I checked myself in the mirror, relieved that the bruising around my neck had finally faded into oblivion. I pushed my fingers against the parts of my throat that had worn fingerprints for weeks, relieved that it didn't hurt to the touch anymore. The move had almost become a nervous habit for me, a reminder, and when I walked into Tryst and found the man responsible for the bruises sitting at a cocktail table with three of his friends, any sense of relief from before left my body like it had been raptured right out of me.

Marigold was working behind the bar, and I gave her a quick hello after dropping my guitar and my messenger bag off in the back room and got to work. Another girl, Shara, who worked with me, had the tables under control, which meant I could stay behind the bar and didn't have to deal with anyone at that table. The crowd picked up as the clock ticked past ten, and Shara was quickly getting overwhelmed with all the bustle around the tables.

I'd kept John, or whatever his name was, in my periphery all night, only letting my guard down for two seconds to take a drink of tea and rest my eyes. It was nearly midnight, and I was beyond tired. I'd been sleeping like shit since the breakup with Alex, honestly…since I'd been cut off in the first place. But the weight of my choices and responsibility had been heavier since Alex, and always at night. Like, in the dark, my choices were clear, and I hated them. I just wanted to sleep, I wanted to be famous, and I wanted someone to care enough to let me have both of those things without having to compromise myself.

"You can do this," I muttered under my breath. "It's worth it."

Taking a drink and letting the tea wash away all the promises I made to myself, I set my glass down on the corner of the bar, back near the maraschino cherries and lime wedges. Maybe I'd call Alex after their trip to the farm, not to ask for another chance, but to apologize. To let him know I'd quit drinking, that I'd quit…

I'd call him to thank him.

"You disappeared." The last voice I wanted to hear broke

me out of my pretend apology tour, and I opened my eyes, stepping back from the bar.

"I've been here all night," I said. "Did you need Shara?"

"I meant off the app."

"I'm not doing that anymore."

He frowned. "Why not?"

"Because I don't want to." I glanced over my shoulder, finding Marigold and Shara bent over a tray full of cocktails. "If you need a drink, I'll send Shara to your table."

"We've cashed out," he said, licking his lips. "Just wanted to let you know I missed you."

I shivered, and not because I was turned on. "Great. Well."

"Take care," he said, his frown flickering into a smile before fading into nothing.

I didn't say anything. I just watched him leave, catch up with his friends outside on the sidewalk. One of them lit up a cigarette, and my nervous system started to settle. The danger had passed, and I had fifteen minutes left on my shift before I could head out for my gig. Shaking off the awkwardness from the encounter, I felt lighter than before. It was relief, I realized. I'd set a boundary it had been honored, and that was more than my dad had ever given me. More than Alex...

No, that wasn't fair.

Alex wasn't like anyone I'd ever met before.

He wanted to push my boundaries, and I liked that about him. The thought of it had turned me on, but only with him... no one else.

I finished my drink, washed the glass, then helped Marigold by slicing up some more limes to get her and Shara through the rest of the night. One day, I wanted to tell her the truth. She was a good boss, friendly and kind, and I didn't want to take advantage of her. I didn't want handouts. I was willing to work; I just needed the chance. I needed to prove to myself and everyone else that I could do it on my own.

After sealing the tub with the last of the limes, I swayed forward, entire body feeling like vibrating Jello. It had to be the exhaustion catching up with me, I thought. I said good-night to Marigold and Shara, then headed to the back to get my guitar and my bag. I banged into the door frame on my way out of the back room, blinking hard and slow to get my bearings back about me.

Something didn't feel right.

But I was more tired than I'd ever been, more emotionally worn down, and I'd quit drinking. My body was trying to make sense of whatever chaos I'd put it through over the past months, and I made a note to take a day off to sleep the next day.

Waving goodbye to Marigold and Shara over the loud crowd, I made it to the front door before I realized it wasn't just me being tired or worn out. There was something very, very wrong. I turned to head back in, grabbing the door frame to steady myself. The bar spun, the sidewalk spun, and warm, calloused hands curled their way around my waist, pulling me upright.

For so long, I'd always imagined my worst nightmare to be hanging up my guitar, putting on a suit, and going to work for my father, but I realized that was nothing compared to the real life nightmare I found myself standing in at that moment. I tried to point inside, tried to shout for help, but nothing was working. My arm didn't move, my mouth didn't open, and then everything went black.

Ford had bought Boston a farm.

It was the most ridiculous and most on-brand thing he'd ever done, and being at the farm alone while all my friends were there and so grossly in love made me want to crawl out of my skin. They'd all given me such a hard time about isolating myself, but they had no idea how insufferable they'd become. Kale's controlling asshole streak had been amped up to eleven from the first day he found out Carter and I were involved with each other, and it hadn't calmed down since. The relationship between Kale and Ford had become contentious at best, with Boston, who was normally immensely level-headed, even being worn down about his brother's antics.

Being stuck upstate with Carter and his husband in the mix didn't help matters, but I could only think about one thing at a time. Dylan's rebuke the last night we'd been together echoed sharply around my mind and I just needed a minute, needed a break, to catch my breath in silence, but there was no escape from my friends—or their happiness.

Kale had been the last to arrive, his presence ratcheting up everyone's nerves more than Dalton Fox's existence ever had. Boston and Ford deliberately poked at him, and by the time Kale raised his voice and shouted at all of us, I was ready to get on my bike and go back to the city.

"I don't care who you fuck!" Kale yelled, at none of us in particular. "I care that you lied to me about it. That you didn't trust me enough to tell me the truth!"

"Maybe you guys should sit down and have a chat," Tate suggested, grabbing Christian and hauling him toward the back door. The two of them went onto the wraparound porch, leaving the five of us alone, staring at Kale like his confession was an actual thing that existed in the space between us.

"I don't think this involves me," Dalton said, giving Carter a wary look.

"You're right."

Dalton nodded and took his leave, joining Christian and Tate on the porch. Our group was once again reduced further and I'd never been more jealous of anyone in my life.

"Not everyone owes you their truth, Kale." I stood up and smoothed my hands down the front of my jeans, thinking about just how many truths I hadn't shared with my friends and why. "You can't fix everyone or everything."

"I don't want to," he countered.

"Then why can't you just let people live?" I asked.

"I care," he choked out, turning his attention toward the door separating him from his boyfriend. "I care too much."

"You can't control it," Ford said. "*I* couldn't control it."

Ford was obviously talking about the development of his relationship with Boston, and Kale's immediate reaction was to open his mouth to argue, but he snapped it closed before any words managed to come out.

"It's not all about you," Carter said gently, the softness of his words making my heart twist in the middle of my chest.

No wonder your ex married someone else.

"You're not the main character in everyone else's story," Brooks said.

I took a step backward, and another, and another.

We were a group of four, but I was on the outskirts and their issues with Kale were not mine. I dealt with him when he'd shown up at my door, red-faced and furious over the idea I'd played with Carter hard enough to leave marks. I didn't buy into his rage or his petty behavior, and I'd long ago made peace with his controlling nature. It wasn't something I tolerated in my life, and I wasn't going to defend him or fight him now.

I slipped out onto the porch, letting the boyfriends who'd assembled there know my friends were still alive and in one piece. Sliding down the wall, I bent my legs at the knee and stared off toward the rolling fields that stretched for acres beyond the back of the house.

It pained me to admit, but I missed Dylan.

And being surrounded by my friends, all so clearly and fully in love, it shifted my own feelings for Dylan into a new perspective. One I hadn't been so willing to acknowledge back home. The developing relationship between him and me had been doomed from the start, built on an uneven foundation. As long as Dylan was struggling for money, fighting to hold on to the thing that meant the most to him, he'd never be able to fully let me into his life. Even if he understood the expectations I had, even if he wanted to meet them, there was always going to be something that took priority over me.

Maybe it was selfish or unhealthy for me, but I didn't want to come second to anything or anyone. I didn't think for one second that any of my friends weren't the first priority of their partners, or vice versa. I'd seen it most recently with Brooks and Tate who had basically entered each other's orbit and never left. The same with Boston and Ford, Kale and Christian, even Carter...Beamer and Dalton Fox.

I was jealous of them. Envious of the way love had come so easy to them while I'd spent weeks trying to claw and scratch it out for myself. I truly believed Dylan wanted to be with me, but I also didn't know if *want* was enough.

I'd never know if I didn't try.

I'd just pulled my phone out of my pocket to call him when there was a commotion from inside the house. Dalton was through the door before I could even get to my feet, but I was quick to push around him. Inside, the two of us found my best friends tangled together, not in a fight, but a hug. I brushed past Dalton and flung myself around the mess of limbs and heads, eyes watering when Brooks' fingers dug into my back and pulled me close.

With my eyes closed and my friends there, it was like it had been before. Back when we'd been inseparable and unstoppable, before our loyalties and allegiances had been tested. Kale, from the middle of the bunch, muttered an apology before we all broke apart like at the same time we'd remembered we weren't alone.

Ford sniffled, and Beamer rubbed the bottom of his right eye. For the first time in what felt like forever, I almost felt at peace. The only thing that would have made it better, made it right, was if Dylan was waiting on the porch for me. If he was with the boyfriends of my best friends...if we were all one group, together and unbreakable.

Even after we all stepped back further, Boston going to Ford, Christian coming for Kale, and Dalton practically running to Beamer, I didn't feel the same separate aloofness that had been wrapped around me for months. The memory of Dylan, even sharp around the edges, lived in my chest and my mind, and if I wanted to make things right with him— which I did—I would. When I got home from the farm, I'd call him. We would talk like two civilized adults, because if Kale could do it, so could we, and then we would try again. I would forgive him for his cruelty and hopefully he would forgive me for being me.

"We have to go." Brooks' voice was low and urgent in my ear, his fingers curled around my wrist. I glanced at him sideways, his stare shifting from me to Kale. "We need your plane."

"What's wrong?" I asked, staring down at the firm way he held me.

"Dylan's in the hospital."

"What?"

Brooks' fingers tightened around my wrist.

"You heard him," Tate spat, all his unspoken accusations following in the heat of his glare. "He was dumped outside the ER, nearly unconscious."

Brooks reached for Tate with his other hand, and Tate moved to him like they were magnets.

"That's all I know," Tate muttered, dropping his face into the crook of Brooks' neck. "That's all they'll tell me until I'm there."

"Who's Dylan?" Kale asked.

Ford sighed heavily. "Don't start now."

"It was an honest question."

"Can we please just use the plane?" Brooks asked, interrupting. "It will get us there faster."

"Sure, yes." Kale pulled his phone out of his pocket and frowned at his screen, fingers flying. "You're good."

"You have some explaining to do," Tate said to me, yanking Brooks toward the door with so much force it dislodged Brooks' fingers from around my wrist.

"And you say I'm bad," Kale said under his breath.

"Dylan is..." I trailed off, not sure how to answer the question because I wasn't sure who Dylan was to me anymore beyond... "He's someone important."

Tate scoffed, and Brooks and I followed him out of the house.

"Please don't ask me," I said to them both once we settled in the car.

They didn't say anything to me, didn't ask me, didn't even acknowledge my presence. Not for the drive to the airfield and not for the flight back to the city. I was an interloper between them, not anyone to Dylan in their eyes besides the man who'd let all three of them down. Brooks had asked me to get Dylan on track and Tate had expected Brooks to pick a man who could live up to the job. Instead, they'd gotten me, and whatever had happened left Dylan unconscious in the hospital.

Was I wrong for reacting to Dylan's words the way I had?

On the short flight to the city, I questioned every decision I'd made when it came to Dylan. From paying him for sex the first time, the second time, to thinking that I could take someone who didn't know better and hold him to a standard he didn't understand. All the missteps had been mine—not his—and if I had a chance to do it over, I would have handled everything differently.

I'd given Dylan enough rope to hang himself when that was the last thing he needed. Brooks had told me as much the day he showed up at my house. Dylan had needed structure and control, and I'd been too nervous, too shaken to give that to him. Too worried about scaring him off to be honest with him—and myself—about what I needed.

Tate continued to ignore me after we arrived at the hospital, rushing into Dylan's room before Brooks and I could even try to get in the door.

"One at a time," the nurse had warned. "He's awake, but needs his rest."

Leaning against the wall outside Dylan's hospital room, I scrubbed a hand down my face, well aware I couldn't avoid the impending line of questioning forever.

"Do you want to tell me what happened between the two of you now or wait until Tate is done in there?" Brooks finally asked me.

The answer was a resounding no, but I owed him—and Tate—the truth.

But still, even after everything, I didn't know if I could bring myself to tell either of them the whole truth. Just like we'd talked about with Kale less than two hours earlier, some truths were meant to stay private. There was a lot about Dylan's situation that wasn't mine to share with Brooks, and enough about my own that I didn't have the words for.

At the end of the day, the trust between Dylan and I had been damaged.

Consent had been revoked.

Vocally.

Repeatedly.

And emphatically.

The door to Dylan's hospital room swung open and Tate came for me, guns blazing, just like I knew he would.

"You promised he would be okay," he whisper-yelled, inches away from stabbing his finger into my chest.

"I tried."

"You tried," he mocked.

Brooks attempted to talk Tate down from his anger, but there was no calming him. If I was the best place for him to drop his confusion and his hurt, carrying that for Tate was the least I could do. All things considered.

"Did not."

"What did you do wrong?" Tate asked. "Why did Dylan change his mind about being with you?"

"That's not for me to answer, and frankly, even if I had the answer—it's not your business."

"He's my best friend!"

"You sound like Kale," Brooks interjected, his tone soft, but the accusation biting. It was enough to zap all the wind out of Tate's sails, and he turned away from me, toward Brooks.

"I don't know him well, but I know that was an insult."

"You cannot control the lives of the people around you," Brooks clarified. "If you try, you will only push them away."

Tate's anger bordered on turning physical, and I recognized the helpless feelings inside of myself too.

"I care about your friend," I said gently, because it was the simplest truth. "I wish I could have helped him more."

"You helped," Tate grumbled a concession that was miserable enough to break my heart.

Had I helped or had I only delayed the inevitable?

"Not enough, obviously."

Tate combed a shaky hand through his hair, throwing himself against Brooks' chest and I again found myself the lone man out.

"He's okay. " Tate shared, relief loud and clear. "He was drugged and left unconscious on the curb outside the emergency room. He said I could tell you this, by the way. I'm not—"

"I know you're not breaking his trust."

"He's even more worried now about paying his half of the rent."

That was just like Dylan, ignoring the real problem to instead focus on something absolutely irrelevant. His rent was a non-issue as far as I was concerned now, whether Dylan liked it or not.

Brooks whispered something to Tate, pushing him back enough to wipe Tate's tears.

"I didn't want to assume, but I figured you would loan me the money to cover it until he's back on his feet," Tate muttered.

"I won't loan it to you, Tate. I'll give it to you."

"I hate that," he said.

"*I'll* give it to you," I offered.

Tate's jaw clicked.

"Fine." He accepted my money far easier than Brooks', which I loved. "Dylan said they want to keep him until tomorrow for observation. He doesn't want me to stay all day. He said he'll call me when he's ready to go home."

"Do you believe him?" Brooks asked

"This time."

"Let's get you home then," Brooks said. "Get you cleaned up and get some food in you and we'll wait for the call."

My feet grew roots, sticking me to my place in the floor as the two of them readied themselves to leave.

"Thank you for trying," Tate said softly, nothing like Kale. "I know it's not your fault."

"I'll try again if he wants me to," I said.

I hoped he wanted me to. I needed him to want me to.

I wanted to make this right, not just for Tate, for Brooks, or for Dylan, but also for myself.

CHAPTER 19
DYLAN

I woke up after Tate left, listening to the steady beep of the heart monitor count off every pump of the stupid organ that had kept me alive. My shoulder ached, but it was a dull sensation so far beneath the surface and below the layers of pain medication it didn't bother me. The Velcro on the arm sling rubbing against my skin was far more annoying than the injury itself.

A torn labrum, the doctor had told me.

They weren't sure if I needed surgery yet, but it had my shoulder out of commission for further notice. Surgery would come with recovery time, and so would no surgery. There was no best case scenario for me.

Not anymore.

The only saving grace was that the hospital had called Tate instead of my parents, because if they found out about my injury, which I supposed would happen once they got the bill from the hospital, I might as well glue my ass to a Herman Miller chair and call it a wrap. They'd also called the police, but I wasn't going to give them any information that would implicate how I'd gotten myself in the situation, so they left soon after their arrival, defeated with no leads or charges to press.

"I know you're awake," the second-to-last person I wanted to talk to said from somewhere near my hip.

I pried my eyes open—they were dry beyond belief—to find Alex sitting on the edge of my bed, one knee up on the sheets, his entire body mapped with exhaustion and worry.

"How long have you been here?"

"I came with Brooks and Tate," he said.

"I meant *here.*"

"Long enough to notice the change in your heartbeat when you woke up and tried to pretend you were asleep still."

"I was trying to pretend I was dead." I let my eyes fall closed again. Keeping them open was too much effort. My shoulder hurt, my ribs burned—on account of two of them being bruised—and my head throbbed like someone was smashing me in the skull with an iron hammer.

"That's one I don't think Tate would forgive me for," Alex said softly, tugging at the shitty hospital blanket and straightening it out over the top of my hip.

I hummed because it was all I had energy for.

The bed shifted, and before I could protest, Alex's hand was around the back of my head and he had the rim of the shitty pink hospital cup pressed against my mouth.

"You need to drink some water," he said, tipping the cup back.

I didn't have it in me to argue. I was so tired of fighting.

The cold water sliding down my throat was the best thing I'd ever felt in my whole life, like it washed away the razor blades that had sprung up since I'd...

Since I'd...

Shit.

"That's enough," I said, trying to shove him off and only hurting myself in the process.

"Settle down," he warned.

"Why are you here?" I opened my eyes into thin slits, rolling my head against the pillow so I could see his face without the overhead lights glaring in my eyes.

He studied my face, then stood, heading for the door with three long strides. He was leaving me. Again. Of course he was. If he didn't want me before, why would he want me now? I bit my lips together between my teeth to stop from calling out for him. But instead of reaching for the handle on the door, he flipped off the lights and walked back to his perch beside me.

Alex sighed at my question, rubbing his chin with the side of his pointer finger, shoulders slumped. "I decided at the farm I was going to call you when I got back into town."

"Why?"

"Because I missed you."

"I'm sure you can find someone else who can hurt your feelings just as good as me, Alex," I said, eyes closing once again, my last encounter with Alex still vibrant and fresh in my mind...unlike the past twenty-four hours.

I don't know why I didn't startle when he touched my face. Maybe I expected it from him, even though I had no idea how I already knew him well enough to know it was coming. His fingers softly dusted across my cheek and down toward my jaw, brushing over the scruff that I'd been neglecting.

"I'd rather nobody hurt my feelings," he said quietly, "but I think it's unavoidable."

My breathing hitched when his fingers skated over the angle of my jaw and made their way to my neck. The bruising was long gone, and thankfully there wasn't anything new to be seen, but his fingers moved over the ghost of them anyway, and that fucking heart monitor started to beep louder, betraying me like everything else in my life.

I was relieved Alex didn't pay mind to the audible proof of how he affected me beyond the smallest twitch of his mouth. He traced his way along my collarbone to the thick black strap of the sling that held my shoulder steady before he stopped, stare flickering up to my face. I blinked slowly, watching the way he watched me, feeling even more vulnerable than I already was.

"Brooks offered to cover your half of the rent until you're back on your feet," Alex said, fingers moving down my sternum, stopping over my heart.

"Tate would never let him."

"You're right, but he'd let me."

"I won't," I argued.

Alex flexed his fingers against the scratchy hospital gown like he wanted to reach into my chest and tear my heart out with his bare hands.

At this point, I'd let him.

"Yes," he said quietly. "You will."

I licked my lips, tears welling up in my eyes before I could stop them. My lashes fluttered, but stopping the tears from escaping was impossible and I was too weak to put much effort into it anyway. Alex left his hand over my heart, using his other hand to wipe the tears away before they fell into my ears.

"Okay," I agreed.

Relief washed out of him, settling over me like a balm that did far more for all of my wounds than anything they would give me at the hospital. I cried harder, silently, and he moved his other hand to my face, using his fingertips to swipe away each and every tear as it raced out of my eyes. He was being so kind, so gentle. I didn't deserve it.

I didn't want it.

But I wanted *him*.

"I'll pay your rent as long as you need me to," he clarified. "But I want you to come stay with me."

I answered him before thinking, "No."

He kept brushing away my tears.

"Green?" he asked.

I squeezed my eyes closed.

He was *seeing* me and there was nowhere for me to go. I was hooked up to monitors and IVs and pain medication drips and I was so fucking tired of fighting...

"I don't mind the fight, Dylan," he said, finger slowing in time with my tears. "But it has to be for both of us."

"I know." The tears had clearly stopped coming out of my eyes because they were all lodged in the back of my throat. "Can I have some water, please?"

Alex made a pleased noise and moved to bring the water to my lips once again. The ice cold liquid didn't do much to wash the tears or the emotion away, but it was enough of a jolt that I was able to drag myself out of the misery of the past twenty-four hours.

The past two weeks.

The past two years...

"Thank you," I croaked after he set the water back down on the table.

"I'm waiting," he said, head slightly cocked to the side, one dark brow arched toward his hairline.

Even tired and tense, Alex was gorgeous.

Even mad at me.

With his dark eyes, a little bit of red around the whites, hidden behind the lenses of his glasses, and I remembered him being without those glasses, trying to blink me into focus.

"I was roofied," I told him. "Or not actual roofies, something like it. I don't remember the name they used."

He clenched his jaw, working it side to side, but not saying a word. I knew the unspoken question was right on the tip of his tongue. It was the first thing I'd asked the doctors after they came back with my bloodwork. Well, the first thing I'd asked about after I realized I couldn't move my shoulder.

"There's no signs of..." I trailed off, expecting another wave of relief to roll off of him, but he remained stoic and still. "Not that it matters."

"Do you know who it was?"

"Does it matter?"

Another click of his jaw. "Does it matter to you?"

"No."

Alex swallowed, Adam's apple bobbing. "Then it doesn't matter to me."

"The nurse said I was thrown out of a car in front of the ER," I said. "Unconscious. Landed on my shoulder and..."

I jerked my head toward the sling since my shoulder surely wasn't going to move.

"The nurse told me her best guess based off the dose they found in my blood is that I was too close to unconscious for it to be fun." I closed my eyes, every word burning. "Either that or they worried I was about to die."

Alex pulled his lips together, worrying them like it was the only thing stopping him from saying something we'd both regret. I hated his silence, but I didn't know if I wanted him to yell at me or tell me it wasn't my fault. Either would have been within fairness considering how we'd left things, and I would take whatever he wanted to give me. Because he said he'd missed me and I missed him, and it was unfair to the both of us for me to keep making that a problem.

"What about your shoulder?" he asked.

"They're waiting to get me in for an MRI to see if I need surgery."

Alex winced, returning one of his hands to the center of my chest. I didn't see the point because the heart monitor gave away every hitch and hiccup.

"I don't know when I'll be able to play guitar again," I finally spoke the words that had been screaming themselves at me since I'd woken up in the hospital bed. More unwanted, hot tears slicked down my cheeks too fast for Alex to catch them all with his fingers. Instead, he hitched me up halfway, wrapping his arms gingerly around me when I pressed my forehead against the side of his neck. The position was awkward and twisted and uncomfortable, but I would have been happy to never move again for the rest of my life. "Is that green for *you*?"

"I'll pay your rent," he said again, ignoring the question while answering it at the same time, "but I want you to stay with me. I want you under my roof."

"Under your heel."

He gave a shake of his head that bumped into mine, but I couldn't see his face to gauge his reaction.

"I want you to let me do what I do best," he whispered.

I was about to ask him what that was, but I was so tired, I slumped against him, and he held my weight with ease. It was more of an answer than any words would have been on their own.

"Green," I told him.

"It has to be for all of it, Dylan." He stroked his hand down the back of my head, fingers tangling their way through hair that was already matting. "None of the shit that happened the last time we were together."

"Green," I whispered again.

"You're not going to like everything. It's not...not like it was when I paid you."

The sex for money had been transactional. It had been Alex scratching an itch. From the haze of the morphine and the exhaustion, I understood the difference between before and also then. I'd gone into a relationship with him expecting more transactions, but the sex we'd had at the beginning of things had been superficial. It was great, but there wasn't any heart behind it. No trust. Alex wanted more than just sex from me, and all I'd given him was the worst part of me.

I owed him an apology, but my mouth wasn't going to form the words until my head was clear.

"I don't like *this*," I said instead, eyes too heavy to open. "Can I lay down now?"

Alex made another sound, then shifted me off of him and back down onto the shitty hospital pillow. He was warmer and softer and...safer...but I didn't want to ask him to stay.

But...

If he wanted me to be in for all of it, then he needed to be in for all of it too. Right? I was allowed to ask for things I wanted, wasn't I?

"Will you stay?" I asked on a yawn.

"Of course," he said quickly, settling me onto the bed and moving to stand up. There was a chair in the corner, but that wasn't what I meant. It wasn't what I wanted.

"No, wait." I couldn't reach for him quick enough. I was tired and my bones hurt. "I meant here."

I lifted one hip, but it was all I could manage.

Alex lay down next to me, first on his side before rotating onto his back so I could lie on my good shoulder and press against him. The wires and tubes were beyond annoying, but he was calm and patient while we worked together to move them out of the way. By the time we got it finished, I would have sworn I'd run a marathon and sleep was close enough to snatch my next breath away.

"Thank you," I whispered, already asleep, but I swear I heard him before I went under.

"Green."

THE NURSE WAS NONE TOO PLEASED WHEN SHE CAME IN TO CHECK ON Dylan and found him half on top of me, drooling a puddle the size of the Atlantic Ocean on the middle of my chest.

"You look like the kind of man who should know better," she chided.

"I'm also the kind of man who doesn't care."

She grunted, then checked Dylan's vitals and updated the white board at the foot of his bed.

"They'll be coming shortly to take him for an MRI and then I expect he'll be released."

"Okay."

Dylan stirred, groaning when he shifted toward his injured shoulder. I used my body to shove him onto his back before he put too much pressure on the injury. The shift involved me climbing out of his bed, which earned the nurse's approval and Dylan's dismay.

"Do you have your keys?" I asked him.

Dylan blinked at me, beyond groggy, mouth pulled into a deep frown.

"To your apartment," I clarified.

"There's a bag in here somewhere," he said.

I looked around, finding the plastic bag on the windowsill. His clothes were folded neatly inside, and on top of his pants I found his dead cell phone, the screen shattered, and a carabiner with four keys on it.

"Are these them?" I asked, holding it up.

"The one with the yellow," he said.

I shoved the keys into my pocket and sat on the side of his bed, the position I'd spent most of the previous night in before lying down beside him.

"They're going to get your MRI done before they discharge you." I told him what the nurse had said. "So I'm going to go get you a change of clothes and come back so we can head out once they cut you loose."

He opened his mouth and slowly closed it. "Okay," he said.

My eyebrows went up because I couldn't believe I'd actually watched the protest die on his lips. He huffed and dropped his head back against the pathetically flat pillow.

"Can I shower there?" I asked.

"Yeah."

"I'll be back in a couple of hours, okay?"

"Tate wanted me to call him," Dylan said, gesturing toward the bag of his belongings. "He wanted to pick me up."

"Your phone is dead," I told him, "but we can go to Brooks' after we leave here if you want to."

Dylan licked his lips. "Yes, please."

The soft agreement did something to me, heat blooming at the base of my spine and between my legs. The hospital was no place to get an erection, least of all with Dylan trussed up in a sling and on pain medication.

And yet...

"I love it when you listen," I said, brushing his hair back from his face and kissing his forehead.

He whimpered, body swaying toward me as much as the sling and the sheets would allow.

"I'll try."

I swiped my thumb down his temple and stood. "It's okay. I like it when you fight too."

Dylan snorted, cheeks flushing.

"Rest until they come get you," I said again. "I'll be back soon."

I was reluctant to leave Dylan, but I needed to get him something to wear out of here that wasn't his dirt-stained work clothes. With one last look, I stepped into the glaringly bright hospital hallway. I stopped at the nurse's station and waited for her to look up at me.

"Where is your billing department?" I asked her.

"Fourth floor, west corner."

"Thanks." I tapped my hand against the counter. "How long do you think until he's ready to go?"

"Probably after lunch."

I checked my watch, relieved that after lunch meant I had enough time to not just get Dylan clothes, but to get fresh clothes for myself as well.

"Thank you," I told her again.

On my way downstairs, I stopped by the billing department and put my Amex on file for whatever his stay ended up costing, then I called a car and headed across town. Stepping into my house felt like a time warp, so jarring to my equilibrium I had to brace myself against the wall to keep from falling over. I'd only been gone for one night, but so much had happened.

So much had changed.

I kicked my sneakers off and jogged upstairs to my bedroom, stripping out of my clothes as I went. Brooks, Tate, and I had departed from the farm in such a rush, I'd left my bag behind, including my toiletries. I did what I could with water and a toothbrush, then hopped into the shower and rinsed the stink and sick of the hospital off. I was looking forward to getting Dylan away from that place, bringing him back and giving him the same treatment, though I would probably be softer with my hands against his skin than I was with my own. Freshly showered, I dressed in a clean pair of jeans and a black t-shirt, then headed out to get clothes for Dylan.

I don't know what I expected to find at his apartment, but it wasn't a dozen empty water bottles strewn across the floor of his bedroom, an unmade bed, and a pile of dirty clothes that reached toward the ceiling. Practically nothing he owned was clean, save for a pair of black basketball shorts that looked like they were probably pajamas, and a t-shirt that was the least wrinkled thing on top of the pile.

Digging under Dylan's bed, I found a duffel bag, and I shoved the dirty clothes into it. I'd deal with getting them washed once he was settled at my house. I noticed his belongings were a mix of designer labels and discount brands, which indicated to me he'd been struggling without his parents' money longer than he'd admitted to me or to Tate. I figured there would be other things he'd want to bring over, but we'd deal with all of that after he was discharged.

The one thing that was notably absent from the mess in

his room was his guitar. He hadn't made any mention of it at the hospital, nor had he asked about it, which led me to believe he either knew where it was or he knew he wouldn't get it back. I imagined the topic would come up sooner rather than later, even though the injury to his shoulder meant he wasn't going to be playing for the foreseeable future anyway.

God.

That had to be the worst of it, and when it clicked into perspective for me, I was suddenly *worried* that Dylan hadn't brought it up at all. Guitar was his life, music, all of it, and to have it physically and emotionally taken from him all at once? It was the one thing he'd been actively trying to avoid for as long as I'd known him.

Sighing, I zipped up his duffel and locked the door behind me.

I made it back to the hospital and found Dylan sitting up in bed, looking more alert than he had the night before. He poked his spoon into a tub of orange Jello, cursing under his breath.

"Do you want help?" I asked, leaning against the doorframe.

"No," he snapped, jaw set.

"Alright." He was going to be a handful. "Well, help is here if you need it."

"Sure."

"Glad to see you're back to your old self." I shoved off the door and stepped into the room, ignoring the glare he leveled at me on my way in. "Did they have something to say about your shoulder?"

"Not yet."

Dylan gave up trying to scoop the Jello out of the tub

and instead sucked it straight into his mouth like the world's largest Jello shot. How it didn't choke him to death, I didn't know, but I definitely wasn't going to make a joke about it.

"They are discharging me before the doctor reviews the results," he said.

I dropped the clean-ish clothes I'd picked up for him onto the foot of the bed.

"I assume you don't want help changing either?"

"You'd assume right."

"Do you want privacy?" I asked.

He shoved the table away from the bed and scowled up at me. "Yes."

"Okay."

I stepped out of the room, leaning against the wall and pulling my phone out of my pocket. There was no way Dylan was going to be able to get his shirt on without help, but I'd let him come to that conclusion on his own. While I waited, I texted Brooks to let him know Dylan and I would be coming over, sliding the device back into my pocket when the nurse brushed past me and into the room.

"Everything okay?" I asked, following her in, my pulse immediately spiking.

"Just time to get Mr. Rivers signed out of here," she said to both of us. Dylan was half out of the hospital gown, boxers on and shorts halfway up his legs. "Careful there, sweetheart. Let me help."

She went to him, fussing over the hospital gown and the sling, far more meddlesome than I would have been...and he let her. He caught my eye over her shoulder, his stare steady and unreadable, but the grimace every time she jostled his shoulder was impossible to miss. I was just about to step in and push her off, but Dylan must have read my intent.

"She's got it," he said through a pained grunt.

So...

This was how it was going to be.

Better to get myself ready for it now than get him home and think it was going to be any other way. I'd told him I could handle the fight, that I liked it, and that wasn't a lie. The question, though, was if he was going to like what the fight got him.

We'd both find out sooner rather than later.

Discharge went quickly and gratefully the topic of payment never came up. Dylan was not going to be pleased that I was covering the stay, but I wasn't about to hear any argument over it either. It was something he'd have to learn to deal with if he wanted to be with me, which he said he did.

He remained silent and cranky the whole drive to Brooks' penthouse, his anger only mounting further when I refused to give him the bottle of pain meds the pharmacy at the hospital had sent him home with.

"I'll take care of this," I told him, tucking the orange bottle into my pocket and out of his reach. The unspoken part of the statement, of course, was...I'll take care of *you*.

Tate was asleep when we arrived, but the sound of our voices in the kitchen must have woke him because he ran down the stairs fast as a flashflood. Hearing his footsteps, Dylan climbed off the barstool he'd been perched on and met his friend with a hug. Brooks and I were on the other side of the island, quietly observing the reunion.

"Do you want some water?" I asked. "Coffee?"

"Water, I think." Tate answered, but got it for himself

before Brooks could manage the task He took a small sip and glanced up at me, eyes clearly still tired. "Thank you for picking him up."

I didn't know what to say, but Tate didn't care to hear it anyway. He took the water over to Dylan, who had moved to stare out the floor-to-ceiling windows of Brooks' kitchen. The two of them huddled together, talking in hushed tones, barely louder than the slow exhale of my own breath.

"Can you do this?" Brooks asked me.

"I can only do what he lets me," I said.

"Is he going to?" he asked. "This time?"

"I think so."

I hoped so.

I knew I could be what he needed, what he wanted. And being those things was also what *I* wanted. It wasn't Dylan filling a hole that Beamer had left behind. It was a new shape, a new space entirely, made especially for him. If we couldn't make things work this time, I was simply going to be left with the void.

"Dylan," I called to him across the kitchen, "it's time for your meds."

I dropped the pill into his hand and slid him a glass of water. He made a show of taking the pill, cursing me under his breath before he swallowed.

"I'm not going to kill myself, asshole."

Then he stalked back to Tate.

Brooks, the asshole that *he* was, laughed at me. Not loud enough for Tate or Dylan to hear. It was a soft noise meant only for my ears, and it sounded half like sympathy, half like understanding.

I flipped him off, finishing Tate's water while the two

friends continued their conversation. It didn't look happy. In fact, Tate looked downright incensed at most of what Dylan had to say, but then the two of them laughed and Dylan took a half step away. He was beyond exhausted, the sag in his good shoulder and the curve of his spine clear indicators he was about to drop.

"I need to get him home," I told Brooks.

"I'll work on softening Tate."

I gave him a tight smile, hoping it would be enough.

"You're a better man than the rest of us, Alex," Brooks said, "I hope you know that."

I didn't want to hear it, so I shook my head and lifted my chin in Dylan's direction.

"Are you ready?"

If he had more energy, I knew he would have had a name to call me, but all I got was a slightly annoyed, "Yes."

I stretched my arm out toward him and he closed the space between us, like there was a line from Tate to me, and Dylan was pulled strung the two. I stopped myself from kissing the top of his head, and even as he grumbled goodbyes to Tate and Brooks, he pressed into my side and whispered,

"Green."

You've never really lived until you had to hold a raw egg against the wall with the tip of your nose. At least, that's what I kept repeating to myself the longer I did it. My shoulder ached in its sling and my molars hurt from how hard I'd been grinding them together, and I'd long ago lost focus on the fine brush strokes that made up the flowered filigree in the silk wallpaper in front of me.

My vision blurred beyond anything I could blink away, and I closed my eyes, wishing I had a better internal clock and some awareness of how much time had passed since Alex hauled me out of bed before sunrise and shoved me into the corner. From the other end of the room, a phone alarm began to trill. The noise—a welcome reprieve after what had to have been hours of silence—startled me to the point of almost dropping the egg, but I shifted and pushed it harder against the wall before it rolled down.

This was the sixth day in a row Alex had woken me up like this, and I knew what was going to come next. Behind me, the sheets rustled, and I wondered if he'd actually gone back to sleep or if he'd stayed awake and watched me the whole time. I never knew what time he actually got me out of bed, so it wasn't even like I could compare once I got to a clock.

His breath against the back of my neck was more jarring than the alarm, his fingertips dusting across my bare shoulders even more unsettling. I worried again about cracking a molar.

"Go cook the egg, Dylan," he said softly.

I shoved my hand between my chest and the wall, pushing back into him with as much force as I could muster. The egg fell into my waiting palm and my shoulder blade connected with his sternum. My injured arm still hurt most of the time, so I made sure to leverage as much weight onto my other side as I could manage. He was expecting it, though, slamming me against the wall with far more force than I'd used with him.

"What's your safe word?" he asked, the question hot against my ear.

"Asshole."

"We would have stopped a long time ago if that were true."

I screwed my eyes closed, rubbing my cheek against the hand-painted textile that lined the walls of Alex's bedroom. I wanted to dig my fingers into the seams and strip it off the wall.

"Juilliard," I grunted.

He pushed me into the wall again. "Are you going to use it today?"

"Not yet."

"Then go cook the fucking egg."

Alex stepped away from me, bare feet padding quietly against the wood floor as he walked out of the bedroom, leaving me alone in the space that was so sickeningly his that it made me ill. His entire house was bland and boring, almost sterile. Every room a copy of the one before it. Every room except his bedroom and his playroom, at least. Both of those rooms had character, even if the character was a fucking domineering prick.

I blinked my eyes open, staring down at the brown egg in the palm of my hand and debating the merits of cracking it right there, smearing the yolk all over the walls and ruining his precious wallpaper that way, but even as I tensed my fingers around the fragile shell, I knew I wouldn't go through with it. Alex knew too, or he wouldn't have left me alone there with the egg in the first place. I decided then that he probably did go back to sleep after he got me up for our little morning ritual.

What was the saying?

Just enough rope or something.

He was already in the kitchen when I got there, sitting at the bar with his stupid little crossword and his stupid little white mug of espresso. Half rumpled from sleep, his hair was unstyled, his cheeks covered in a day's worth of growth. He had on a pair of plaid sleep pants and his glasses. Nothing else. I swallowed down the way I wanted to salivate at him because leaning into how much I still wanted to fuck him wasn't going to get me anywhere besides back in the corner.

Alex hadn't touched me since I was discharged from the hospital.

Well...

Except to spank me.

Which he did more often than not and also harder than I thought I deserved. Standing in the corner with my nose against the egg should have been a reward for how bruised my ass was. If he'd wanted to be truly cruel, he would have made me sit on the floor.

With my back to him, I turned on the stove and dropped a pad of butter into the small cast iron pan on the front burner, determined to not let the very simple task get the better of me again. Six days with the egg against the wall, six days of being told to cook the egg after I'd served my time in the corner. The first five days had ended with the final product destroyed, stuck to the pan and mangled beyond recognition, which in turn ended with Alex strong-arming me over his knee and spanking me until I cried. He was always careful with my shoulder, but never with the rest of me. I knew there had to be a lesson in it somewhere, but I was too angry with him to find it.

If I turned off the stove and gave him my safe word, the whole ruse could end. He wouldn't lay a hand on me after that. He'd probably help me pack my shit up and then drive me to Chelsea on the back of the sleek black motorcycle he favored over a car. The word was right there on the tip of my tongue, but the egg was in my hand and the butter had started to melt, and I wasn't a quitter.

Or...I didn't want to be anymore.

Walking away from my family had basically been the same as quitting my entire life, and at the time, I hadn't realized the implications of the decision. I wasn't stupid. I understood the concept of money and knew I needed it to survive, but I'd grown too complacent with the pad of the monthly deposits my dad made into my bank account. I hadn't put together how much I relied on him. How incapable I was of taking care of myself.

Alex was taking care of me now.

Even if I didn't understand the how of it. Even if I hated him and fought him at every turn.

Even if I resented him for it.

His pen clicked, the point retracting.

"The butter is going to burn," he said simply.

I swallowed, staring down at the pan. The butter was still golden, bubbling and racing around from edge to edge like an air hockey puck. Maybe if the butter burned, the egg wouldn't stick. I didn't know shit about cooking—we'd always had help —but I wasn't above trying something new to see if I could avoid getting my ass spanked raw for the sixth morning in a row.

"Shut up," I told him, frowning at the butter as the bubbles turned a darker shade of gold before going brown.

I cracked the egg on the handle and dropped the contents into the pan. The burning butter popped and sizzled, the egg immediately turning white around the edges. I threw the shell into the trash can and grabbed the spatula out of the drawer.

"You think you know best, Dylan," Alex warned, "but you don't know shit."

I wanted to beat him with the fucking overpriced wooden spatula, but knew nothing good would come of that, so I shoved the flat tip against the egg to flip it before the edges of the egg burned and curled. The egg didn't flip. The spatula skittered across the pan, dragging chunks of egg all the way across.

"Fuck."

The pen clicked open, and the point scratched against the newspaper...Alex back at his precious crossword again. He waited in silence until I'd given up on the egg entirely, turning my back on the burned disaster and staring at his fingers, resting against the white marble countertop.

"Are you finished?" he asked.

"Yes."

"Were you successful?"

"You know I wasn't," I ground out, fisting my hands at my sides. My safe word was again on the tip of my tongue, but it was like my jaw had been wired shut. I wouldn't have been able to utter it even under threat of bodily harm.

The first time Alex and I slept together, I hadn't known what to expect. He warned me that it wasn't going to be a normal, vanilla flavored, roll in the hay and that had been fine. Afterward, I'd been confused, a little scared, but not of him. Of myself.

Alex had intentionally hurt me during sex, he'd demanded I demean myself for his pleasure, and I'd not just complied... I'd enjoyed it. I'd gotten off more than once, my body ramped up past eleven even as pair shot through me for how hard he had my nipples between his fingers.

Sex with Alex, penetration or not, left me feeling in control of my life in ways that I'd almost forgotten. This shit, though, with him dosing out my pain medication for me, making me cook for him and clean for him, this shit with the eggs in the morning and the spankings that followed...there was control here, but it wasn't mine.

"Were you successful?" he asked again.

I bit the tip of my tongue with my incisors, the taste of copper flooding my mouth. "No."

He set down the pen and stood up. My fight or flight threatened to kick in, and I had to mentally command myself to not run away from him. I knew what was coming, I knew it would hurt, but I knew it wouldn't last forever.

I knew I was safe.

He came around the edge of the island and instead of grabbing me like he had the days before, he simply cocked his head toward the stairs. I swallowed, understanding immediately what he'd asked of me. He wanted to know if I was going to come of my own free will or if I wanted to fight him on it again.

"Where?" I rasped.

"Playroom."

Just like I'd willed my feet to stay put, I had to next will them to move. One muscle at a time, I managed to walk toward him, then past him. He took the spatula out of my hand and started off behind me. I took the stairs to his playroom and stood in the center, shoving my boxers down to my ankles before stepping out of them. I knew I wasn't allowed clothes in here.

The room was his favorite space in the house, but even he looked out of place down there in nothing more than his cotton pajamas. He pulled the spanking bench away from the wall, which was an expensive and glorified wooden saw horse, painted black and covered in soft, pebbled leather, and made for fucking. It was the only soft thing in the whole room.

Alex clucked his tongue against the roof of his mouth and folded his arms over his chest. Waiting. The way he held himself made his pecs and biceps bulge, and my cock, even knowing what was coming, twitched against my thigh.

"On it?" I asked, voice cracking.

"On it."

His eyes scanned my face as I climbed onto the bench and

folded myself over it. He had O-rings on either leg designed for restraint, but he also had handles. He'd fucked me on the bench once, back before everything in my life had gone to shit. I didn't think he was going to fuck me today, but his cock tented his pajamas so I at least knew he was thinking about it.

"Scoot down more so your bad arm isn't pressed against your chest," he said.

I slid down so the top half of my chest and my head hung over the edge, stretching my good arm down to reach one of the thick steel handles, curling my fingers around the metal. It quickly warmed under my touch and I closed my eyes, sucking in a slow breath.

"Okay," I said.

My shoulder hurt. It always hurt, and I started to wonder if it would ever feel normal again. I didn't need surgery, but there was going to be weeks of physical therapy, and even then...the reality of that crushing possibility was too much for me to process, so instead, I welcomed the burning sting of his hand against my ass to spank it right out of my mind.

"Why are we down here, Dylan?" Alex asked, having moved around behind me. He pressed one of his fingers into what felt like a particularly deep bruise in the center of my left ass cheek and I grimaced, tightening my grip on the handle.

"Because I ruined breakfast," I answered.

"Why else?"

I swallowed, tears already leaking from the corners of my eyes.

"Because I want to be," I whispered.

"And I want you to learn how to cook a fucking egg," he said sharply, landing a biting slap against that bruise on my ass cheek with his stupid fancy spatula. It was far less painful than the heavy sting of his palm, but one hundred strikes of the spatula later, the pain blurred into itself and Alex could have dusted a feather against my ass and I would have cried out for how much it hurt.

Alex breathed heavily, wailing down on my ass until the spatula cracked in two. The top half landed against the floor with a deafening crash and I sucked in a breath during the pause.

"Dylan."

I shook my head. I wasn't ready to be finished.

Alex sighed, brushing his fingers over my ass before resuming his pace, this time using his hand instead of the spatula. He spanked me so hard the whole bench dragged across the floor from the force of it, and it hurt.

It hurt.

It *hurt.*

It hurt until it didn't hurt anymore, and then everything felt like heaven, like I was lying in a cloud of silks and velvet, and I let out a loud and watery cry for peace.

"Thank you!" I shouted at him, even though the words didn't sound real to my ears.

He stopped mid-swing. I felt the air push against my tender and probably bleeding backside in lieu of his palm. I sobbed again. I thanked him again.

I thanked him.

Alex's next breath rumbled through him all the way down to his fingers. He pulled me up into a seat, letting me lean against his bare and now sweaty chest to catch my breath. It always took me awhile to stop crying after we finished, and

Alex diligently stroked my hair and kissed the top of my head while I settled back into my body. He always waited until I pulled away from him to go. He never pulled away first. I didn't know if he was aware he did that or not, but I sure was.

"You need a bath today," he said into my hair, "not a shower. You need to soak that bruising."

I didn't say anything, but I didn't fight him when he helped me stand. He followed me up the stairs to his bedroom, one step behind me the entire way in case I stumbled or fell.

I was safe.

I braced myself against the edge of the sink while Alex filled the tub with warm water. He poured in some Epsom salts and some herbs, using his fingers to swirl the mix around. His palm was as red as a strawberry, a sharp contrast to his otherwise tanned complexion. He held it out to me, not groaning or grunting when I grabbed onto his hand for balance climbing into the tub.

Sitting down in the massive soaking tub hurt far more than the spanking had, the salt and the herbs immediately starting to relax my muscles and tenderize the bruises. My face was damp from the tears, and I slipped under the water, eyes closed tight and lungs full of air. I counted to forty-nine, wondering what it would feel like to drown right there in his bathroom. My lungs ached, fighting against my brain to get air, and at the very last moment, I pushed my head back above the surface.

Alex was still there, sitting on the closed toilet lid, his crossword now in hand.

He'd left me alone under the water, but he'd come back.

He knew what I would and wouldn't do.

I was safe.

"Thank you," I said to him softly. He accepted my thanks with a nod, and I was grateful...because it was the only thing I had to give him.

DYLAN SLEPT PEACEFULLY ON HIS BACK, EVEN THOUGH IT HAD TAKEN him some time to settle in on the bruising. I watched him, leaning against the bedroom wall and shaking the ache out of my hand until he started to softly snore. He was so peaceful when he slept, so non-combative, but I understood his need to fight for control. The fear of losing it before you realized how much you stood to gain…

I wasn't submissive—I never had been—but Beamer had explained it to me enough times that I understood the choice of walking up to the precipice and either fighting like hell not to fall or jumping off with your eyes wide open. My phone buzzed quietly in my pocket, a reminder alarm that I had lunch plans with my friends.

All of them.

Since the weekend at Boston and Ford's farm, Kale had been making a concerted effort to be a decent human, which was unsettling half the time and welcome the other half. It was a fine line, and I recognized he tried not just for his brother or Christian, but also for himself. I was hesitant to leave Dylan unsupervised, I hadn't let him out of my sight since he got home from the hospital, but that cry had really taken it out of him and I figured he'd be asleep until nearly dinner time.

Dylan slept like garbage at night, but I didn't know if that was a side effect of the hospital or the assault. He didn't want to talk about it, and that was one thing I wasn't going to force, but I had strongly encouraged—or demanded—he start therapy. He hadn't used his safe word, so I'd gotten him set up with twice a week sessions to start, but he'd said the doctor said they could move to once a month after another few weeks.

I also didn't make him talk to me about his sessions. Those weren't for me anyway. Whatever work he did with the good doctor was for him, not for me. The only thing that mattered to me was that he was whole, because the thing developing between us wasn't fit for half a man.

Dylan let out a loud and rumbling snore, the tension between his brows finally relaxing. He was sound asleep, so I set the broken spatula down on the bedside table and walked quietly out of the bedroom. He knew I was leaving. I'd gotten dressed while he brushed his teeth, and I was relieved that his eyes didn't spark with rebellion. There'd been a brief flicker of...something, but it was gone just as fast as it had flared to life.

Even though I told him where I was going and how long I'd be gone, I left him a note on the kitchen counter with the same information. I had half a mind to tell him to spend his downtime searching information on how to cook an egg in a cast iron pan, but it would have defeated the purpose of the whole exercise.

Dylan needed to learn how to ask for help.

For as long as I'd known him, he'd had a stubborn streak a mile wide, and if he wanted things to work with me, it would have to shrink. I didn't want to break him of it completely, I wasn't lying when I said I liked the fight, but he was his own worst enemy and he was too blinded by his own preconceptions about himself to see it. Helping him get there was the best thing I could do for him, whether he believed it or not.

The motivation wasn't entirely pure, though. Because if he and I were to stay together in the ways I wanted and the ways *he* needed, he had to get over himself first. Even though he took his punishments as well as any other partner of mine ever had, he didn't understand the point of them. He cried through them, the pain giving him a chance to cry out all the feelings he couldn't express otherwise, but the fight was still against himself instead of me.

I left the note for him on top of my unfinished crossword, leaving out the internet search suggestion. He'd barely been on his phone anyway since coming home, and I doubted he would pull it out to google how to cook an egg. I made it halfway to my door before my own unease set in, the prospect of leaving him alone almost enough to make me crawl out of my skin.

"Idiot," I said, turning back and throwing the note into my trash can.

I pulled my phone out of my pocket and fired off a text to my friends.

> Meet me here instead.

FORD

> Where is here?

KALE

I imagine he's home with his adopted
little pet.

I'm home

BROOKS

But I was looking forward to eating.

KALE

Eat Tate.

BROOKS

I think I liked it better when you were being a
sullen piece of shit.

I regret all of you.

But I'm not leaving, so come over or go
without me.

BROOKS

Do you have food?

KALE

He's keeping another human alive over there,
of course he has food.

I gathered the consensus the three of them were going to make their way over to my house, and if Dylan had been awake for the whole thing, I would have cooked them all eggs in the cast iron to prove a point, but he was sound asleep, so I settled on throwing together a salad and some sliced meats and cheeses. I carried all the trays and bowls out to the back yard, wanting to give Dylan as much quiet in the house as I could. I knew from first-hand experience, the full body releases he'd been having this week were extremely physically taxing.

Ford was the first to arrive with a paper grocery bag full of apples, undoubtedly from the farm. He shoved the whole thing against my chest and grinned, closing the front door behind him and right in Brooks' face.

"Prick," Brooks grumbled, brushing past him with a bottle of wine in each hand.

Ford chuckled and followed me through the house. I left the apples in the kitchen. Maybe I'd give Dylan a break from eggs and let him try his hand at apple juice. Ford grabbed one out of the bag and bit into it, holding it between his teeth so his hands were free to get four wine glasses out of the cabinet by my sink.

Tears prickled against the backs of my eyelids and I left the two of them in the kitchen so they didn't see me cry. It wasn't a full cry, but enough tears leaked out that either of them would have called me on it, if not both. It had just been so long since everyone had been over, since I'd bothered to invite them. The only thing missing was Beamer, and the more time and space between us, the more I started to miss him as a friend, not a lover.

"Thanks for helping," Ford said, coming up behind me and setting the glasses down on the table. Brooks had the wine opener in his hand and I cast them both an unamused sideways glance.

"I'm hosting."

"Because you didn't want to leave." Brooks' stare flickered up toward my bedroom window on the third floor.

"He's asleep," I said. "We had a long morning."

"How are you dealing with that?" he asked.

Ford took one of the wine bottles out of Brooks' hand and poured us each a glass before sinking down into one of the chairs and stretching his legs out in front of him.

"I forgot how nice it was here," he said, taking a drink of the wine and smacking his lips.

I looked at him, looked at Brooks, looked at my home...

"So did I," I said, clearing my throat. "And I'm dealing with that the best I can. With him."

"I don't know a single thing about this little pet of yours," Ford said.

"He's not a pet," I corrected, even though he very much was. I didn't want my friends to get in the habit of reducing him to a stray when he had the potential to be so much more.

"About this Dylan of yours," Ford corrected.

That wasn't much better, but...

"He's Tate's best friend," Brooks answered.

"In over his head with life a bit." I didn't want to give his whole story away, but after we'd hijacked Kale's plane and fled the farm the weekend before, Ford deserved as close to the truth as I could get without betraying confidence. "He can tell you whatever he wants whenever he wants."

"Happy to see you're tightlipped as ever," Ford teased.

"Didn't we just talk about letting people have their own shit?" Kale's voice rang out crisp and clear from behind me, and I swiveled around to see him standing in the doorway with an amused grin on his face. "The door was unlocked, so I let myself in."

"Happy to see that even with everything that has changed, some things never will," Brooks muttered, pouring a fourth glass of wine and sliding it toward one of the empty seats at the table.

"How's Dylan?" Kale asked, taking the seat beside Ford, whose shoulders tensed for half a second before settling back to their normal positioning.

"Asleep," I said.

"And still you couldn't bear to leave?"

"Let him be," Brooks warned.

I swallowed, throwing him a sidelong glance. Of the four of us, Brooks was the only one who knew the details of what happened last time I'd left Dylan alone, when I'd let my own pride get the better of me. Sometimes at night, while Dylan slept soundly in my bed, I wondered if it had been my shortcomings as a dominant or my shortcomings as a man that had caused me to safeword on him that day and send him on his way. If I'd been more levelheaded, less emotional...I struggled to find the source of the flaw.

"Stop it," Brooks said under his breath, just to me.

I forced a smile that settled into something real enough, then chased my own doubts back with a drink of wine.

"Tell me about the farm," I said, swiveling to face Ford. "I want to hear all about how rural life has domesticated you."

"It helps now that Brooks brokered a deal with Lang over the soup kitchen."

I bit my lips together between my teeth, Dylan's father's surname not lost on me.

"What happened there?" I asked.

"He owns the place Boston had been levering most the donations to," Brooks explained, "and taking donations would have ruined the way he was cooking his own books to evade taxes."

"Boston was insistent, though," Ford picked up the explanation. "He's friends with the manager, and that was where they wanted the produce to land."

"We got him in the end." Brooks and Ford clinked their glasses together.

It was impossible for me to not think about how those negotiations could have just as easily had Dylan on the other end of the table from my two best friends. It was his passion for creating music, for living his life for himself, that had kept him away from his father's dealings for so long.

I finally understood the absolute desperation he must have felt. That he must still be feeling.

"Where'd you go?" Kale asked me, titling his head to the side while Brooks and Ford lapsed into a conversation about whatever scheme they'd used to get what they wanted out of Dylan's dad. I wondered if they knew who they were talking about...

"Just thinking," I said, raising my glass.

Kale exhaled and rolled his eyes, taking a drink of his wine.

"You look...happy," he said. "Happy, but tired."

I shrugged.

"I have to be honest, Alex." Kale grabbed the bottle of wine and topped off both our glasses, ignoring Brooks and Ford entirely. "I've always been a little jealous of you."

I scoffed. "Jealous? Of me?"

He glanced up at the top floor of my house, the shadow of the roofline washing the yard in shade.

"I like things handed to me." He smiled, a little coy. "If they're not freely given, they're freely taken."

"Are we talking about your kidnapped prince?"

"Hey, now. He came on his own accord."

Kale was insufferable on his best day.

"I bet he did."

"It wasn't a sex joke, though..." He chuckled. "I meant that

I'm a lazy, spoiled man, and you've never been afraid to work for it."

I followed his stare up to my bedroom window.

"Is that what I'm doing?"

"I think we both know it is," he said.

At the same time, Ford reached for the bottle of wine, making an outraged sound when he picked it up and found it empty. Kale laughed at him and took a drink, leaning back comfortably in his chair and turning his attention to the small fountain against the back wall.

I hadn't looked at my relationship with Dylan as work, but that helped put it in a new perspective for me. That was really what he needed, after all. Someone to show up for him and fight for him when he couldn't do it for himself. I was a man of many means and resources...it was the least I could do.

My showing up had nothing to do with my feelings. It was too soon for that.

"You're so greedy," Brooks said to Kale, twisting the corkscrew on the second bottle of wine. "Alex would give me the shirt off his back if I asked for it and you won't even leave me a drink of wine on a hot spring day."

I opened my mouth to argue, but Kale shot me a knowing look, one brow raised.

There wasn't much I wouldn't do for my friends. And even less that I wouldn't do for Dylan.

Maybe it wasn't as soon as I thought.

WHEN I WOKE UP, THE CLOCK TOLD ME IT WAS THE MIDDLE OF THE afternoon. My shoulder hurt, but it was the same kind of dull throb I'd gotten used to over the week since my discharge. The lights in Alex's bedroom were off, but the windows were east facing and I could tell by the gray and blue shadows across the floor the sun was on its way to the other side of the house. Somewhere inside, a door closed, and I rolled onto my back, staring up at the ceiling.

I was due for a pain pill, which meant it was only a matter of time before Alex came looking for me. Thankfully, his egg-based punishments were saved for the morning. The rest of the day, he was content to let me find snacks or he ordered takeout for us. Admittedly, though...I was starting to go a little stir crazy. His house was gorgeous and large, smaller than where I'd grown up, but far bigger than my apartment with Tate, so there were always places to go, but I'd been out of work since my hospital stay. I'd gone from having two steady jobs and the occasional music gig to no jobs, no gigs, no nothing.

Alex's footsteps grew louder as he made his way up the stairs. I was already familiar with the soft tread of his footfalls, and I turned toward the door just as he twisted it open. He had a glass of water in one hand, the orange pill bottle in another, and his face was flushed and pink.

"How long have you been up?" he asked, sitting down on the edge of the bed.

I scooted into a seated position and held out my hand for the pill. "Not long."

He passed me the water and I took a swallow, sending the pill down my throat.

"You look like you have something you want to say."

I handed him back the glass and gave him a small shrug with my good shoulder.

He clearly didn't like that response, reaching forward and brushing my hair away from my face. "I thought we made some progress this morning."

Shifting my weight, I found myself reminded of exactly how much progress we *had* made this morning. Not with the egg, but with the way I'd cried bent over his bench. It had been embarrassing the first time, but now it was like opening a drain and letting out everything that I'd accumulated for no good reason. The release I found from playing with Alex was beyond anything I'd experienced our first two times together, and it was enough to pique my interest in him further.

The thing about Alex was he was always full of surprises. I thought I understood him the first time I took his money, then I thought I knew him better the second time. When we argued before my injury, I clearly knew enough to hurt him, but the Alex that showed up at the hospital...he was a different man entirely. This new version of Alex was so much more whole than what he'd given me before, and I was far too broken to hold him safely in my hands.

"It's just me," I said softly, pressing my fingers into my thigh, playing through the chords of a song I hadn't had a chance to write yet. "I know this is probably stupid, but...do you know what happened to my guitar?"

"I didn't see it at your apartment," he answered.

I stilled the melody. "I had it with me when..."

"It wasn't at the hospital either."

I swallowed thickly, fighting back another surge of tears. That was an additional unexpected result of my stay with Alex. I cried. Constantly. To call me hyperemotional would have nearly been an understatement. It was as if the first time he spanked me he'd flipped a switch that never quite turned off. I was always primed for a fresh wave of tears, even if I didn't know what had caused them in the first place.

"You can't play right now anyway," he said quietly, brushing wetness off my cheek. I wanted to tell him it was useless, because as soon as it was gone, two more tears took its place.

"I know, I just..."

"What kind of guitar was it?" he asked. "I can get you a new one."

"You don't need to buy me a new guitar," I said.

"Green, Dylan?" Alex arched a brow at me, and I swallowed back another protest.

"It was a Martin D45."

"Thank you." Alex nodded. "But you still can't play. Probably not for a while yet."

"They said six to eight weeks," I told him, reminding

myself that two months was nothing. It was no time at all. It was the same amount of time I'd known him.

"You'll have it tomorrow," Alex said, "but you're not allowed to play it until you're cleared for that range of motion."

"But I'm cleared to bend over that bench of yours to get spanked every morning?"

Alex sighed, body swaying away from me.

"And speaking of that," I continued, sliding my back straighter against his headboard. "Why won't you touch me?"

"I touched you two minutes ago."

"Like *touch me*, touch me," I said, shoving the sheet down past my hips to reveal the sleepy bulge between my legs. "You haven't fucked me, touched my cock, nothing since the hospital."

"No," he agreed. "I haven't."

"Why not? Do you think that because of what happened... You know that they didn't...the hospital checked..."

"Dylan, stop," He reached up and pressed his fingertips against my lips. Touching me again, almost as if to prove his point. "Even if something had happened to you in that way... that doesn't have anything to do with it."

I smacked his hand away from my mouth. "Why then?"

"Because you can't always get what you want when you want it."

"You think I don't know that?"

"If you could have your way, what would you have right now?" he asked. "What would your life be like?"

"I'd be a famous musician," I said automatically. It had been the answer for as long as I could remember. "I wouldn't need my parents' money. I wouldn't have to worry about when the next gig was coming up. I wouldn't have to worry about finding gigs at all. They'd be calling *me* to come play, all across the country. Around the world."

My heart hammered against my chest, shoulder finally feeling numb, unlike the backs of my thighs and my ass. That was a pain I welcomed, though, one I could manage and make sense of.

"And that is why, Dylan," he said simply.

"Why? Do you think you're too good for me?"

He rolled his eyes, standing up and smoothing his hands down the front of his jeans. His fingers trembled when they reached his knees and he was quick to pull his hands back, but I'd already seen. His cheeks were still flushed, his jaw now tense.

"I am not interested in doing things by half," he said. "Not anymore and not ever again."

"What does that even mean?"

"Your future is about you, as it should be. But if there's no place for me then, there is no place for me now," he said.

It was instinct to argue, and my mouth opened before I even knew what I wanted to say. But any argument died in the back of my throat, and Alex reached forward and pressed his fingers against the bottom of my chin until I snapped my mouth back closed.

"I'll give you what I can afford, Dylan," Alex whispered, mouth twisted into a grimace. "Nothing more."

I bit my cheek, another fresh wave of tears welling up. My face crumpled, and Alex's arms were around me before the first sob fell out of my mouth. I was grateful, in that moment, that affection was something he could afford me, because the thought of crying alone on his bed was too much for me to handle.

"You're okay," he soothed, kissing the top of my head and stroking his hands down my spine. "You're okay and you're safe."

That sent another wash of tears out my eyes, and I curled my good arm around him, fingers digging into the rich cotton of his t-shirt.

"You smell like sunshine," I mumbled against his chest, smearing tears and snot all over him.

"I was sitting outside," he said.

"Can I sit outside?"

Alex huffed a laugh into my hair and rested his chin against the top of my head. "Of course you can sit outside."

"Now?"

"Is that what you want?" he asked.

I clutched his shirt tighter. "Yes, please."

He let out a quick, low groan, then shifted out from underneath my weight. There was the promise of an erection growing between his legs. I could see it, feel the heat of it, but he adjusted himself with one hand and helped me out of bed with the other. Even though I didn't need help walking, Alex helped me anyway. One hand pressed softly against the small of my back as we made our way downstairs.

There were two empty bottles of wine on the table out there, four empty glasses, a mostly eaten tray of meat and cheese. Alex's usual crossword sat finished in front of one of the chairs, pen clicked closed on top of it.

"You had company?" I asked.

"Brooks, Ford, and Kale came over for a bit," he said.

"I didn't hear you."

"Good." He pulled out a chair for me and I sank down into it gratefully. Even though the sun was already working its way toward the other side of the house, the brightness of the sky was welcome after being inside for so long. The fresh air would have been enough on its own, and I tipped my head back, sucking in a deep breath.

Alex sat down across from me, stare appraising. "You've been cooped up all week."

"I know."

"You should get out more."

"You should let me out more," I countered.

He pursed his lips, unimpressed. "The only thing I've dictated since your arrival is your morning routine. Everything else has always been up to you. The morning is up to you, as well. If you wanted to get technical about it."

"You don't have to remind me," I grunted.

"Clearly, I do." He leaned back and curled his fingers around the arms of the chair. "You're not a prisoner here, Dylan. I thought you wanted to be here."

"I had different ideas of what it would be."

"That seems to be a trend with us," he said.

"I wish sometimes..." I looked down at the table, at his crossword. I'd taken his seat—or he'd given it—without even asking. "I wish we could start over."

"I thought we had."

"Not fully," I said, glancing up at him. "Not really."

Alex reached for the half-eaten meat board and rolled a piece of prosciutto with his finger. "Start over how, then?"

"Maybe we met at the bar that night and I wouldn't have slept with a patron."

That earned me a smirk and a quick adjustment of his glasses.

"My loss there," he murmured.

"Maybe it's another world where we met under different circumstances." I shrugged my good arm, exhaling loudly when he passed the rolled up slice of meat to me.

"A world where you're a famous musician and I'm out for a night with my friends?" Alex cocked his head to the side, mouth quirking up in the corner. "I'm so captivated by you that I wait for you after the show and buy you a drink?"

"I don't drink anymore," I told him.

His expression made it clear that the revelation was news to him, but for some reason, he didn't press it. Didn't ask how long ago I'd made the decision.

"I wait for you after the show," he started over again, "and give you my number. I ask to take you out on a date."

"Where do you take me?" I asked.

"Wherever you want to go."

Even born from privilege, that was a life that could have never been mine. Just because my upbringing hadn't given me anything of note didn't mean the rest of my life had to remain unremarkable. It was okay, I imagined, to feel sorry for myself for a little while. To cry every morning about the future that I'd never even had a chance at, every strike of Alex's hand against my backside pushing it out of me. Maybe one day, all of those lost dreams would be gone and I'd be able to focus on the reality in front of me instead of the pipe dreams in my head.

My fingers dropped to the table, pressing out another series of chords I'd not yet had a chance to put to paper. It was part nervous habit, part hope.

"Could we still maybe start there?"

Alex worried his lower lip between his teeth, a thousand thoughts I'd never make sense of racing through his mind, barely visible in the dark brown of his eyes. He scratched the corner of his mouth, head tilted in question. The silence stretched for what felt like hours. I wanted to take it back, so I didn't ruin whatever the thing between us actually was with dreams of what I wanted.

"I would like that," he said carefully, looking up at me even though his face was downcast toward the table. There was a glare on his glasses that made it hard to see his eyes. "But I'm not sure if you're there yet, Dylan."

"Forget I said anything."

"No." He raised a hand to stop me, shaking his head. "That's not what I said. That's not what I want."

"But you don't want me."

"I do want you." Alex dropped one of his hands into his lap, immediately reminding me of the erection from upstairs. "I want you more than I should, but...it has to be right."

"You have to be able to afford it," I repeated his statement from earlier.

"I have to be able to afford it." He licked his lips, exhaling and turning his attention toward the sky. "Don't for one second think that I don't want you, Dylan. It's not that at all. Do you believe me?"

I didn't need to see his face to know the truth of his words.

"I believe you."

THE NEXT MORNING, DYLAN FOUND ME IN THE KITCHEN JUST BEFORE seven a.m., his eyes half-closed with sleep and his hair sticking up in every direction possible. He rubbed at his left eye with his right hand, swaying on his feet in the doorway.

"Good morning," I said, setting down my pen.

"No eggs today?"

I gave him what I hoped read as am unamused smile. "You ran through a dozen eggs in six days."

"I only ruined six of them," he said. "What do you mean?"

"I have to eat, Dylan." I picked up my coffee and took a sip, eyeing him over the rim of the mug. "Just because you have a good cry and go to sleep afterward doesn't mean I starve."

He swallowed. "Oh."

"Sit down." I climbed off my bar stool and pointed at it. He shuffled toward me and awkwardly got himself onto the seat. He smelled like my soap, my laundry detergent. I breathed him in before putting space between us to get him a cup of his own coffee.

I meant everything I'd told him yesterday. I wanted him.

Truly, I wanted him as much as I'd wanted Beamer, if not more, but it wasn't right. Dylan was still too angry, too volatile, to be safe for me. He was drowning in the middle of the ocean, even though there was a life raft in his line of sight. I couldn't give my heart to someone with less than zero sense of self-preservation, no matter how much I wanted him.

I slid the coffee in his direction, propping my hip against the far counter so I could watch him. It had become one of my favorite hobbies, most of all watching him when he didn't know I was. Because Dylan spent a lot of time watching me, especially when he didn't think I noticed. I was curious to know what he saw when he looked at me, the things he thought about.

I rinsed my mug out, washing a sliver of my sanity down the drain with it. My back still to Dylan, I asked him, "Why do you want me?"

He made a rough sound in the back of his throat, and I braced myself against the counter, unsure of what was the best answer and what would be the worst.

"I don't know," he said simply.

"Try."

"You're attractive," he said, and I threw an unimpressed glance at him over my shoulder. "You're good in bed."

I turned and folded my arms over my chest, ready to call the whole conversation off.

"Plenty of people meet that criteria, Dylan. Hell, *you* meet it."

His cheeks burned and he tucked his chin toward his chest in embarrassment.

"You haven't left me," he said next, quietly.

"I threw you out."

"I deserved that."

I snorted.

"I've done nothing but argue and fight with you since the hospital," he went on.

"Since before then," I interrupted.

He rolled his eyes, but there wasn't any malice in it. "And you've just…taken it."

"You won't fight forever."

Dylan clenched his jaw, swallowing hard and screwing his eyes closed. "It feels like it sometimes."

"It's exhausting," I said, not a question.

He nodded, a tear sliding out from the corner of his eye.

Apparently we didn't need quiet time and eggs and spankings to get him where he needed to be the most. I knew Dylan hated the emotion that came from our morning routine, but he'd been running from his problems for years and the only way to solve them was to really sit with them. I had no idea what he thought about while I left him in the corner with his nose against those eggs, but by the time I wrestled him into the playroom every day, he was beyond ready to let go of it. The only surprise to me was that he still had so much anger inside of him to work through.

"Do you think you brought it all on yourself?" I asked.

He swiped at his cheeks, not fast enough to keep them dry. "I don't know."

"Yesterday you told me you wanted to start over. Don't do that by lying to me."

He glared at me, but it was tired. "Of course I brought it on myself. If I would just do what I was told…isn't that what you want from me too?"

"I want you to want to do it," I told him. "Your father wants to control you."

"Isn't that what this is?"

"Are you green, Dylan? Or is there another word you want to tell me right now?" I asked.

"I'm green," he said, hooking his finger around the handle of the mug and spinning it in a half-circle.

"Then that's not what this is."

I didn't think that needed saying again, but every day with Dylan was a new one. He was working through some big feelings in my playroom, and I hoped he got to a resting point soon. Partly because he needed the break, partly because I was a horny and selfish asshole and I wanted to get him underneath me again.

"I know," he sighed. "I'm sorry for saying that."

It may not have registered at all with him, but the easy apology, the unprompted correction, it was the biggest step in the right direction he'd made since getting discharged from the hospital. He deserved a reward.

"Go to the bedroom and strip," I said abruptly, pushing off the counter before I thought better of the reward I was about to offer him.

"What?"

"You heard me."

Dylan cursed under his breath and scrambled off the stool, nearly crashing his forehead into the corner of the marble before righting himself and practically running to the bedroom. I chuckled, not sure exactly what he expected to happen next, but endlessly amused by his enthusiasm.

When I got to the bedroom, after rinsing his half-finished coffee and putting away my crossword, Dylan stood awkwardly in the middle of the bedroom, naked and shifting his weight like a flamingo on one leg. His shoulder was still in a sling, though he'd just been cleared to take some time out of it around his physical therapy, but beyond that he was bare. His cock jutted out toward the window, quickly getting thick and hard, precum shining on the tip.

"This is a reward," I told him, pushing the waistband of my sleep pants down below my cock and balls, "not a concession."

"Reward?"

"In the kitchen, you edited your own behavior when you did something wrong. You apologized without being prompted. That shows me that you're learning, that you're listening."

"You're nothing like my dad," he rasped.

"I know that." I closed the space between us, walking Dylan backward until his shoulders hit the corner where he normally spent his mornings with the egg. He moaned when our bare chests pressed together and the sound was so divine I wanted to drink it every day for the rest of my life. "I'm nothing like anyone."

"You're amazing," he whispered, tilting his head back and closing his eyes.

"That might be an overstatement, but I'll take it."

"So patient—"

"Dylan, put your good hand flat against the wall."

He slammed his palm against the wall, the position arching his back and pushing our bodies that much closer together.

I licked my palm and reached down, taking both of our

cocks into my loose fist and tightening my hold until his knees gave out.

"Patient," he said again, eyes closed and jaw slack.

"Tell me more about the kind of man you think I am." I kissed his temple, resting my forehead against the wall to lock us both in place. I gave a slow stroke up both our lengths, breath shuddering out of my lungs on the exhale.

"Generous, tolerant." He grunted. "I already told you that you're a good fuck."

"I'm more than good."

He hummed, turning his head to the side and knocking it against mine.

"I don't know how to explain the—" His breath hitched when I twisted my fingers around the leaking tip of his cock. "—explain the things you make me feel."

"Try."

"You make me want to be better," he blurted, the words trailing off into a moan.

I kept stroking both of us off, grip unforgiving to stop me from flying out of my bedroom and into another stratosphere. I hadn't forgotten how good it felt to have his body against mine, and it was far from the first time I'd seen him naked, but my brain had somehow shrouded what pleasure with Dylan felt like. Much like how he found himself at a loss for words, I was often the same when it came time to describe what he meant to me, the things he made me feel.

Another version of me would have talked to my friends about this. It would have been a night at The Black Door with a handful of drinks between us, easy flowing conversation and understanding, but ever since...ever since Kale had met Christian, since Beamer's husband showed up...I hadn't had it. I realized, with my balls heavy between my legs and Dylan's breathy little moans growing louder in my ears, that I missed my friends, but I also understood there was no going back.

Dylan couldn't go back.

I couldn't go back.

There was only forward, onward...hopefully upward.

Acting the way I had before, being the man I used to be, there was no way of telling if that would serve me and save me on that road or if it would set me back and cause me to stumble. With our wetness swirling around my fingers, I realized I had to look at the facts.

Dylan had said more than once today I was the patient one, but he was just as patient, just as generous. He offered me just as much grace. Whether he understood that our time together was just as much for me to work my own shit out as it was for him, I wasn't sure, but did that really matter? He'd given me more than I asked for, maybe more than I deserved.

"Say that again," I told him.

"You make me want to be better," he repeated quickly.

"You make *me* want to be better."

Dylan whimpered. "Not sure how you can be."

"I could be braver," I whispered against the shell of his ear. "I could trust more."

"Alex."

Dylan's jaw quivered and he tipped his head back, mouth open and searching. It wasn't even a thought to angle my face toward his, to slant our mouths together and kiss him. Our tongues tangled and he slammed his hand against the wall, three times in rapid succession, body pushing toward mine for more connection, more skin.

"Settle down," I breathed into this mouth, my hand still sliding torturously slow up and down the length of our erections. With my other hand, I brushed his tangled hair back from his face and pressed his head against the wall.

"I'm going to die if you don't let me—"

"I won't allow it," I said, deepening the kiss to stop him from saying something else absurd.

My entire body trembled, my tongue tracing around the backs of Dylan's teeth, tasting every inch of him I could reach. I wanted this man. I wanted him more than I had common sense anymore, and maybe this new road meant I didn't have to deny myself those things. There had to be a reason the feelings were there. Had to be a point to Dylan's constant reappearances in my life, the connection, the orbit.

Picking up the pace, I began to stroke us both off in earnest.

I didn't want to stop.

I wasn't going to.

"Alex," he groaned my name back into my mouth, going still beneath me.

"Yes, pet?"

He let loose a long and nonsensical stream of obscenities as spurts of cum shot out of his cock and painted my hand. He spilled onto both of our stomachs, the wet heat of him enough to draw my own orgasm out. Tightening my hand, I grabbed his face and kissed him until I couldn't breathe, my own cum shooting hot and long against his stomach, his chest.

I kept my hand around us, our mouths together, until it was easier to breathe until I could stand again, until I could see. The earth had shifted beneath my feet and when I finally let Dylan go, he slid down onto his ass with a grunt, right hand still pressed flat against the wall.

And everything for me...had changed.

My legs were still shaking when Alex stripped me the rest of the way out of my clothes and walked me into the bathroom. I didn't have it in me to fight him on anything, not even when he carefully loosened the straps on my shoulder sling and slid it off.

After he got us both off, he'd pulled his pajamas back up, his cock still half-hard against the soft cotton. He reached around me and turned on the shower, then he sank down onto the closed lid of the toilet, palms resting damp on top of his thighs.

"Can you wash on your own?" he asked.

"No," I lied.

He arched a brow at me, and I backed away from his scrutiny, one step after another until I was in the shower, water raining down on my head. Tilting my chin back, I closed my eyes and let it spray across my face.

"I can," I told him without being prompted, "but I don't want to."

"What do you want?"

Scrubbing a hand down my face so it was safe to open my eyes, I leveled an exhausted look at him.

"I want you," I said. "I thought that was clear."

"I wanted to make sure you meant it when you weren't trying to get off," he murmured.

"Am I so untrustworthy?"

"I'm so untrusting," he corrected, pushing up from his seat and discarding his pajamas into the pile of clothes I'd left on the floor. "But I'm trying."

"So am I."

Alex set his glasses on the counter, squinting and scrunching his nose the way he always did when he was trying to adjust his eyes. Without much thought at all, I reached out and grabbed his hand so I could pull him into the shower with me. I didn't think he really needed any kind of guidance to find his way around his own house, but something had shifted between us in the bedroom and I didn't want it to go back to how it had been before.

"What happens now?" I asked.

He hummed a little sound I couldn't make sense of, then he lathered some soap in his hands and set to work cleaning the cum off my chest and stomach.

"Why have you put up with me so far?" he asked, and I felt it was an answer to my own question, but I wasn't quite sure.

"What do you mean?"

Alex lifted my right arm and slid his soapy fingers over my armpit, around the back of my shoulder, and down my flank. "The eggs, the spankings, all of it...all of me. Is it just because you don't have any other options?"

I jerked my shoulder so he'd let go of me. "I have plenty of options. I could stay with Brooks and Tate, I could stay home, I could call my parents—"

"That's hardly an option," he interrupted.

"The first two are."

Alex licked his lips and grabbed my arm again, this time to clean the crook of my elbow, the bones in my wrist.

"Why me, then?"

In the back of my mind, I'd always known this conversation would come sooner or later. I'd been asking myself for weeks, months at this point, and I wasn't much closer to an answer than when I'd started.

"After our first time together, I went home and got hard while I scrubbed the shower," I answered. A small smile flitted across his mouth, and he twined our fingers together, cleaning me there next.

"How was that for you?"

"Confusing."

He chuckled. "I bet."

"I don't understand a lot of what you want. At least, I don't think I do—"

He cut me off before I could finish. "I think you understand just fine, Dylan."

Alex dragged his soapy hands back up my arms, across the front of my chest and down, fingers twisting gently around my hard nipples. I groaned, leaning into him and, to my surprise, he took my weight willingly. I flattened myself against his chest, sliding my good arm around his waist. Something had him faltering, and it was a breath, then two, then three before he wrapped his arms around my shoulders in return.

"I know my life is a shit show," I mumbled against his collar bone, kissing away the words as soon as I said them.

"Mine isn't much better."

"I meant what I said before." I tipped my head back, using my knee to shove him backward and out of the spray enough that I could look up at him. He couldn't see my face as clearly as I could see his, but I found every answer I needed in the soft wrinkles around the corners of his mouth.

"You say a lot."

"About wanting to be better for you."

He swallowed, nodding but not saying a word.

At first, I'd wondered if it was some driven and jealous part of me that wanted more, wanted to mold myself into someone better than the man he was so clearly still in love with. But the first night I'd spent in the hospital had erased that theory right out of my head. I didn't want Alex to want me because I was better than someone else—I wanted him to want me because I was good enough on my own. I wanted to be able to fight him and know that it wasn't going to push him away.

My parents, the two people who were supposed to love me unconditionally in this life, had been so willing to cast me aside as soon as I went against their ideas for who they wanted me to be. I didn't want Alex to be like them, even though he'd never done anything to show me he was.

I didn't trust it, but I *wanted* to.

I wanted to trust *myself*.

I'd made so many bad decisions over the past year, I didn't think I could bear it if Alex proved to be one more on that list.

"I owe you an apology," he said, startling me out of my own head.

"For what?"

"The night I used a safe word with you." He worried his lips together, rubbing them between his teeth, eyes squinted half-closed.

"I was out of line."

"You were," he agreed, "and I was within my rights to stop things, but...I shouldn't have sent you away, I just..."

"You don't have to apologize," I assured him, mostly because I didn't think I deserved it, but also because it made my skin tingle to see a man like Alex struggle to find words for anything.

"I do. I just..." He trailed off. "Let's get out of the shower. I think I left my brain in the bedroom."

I laughed at that, an unexpected peal of laughter that echoed around the bathroom. Alex smiled at me easily, almost relaxed, and he finished washing me up in silence. Once the water was off, he dried me with as much attention as he'd used to get me wet, and I padded barefoot into the bedroom while he knotted his own towel around his waist.

Sitting down on the side of his bed, I let my arm hang without the sling, testing the pain in my shoulder and finding it tolerable. If anything, the unexpected bites of heat in my muscle kept me alert and grounded in the moment. I wanted to be fully present for him.

For myself.

"I know you don't understand the why of a lot of this," he said, two steps short of pacing. "But what I did that night was wrong. Almost inexcusable."

"You're excused," I said.

He put his glasses back on, which made it easier for him to

roll his eyes *at* me instead of in my general direction, which made me smile.

"I let my emotions get the better of me."

"I always let mine do that," I told him.

"You're allowed."

"And you're not?" I cocked my head to the side. "That doesn't make sense."

"In this dominant sort of role, it's a different expectation," he explained.

"I don't want you to pretend with me," I said, standing and taking a step toward him before he walked a hole in the expensive rug. "That sounds like pretending."

"It's being mature," he offered. "Responsible."

"You are."

"For you," he said, covering my mouth with his hand. My eyes went wide, blood immediately running hot in response to the press of his palm against my lips.

"Being responsible for you."

I huffed a breath out against the side of his pointer finger, and he put his other arm around my waist, pulling my body flush against his, save for our arms between us.

"That's why the pills," I mumbled against his palm. He dragged his hand down to my chin so I could speak and I repeated myself. "The pills, the punishments, the rules."

"Yes."

"Keep going." I put his hand back over my mouth, smiling against his palm when his lips lifted into one of his own.

"I've never pretended with you," he said next. "I've wanted you from the first time I saw you. I wanted you then and I want you now."

I nodded.

"I want you to let me take care of you."

I licked his palm, and he turned his hand from a gag into a tight grip, digging his fingers into my cheeks until my mouth puckered like a fish. I was so fucking hard, my cock leaking against Alex's thigh.

"I want it to be my job to tell you what you want and when. To give you what you need."

My cock jerked, and I shuffled my feet forward, trying to get closer to find some friction. He'd just gotten me off fifteen minutes earlier, but I was ready to go again. Ready to go for him, because when he talked to me this way, about these things, my body responded even if my brain was slow to catch up. I shouldn't have gotten aroused from the things he said. The idea of being beholden to another person again, subservient in any way...it was exactly what I'd been running from, but with Alex, it didn't sound scary.

It was safe.

"Settle down, Dylan," he whispered, leaning in so his breath burned against my mouth. "That's not what you need right now."

"Yes, it is."

He dug his fingers harder into my cheeks and I groaned, knees quaking.

"Are you sure this is what you want?" he asked, eyes searching my face for a lie he wouldn't find. "You want me, and you want me like this?"

He released my face, stroking his fingers down my cheeks, over my chin, until his fingers came to rest against my throat. I closed my eyes, shivering, though I was unsure if it was from his touch or from a memory I'd been trying to forget. Maybe it was a little bit of both and maybe that was okay.

"I want *us* like this," I whispered.

The words were barely out of my mouth when he kissed me again, slanting our lips together and spearing his tongue so deep into me that he swallowed down any other words I'd meant to say. I grabbed his hip with a high-pitched cry, flattening myself against him to search out every physical point of contact I could find.

Alex walked me back until my legs hit the bed, and he slowed then, carefully lowering me down onto the tangled sheets so I didn't jostle my shoulder again. I scooted back to make room for him between my legs, and I didn't need to ask what was next. He reached into the nightstand for a bottle of lube, and then slick fingers were between my legs, his hot mouth against mine once again.

"Green, Dylan?" he asked.

"Neon fucking green," I promised, spreading my legs wider as he pushed his fingers into me.

Arching off the bed, I fought against the weight of Alex's body, but as with all things, he was a formidable opponent. He pinned me down, determining the angle of his penetration, the pace of his thrusts. His fingers stretched, but I was desperate for more. A cold sweat beaded against my temple and precum smeared across my freshly clean stomach as he coated his cock with lube and replaced his fingers with the thick girth of his erection.

Seating himself inside of me, long and hard and bare, Alex pressed his forehead into the sheets beside my head, moaning my name as a shiver tore through his entire body. He stilled, heart beat pulsing in his cock, stretching my rim with every pump, and I shivered beneath him, wrapping my legs around his waist and silently begging him for more.

Begging him for everything.

CHAPTER 26
ALEX

Dylan fell asleep shortly after I came inside of him, but sleep was the last thing on my mind. As much as it pained me to leave the warmth of his naked and decidedly non-argumentative body, I did it anyway. Pulling my pajama pants on, I closed the door quietly and shuffled barefoot down to the kitchen.

I'd been working on the same crossword for days, my brain not focused enough to understand the clues, let alone try to figure out the answers. I sat down at the table anyway, pen in hand, and the first clue I went to might as well have been a gunshot through my kitchen window.

One-sided romantic feelings. Ten letters.

"For fuck sake," I muttered, shoving the crossword puzzle off the edge of the table and getting up for a drink.

Whiskey was the closest thing. Unfortunately, so was my cell phone. Forgotten on the counter beside the sink. Without thinking too much about it, I took both items back to the table. I poured a drink, swiped through my contacts, and pressed call before I could talk myself out of it.

"Good morning, Alex." Beamer's low baritone rumbled through the phone, vibrating the bones in my hand.

"Beamer."

He hummed. "Been awhile since you used that name for me."

"The other felt inappropriate," I said, taking another swallow of whiskey. "All things considered."

It was barely the afternoon, but Dylan had started to make a habit of sleeping through the late morning. It was my own fault, I knew. Getting him up before sunrise to balance an egg against the wall was one thing. Forcing him to confront his shortcomings by being unable to cook it properly, another. And spanking him until he was out of tears and strength... well, it was enough to send anyone back to bed before lunch.

"Probably so," Beamer said.

I could hear the smile in his voice.

"I missed you at the farm. I'm sorry you had to leave early."

I'd done everything I could to avoid him and Dalton when we'd all arrived at Ford's place upstate, and Dylan's hospital stay had only served to rush me out of there even sooner than I'd planned.

"I didn't say goodbye on purpose," I admitted, taking off my glasses so I could rub at the corners of my eyes.

"I assumed."

"I'm sorry for that," I said.

"It's...it's not okay, Alex, but it's fine."

I scoffed. "It can't be both."

"It can, and it is," he pressed.

I imagined him sitting on a couch in a house I'd never seen, comfortable and barefoot, that fucking wedding ring on his finger. I hadn't wanted to marry him. I didn't want to marry anyone, but still the thought of it...

"How is..." he trailed off.

"Dylan," I supplied, slumping back against my chair. "His name is Dylan, and he's...getting better."

"Was he hurt?"

"Yes, but not as badly as we thought." Swallowing, I tipped my head back and stared at the recessed lights in my ceiling until all I saw was fireworks. "He's better every day."

"Is he there with you?"

"Yes."

"I'm glad for that," Beamer said gently. "You need that."

"I—" I stopped myself, because for months my response would have been a correction. It was muscle memory at this point, but the words burned in my throat like a lie, and I glanced toward the stairs, worried somehow that Dylan might have heard them or that he could have known.

"You deserve that," Beamer said.

I wanted to argue with him, but after the morning I'd just had, after the days and weeks I'd lived through since Beamer left, I'd finally started to believe it.

"He's not experienced," I said, chuckling under my breath. "Are we even allowed to talk like this?"

"That's between you and him." A short pause. "Dalton knows where my loyalties lie."

I pressed my hand against my sternum, rubbing a soft circle over my heart even though the words didn't hurt me as much as they would have half a year before.

"I feel out of my element with him sometimes," I said.

"I can't imagine you ever being out of your element."

"You've been gone." I snapped my mouth closed, clearing my throat to try and drown some of the aggression that had fallen out. Taking another drink of whiskey, I started over. "It's...I..."

"It was hard on you," he said sympathetically.

If I closed my eyes, I could feel the hot press of his body next to mine still, but my brain was quick to remind me I had a different body upstairs, a better body. Not in the physical sense, not meaning one of them was better than the other, though maybe...Maybe Dylan was a better match for me. But it wasn't a fight between the two of them, and I'd long stopped weighing one against the other. It was more just the fact they each existed. Beamer had one piece of me, one part of my life, and Dylan...he had the rest of it.

The rest of me.

"I was fine," I lied.

"That's not what Ford said."

"Fuck Ford."

He gave another laugh, a full sound that once again vibrated through me. I put the phone on speaker and set it on the table. If I woke Dylan, that would be fine. I wasn't trying to hide from him, and he'd already thrown his barbs about Beamer at me. There wasn't anything more for him to say that he hadn't already. But even if there were, I didn't think he would.

Not anymore.

"I wasn't fine," I admitted, "but I am now."

"Because of Dylan?"

"For Dylan," I said simply.

Beamer stayed silent, and I worried my tongue across the front of my teeth, back and forth and back and forth, my hands nervously spinning my whiskey from one side of the table to the other.

"I've been trying, you know..." I laid my head down on the table and closed my eyes. "Trying to take back the parts of myself that I'd given you because he deserves something whole. I deserve to be whole."

On the other end of the call, he breathed softly, steadily.

"I'm trying to find a place for him to exist here," I said.

"Sounds like you already have." Beamer exhaled. "Can I speak freely?"

"I think we're past you asking me for permission to do anything."

He chuckled. "I didn't know it, not back when you and I got involved with each other, but I wasn't whole then. I wasn't myself. Not fully."

"I'd disagree."

"It's not up for debate," he said. "Dalton had stolen a piece of me long before you and I even fell into bed together. I think both of our lives, yours and mine, even his... it was just a whole lot of chasing when we knew the answers all along."

"And what was your answer?" I asked, rolling my forehead onto the table and smashing my nose into the wood.

"For a moment, you." Beamer paused, and I bit the inside of my cheek until it was ready to bleed. "But for always...him."

"I'm happy for you," I said, even though it sounded like a lie because of the tears in my voice.

"I know you are. And I want to be happy for you. Should I be? Can I be?"

I forced myself to sit up straight, wipe away the tears that I never had a chance of stopping. Beamer deserved an honest answer, and as he always had, he gave me the time to find it for him.

Through blurry and wet eyes, I looked toward the stairs, quietly counting how many steps it would take me to get to my bedroom. Counting how many breaths it would take me to get to Dylan, asleep and spent in my bed. I knew if I went up there and pulled back the sheets, spread his legs apart, I'd find my cum trickling out of his ass. Pride and heat flared up my spine at the thought of it, at how good I'd done. How well I'd taken care of him, but...I knew that wasn't what Beamer meant with the question.

I closed my eyes and forced my brain to wipe all of that away.

Imagined a morning when I was alone in my house with my phone and my whiskey and my unfinished crossword, where my bed was empty and cold without me in it. Was I good enough, deserving enough, strong enough to truly be a better version of me than I'd been before taking Beamer into that bed?

It was hard, not impossible, but hard still to separate my opinion of myself on my own from my opinion of myself with Dylan. At first, he'd been a rebound, a quick fix. That was one of the reasons I'd been willing to play. I wanted to get Beamer and the things that reminded me of him out of my system. But what I'd learned was *I* reminded me of him. The things we did together were things I'd done with people before him, things I'd done recently with Dylan.

That didn't have anything to do with them, so much as it had to do with me. Of course, anything I did with any partner ended up being mutually beneficial, but it was driven by my wants and my needs. I used to worry that was selfish, but maybe not as much anymore. Because if I was any different, if I was lesser, I wouldn't be able to do the things I did. I wouldn't have had the fortitude to let Beamer walk away, wouldn't have been strong enough to fight my own brain when it came to Dylan.

I wanted Dylan more than I'd ever wanted Beamer, I realized, but Beamer had been convenient, he'd been understanding. Dylan always had been—and always would be—work. That didn't scare me. If anything, it turned me on to watch him fight his own brain to break the cycles he was tired of repeating. So terrified of being beholden to his parents, he'd put his entire future in my hands before he even understood what he'd done.

"Yes," I finally answered. "I think you can be."

"And can you?" he asked. "Can you be happy for me?"

"I've never not been happy for you," I promised, scrubbing a hand down my face. "I was hurt and I was jealous, but I've always been happy for you, Car. I've always wanted the best for you, even if it's not me. Even before it was me."

"Car," he murmured. "That sounds better out of your mouth than Beamer."

"I know you hate the nickname, but Carter..." I trailed off, swallowing thickly. "It wasn't mine anymore."

"Not in that way, no," he said, "but I miss my friend, Alex. I want to be friends again, like we were before."

"Is your husband okay with that?" I asked, a spear of jealousy lancing through me at the thought of what I would do if someone Dylan had fucked before wanted to be his friend.

"Like I said, he knows where my loyalties are." He paused. "With him, and my friends. As they've always been."

Another unwanted wave of tears leaked from the corners

of my eyes, and I gave up trying to slow them down. Chin quivering, I screwed my eyes shut, nodding at the forgiveness I didn't even realize I'd been waiting for.

"I've missed you," I told one of my closest friends. "I've missed you so much."

On the other end of the call, Beamer, Carter..Car...he sniffled, but I could hear the smile in it.

"I'm right here, Alex," he assured me. "Right where I've always been and where I'll always be."

"Fuck," I cursed under my breath, taking a quick swallow of whiskey and giving my face another wipe. My eyes were already feeling tender to the touch, and while I wouldn't lie to Dylan about the conversation if it came up, I didn't necessarily want to have to explain it to him either.

"You're one of my closest friends, you know."

"I know," I whispered. "You're one of mine too. You were like...the blueprint."

"How so?" he asked.

"You were like... the *promise* of everything I wanted."

He made a content noise that sounded like a soft hum through the phone. "And Dylan?"

"I think I'm in love with him," I admitted out loud for the very first time. The words sounding foreign, but still so very right to say.

"I think you are too," Car said gently. "And I'm so fucking happy for you."

CHAPTER 27
DYLAN

ALEX WOKE ME BEFORE SUNRISE THE NEXT DAY, BUT INSTEAD OF WITH an alarm, it was with two slick fingers gliding up and down the length of my ass crack.

"Oh, good," he murmured into my hair, rolling me onto my back and notching himself between my legs. "You're awake."

"Convenient," I agreed, arching against him with a moan.

Both of his fingers pushed into me, and I spread my legs wider, still pliant from sleep and from the amazing fuck he'd finally given me the night before.

"You'll be begging for the egg by the time I'm done with you today." He pulled his fingers out, tracing his way to my balls and the base of my already erect cock.

"I find that unlikely."

He made an amused sound, quickly taking himself to the other side of the bed and leaving me hard and exposed... wanting.

"Get up," he said, "we've got to get going."

"I was trying to get going."

"Time is short, Dylan," he said, tsking his tongue against the roof of his mouth before padding naked toward his closet.

Rolling onto my side, I blinked a few times to get the sleep out of my eyes so I could watch his ass shift with each step. It was still dark outside, the sky barely changing into that soft orange that came after the purple of night. It had been so long since I'd seen it after it being a normal sight for me for years. Bartending, getting off at four or five in the morning meant my schedule was the opposite of most people's in the city. I had the sunrises to myself most of the time, sleeping through the oppressive and loud heat of the morning as often as I could.

"When can I go back to work?" I asked, pushing myself into a seated position and flexing my toes against the floor to orient myself before daring to stand.

Alex came out of the closet, fastening the button on a pair of dark black jeans. "You don't have to go back to work."

"Are you telling me I can't?"

He had a black shirt on, tight and soft looking, stretching across the broad swell of his chest and the muscles in his arms. With his black-framed glasses, he looked every bit the handsome prick he'd long ago proven himself to be. Alex ran a hand through his hair in lieu of a brush, staring at me intently.

Finally, he said, "Yes."

I swallowed, waiting for the blow of his confirmation—or his refusal, depending on how I wanted to look at it—to land, but the hit never came. Picking at a loose cuticle on my thumb, I kept my attention downturned toward my hands in my lap. I didn't hate bartending, but it had always been a means to an end for me. It was quick chunks of money meant to cover my expenses so I could focus on music. Losing it...was not really a loss. And for what might have been the first time, I remembered if I looked at Alex and told him Juilliard, I would be more than welcome to walk out of his house and go back to work at Tryst or The Black Door, or wherever I wanted.

The only thing stopping me was me, and I meant that in *all* ways.

"Okay," I said, standing. I hadn't bothered re-dressing after the last time we'd had sex the night before, so I was already naked in front of him, my cock still hard from his teasing.

His eyes widened briefly at my response, but he schooled his face quickly, tugging at the hem of his shirt.

"Get dressed, Dylan," he said. "Be quick about it."

"Okay," I agreed again, heading into the closet.

Alex had a walk-in closet to rival the size of my bedroom in the apartment Tate and I shared, which wasn't saying much, and he'd made room for my clothes right alongside his. It was funny, I thought as I dressed, that even though we had shirts from the same designers, I was practically destitute, saved only by his good will.

I stumbled my way into a fresh pair of underwear and clean jeans, struggling less with getting a shirt on than I had in the days since my injury. My fingers itched with the absence of my ability to play music, but much like my question about going back to work, I knew my question about playing again would get the same response. I'd been cleared for limited movement, but the physical therapist wasn't on board with guitar quite yet. It was the longest I'd gone without picking up an instrument of any kind since I started lessons, and it was beginning to wear on me.

I found Alex in the bathroom. He'd just finished brushing

his teeth and he stepped to the side so I could go through my own morning routine. Glancing up at me in the mirror, he caught my stare, eyes curious.

"What's on your mind?" he asked.

"Besides waiting for you to whip an egg out of your pocket and shove me into the corner?" I asked.

"I told you I'm fresh out of eggs."

I licked my lips, squirting a blob of toothpaste onto my toothbrush. "I want a piano."

He smiled at me, lip quirking as I brushed my teeth. He didn't say anything, just watched me until I spit the toothpaste into the sink and rinsed my mouth, returned the brush to the cup beside the faucet, wiped my mouth dry with a hand towel.

"What kind?" he asked.

"A Clavinova."

"Alright."

I bit the inside of my lip, turning away from the mirror and leaving him alone in the bathroom. I clearly didn't even need the egg anymore, or the spanking, because I found myself hit with the same wave of emotion that often found me bent over the bench in his playroom even without it. I went downstairs to the kitchen and made us both coffee, tapping a beat against the edge of the countertop while I waited for the machine to warm up and percolate. Alex met me there, taking the carafe and pouring it into a thermos before I could reach for mugs, then he slid it into a small black backpack, which he handed off to me.

"Get us some snacks," he said, leaving me alone again in the kitchen, the scent of coffee still fresh in the air.

Hungry, tired, and horny, I shoved two muffins and some

fruit into the backpack alongside the thermos, then zipped it up and padded through the house until I found Alex again in the living room.

"Aren't you going to ask me what we're doing?" he asked without looking up from lacing up a pair of black leather boots. "Where we're going?"

"I didn't really think I had a say, so I didn't see the point." I dropped the backpack behind the couch. "Should I put my shoes on too?"

"Yes," he said, standing again.

I put on my sneakers, grabbing the breakfast backpack again before joining him in the foyer. He shrugged his way into a black leather jacket I hadn't seen since the first night I met him. It was a cherry on top of the all-black look he had going on, and my cock, which hadn't quite settled down, surged back to life. I made a show of palming my cock, trying to still the hot energy building between my legs. Alex's stare flickered down to my hand, but he ignored my need. Instead, he pulled a jacket down from the hall closet and tossed it at me.

It was new, I realized, leather like his, but otherwise unworn. The material was loud beneath my fingers, and he watched me quietly while I struggled my left arm into the sleeve. Once I was suited up, he came toward me and fastened the zipper, tugging it up to my sternum and jerking me around a bit until I blinked up at him.

I would have given up the piano he'd so willingly offered to buy me to know what thoughts were in his head at that moment, but I knew I'd get one of those things far more easily than the other.

"What?" I rasped, asking him anyway.

He smiled softly at me, tipping his chin down and pressing our mouths together with a kiss. It was hungry, but not demanding, and like always, I melted into him. But as quick as he'd started, Alex broke the kiss, pulling back enough for me to see how dilated his pupils were. It was some kind of relief to be reminded I wasn't the only one affected here. That he was just as turned on and desperate for me as I was for him, even though we offered very different things to the other.

"Nothing," he said, kissing the corner of my mouth while he helped me get the backpack on.

"Where are we going?" I asked, unsure if I meant overall or in that moment.

"Now you ask?"

I nodded, swallowing and stepping back so I could breathe.

"You tell me the answer," he said softly, pulling two motorcycle helmets out of the closet and pressing one into my waiting hands.

"Wherever you want," I said.

"Good answer, pet."

A shiver raced up my spine, and I didn't miss the way that pleased him. The way his fingers flexed like it took work to stop himself from touching me. The way his nostrils flared, the way his Adam's apple bobbed when he swallowed.

"I'm ready," I told him.

"I know. Come on."

I followed him outside, leaning against the wrought iron fence while he locked the house up. In all the time I'd spent at his house, I'd never noticed the slim street level door, tucked halfway beneath the stairs that led to his front door. It was clearly meant to be a storage room of some kind, and Alex used it well. I stepped out of the way, watching as he wheeled a sleek, black motorcycle onto the sidewalk.

"You have to hold on tight," he said.

I'd never been on a motorcycle before.

"Okay."

He walked the bike onto the street between two cars, and the way he flung one leg over the machine and used his other to shift the weight of it onto the center of the two wheels was one of the sexiest things I'd ever seen in my life.

"Helmet on," he said, beckoning me toward him.

I fitted the helmet over my head, gooseflesh breaking out down my throat when his fingers swiftly latched the strap beneath my chin. When he was satisfied it was on me properly, he put his own helmet on, adjusting the frame of his glasses beneath the thick padding until he got them comfortable.

"Swing over behind me," he said, voice muffled through the helmet.

My dick was so hard it hurt, my head fuzzy from how disproportionately turned on seeing Alex on a motorcycle made me. But I followed instructions, managing to barely lose my balance as I shifted up to get onto the small seat behind his.

He swiveled, pulling my right arm around the front of him until my fingers rested on the soft leather that wrapped his stomach.

"Can you do both?" he asked.

I probably could have gotten my left arm around him, but it pulled the muscle more than I knew it was supposed to. I settled my hand on his hip, and he looked down and nodded.

"If it hurts, we don't have to go."

"I want to," I told him.

I'd been doing physical therapy and my shoulder was healing as much as it should have been. I couldn't lift anything or do strenuous rotation or anything like that, but sleeping was easier and so was getting dressed. I could manage a motorcycle ride, especially if it meant I'd have to be pressed against him, breathing him in for God knew how long.

"I know you *want* to."

"It doesn't hurt," I promised, adding for good measure, "I'll tell you if it does."

"I'm trusting you."

Even through the lens of the helmet, his expression was serious.

I swallowed and nodded. "I know."

"Okay," he said, turning on the bike. The engine roared to life between our legs, and it would be a wonder if I made it to our destination without coming in my pants. From the vibration and the heat of him, the newness of things between us...it was everything.

I bent forward enough to press my stomach against his back, one arm all the way around him, the other as far as my injury would allow.

"I'm ready," I shouted so he could hear me over the noise and through the padding of the helmets.

He nodded, patted my hand, and sped off down the street.

CHAPTER 28

ALEX

It took us less than an hour to get out of the city, and once we made it to Harriman State Park, I down-shifted the bike and pulled into a parking spot. Dylan climbed off the back of the bike, struggling with the strap on his helmet but, as usual, refusing to ask for help. I let him fight it for a bit before reaching up and undoing it for him without being asked. His shoulders sagged on an exhale, but he managed to fight the helmet off with one hand. I pulled mine off and re-adjusted my glasses, scrunching my nose and looking around.

"Wow." Dylan looked around, scrubbing a hand down his face. "It's so pretty here."

It was pretty, which was one of the things I liked the most about it. I also liked that it was out of the city without taking hours to get to, the bike helping cut down the time, of course. The ride itself was scenic, and after arrival, there were lakes and trails galore. I'd come out here after I got my motorcycle license with the intent to get lost on more than one occasion, but with Dylan, it was the last thing on my mind.

"I come here often," I told him. "I thought some fresh air would do you some good."

He made a derisive noise in the back of his throat. "What gave me away?"

"The listless way you roam the halls paired with your habit of sleeping half the morning away."

"You're exhausting," he said, rolling his eyes.

For what might have been the first time, there wasn't any cruelty in it, though. And I didn't look for any hints of it hidden under the surface. I'd spent the past week putting Dylan through it, and we both knew it.

"Let's go find someplace secluded to have our coffee," I said.

I locked the ignition on the bike and Dylan set off, walking alongside me as I found a trail that looked easy enough for us to manage with helmets in hand. I tuned into the sound of Dylan's footsteps beside mine, the way he shuffled more than stepped, the soft huff of his breath when he quickened his pace to catch up if I went too fast for him. He didn't argue, didn't complain, and I thought maybe for the first time we had turned a corner with things.

It felt that way to me.

Something about the last time we fucked had been different. It almost felt blasphemous to call it fucking, but none of the other words seemed to fit. I'd told Car I thought I was in love with him, and his ready agreement had caught me off-guard. He wasn't here, he hadn't met Dylan, he didn't know the half of what happened since he'd left, but somehow he still knew? I had thought about calling Brooks, asking him his opinion of the matter since he probably had the most experience—besides mine—with Dylan. But before I could even dial the phone, the answer sounded loud and clear in my mind.

I was very much in love with Dylan Rivers so, no, I hadn't *just* fucked him, but there was no way I would tell him that. Everything about the state of our relationship was messy and unconventional, and we were just getting into a new kind of calm about things. I wasn't going to screw that up by telling him I was in love with him. Those kinds of feelings would change everything. I'd watched it happen with every single one of my friends, for the better, but still...

Dylan was healing from an injury that was just as emotionally traumatic as it was physical. His life was in a state of upheaval and I wasn't arrogant enough to think I was the only thing keeping him grounded, but I was a big part of it. I wouldn't risk ruining his sense of safety and security to confess my feelings for him.

If they were real, they would keep.

After a twenty minute walk, we found a small trail that veered off from the main path, and I bumped my shoulder against his so he took it. There was a small bridge over a creek that was nearly dried up, and a few hundred feet farther, it opened up into a small overgrown meadow.

"I don't think anyone knows this place is here," Dylan said, mouth settled into the softest and happiest smile I'd ever seen on him.

"We do."

I shrugged out of my jacket and set it down on the grass, then I helped him out of his backpack and watched him do the same. We sat down and kicked out our legs, then I set to the business of pouring coffee for both of us. The sun had crested over the hills on the ride up, and the soft golden rays cast the little field in a beautiful orange and yellow glow.

I put my hands behind me to lean back and stretch, watching out of the corner of my eye as Dylan moved to mirror the pose on instinct before realizing that his shoulder made it impossible. He grunted and frowned, straightening his spine and taking a drink of coffee.

"Come on," I said, angling myself to the side so our shoulder blades matched up. He pressed his back against mine, sighing in relief. More than anything, I wanted Dylan to learn to ask for help, but I didn't think the word was in his vocabulary. I'd spent a week watching him struggle with eggs and clothes, fighting the noise in his mind at every step. To me, it seemed the only time his brain went quiet was when he was in the playroom or on his back.

There were worse things.

We sat together quietly, drinking coffee and staring out at opposite sides of the meadow and listening to the birds chirp their good mornings to each other. He reached for the backpack and pulled out a muffin, twisting his arm around to hand me one before taking the other for himself. That stupid four-letter word twisted itself around in my chest again, and I chased it down with another swallow of coffee.

"Are you my boyfriend?" he asked me next, hand flat against the ground, fingers tensed nervously against the bunched arm of my jacket beneath us. I dropped my hand down next to his, stretching my pinky out toward his. His skin was warm, and as soon as we touched, the nervous twitch of his fingers went still. My own heart skipped and then slowed, settling into the most comfortable and strong beat against my ribs, repeating that word to me over and over again with every pulse.

"Do you want me to be?" I asked.

"I want to know what you want before I answer that." He bumped the back of his head against mine.

"I want you."

"As a boyfriend?" he pressed.

I hooked my pinky around his, bringing more of our hands into contact. "As however you'll have me."

"That's not an answer," he murmured, grunting as he raised his injured arm to get a drink of coffee.

"What do *you* want, Dylan?" I asked instead.

He was at a disadvantage, reliant on me for so many things. It didn't feel fair or reasonable for me to be the one leading the conversation with my own, selfish wants.

"More," he rasped, overlapping more of my hand with his own.

"More of what?"

"More of everything."

All of our fingers were threaded together, an awkward reverse hold that felt more perfect than anything else ever had before. I gave him a squeeze and closed my eyes, using his body for as much support as he used mine.

"What is everything?" I asked.

Dylan sighed, chewing another bite of his breakfast and swallowing.

"Did I ever tell you after the first time we were together I went home and cleaned my shower?"

I huffed out a laugh. "No?"

"I cleaned my shower and it made me so fucking hard, Alex." The next sound that left Dylan's mouth sounded almost like a whimper. "It made me hard and I jerked off about it."

"Why?"

"I wish I knew," he said. "But you made me clean my cum up off the floor and it was one of the hottest things I'd ever done."

"What part of it?" I asked, genuinely curious. "Most people would have found it demeaning."

"Well, it kind of was." Dylan shrugged his good shoulder against my back. "That's why it's all so confusing for me. But it also feels really simple at the same time."

"Explain."

"Like, there's a thing you need done and you tell me about it, and then I do it. It's easy."

"There's nothing easy about getting on your knees for another man, Dylan."

He answered that with a sardonic laugh under his breath. "For you, maybe."

"There's nothing wrong with liking what you like."

He exhaled softly, and we sat quietly for another few minutes. The muffins were gone, and I poured out what was left in the thermos into our cups. The coffee was quickly cooling down and the air was warming up. The ride back to the city would be nice, but I wasn't in a rush to leave the calm comfort of the secluded, off-trail hiding place we'd found. The way I felt in the meadow was how I felt about kink. Somehow hidden, but in the open at the same time.

Private, but not hiding.

"What was it like with your ex?" Dylan asked, the words soft and measured, like he'd been thinking about them for far too long.

Nerves prickled at the back of my neck at the question, and I was glad we weren't face to face because I didn't have a chance at stopping the way my nose scrunched at the question. The last time Dylan brought up my ex, I'd thrown him out.

"We were friends for years," I said.

"Are you still?"

"Getting there."

Dylan hummed, repeating his initial question, "What was it like with him? Did you do the eggs with him too?"

His elaboration gave me all the information I needed about the intent behind his line of questioning. Dylan was comparing himself, which was a foolish undertaking. He and Car couldn't have been more different, even in all the ways they were the same.

"No eggs," I said.

"Why?"

"It wasn't what he needed."

"But it's what I needed?" Dylan asked.

"Wasn't it?"

He swallowed, entire body moving with it. "What did he need?"

"Dylan..." I paused, knowing it was important to choose my words carefully. "I wouldn't tell other people the details of what we do together, and I'm not going to tell you details about what he and I did either."

He grunted. "That's fair. But like..."

"Are you trying to ask about the Dom/sub aspect of my relationship with him?"

"Yes," he answered, sounding relieved.

"He was...is...submissive. I was his Dom."

"Like you are with me?" Dylan asked.

My chest felt hollow and full all simultaneously. I realized in that moment, I wanted to see his face, but I somehow also knew Dylan needed the anonymity to get through this line of inquiry, so I flexed my fingers against his, our hands still joined, letting him know it was okay for him to ask his next question. Facing away from him had also made it easier for me to talk about my past too. Maybe it was the best thing for us, in that moment, to be vulnerable without being scrutinized.

"Similar, but not."

"Why did you break up?" he asked next.

"He was in love with someone else," I said.

The details were irrelevant. The facts were the same. And even as the answer left my mouth, I knew what question was coming next. I steeled myself against my own feelings, ready for it when it came.

"Were you in love with him?"

The truth came far easier than I'd expected it to.

"The idea of him, I think," I admitted.

"Are you in love with me?" he asked, laughing at himself before speaking again. "Never mind, don't answ—"

Yes.

"Yes."

Dylan's laugh died in his throat. "What?"

"Yes, I'm in love with you."

"Oh."

It was my turn to laugh, palm sweating against Dylan's. "It's okay if you don't—"

"I love you too," he blurted, turning at the same time as I did so quickly he almost fell right onto my lap. I caught him, both hands cradling his face to keep his eyes on mine. "But why?"

"What?"

"Why do you love me?" he asked, gaze worried and searching.

"It was impossible to not," I told him honestly. "I don't think I ever stood a chance."

"But *why*?" He pushed forward against my fingers, eyes wide.

I stroked my thumb beneath his eye, unprepared to find words for something that simply felt *right* all the way down to my bones.

"You're the bravest man I've ever met," I told him. "You're strong and stubborn."

"I'm not brave."

"You're here," I reminded, pressing my thumb against his cheekbone. "You're *here*."

I meant in that moment, in my life. I meant *with me*.

"I was so mean to you," he argued. "I still am."

"Not today."

He breathed out, a soft smile flashing across his mouth before he fought to point his chin toward his chest, escaping my scrutiny.

"If you meant it, you would leave," I said simply. "I know that and so do you."

"I don't want to leave," he whispered.

"Like I said...brave."

"Stubborn," he said instead.

"You can be both. You *are* both. You can be anything you want, Dylan."

"I just want to be with you," he said. "I want you to be my boyfriend."

"I'm yours," I promised.

"I want you to be my Dom," he said next, words shaky.

"I'm yours, Dylan," I said again, leaning in and pressing our mouths together in a quick kiss. "In every way you want me."

He moaned against my lips, swaying forward and chasing after a better kiss.

"Does this mean I get my piano today?" he asked.

"I already ordered it," I told him. "It means when we get home, I'm taking you straight into the playroom."

"Fuck, alright." His lashes fluttered, cheeks flushing. "Yes, please. Thank you. I love you, Alex. What the fuck?"

I laughed quietly, kissing him again.

"I love you too, pet."

He loved me.

I repeated it over and over in my head the entire ride back to his house, my arms wrapped around his midsection the whole time, right one tighter than the left still. Sometimes, he'd let go of the bike and pat his hand against my knuckles, squeezing and using his body to once again offer up the confession he'd given me in the meadow.

When we got back to the city, there was a man in front of Alex's house, leaning against the railing with his arms crossed and an annoyed look on his face. He was dressed as well as Alex and Brooks ever were, but I didn't recognize his face. I realized Alex hadn't introduced me to any of his friends. How could he love me if...

He pulled the bike up to the curb and cut the engine. After an hour of the engine rumbling and the wind whipping around my head, the silence was deafening. I pulled off my helmet and climbed off the bike, standing to the side while Alex rolled the motorcycle back into the storage shed. He locked the door and pulled his own helmet off, tucking it under his arm and turning toward the man with an outstretched hand.

"You owe me," he said to Alex, dropping a folded stack of papers into Alex's waiting palm before turning his stare toward me.

I swallowed nervously, immediately aware of the weight of his appraisal as it dragged over me.

"Stop it," Alex warned.

The weight lessened.

"You're the infamous Dylan then?" the man said.

"Infamous?"

"I can go back to being a recluse and you can go back to being friend group enemy number one if you liked it better that way, Kale," Alex snapped.

Ah.

I'd heard about Kale, who was probably more infamous than me, but I was high on the morning, on the revelations that were fresh between Alex and me, and I wasn't interested in soiling any of that by digging in and poking at what I knew about him.

"Ignore him," Alex said, this time to me. He shoved the folded-up papers into his pocket and started up the stairs, leaving Kale on the sidewalk.

"You're welcome, you know," Kale said, as if he hadn't been dismissed. "It's not like I had anything better to do besides accept delivery of a piano for you."

My heart skittered and jumped, then stalled out entirely.

"A piano?" I croaked.

"You asked for one," Alex said simply.

"Yeah, like four hours ago."

"Jesus," Kale muttered under his breath, looking at Alex, then at me.

"Oh, like you're any better," Alex said.

That got him a quick flash of a smile. "No, you're right. I'm far worse."

"Thank you," Alex told him.

"It's in the guest room like you demanded."

Alex rolled his eyes, and my sweaty fingers slipped against the helmet. "I didn't demand," he said.

"You always demand," Kale responded.

"You do," I agreed, which earned me a sharp look from Alex and an amused one from Kale.

I held Alex's stare, my heart finally falling back into its usual pace as Alex's expression softened, and then darkened.

"Inside, Dylan," Alex said quietly, and I gave Kale a quick nod before passing both of them and heading into the house.

I listened to the quiet rumble of Alex's voice as he answered whatever Kale said next, setting my helmet down on the couch before collapsing on it myself. Kicking off my shoes, I leaned back and closed my eyes waiting for Alex, who followed less than five minutes later.

"I'm surprised you're not in the guest room," he said, bending down to unlace his boots.

"I didn't know if I could."

"It's your piano," he said.

"It's your house," I countered, sitting up to see him better.

He worked his jaw back and forth, pushing his glasses up the bridge of his nose.

"Do you really find me demanding?"

"Yes," I rasped.

"Do you like it?"

"Very much, I think," I admitted.

There was so much more to my relationship with Alex than simply whatever kind of confessed love existed between us now. There was an undercurrent of control and power that weaved its way around us constantly, and even if I didn't always understand the tide and the flow, I wanted it. I welcomed the force and the severity of it because, the majority of the time, it was the most reliable thing I'd ever had.

Even as a child, I'd always known my parents' money was a fleeting thing. I didn't think it also meant their love was fickle, but I understood there were expectations and requirements. If I performed well, I won a prize. Whether that prize was their attention or something tangible didn't matter. I understood the logistics of give and take, and my relationship with Alex was just another example of that.

But at the same time, it felt unfair to discredit him so. To compare him to the transactional interactions that had made up my life before him. Alex would suffer as much a loss as I would if things ended between us. I could see the truth of that in his eyes and the sometimes tense stretch of his shoulders when I got too pushy with him. Just as I was afraid of pushing him too far one day, I was fairly certain he was also afraid of standing too strong against me.

"Go upstairs and make sure it's tuned," he said. "It should be. Then wait."

I smiled and jumped off the couch, the excitement of being able to play an instrument again, let alone piano, was enough to have my hands shaking. After moving to Chelsea, I knew there was no way I would have room for a piano in the small apartment I shared with Tate. Sure, I could have just not rented to him in the first place and turned the second bedroom into a music room, but the tradeoff was worth it. I'd gotten a best friend out of the deal, even though I'd been horrible to him over the past few months.

Tate and I had talked enough to clear the air over the way I'd lied to him about our money situation, but beyond that... not much. He was so happy with Brooks, I didn't want to ruin that with my own mess, and I still wasn't sure how to explain Alex to him. Though, I wondered how Alex explained me to Brooks sometimes too.

Out of breath with my heart threatening to burst out of my chest, I found the piano in the guest room, tucked against the far wall. The window was open, bright rays of afternoon sun streaking down across the rich black of the instrument, and I knew before I even pressed the middle-C that it was already perfectly tubed. I'd told Alex I wanted a piano and he'd taken me out of the city for a picnic breakfast and brought me home to the thing I wanted most in this life— besides him.

The moment didn't feel real, and I had to sit on my hands to stop myself from playing a whole song. My left shoulder burned, but it wasn't as glaring of a pain as it had been days before. The doctor said the injury would heal on its own, and the fact I didn't need surgery was a relief. The angle and control I needed for guitar was still too much of a stress on the muscle, though, but with a piano...

I would survive the waiting.

Though, I didn't think I'd survive the wait for Alex, who had yet to make it upstairs.

Opening my mouth to call out for him, his name died in my throat before I could say anything. This was deliberate. It was a test. Maybe a test for the both of us, I wasn't sure. Instead of looking at the gleaming keys, I turned my stare toward the window, the sun, the clouds, the sky...

"Do you like it?"

Alex's voice in the doorway startled me and I jumped, head jerking around to face him. He leaned against the door frame, half changed out of the clothes he'd worn on the ride. No shirt, no socks, barefoot with his legs crossed at the ankle and his arms folded casually in front of his chest. His hair was tousled from the helmet, his eyes clear behind the lenses of his glasses.

"It's perfect. Thank you."

"Did you want to play something?"

"So much," I said, unable to stop my lips from curving up into a smile. Though, if he didn't let me play, I'd survive it. Just knowing it was here, having it close, that was almost enough to hold me over until he decided I could. I hadn't realized... hadn't understood just how much music meant to me. That sounded like such a silly thing to say, considering I'd given up almost my entire life because of music, but in the stress of it, I'd lost sight of the passion.

Alex pushed off the door, nodding and crossing the room. He traced his tongue across the front of his teeth, the dark glint in his eye turning devious. He dragged a chair from across the room, notching it up behind the piano bench and sitting down. It put us almost at the same height, a few inches between our bodies. He was careful to not knock his knees into the bench, leaning close and going entirely still.

"Play, then," he said simply.

Tugging my hands out from beneath my legs, I did a slow shoulder rotation, one of the ones I'd been working on in physical therapy. Another burn, but nothing that wasn't manageable. I wouldn't overdo it, and even if I tried, Alex wouldn't let me. I knew that down to my bones.

I set my fingers against the keys and he set his against my waist.

"Play," he said again, the tone brokering no argument.

Of the thousand songs I knew, my brain gave me notes for one of the hardest, and I quickly fell into the soft melody of Nocturne in E-flat Major by Chopin. It had always been one of my favorites because it was hard for everyone else, but not for me. There were parts that required work, but the notes rang together so beautifully there was never a question in my mind if the payoff was worth the effort.

I made it through the song with a few minor hiccups, which I doubted Alex would have ever heard, then I set my hands together in my lap. His were still on my waist, finger-tips curling around the curve of my ribs.

"Were you happy with that performance?" he asked.

"It wasn't perfect."

"I don't imagine it ever is."

"It wasn't up to my standards," I told him.

"You have a tear in your labrum, Dylan," he reminded me. "You haven't played piano in how long?"

I cleared my throat, cheeks burning. "Nearly a year."

"Nearly a year," he repeated, ending with a knowing hum. His fingers finally moved, startling me for how still they'd truly been. He reached around my front, undoing the button and the zipper of my jeans. Making no move to tug them down, Alex reached into my underwear and pulled out my cock, letting it sit soft and warm against my thigh. "Play it again, then."

I played through it again, this time with my dick out and his fingers so close to my bare skin I could feel the heat of him, but not the actual touch. I made more mistakes the second time, of course, because I was distracted. Thinking more about how much I wanted him than how much I wanted to do justice to Chopin.

"That sounded worse," he said after I finished.

"It was."

I'd gotten half-hard during the last round of the song, partly on account of the fact the piano was a dream, but mostly because of Alex and the way he hovered, the way he teased. At my confession, Alex dusted his fingertips up my thickening shaft, humming thoughtfully in my ear.

"Do it better," he said, finally, *blessedly,* wrapping his fingers around my erection.

My entire body trembled at his touch, and I was ten seconds into my third attempt at the song when he stroked his hand from my root to my tip. My fingers splayed on their own accord, absolutely butchering the perfection of the song, and as I went still, so did he.

"Do you need a break?" he asked.

"No."

I reset my hands and started in again, ready for the tight squeeze of Alex's hand when it came. My fingers barely faltered, slipping off by a quarter before finding the rhythm again. From behind, Alex stroked my cock until I reached the end of the song, not stopping when it ended.

"Was that the best you could do?" he asked me next.

"No." My back bowed, and I ached to lean back against him, to let him wipe away every thought that had ever existed in my brain before him and every thought that would come after.

"Again then, pet," he said.

The endearment—or whatever it was—sent a shiver all the way down to my toes, and I set my hands against the keys again and played. Alex's touch was soft and slow, deliberate with the weight and the tease, and I lost count of how many times I played through with new and different faults every time.

"I thought you were good at this," he whispered, the tease light in his voice.

"I am when I'm not distracted."

"Life is a distraction." Alex stretched his fingertips to my balls, pressing until I groaned. He leaned forward and set his chin against my shoulder, lips hot against my ear. "Play it again, pet."

"S'hard."

"You are," he agreed, giving my dick a squeeze. "But we're going to do this until I'm tired of hearing it."

"I could never get tired of it," I said, taking a breath and forcing my fingers to start once again into the song.

"The song is fine," he whispered, sinking his teeth into my ear, "but I meant tired of hearing *you*."

As if on cue, he gave a sharp flick of his wrist that somehow sent me straight over the edge. I lost the song entirely, lost my mind as cum spurted out of my dick, streaking across his hand, even up to the piano keys. I hadn't even realized my orgasm had been so close, and I trembled against him as he milked the whole of it out of me.

"Oh, fuck." I fell back against him, head landing on his shoulder, and Alex chuckled, quick to shove me forward, back upright on the bench.

"I'm not tired of it yet," he said, sticky fingers still moving up and down my length. "Not tired of you. Now, do it again."

Even while Dylan's fingers stuttered through the notes, mine held steady around his cock. Sweat beaded on his temples and his entire body trembled as I wrung a second orgasm out of him. My own dick ached for attention, pressing hard enough against the fly of my jeans to bruise. In front of me, Dylan mumbled something mindlessly, shoving his hair away from his face and readying his fingers once again on the keys.

"Can you play standing?" I asked.

"Yes," he rasped.

"Good."

I kicked my chair back toward the bed, flung the piano bench toward the wall, and went to my knees behind him. Releasing his cock, I spread his ass apart and speared my tongue straight into his asshole. Dylan cried out, dragging his fingers against the keys in a loud smash of noise that sounded nothing like the song he'd been playing.

"If you stop, I stop," I whispered, returning my mouth to his hole only after his fingers returned to the keys.

Above me, Dylan groaned, legs shifting awkwardly as he tried to keep his balance, to keep playing. When I pushed a finger into him, his fingers splayed across the keys, he cursed under his breath and started over.

"Good pet," I whispered against his dripping asshole, adding a second finger when he'd nearly made it through the song.

The wail he let out drowned any sound his fingers would have made, and then the piano went quiet. Dylan whimpered and panted, and I pulled my fingers out of him entirely, rocking back onto my heels and wiping my mouth with the back of my hand.

"Green?" I asked, when he hadn't moved for nearly a minute.

"My dick is so fucking hard, I want to cry," he said, dropping his chin toward his chest and letting out a shaking exhale. "I'm green."

"I won't stop if you cry," I warned him.

"I know."

And he started to play again.

When I'd sent Dylan upstairs ahead of me, I'd had the foresight to stop in my bedroom and get a bottle of lube, which I pulled out of my pocket and flipped open. I squirted a fair amount onto my fingers, then wrestled my throbbing erection out of my pants and slicked some more down my length. Pushing forward, I shoved two fingers back into him with so much force he rocked up onto his toes, barely missing the key his right ring finger had been aiming for.

He cursed under his breath, the words trailing off into a whimper when I pulled my fingers out of him and stood, pressing my chest against his back.

"Why did you stop?" I asked, banding an arm around the front of his chest. He was short enough that I had to bend my knees to get my cock between his cheeks, and I didn't bother waiting for him to answer before impaling him with my dick.

Dylan shouted my name, right arm flying out to brace himself against the body of the piano as I seated myself inside of him. My right hand curled around his hip, pulling him down against me until it was hard for me to breathe for how overwhelming the feel of him was. Sweat trickled down my spine, my breath skittering out of my lungs as I accustomed myself to the too-tight grip of his body.

"Play it," I whispered into his ear, fighting myself to stay still.

I needed Dylan to get through the song as much as he could because I was seconds away from shooting my load deeper than any man ever had or would again. His muscles fluttered and gripped me like butterfly wings made of iron, pulsing in time with my own heartbeat, which I could feel in every part of my body.

I'd listened to Dylan masterfully play his way through the Chopin piece more times than I could count, and when he neared the end without a mistake, I gave in to the thing both of us wanted the most. Pulling out so the tip of my cock teased his rim, I shoved back inside with so much strength it picked him up off the floor entirely.

Dylan cried out, scrabbling against the piano to steady himself, but not lost enough to pleasure to trust the strength of his injured arm to give him balance. Realizing I couldn't fuck him the way I wanted, I pulled out and stepped back.

"No!" he shouted, turning toward me just as I spun him around and grabbed him underneath his legs. Lifting him from the backs of his thighs, I dropped his ass onto the keys and pushed back into him.

"No, what?" I asked, leveraging his weight against the piano so I could rut into him. The keys smashed beneath him, the tune just as gorgeous as it had been when he played Chopin for me.

"No, don't stop," he whispered, dropping his forehead against my shoulder.

"I should have made you play all day," I said, thrusting my hips upward. My legs burned from the angle and the bend, but I was less than a breath away from coming anyway.

I could handle it.

I *would* handle it.

"I would have," Dylan said, mouthing the promise against my collarbone, his teeth gnashing against it.

We were so unsteady, so off-balance.

"Hold on," I said, grabbing him under his legs again and lifting him off the piano. Dylan wrapped his arms around my neck, mouth still hot on my collar as I carried him to the bed and laid him down as gently as his shoulder needed and as rough as I wanted.

"Please," he pleaded, lips moving against my skin.

"I've got you," I promised, using my hips to spread his legs wider. My jeans were still on, but I wasn't going to deal with getting them off now that I was already buried inside of him.

"I know."

"Mark me there," I told him, curling my fingers around the top of Dylan's head to hold him in place so I could fuck him deeper. "Make it hurt."

Dylan groaned, closing his lips around my collarbone and biting down hard with his teeth. The shock of pain rippled through me like I'd touched a live wire, and I pumped my hips into him two more times before my cock thickened and emptied. I fucked him so hard, Dylan's ass was lifted off the bed, my balls hot against his skin as I filled him. He thrashed beneath me, spreading his legs wider like it would let me deeper, and I reached between us to stroke his cock through another orgasm.

He yelled at me, cursed and writhed. He had to be so tired, so oversensitive, but he didn't ever ask me to stop. After he let out his pretend protests, he sealed his lips around the spot on my collarbone again, bearing down even harder when I finally managed to draw another orgasm out of him.

He burst into tears at the release, his legs unwrapping from around my waist, his arms from around my neck. Against the white bedding, Dylan went absolutely slack. The rapid strum of his pulse against my fingers was the only sign he was alive at all, that and the way his cock thickened and pulsed as trickles of cum leaked out of his slit. As my wits came back to me, the marks from his teeth turned from pleasure to actual pain, and I was careful to disentangle myself from him before rolling over onto my back.

"Dylan." I pressed my fingers over the divots from his teeth, shivering at the way the mark of his mouth against my skin had me feeling.

"Hmn?"

He was going to hate me.

"Go play it again," I said, forcing myself up and out of the bed.

I dragged the piano bench back into place and reset the chair in the corner of the room. The last thing I needed was for him to come again, so I sat down in the chair and finally kicked my pants off.

"Are you serious right now?" he asked, eyes closed and limbs splayed like a starfish. Even his left arm was stretched more than I'd seen it since the accident.

"Very."

Dylan sat up, his body swaying. He slid off the bed, made his way to the bench, and sat down. With his eyes still closed, he set his fingers on the keys, then he played me the most beautiful version of Nocturne that I'd ever heard. When he finished, he exhaled softly, shoulders sagging as he dropped his hands into his lap.

"How was it?" he asked.

"If I didn't love you before, I would love you now," I said.

He turned his head to the side, lashes still fanned out across his cheeks. "Because of the song or the sex?"

"Because of you."

Dylan licked his lips and turned his face back toward the piano.

"Do you want to clean up first or eat?" I asked him.

"Eat," he said softly.

"Alright." I was still hard and I took my cock into my fist, pointing it toward his back. "Come here, then."

Dylan spun around on the bench, rolling his eyes when he saw what I had in mind for him.

"That's not what I meant."

"I know," I said. "Now come here."

He closed the space between us, sinking down to his knees in front of me and taking my cock into his mouth without being told again. Threading my fingers through his hair, I lifted off my seat, pushing all the way into his throat on the first thrust.

"Oh, fuck, pet. Dylan. Jesus. Your mouth."

He'd sucked a bruise into me during sex, and he set to work on my cock with the same level of intensity, bobbing up and down my shaft, all the while leaking spit down my balls and licking it up with his tongue. Dylan made an absolute mess of me, and I loved him even more for it.

"Can I come in your mouth?" I asked, the end *very* close.

In response, he reached behind his head and covered my hand with his own, pushing himself deeper down my shaft.

I groaned his name, told him I loved him, and cursed him... all in the same breath, then I spilled onto the back of his tongue. My hips jerked and I fucked my cum down into his throat, into his stomach, relishing the way he smiled around my shaft while he cried. After the tremors of my orgasm rolled through me, I wanted nothing more than to haul him onto my lap and hold him until we both fell asleep, but the chair was uncomfortable and we were both covered in sweat, cum, and dirt from the ride.

"Eating," I said, pulling my cock out of my his mouth and tracing the tip across the outline of his swollen lips.

"I just did," he murmured, falling onto the side of his legs and resting his head against my thigh.

I carded my fingers through his hair, wondering if there would be any real harm in rearranging the aftercare and letting him nap awhile first.

"Do you need water?" I asked.

He licked his lips and nodded.

I helped Dylan into the guest bed and went to the kitchen, grabbing a glass of water and the newspaper. By the time I made it back to the guest room, he was sound asleep on his back, spread across the whole bed like he had been after he came. I set the water on the nightstand beside him, then settled into the chair with my crossword.

The newspaper remained folded in my lap, pen clutched in my hand, because as much as I'd planned otherwise, in this and in so many other ways, I couldn't tear myself away from Dylan Rivers.

And I was surprised to find I no longer wanted to.

Playing piano hurt my shoulder, but there was no way I would ever tell Alex that.

He wouldn't let me near a guitar until I had explicit clearance from my physical therapist, which I'd yet to receive. I was still on limited mobility, but I didn't have to wear the sling anymore, which was a blessing and a curse at the same time. Every day I woke up feeling a little more like myself... and a lot less like myself I'd gotten so used to the kind of attention and care being in a relationship with Alex brought me, but there was no way it could last forever.

Three weeks after the day he bought me the piano, I woke up before him. It was an unwelcome first, especially on a Saturday, and I debated staying in bed but I couldn't force my eyes to stay closed. Carefully, I slid out from beneath the covers, pulled my cell phone free of the charger, and padded barefoot down to the kitchen. The cast iron was on the stove and there were eggs in the fridge, but it had been weeks since I'd even thought about holding that egg against the wall before ruining it on the spitting hot pan.

Instead, I made myself coffee and collected the newspaper from the porch for Alex. I flipped through the newsprint searching for the crossword, but my finger skittered to a stop when I caught a familiar name in one of the articles.

My father.

I wanted to say it had been ages since I'd thought about him, but that would have been a lie. I thought about my parents every day, thought about the life I used to have and the one I wanted. Thought about the life I *had*. Since my injury, I'd been living in a constant state of nervous fear while I waited for a call from my dad—or his assistant—about what I knew had to be a massive hospital bill. Every day that passed and the call didn't come, I felt better, then I felt worse. Did he not care about what happened to me that would have sent me to the hospital and warranted all those tests and that ongoing therapy? If he did care, why would he pay for those bills so freely and not my rent, not my groceries? The mercurial way of his love gave me whiplash, and I hated myself for not knowing which outcome was preferred.

What I truly wanted was a world that didn't exist. One where my parents were proud of me for breaking free of the mold and choosing to pursue music even though it was risky. My father had made all his wealth from mergers and money management, surely he would appreciate the outcome of a well-managed risk. That couldn't have been further from the truth, though. So, instead I was on my own until Alex showed up and either ruined—or made—my life.

Propping my elbows on the counter, I rested my head in my hands, digging my fingertips into my temples until it hurt. I wasn't unhappy with the turn my life had taken. I loved Alex, that was the truth, and if it wasn't for my dad cutting me off the way he did, I never would have had the opportunity to even meet Alex in the first place. Sure, it was safe to assume with Tate and Brooks our paths would have crossed sooner rather than later, but I didn't know what that would have looked like for either of us.

Alex had also been at a low point when we met. Like the hands of fate had given up on us both before throwing us together in some kind of last-ditch effort to allow us some shred of happiness. Luckily, he was strong and had grabbed on for dear life, hauling both of us up and out of the pit we'd found ourselves in.

But now...

Now what?

Coffee, first.

I poured a mug for myself and carried it out to the back yard. It was still early, the sun barely pinking the sky, but the air was already thick and warm. I sat down at the table in the back, then I pulled my phone out of my pocket to text Tate.

> Hey, I miss you.

Three dots popped up almost immediately, and then a reply.

TATE

> I miss you too.

> You're up early.

> Brooks is a runner, sometimes I sleep through him leaving. Sometimes I don't.

> Oh.

I realized in that moment, I'd been a horrible friend. I didn't know anything about the man my best friend had fallen in love with.

How are you? Why are you up so early?

Alex used to get me up early and I'm just used to it now.

Used to?

Did you two break up?

I snorted, the idea of me and Alex breaking up was absurd because the thought of me and him being together in the first place was still something I struggled with. Not because I didn't want it or trust it, but because, on paper, I didn't understand it. We worked in private. I didn't know if that would hold up in the real world, like once my arm was healed and I didn't need to be taken care of.

Even though I'd gotten used to it.

Even though I wanted it to continue.

No. He just lets me sleep in now.

That's nice of him.

Was it?

Rolling my head around to crack my neck, I played with the idea of Alex letting me sleep in as being a *nice* thing. My first thought had been that I'd made him unhappy somehow or that he'd grown bored of me. I hadn't worried about it when he stopped with the eggs because we'd talked about that, but a couple months in now...was the novelty of *me* wearing off?

Inside, I heard a toilet flush.

Alex was awake.

Without thinking, I went into the kitchen and poured him some coffee, taking it out to the yard and setting it down at the seat across from mine. I'd left my phone on the open newspaper, my brief distraction from the article about my dad that I hadn't bothered to read. I flipped the paper to the crossword and folded the section into quarters, tucking the edge under Alex's coffee, then I went back to my phone.

> Can we get together soon?

TATE

I didn't want to push.

> You never cared about pushing before.

It's different now.

Yeah, it was.

I caught movement from the corner of my eye, and I looked up in time to see Alex shuffle into the kitchen, half-asleep. He had his glasses on, hair sticking up every which way, and he wore nothing more than a pair of gray sweats that were hanging on to his hips for dear life. Unconsciously, I licked my lips, biting the bottom one between my teeth as he came close enough to the door for me to see the dark trail of hair that led down past the waistband.

Alex looked around the kitchen, stare lingering on the coffee pot before drifting toward the cracked-open back door. When he saw me, I set my phone down, chest constricting as he smiled softly at me and headed outside. Like always, my breath caught when he got close, and I blinked up at him... helpless.

"You're up early," he said, running his fingers through my hair so gently I almost purred.

"You're up late," I corrected. His fingers flexed against my scalp. "I made coffee."

Alex hummed, easing me off of my seat and onto my knees. It was second nature for me to grab his thighs and rub my cheek against his sleep-hard cock. Shifting, I mouthed his length through the soft material of his sweats, my own dick thickening and pulsing to life.

"Sometimes I worry that you're not real," he murmured, petting the back of my head while I tried to get his pajamas wet enough that I could feel the swell of his cockhead through the material.

"I'm real," I whispered, fingers working their way up to the waistband of his sweats. "Let me show you."

He nodded and I tugged his sweats down low enough to reveal his erection, which I swallowed into my mouth before he could stop me. Alex groaned, hips pumping forward as I swirled my tongue around his thickness. He was so hot and getting thicker by the second, the taste of cum and lube from the night before still musky against my tongue. Reaching down, I palmed my cock, groaning when the heel of my hand made contact with my shaft.

"Hands, pet," he warned, and I sighed around his shaft, raising both hands above my head. A twinge of pain raced through my left arm, but not enough to make me lower it back down. It wasn't any more than if I'd slept on it weird, which was a relief to me considering how it had been a month ago.

He curled his fingers around my wrists. "How's your shoulder?"

"I'm fine."

"You winced when you raised your arms."

"It's better than before," I promised, licking the slick tip of his cock.

Alex chuckled, giving me a quick nod of his head to continue. I took him back into my mouth with a low moan, licking down his shaft until I got as much of him into my mouth as would fit.

"I love how you suck me," Alex said, teasing the fingers of his free hand through my hair. "Love how you get on your knees for me without being told."

It was a change, that was for sure.

Before, kneeling for Alex had felt like getting down onto broken glass, but now...it felt more like home. There was comfort and safety on my knees, protection in the trust I had for him. On my own, I'd come so far since the first time he and I had been together. There was still so much about the things he liked and did that I didn't understand, but sometimes I wondered if I needed to understand. Would it be so bad for me to leave the why of it to him and just take what he decided I needed?

It was the loud voice in the back of my head that sounded like my father that always brought me back around and made me question everything. Why was it okay for Alex to control my life and make decisions for me, but not my dad? Why did I let Alex treat me the way he did without arguing? To a normal person, an average person, things between me and Alex could look like abuse, but nothing could have been further from the truth. Even if I didn't understand it, our relationship was love.

And that was all.

"Dylan," he grunted my name, burying himself into the deepest part of my throat and cradling the back of my head with a steady hand. With my mouth wide and my jaw aching, I blinked up at him through teary eyes. It was hard to breathe, hard to think, and I didn't care.

I didn't want to do any of those things.

All I wanted was to love Alex, and be loved in return.

Alex's hips bucked forward, and he let go of my head, using his hold on my wrists to pull away enough to get his cock out of my mouth.

"Stick out your tongue," he said, barely getting the words out before the first jet of cum shot out of his dick. His orgasm sprayed across my lip before he redirected the rest of it onto the waiting flat of my tongue. Cursing under his breath as his cum pooled in my mouth, Alex shot the rest of his load, entire body shivering with the last pull. I opened my eyes, blinking up at him. My own cock was so hard it hurt, throbbing with far more need than my shoulder ever had.

Alex sank to his knees in front of me, grabbing my face with both hands. His cheeks were flushed beneath the day-old stubble, pupils wide and dark behind his glasses. His mouth was half open, lips slick with spit. Drool slid from the corner of my mouth, and I moaned, lashes fluttering. Alex leaned in and licked up the spit that had escaped down my chin, then he slanted our mouths together and kissed his cum right off my tongue.

It was the sexiest thing I think he'd ever done, and I trembled, opening my mouth wider for him. Alex licked past my lips and scooped up all of his release, swirling it around with his spit before letting it spread back into my mouth. The flavor of him exploded on my taste buds, and I grabbed his wrists to make sure he didn't take his hands away from my face. Deepening the kiss, I closed my eyes and gave myself over to him entirely.

It was different, I realized, because it was love at the heart of Alex's control, not possession, at least not in the way it was with my dad. Alex wanted to possess me, and he did, but it was to treasure and spoil, not to demean and diminish. From the very first time, he'd always had my best interests at heart, maybe even before his own. That was why he'd sent me away, why he'd made the choices for us that he had.

With that in mind, instead of asking for my own release when he ended the kiss, I pressed my lips together and smiled at him softly. I was just as drunk as if he'd let me come, the release secondary to everything else that happened between us.

"Thank you for the coffee," he said, helping me to my feet. He tucked his softening cock back into his pajamas, ignoring mine entirely save for a single passing glance at the bulge between my legs.

"I got your crossword too," I mumbled hoarsely.

Alex settled me back into my chair, coffee and cellphone with unread messages from Tate still waiting for me.

"I know you did, Dylan." He walked around the table and sat down, clicking open his pen and looking down at his crossword. I don't know if I expected him to say something else or not, to thank me, but the corner of his lip twitched into a ghost of a pleased smile... and that was more than enough.

For what might have been the first time since I'd met him, Dylan looked at peace. Sitting across from me in the back yard, sipping his coffee and staring at the stone fountain against the far wall. His shoulders—including the injured one —were relaxed and there wasn't a single frown line to be seen around the corners of his plump lips. He closed his eyes, unaware I watched him, tipping his head back and letting out the quietest sigh. His throat worked as he swallowed, and I clicked my pen closed, setting it on top of my nearly finished crossword.

"Are you happy, Dylan?" I asked.

He didn't move, but he smiled softly. "Yes."

"Your shoulder is getting better," I said, which wasn't news to either of us. My observation brought his chin toward his chest, his eyes crinkled in worry as he locked his eyes on mine.

"Yes."

I licked my lips, reaching for my coffee.

"I can start with the guitar again soon," he said.

"Yes."

"Maybe some shows," he said next, "some gigs again."

"Whatever you want, Dylan."

He angled his head to the side, and it blew my mind how different he looked from the man I'd met at Tryst. Even with his hospitalization and physical therapy, he'd put on weight and gained some color in his cheeks. Not that he was unhealthy before, but he looked better taken care of now and it was impossible to ignore the way pride swelled in my chest at the change. Dylan bit the tip of his tongue, working his jaw back and forth while he watched me, and I found myself curious to know what he saw in me...besides my money.

I took my glasses off and rubbed the bridge of my nose.

"How long are you going to pay my rent in Chelsea?" he asked after I set my glasses down on the table.

I would have preferred to see him for that question, but the strength had mysteriously gone out of me. "Until you tell me to stop."

Dylan looked down at his hands, tracing the edge of his thumbnail over a callous on his middle finger.

"You know," he said after taking a slow drink of his coffee, "that apartment was supposed to be the start of my life."

"Wasn't it?"

"It feels like I've just been backsliding." Dylan smiled at me weakly before looking back to his hands. "I didn't want to be beholden to my dad and his money and now I'm beholden to you and yours."

I knew there had to be a right thing to say to that assertion, but the words were lost to me. Dylan kept talking before I could even bother to weave a sentence together, but I wasn't sure if it was a blessing or a curse.

"It doesn't bother me the same way, though."

"No?"

He huffed a laugh. "Sometimes I feel like it should, but you're nothing like him."

"No, I'm not," I agreed. I didn't need to know Russell Lang personally to know that.

"I love you." Dylan scrunched his nose.

"I love you."

"I don't trust it, though. Like..." Trailing off, he drummed his fingers nervously against the edge of the table, the words and thoughts abandoning him.

I bit down on the inside of my cheek to stop myself from pressing him on the statement. The wheels were turning and I could tell he was close to talking himself around to a revelation that would either make or break us.

"Before, the first times, when you were paying me...that made sense because there was an even exchange."

"I'd hardly call the money I gave you an even trade for what you gave me."

Dylan snorted, rolling his eyes. "What did I give you?"

"A second chance."

That seemed to stop us both, and I fumbled my glasses back on while he sucked in a breath heavy enough to lift his shoulders toward his ears.

"Agree to disagree," he said, continuing before I could object. "It was a transaction, either way. And then I was so cruel to you—"

"Already forgiven."

"So cruel, Alex," he repeated, leveling me with a sharp look that let me know he still carried immeasurable guilt over that argument we'd had before I used a safe word with him. "Then when I got hurt...that was also..."

"Taking care of you after that was me doing right by you."

"Charity?"

"Selfishness," I corrected him. "A way to get what I wanted."

Another swallow, another click of his jaw, and I found myself desperate to know what song he was playing against the edge of the table with his trembling fingers.

"Whatever it was, I'm almost done with physical therapy now." As if to demonstrate, he gave a slow and short rotation of his left shoulder. "So, what next?"

"I suppose that's up to you."

"I thought you were the one in charge. You're the Dominant."

"I am. It's my job to make sure you have what you want. What you need."

"And what's that?" he asked, voice low and cracking.

"I can't make that decision for you."

"What about what *you* want?" he asked, dropping his hands into his lap. "Doesn't that count for anything?"

"It counts for everything. Just like what you want."

"And what do you want?"

"You," I said, pushing the chair back and standing up. I jerked my head toward the door and Dylan shoved his chair back.

Following me inside without another word, I listened to the way his feet shuffled against the wood floors as we headed upstairs to the playroom. I was still half-hard from the enthusiastic blow job he'd given me earlier in the morning, and even as he'd sat at the table and dribbled his heart out between us, the bulge between his legs hadn't yet faltered either.

"I want you," I said again, giving the waistband of his sleep shorts a yank down past his knees. He stepped out of them silently, standing naked in front of me. Dylan was so much more sure of himself now than he'd been before. Even with our history between us and the weight of his worries bearing down on our shoulders, none of that seemed to matter within the four walls of my playroom.

But I needed them to not matter everywhere else.

"How can I make you believe that you're it for me?" I asked. "What do I need to do?"

He squeezed his eyes closed, shaking his head quickly, a tear escaping from the corner of his dark lashes. "I don't know."

Scrubbing a hand down my face, I looked around before making a quick decision to change course, and I hoped it was the right one.

"Out," I said, frowning. "Up to the guest room."

"I don't want to play piano."

The set of Dylan's jaw made it clear to me he was itching for a fight again, and I was happy to oblige him. I knew now that he didn't fight me because he was really angry or unhappy with anything; he did it because he wanted to make sure I wasn't going to walk away from him when his mind got the better of him.

"Shut up." I dropped my pants onto the floor beside his and then grabbed his good arm, hauling up out of the room and up the next flight of stairs toward the guest room.

"Ouch," he grumbled, knocking into the banister.

"Green?" I asked.

"Not *not* green," he muttered.

I kicked the door to the guest room closed behind us, giving Dylan another shove across the room. There weren't a lot of furnishings in there—a queen size bed, a nightstand, his piano, and a full length mirror tucked into the corner beside an overstuffed arm chair. Walking around him, I moved the mirror from the corner to the wall so it faced the side of the bed, bringing Dylan's weary scowl into focus.

I pulled lube from the nightstand and sat down on the edge of the bed, wetting my hand and stroking my cock. I held his stare in the reflection, his entire body swaying as he watched me jerk myself off.

"I can do this with you every day if it's what you need, *pet*," I said, emphasizing the endearment that had felt so natural with him. At the sound of it, he shivered, his erection slapping against his stomach. "But I'd honestly rather we get to a point where you understand what I mean when I tell you I love you."

He licked his lips, and I shoved the lube across the bed toward him.

"Come over here," I demanded. "Get yourself ready for me."

Dylan picked up the lube and came around to a spot between my spread legs. His cheeks were dark pink as he slicked the fingers on his right hand, reaching around to tease them through his crack and around his hole.

"Bend over so I can watch." I didn't give him a chance to make the move on his own, instead threading my fingers through the hair at the back of his head and shoving him face first into my lap. His hot lips and stubbled cheek dragged across my thigh, but my attention was caught on the mirror, the reflection of his fingers pushing into his hole and prepping himself for me.

He moaned quietly when he pushed all the way inside of himself, and I tightened my fingers into his hair.

"What are you doing?" I asked him.

"Finger fucking my asshole."

"Why are you doing that?"

"You told me to," he rasped.

I hummed, petting down the hair I'd tangled at the base of his skull. He was knuckle deep into his hole, the sight enough to make my dick leak against his cheek.

"That's all you need to do to keep me happy," I whispered. "Just do what you're told."

"Yes..." He went quiet, the hiss of an unspoken word dying off with his silence.

"Say it," I prompted, pulling him up and spinning him around on my lap. With one hand on him and one on my shaft, I replaced his fingers with the tip of my cock, slowly lowering him down onto my lap. "Just do what you're told, pet. That's all I want."

He ground his molars together, head falling back as he sank down fully around my erection. When he was fully seated, I took a moment to admire the shape of our reflections. My chin on his shoulder and his head thrown back so he didn't have to see us at all. I admired the way his skin was paler than mine, how his legs were more slender. Reaching around, I traced my finger along the place where our bodies joined, and Dylan groaned, shivering and clamping down harder around my shaft.

"Look what you do to me," I whispered, waiting until he looked at our reflections to lift him off my lap. Inch by inch, my cock slid out of him until only the tip remained sheathed. "Look how hard you make me when you let me love you the way you need me to love you."

A shiver tore through him, shaking me down to my bones.

I'd told him once I would only give him what I could afford, and there was a time when my heart might not have made the list. Any chance I had to save myself had come and gone with the fleeting quietness of the way he moaned and breathed in his sleep, when he was beneath me. There was no cost that was too great now.

"I love you," I promised him, "and that means more than you know."

Dylan swallowed, another tear leaking out from the corner of his eye. Using only our reflections to find my way, I reached up and swiped it away, sliding my finger into my mouth to taste him.

"And I will keep loving you until you know it," I swore, "until you understand."

"Why?" he croaked.

I slid him back down until he was once again fully stretched around my cock.

"Why not?"

"What's in it for you?" he asked, voice watery.

"This." I leaned back to rest on my hands, keeping sight of us both still in the mirror. "Ride me. Oh, fuck. My perfect little pet, so desperate to be loved. To be needed."

He shook his head, more tears falling, but he lifted up and slowly started to fuck me, sending shockwaves up my spine every time he sank down around me.

"I will never *not* love you," I whispered into his ear. "My heart is not returnable, Dylan. This is not a transaction."

He didn't need to speak for me to know the thoughts racing through his mind, and he didn't need to tell me he understood because the change in his body was proof enough. Heat flared through him, radiating out like a lava spray over every inch of my skin where we were connected. He picked up his pace, stare still locked on mine in the mirror. I shifted up, reaching around and collaring my hand around his throat to slow his pace. He was too hot, too sweet, and I wasn't ready to come yet.

"I am in love with you." I kissed the words against the shell of his ear. "I will pay rent in Chelsea as long as you want me to, but this is where I want you. In my home, on my cock."

Dylan's chin quivered, hips stuttering.

"I will remind you every day until you believe it," I said, "until you trust it."

"I do trust it."

"Until you believe it," I corrected myself.

Dylan screwed his eyes closed and opened his mouth, a low wail falling out as his cock went rigid and spilled over his stomach.

"Watch," I warned, waiting until he pried his eyes open and forced his attention back to the mirror.

His stare darted from his face to mine, down to the way his cock was still spasming and shooting out jets of cum. I grabbed his hips and lifted him, snapping my own hips up roughly into him. Dylan cried out, catching my gaze in the reflection, and the wide-eyed hope that poured out of him was enough to send me over the edge. I slammed him back down onto my lap, fingers digging into his waist as I came inside of him.

Still in the overpowering throes of my own release, I sank

my teeth into his ear until he shivered on my lap, and then I said, "I love you, and there will never come a day when I don't."

He blinked hard, licking his lips.

I ran through the conversation we'd just had, realizing that with Dylan's shoulder on the mend, he was expecting the other shoe to drop. Every other relationship he'd had, save for Tate, but including his parents, had been a transaction or a trade. He wasn't expecting that from me because of any shortcomings on my part or his, but only because it was all he knew. I needed to show Dylan what the next stage of our relationship would look like, when we were together freely and by choice, not by need.

Regretfully, I lifted him off my lap, using my fingers to push any cum that had leaked out of him back inside. A last burst dribbled out of my cock, and I swiped it clean and pushed it inside of him for good measure before giving him a gentle push toward the door. He kept his eyes on my reflection for as long as he could, turning to face me directly when I'd pushed him too far from the mirror.

"Let's get you cleaned up," I told him, giving my shaft a squeeze and pushing myself to my feet. "We're going out."

CHAPTER 33

DYLAN

AFTER A SHOWER THAT ONLY INVOLVED SOAP AND SHAMPOO—NO more orgasms—Alex sat on the edge of his bed and watched while I got dressed. I could tell he paid extra attention to my shoulder mobility, and so did I. Always aware of every twinge and ache in the muscle, the tenderness was almost nothing more than a memory. I tried to ignore what my brain thought that meant, listening instead to the promises Alex made me about what it *did* mean.

"Where are we going?" I finally asked him when we'd made it down to the living room and I'd laced up my sneakers.

"Lunch," he said, not looking up from his phone.

I scratched my forehead, waiting for him to elaborate.

"Brooks and Tate are going to meet us," he finally said, sliding his phone into his pocket. Alex pushed his glasses up the bridge of his nose, eyes worried until he saw me smile, and then everything relaxed.

"I was just texting Tate this morning while you were asleep," I told him, jumping up off the couch.

It was the first burst of energy I'd felt since getting hurt.

Alex hadn't been keeping me prisoner or anything like that. I could come and go as I pleased, but I hadn't pleased. Things with Alex felt like a bubble, and I feared if I went too far out of the bubble, it would burst. Having lunch with Tate and Brooks seemed like a safe step. My best friend and one of his best friends.

"How fortuitous," he murmured, smiling gently and holding his hand out for me. Threading our fingers together was easy as breathing, and he pulled me against his chest like it was my home. I closed my eyes and breathed deep, the scent of his soap and detergent filling my nostrils, immediately putting me at ease.

"I called a car because I didn't want to deal with the bike in the city."

Alex kissed the top of my head before detangling my arms from around his waist and giving me a nudge toward the front door. Sure enough, there was a black town car idling in the middle of the street waiting for us. An unexpected tangle of feelings exploded in the middle of my chest, the concept of a hired car both familiar and foreign at the same time.

Once we were tucked safely in the back of the car, I dropped my head against the headrest and closed my eyes, letting out a long breath. Alex reached over and took my hand, giving it a squeeze.

"What's wrong?" he asked.

I pried one eye open and angled my head toward him. "Why do you think something's wrong?"

"Because I know you," he said, huffing out an amused breath.

I swallowed, letting my eyes close again. I focused on the

feel of Alex's hand against mine and the steady in and out of his breaths. The explosion in my chest settled into a simmer.

"Life is just weird sometimes," I told him with a lopsided shrug. "I grew up like this with big houses and rented cars, and I don't understand how something can be second nature and brand new simultaneously."

"Maybe you're not the same person you were before."

I licked my lips, gnawing on the bottom one until it felt raw.

"At least I know you're not with me for my money," I said with a self-deprecating laugh.

"And I know you're not with me for mine either."

I arched a brow, and Alex snorted a laugh.

"You would have rather walked over burning and broken glass than woken up with me in your room at the hospital," he said.

"That's not true." Then he raised a brow back at me, and I sighed inwardly. "Okay, you're not wrong. Maybe just broken, though, not burning too. It wasn't that serious."

"You know, Dylan..." Alex squeezed my hand. "Sometimes I wish..."

Before he could finish his thought, the car rolled to a stop in front of a ridiculously expensive-looking cafe, the kind my father frequented, where people had martinis with their lunch and then went back to the high rise offices and did a whole lot of nothing, getting paid more than I ever would.

"What do you wish?" I asked.

He gave me a small smile. "We'll talk about it later."

"You can't do that," I complained, falling out of the car after him. He glanced over his shoulder at me, rolling his eyes and tightening his fingers through mine so he didn't let go of me even as we exited the car.

"I'm pretty sure I can do whatever I want," he said, pulling me toward the front door of the restaurant. "That's literally our thing."

"Not if you're mean," I said.

He snorted.

"Mr. Burke," the host greeted Alex with a flirtatious smile that held a little too much recognition for my tastes. "Mr. Brooks is at your usual table."

"Mr. Brooks?" I asked.

"It's his last name," Alex said, walking us through the small restaurant to a booth in the corner. "Didn't Tate tell you?"

"No," I said.

"Astor," Alex greeted his friend, giving me a wink.

Astor Brooks.

Weird.

"Fuck off," Brooks said in response.

Tate jumped up from beside his boyfriend and wrapped me up in a hug so forceful it pulled my hand out of Alex's. Even without his touch, he was still close enough for me to feel him, like he was in my bones somehow.

Magnetized.

"I missed you so much," Tate whispered into my neck.

"I missed you."

"Are you good? For sure?" He pulled back enough to give me a worried onceover that looked so serious it had me laughing at him.

"For sure," I promised him.

"I have to go to the bathroom," he said to no one in particular, but before he finished the announcement, it was clear he was taking me with him.

Alex gave me an approving smile, sliding into the booth opposite Brooks and waving me off. For a moment, I was another version of myself and my shoulder had never failed me a day in my life. Tate and I had just moved into our apartment in Chelsea and I'd gotten hired at Tryst...there wasn't anything that could stop us.

Tate pushed me into the bathroom, reaching behind me to lock the door. Of course the restaurant was the kind of place that had private bathrooms. Jumping up on the sink to sit, Tate eyed me expectantly. I leaned back against the door and folded my arms in front of my chest.

"What?" I asked, a smile already tugging at the corners of my lips.

"What?" he repeated back to me, tone dripping with mockery. "Tell me *everything*."

"Everything about what?"

"About Alex."

I scrubbed a hand down my face, tingles pricking up the back of my neck just thinking about Alex and the things I knew Tate wanted to know. It wouldn't have been the first time we talked openly about the kind of sex we were having, but most of the time it was him talking about the sex he was having, not the other way around.

"What about him?" I asked, heat flooding my cheeks.

For some reason, I found myself wishing the conversation was about literally anything else. I would have rather talked to Tate about his sex life with Brooks or sang him another song about desperately needing to get railed by the man who'd taken his virginity and disappeared into the night.

"I've met their whole group." Tate was talking a mile a minute like we'd just seen each other yesterday, like I hadn't been deliberately lying to him after isolating myself from him for weeks. "Ford is great. He's a little sarcastic to them sometimes, but he means well. Kale is kind of a prick, but he grows on you. They were all fighting awhile because of, well…"

He trailed off, scrunching his nose together like he'd said something he shouldn't have.

"Because of what?" I asked.

"Uhm. Well. Because of Alex." He shrugged, like I should understand.

"What about him?"

"Alex and Beamer," he said.

I didn't need to connect the names to know Tate was talking about Alex's ex, the one who'd sent him into the reclusive spiral that had brought us together in the first place.

"I know about it," I said, the thought of Alex and his ex not tasting as bitter as it used to. "Kale was a prick about it?"

Tate visibly relaxed. "He's a prick about everything."

"I love that for him."

"I know about everyone, but Alex is kind of a wild card."

I worried my lower lip between my teeth, dragging my tongue across the spot I'd already bit nearly raw. Banging my head against the door, I pressed my fingertips against my closed eyelids, letting out a curse under my breath. I so desperately wanted things to be normal with me and Tate again, but I was standing in a ten-by-ten room with him, a giant wall between us. I was the one who'd built the wall and mortared it solid. Tate, the whole time on the other side trying to chip away at it with his bare hands while I kept layering it on.

Letting my arms fall, I blinked my best friend back into focus, smiling when I caught sight of his wide eyes and hopeful expression. He was the same as he'd always been, ready for me to join him.

"He's the best sex I've ever had," I told Tate, huffing out a laugh when he clapped his hands together like a giddy schoolgirl. "Like, consistently. Every time. It's never a miss. He's fucked me while I played piano for him."

"Oh, my God."

I nodded, blood rushing between my legs at the memory alone.

"What else?"

"You want more than that?" I laughed, pushing away from the door. Tate slid closer to the sink and I managed to haul myself onto the counter beside him.

"I want everything."

"The first time we hooked up, he spanked me until I cried and then made me clean my cum off the floor."

"Oh, my *God*, and you licked the floor?"

"No. Oh, God." I laughed, angling my body toward him so our knees touched. "He literally made me clean it. Like with bleach and a rag."

Tate slapped his hand over his mouth. "Shut up."

"Swear. And it made me so hard." I covered my face with my hands and leaned into him, dropping my forehead against his shoulder as I burst into an uncontrolled fit of laughter. "Like, what is wrong with me?"

"Brooks makes me cry before I come," he said, knocking the side of his head against the top of mine.

"In a good way?"

"The best way."

I thought about all the times Alex had made me cry and wondered if it was the same for Tate or different. If he found the same kind of rest and release that Alex always managed to give me with it.

"It's amazing," I said softly. "He's amazing."

"Does he make you happy?" Tate asked, jumping off the counter and forcing me to look at him. His expression had quickly turned serious, brows knit together. "You were so angry before."

I sighed, giving him an honest smile.

"I wasn't angry with him," I said. "I was mad at myself… for about a thousand different things and I took it out on him."

"That's good of him then."

"What do you mean?"

"He knew you needed to let it out." Tate's eyes crinkled in the corners. "And he knew he could carry it for you."

I swallowed thickly, the truth and weight of Tate's statement landing on my shoulders like an anvil. I'd been horrible to Alex before, and even though I'd apologized, I hadn't ever stopped to think about the fact he'd faced me willingly through the whole thing. It went so much more beyond the things I'd said before I got hurt. The way I'd treated him after, and he'd bore all of it so I didn't have to hold it any longer.

"Oh, fuck," I grumbled, dragging both hands down the front of my face as realization dawned.

"He loves you," Tate said, patting my knee.

"I love him."

All Alex wanted was for me to believe in the love he had for me, and I'd fought him and struggled through it, too caught in my own head over the whole thing. And fifteen minutes in a bathroom with Tate had thrown all of it into the sharpest and clearest focus possible.

"We have to get back to the table," Tate said, phone in hand when I looked up at him. "Brooks said the food is ready and they're waiting for us."

"I didn't even look at the menu," I said, jumping off the counter.

Tate unlocked the bathroom door and threw a knowing glance over his shoulder at me.

"You don't need to look anymore, do you?"

I waited until Tate and Dylan disappeared around the corner before settling into my usual seat, opposite my usual lunch companion.

"It's good to see you among the living," Brooks said, shoving the menu toward the edge of the table without bothering to open it.

"Is that a dig about Beamer?" I asked, flipping my menu open and looking down at it even though I knew the entree options by heart.

Brooks snapped it closed and pushed it toward his. "It was a commentary about how you've been holed up at your house since Dylan got out of the hospital."

"I swear you were just over." I tapped the side of my temple like I was trying to recall the event in question. "You drank two bottles of wine in my back yard."

"I had help."

I flipped him the bird, smiling. "So you do remember."

"As if I could ever forget your smiling face." Brooks flagged down our normal waiter. "But you know what I meant."

"Gentlemen," Tony, our waiter, greeted. "The usual?"

"Yes," Brooks answered before I could. "And a water for my partner, and…"

"Water for mine," I added.

"Happy to see you both with company today," Tony said.

I picked the menus up and passed them off, knowing neither of us was going to look at them and not expecting Tate or Dylan to be back in time to even bother looking.

"We can order while you're here," Brooks said, giving me a knowing smirk, which I did my best to avoid. "I'll have the steakhouse sandwich and my partner will have a cheeseburger."

"And you?" Tony asked, turning his attention to me.

I sighed, knowing I was about to answer all of Brooks' questions simply by ordering Dylan's lunch.

"Strawberry chicken salad and a grilled chicken on focaccia," I said.

"Right away, gentlemen."

As soon as Tony walked away, I shook an unimpressed finger at Brooks. "Don't start."

He laughed, holding up his hands. "I didn't say anything."

"You didn't need to."

"Things are going well then," he said.

I rolled my eyes.

"He was so temperamental the last time I saw him," Brooks went on.

I crossed my arms in front of me, knowing he wasn't going to stop until he felt he'd properly put me through it. Maybe I deserved it, having been in hiding so long after things with Car had gone south and then once again after taking Dylan home. But I didn't think Brooks could truly blame me for it.

"He still is," I said , defenses weakening.

"But you're up for the job."

"You knew I was the whole time."

"I knew you needed to be needed," he said, cocking his head to the side. "And Dylan…"

"Yeah." I swallowed, nodding.

"Things are better?"

"Things are really good, Brooks." I groaned, letting out a breath that rattled my lips. "I love him."

My best friend bit his lips between his teeth, fighting back a smile. I wondered if he'd bet anyone about the over/under on me falling head over heels for Tate's best friend. I'd just been a pawn in his little chess game the whole time.

"Say it," I prompted, swirling my hand in a loop so he would get it over with.

Tony brought our drinks, which offered me little reprieve.

"I don't have anything to say." Brooks grinned. "I'm just happy. Love looks good on you."

"I didn't say he said it back."

"Of course he said it back or the two of you wouldn't be here."

I bumped my head against the padded cushion of the booth, raising my glass to take a big drink of water. Swallowing, I debated the merits of throwing the rest of the contents in Brooks' face, but I knew he meant well. It was easy to be smug when you'd had the upper hand the whole time.

"It hasn't been easy," I finally said, shrugging. "But he's worth it."

"Of course he is."

"I talked to Beamer too."

That shut him up, and I smirked at him, glancing toward the bathrooms to see if Dylan and Tate were on their way back, but there was still no sign of them. I hoped Tate was going easy on him after how long it had been since they'd seen each other. I also hoped Tate didn't dislike me for his earlier assumptions about my relationship with Dylan. Things were complicated, or at least they had been before, and I knew I hadn't made the best first impression when it came to how things were between us. But Brooks had been right, it was what I needed…and what Dylan needed too. He needed to know I would fight for him and with him, and I had. I would.

"Aren't you going to ask me how that went?" I prompted, brow raised.

Brooks took a drink and steadied himself. "I'm offended I even have to. You know there was a time where I was the first person you called after something like that."

"Don't tell Ford."

Brooks snorted.

"It was good to talk to him," I said, glancing again toward the bathrooms. It wasn't that I was hiding the conversation from Dylan, but things were so fresh with us I didn't want him to think I was focused on someone other than him. Car and I were in a good place, or at least on our way to it, and I didn't want to jeopardize that over any misplaced jealousy. "Cleared the air a bit, I think."

"That's good."

"He told me I loved Dylan before I was ready to admit it to anyone."

Brooks tried. Bless him, he tried to stifle the smile that threatened to split his face in two, but he'd never been good at hiding his hand. Once the expression broke free, I rolled my eyes at him and reached for my water, spinning the glass around. It was heavy, the ice clinking against the sides, condensation slippery against my fingers.

"I hope you don't think that just because he's head over heels for that California prick, it means what the two of you had was any less special," Brooks said.

Car's voice was quiet in my head, kind.

Dalton knows where my loyalties lie.

That was great for him, for me...but did Dylan know where mine were? Did he trust it? I chewed the inside of my cheek, realizing that Dylan and I had done a good job about speaking to each other with half-truths and almost-promises. He deserved everything, though, and I wanted to give it to him.

I wanted to take it from him.

"He's a friend," I said to Brooks, meaning it for the first time in months. "We're friends."

"Good." Brooks pulled his phone out of his pocket and set it on the table just as Tony walked over with a tray full of food. The boys were still in the bathroom talking about lord knew what. As the food was served, Brooks tapped out a quick text on his phone before returning it to his pocket. "I texted Tate to come back."

The strawberries on top of Dylan's salad were as red as if they'd come out of a cartoon. I stared down at them, imagining the ripe juiciness of them.

"We should go back to the farm," I said. "A do-over."

Brooks chuckled, getting up from the booth to make room for Tate to slide in. He hadn't even looked over his shoulder to see them coming. Somehow he just *knew* that Tate was there and, fuck, I envied their connection even as I stood on my own accord, making room for Dylan to take his seat. He gave me a soft smile, looking happy and relaxed.

"Everything okay?" I asked, taking my seat and smoothing my napkin back over my lap.

"Everything's great," he said, bending over his salad and taking a deep breath. "Oh, God, these strawberries are wild. This looks delicious."

"They look fresh," I rasped, watching with careful focus as Dylan speared one of the strawberry slices with his fork. His lashes fluttered as his lips closed around it and heat pooled dangerously low in my belly.

"They're the best strawberries I've ever had," he said, stabbing another slice with his fork and shoving it toward me. "You have to try one."

From the corner of my eye, I could see the amused look on Brooks' face, but he graciously chose that time to stay silent. I licked my lips and opened, letting Dylan feed the strawberry slice into my mouth. It *was* delicious. Juicy and sweet and probably the ripest piece of fruit I'd ever had in my life.

"You have good taste," Dylan said, eyes locked on mine. "This is better than eggs."

"Up for debate," I murmured.

"Get a room," Tate griped from across the table, letting out a pained *oomph* when Brooks delivered a sharp elbow to his ribs.

Licking my lips, I forced myself to look anywhere but Dylan because it was far too simple, too much like second nature already, to make him my one and only focus.

"Speaking of strawberries and rooms, Alex just proposed a return trip to the farm," Brooks said, which had Tate immediately perking up. "A do-over, as it were."

"A first time for me," Dylan said, clearing his throat. "If I'm invited, of course."

"Why wouldn't yo—" Tate started to ask, only to get cut off again by another gesture from Brooks.

"You're invited," I said softly, turning to Dylan and taking his face into my hands. His cheeks were flushed, maybe from the conversation he'd had with Tate in the bathroom, maybe from the strawberries, or maybe still...maybe from me, from my hands on his skin, my fingers against his cheeks. "Everywhere I go, you have a place."

He rubbed his lips together, the outline of his teeth almost visible through the thin skin.

"I want you to come," I said next, giving him a small smile.

"Yeah?"

I nodded.

"Your friends must have a bad impression of me after last time," he said, ignoring the fact that one of my friends was sitting directly across from us and obviously had no problems with him at all.

"I love you," I reminded him. "That's what matters."

"No one has any feelings about you at all yet," Brooks said, crunching the toasted bread of his sandwich between his fingers. "Beyond gratitude."

Dylan fought against my hands on his face, almost yanking his entire body to swivel so he could look at Brooks instead of me.

"Gratitude?"

The air sucked out of the room, my lungs suddenly too big for my chest, my mouth and nose fully incapable of getting enough air into them for me to breathe. I opened my mouth to protest whatever Brooks was going to say next, but no sound came out, just a tired little croak that no one besides me even noticed.

"You brought him back," Brooks said simply. "More than any of us could ever do."

Then he bit into his sandwich like he'd said the sky was blue or the grass was green. Dylan swallowed nervously, clearly unsure of what to say to that, but also knowing Brooks had effectively ended the conversation with his silent dismissal. He picked up his fork and shoveled around some lettuce until he'd assembled a bite that had a little bit of each ingredient accounted for on the tines. I watched him eat, feeling proud and horny and weak and whole. Love was a terrifying feeling, I realized. Consuming and draining and so fucking necessary.

"You brought *him* back," Tate said, stare locked on my profile.

Dylan's cheeks flushed almost as red as the strawberries in his salad, but he didn't say anything to that. Just took another bite, chewed slowly and swallowed before reaching for his drink and washing it all down with a large sip of water.

Parched.

Love had me parched.

I threw a sideways glance at Tate, just long enough to watch him smile before shrugging one shoulder at me. He bit into his burger and moaned happily, wiping some melted cheese from the corner of his mouth.

"This is so good," he said to Brooks, who smiled softly. "You picked good."

"You picked good too," Dylan said.

I swallowed, like time around us had stopped and started up again before I'd even had a chance to notice. My lungs fit in my chest again, my heart beat steadily, if not a little faster than normal.

"What?"

"The salad," he said, offering me another strawberry, eyes sparking as he watched me come back into my body. "It's the best I've ever had."

WHEN WE GOT HOME FROM LUNCH, ALEX COULDN'T KEEP HIS HANDS off of me. As soon as the door to his house was locked, he was on me. My back landed against the wall and his tongue was in my mouth, his fingers scrabbling at my pants. I arched into him, the taste and smell and touch of him the most all-consuming thing I'd ever known.

"I'll pay for your apartment as long as you want to keep it," he said, breathless between nips and licks against the side of my neck. "But I want you to live here with me."

"Don't I?"

He smiled against my throat, the feel of his teeth against my Adam's apple bordering on dangerous. I knew he wouldn't hurt me beyond the ways I wanted him to, but the threat was there, enough to send a shiver up my spine and down through my fingers.

"You know what I mean."

"I don't think I do."

Alex hummed, sliding his hand up between us and

collaring my throat. He pressed me back against the door and leaned away enough to look at me. His pupils were dilated, black as the frames of his glasses as he dragged his stare over every inch of my face and then down my throat and back again.

Alex cocked his head to the side, baring his teeth. "Is there something you need, pet?"

"You."

"You have me," he said. "I'm yours."

Alex's fingers flexed around my throat and I sagged against the door, shuddering at the way his thumb and finger dug into the underside of my jaw. He cocked his head to the side, studying me silently, gaze roaming over my face, lingering on my lips before moving back to my eyes.

"I see," he said, even though I hadn't said anything. Even though all I'd done was breathe, swallow against his palm.

"See what?"

He nodded knowingly at me, tightening his grip on my throat. It was reflex to reach for his fingers, to try and pry him off my windpipe, but I wrapped them around his wrist instead.

"I don't mind proving it to you," he whispered, leaning in and pressing a deceptively soft kiss against the corner of my mouth. "I tell you I'm in love with you, that I want you to move in with me. It's not enough?"

"It is," I protested.

"Liar."

Alex sank his teeth into my lower lip, biting down until there was nothing more to do besides try to shove him off of me entirely. He held my throat, my stare, until my vision began to fade around the corners, darkening as saliva splattered out of my mouth with every ragged attempt at breathing.

"Go upstairs," he whispered, dragging his tongue across my lower lip, cleaning up the mess I made trying to fill my lungs. "Strip out of your clothes and go get yourself ready for me."

"In the shower?"

"I want you empty as you've ever been," he said, licking his way up my jaw to my ear. "I want to make sure that the only thing inside of you tonight is me."

Alex let go of my throat and I gasped for breath, sucking in a lungful of air before kicking off my shoes and heading for the stairs. My pants were already halfway undone, and in the bedroom, I made quick work of the rest of my clothes. My cock was hard as Alex ever made it, which wasn't anything new, but in a way I couldn't explain, something was different than the times before. With trembling and nervous fingers, I fussed with the shower attachments required for me to do what he'd asked.

It was far from the first time I'd ever done it, not even close to the first time he'd asked, but by the time the water ran clear, it took all my strength to hold myself upright. My entire body was on high alert, unsure of what was coming while knowing—at the same time—everything had changed. Maybe it was a change in me, I didn't know. I didn't have the brain cells to think about it because when I stepped naked and empty into the bedroom, wet hair still dripping onto my shoulders, I lost the ability to think at all.

While I prepped myself, Alex had made his way to the

bedroom. He was naked, that thick and erect cock of his in hand while he aimlessly stroked it, stare focused on the bathroom door I'd just emerged from. I sucked in a breath and stumbled, coming to a stop with over ten feet between us still. When he saw me, he let go of his cock and wiped his hands.

"I'm not scared of you anymore," he said, his tongue sliding back and forth across the front of his teeth.

"I didn't know you ever were."

He pursed his lips like the statement should have been laughable, but I'd meant it seriously. I couldn't imagine any world where a man like Alex Burke was scared of a man like me. I threw away a cushy and secure life for a dream and a prayer, and I'd managed to throw that away too. I had nothing beyond whatever he wanted to give me, and that didn't sound very intimidating at all.

"You're too brave for your own good," he said softly. "I wonder if that's where your stubbornness comes from."

"I'm hardly brave."

"You're here." Alex's cock jerked, slapping against his stomach.

"I'm here."

"I know myself better now," he said next, "because of you, I think."

"You don't have to lie."

He lifted a finger to silence me. "Stop talking."

I bit the inside of my cheek, swaying on my feet.

"Unless it's your safe word, don't say another fucking word unless you're certain it's something I'll want to hear." He paused, eye twitching. The space between us as insurmountable as the Grand Canyon, as small as a thimble. "It should go without saying, but if you need to safeword, I *want* to hear it."

"I understand," I told him.

He stared at me another second longer, then pulled my pillow off the bed and threw it onto the floor between us.

"On your stomach," he said, jerking his chin toward the floor. "Ass in the air."

"Yes, Sir."

The word was out of my mouth with absolutely zero thought. It fell out like it belonged with the yes, and a rush of adrenaline flooded outward through my limbs. I took three steps to the pillow and went to my knees, looking up at him.

"Was that green?"

He nodded quickly, head jerking. "Very."

I bent myself over the pillow, keeping my left arm folded between my body at the pillow. My ass in the air, I spread my legs and dug my knees into the carpet. Alex didn't move, waiting, stoic in front of me until enough of my nerves settled and I went still. The air conditioner kicked on, a blast of cool air ghosting over my exposed skin, and I shivered, rolling my forehead across the rug.

Alex walked around behind me, getting something out of the nightstand that I couldn't see. When he kneeled down behind me, the heat of him burned the backs of my legs.

"Do you remember the first time we slept together?" he asked.

"Yes."

"What were you thinking? During and after?"

"How much I liked it, how much I wanted it." I swallowed. "How much I wanted you."

"Why me and not someone else?"

Something cold brushed over my asshole and I startled, almost flying off the pillow, but he'd anticipated the jump. His palm pressed against the small of my back, urging me back into position overtop of the pillow. His question was fair and I wanted to turn it back around on him, but his lube-slick finger was back at my entrance, swirling around my rim before sinking inside.

"No one touches me the way you do," I said, words trailing off into a quiet groan. I turned my head to the side, resting my cheek against the rug and staring at the wall, wishing I could see him. Wishing we were in the guest room with the mirror that told all of our secrets to each other whether we wanted it or not.

"I find it hard to believe no one has ever fucked you with their fingers before," he said, adding a second and drawing a gasp from the deepest part of me. "Or their cock."

"The way you do it," I corrected, pushing back against his hand.

"Stop it." The fingers splayed across the small of my back inched toward my ribs, pinching the thin skin there until I winced. "The first time we were together, you hated that you liked it. That you liked me."

I didn't think I had anything to say in response that he'd want to hear, so I stayed silent.

"I hated that I liked you too," he whispered, drawing his fingers out and dragging them down toward my balls. Alex cradled my sac in his hand, testing the weight before closing his fingers around my balls and giving a less than soft tug away from my body. I cried out, in pleasure not pain, and my cock shot a burst of precum against the pillow.

Something new pressed against me, something hard and unforgiving. It was a toy, I realized with a start when it began to vibrate against my rim. Alex traced the shape of my entrance before sliding it into me with a satisfactory pop of my muscles around the flared base. The inserted part buzzed slow and steady against my prostate, the exterior piece pushing hard and insistent against the sensitive patch of skin between my asshole and my balls.

"Green?" Alex asked, taking both of his hands away and leaving me on the floor with that buzzing sensation already threatening to set me on fire from the inside out.

I squeezed my eyes closed and sucked in a breath, nodding.

"Green."

The first part of the color had hardly rolled off my tongue when Alex's hand landed against my ass with a crack so loud it bounced off the walls and echoed through the room. I should have known it was coming because Alex was predictable in his unpredictability. It had been so long since he'd spanked me, and with the first strike of his palm against my ass, he shoved all of the worries and feelings I'd been carrying in the pit of my stomach closer to the surface.

After the first hit, he paused, and I knew he was waiting for me to call him off if I needed it, but the thing I needed from him most was...

"More, Sir," I begged.

He spanked me a second time, a third, a fourth.

"You have no idea what it does to me to hear you call me that," he rasped.

Five.

Six.

Seven.

The pillow beneath my hips was soaking wet from my arousal, the vibration in and around me enough to already have me on the cusp of an orgasm.

"I'm close to coming," I warned.

"You can come as much as you want," he said, voice darkening when he let out a low laugh. "And then you can come as much as *I* want."

I dug the fingers of my right hand into the rug like I could brace myself for the onslaught, but there was no preparation, no retrofit that would hold me up through what Alex had in store. Somehow, in my bones, I knew I just had to give up and take it. But it wasn't in a bad way. I wanted it. I needed this so badly from him, to believe...

Eight.

Nine.

Ten.

Eleven.

His palm was hot against the tender place where my thigh turned into my ass when I came for the first time. The orgasm ripped through my entire body, from my toes to the top of my head, shaking me in rolling waves as I shot my load into the already ruined pillowcase.

I screamed, arching up off the floor and bracing myself with both arms, good and bad. My left shoulder didn't hurt at all. Nothing in my body hurt. I was pleasure, pleasure, perfect fucking pleasure, and Alex hadn't stopped spanking me. I lost count of the times he brought his hand down on my ass, briefly being aware that he tired out and changed sides before starting again with the same level of ferocity. Sweat beaded on my temples, and every strike of his hand against my bruised and tender backside was as perfect as a hug, tender as one of his after-sex kisses. The vibrating toy in my ass might as well have been a part of me, because Alex sure was.

"Green, Dylan?" he asked me.

I didn't realize I'd started crying until I opened my mouth to reply to him and the word came out sounding wet.

"Green," I promised. "Green. Green. Green."

CHAPTER 36
ALEX

Dylan's ass was purple and red, speckled with bruises shaped like my fingers and patches of gooseflesh the size of my palm. He'd come twice already, though I wasn't sure if he had even registered the second one. When I pulled the vibrating massager out of him, he whimpered, pushing his hips back toward me.

He was flying, and I was right there with him.

Pouring lube over my cock, I lined my head up with his quivering gape and pushed inside. Even with the prep I'd done with my fingers and the toy, his body was still the hottest and tightest place I'd ever been.

"Bear down, pet," I reminded him, petting my hands down the small of his back.

He murmured something mindless, but his body relaxed around me and the rest of my length punched inside of him.

Fuck.

"I believe it," he murmured, eyes open but stare focused somewhere far beyond the bedroom we were in.

Falling forward, I braced myself over top of him, putting my hand over his and tangling our fingers together.

"What do you believe?" I asked, dragging my nose through the trails of sweat and tears along his cheek. He was a mess. He was perfect. He was mine.

"You love me."

I hummed, pumping my hips against the bruises I'd just made, shivering with every moan and groan that fell out of his mouth. Dylan was so far gone I worried he might never come back down, but he flexed his fingers against mine, and that was enough of a reminder that for as high as we both were, we were still very present in the moment.

"I love you," I confirmed, snapping my hips, setting a pace with short and shallow thrusts that fucked my cock into his tightness and his slippery cock into the pillow beneath him. He grunted, hole clenching down around my dick. Bending over Dylan entirely, I pressed a kiss against the back of his sweat-slick neck. "And I love that you don't even know that you're coming."

"I'm wh—"

His words were garbled, and I reached my arm between the pillow and his stomach, catching spurts of his most recent release against the tips of my fingers. I banded my other arm around his chest and pulled us both upright. Rocked back onto my heels, Dylan sank fully down around me, opening his mouth but letting no sound out. I traced my cum-sticky fingers across his lower lip before pushing them into his mouth, flattening his tongue until he gagged.

Everything about him was perfect.

Perfect for me.

Dylan choked around my fingers, mostly dead weight on

my lap, but I couldn't blame him. I'd spanked and fucked him nearly senseless and I wasn't anywhere near being finished with him.

"Suck," I demanded, shoving my fingers deeper into his mouth until he sealed his lips around my knuckles and did what I'd asked.

Leaning back enough to hold us both upright, I let my other hand wander down his chest, stopping to tease and tweak his nipples before reaching his inner thighs. Dylan's cock burned the side of my hand like a hot poker, cum stains drying on his stomach, his legs, and his balls. Using my fingernail, I scraped some cum away, then sank my fingers down around the smallest sliver of skin I could grab. I pinched him so hard it hurt me, and every muscle in his body constricted and released.

The unforgiving hold of his channel around my cock sent a shockwave through me, and I clenched my jaw together, lifting off the floor to fuck my cock into him deeper.

"That's a good pet," I praised, releasing my fingers and moving an inch higher. "Just like that."

I pinched him again and he cried out so loud I thought the windows were going to shatter. Another wave of tension through his muscles and then the inevitable release. Dylan cried and stopped, started again and then stopped once more. I was relatively certain any feelings inside of him were now smeared across his skin, which was a clean slate for us both. Beneath our combined weight, my thighs shook, tense and aching. My mind was focused on Dylan and Dylan alone, but also treacherously close to going entirely blank to the point the only thing left in me was the unhinged need to mark him as mine.

"Do it again," I whispered, moving to a new spot and delivering another sharp pinch. He sobbed, but his body tightened down around mine like a vise. Baring my teeth, I dragged them across the back of his neck, ready to bite. "Make me come, Dylan."

I pinched him again and he sobbed, muscles clenching down around me harder than before. I moved my hand closer to the inside of his leg and found a new spot to torment, sinking my teeth into the side of his neck when the orgasm finally crescendoed at the base of my spine.

Dylan screamed my name, his body seizing out of his control as a weak burst of cum leaked from the tip of his cock, sliding down until it spread across my fingers. He was spent and he was as much mine as I was his. I came with a roar, which should have been embarrassing, and probably would have been were it not for the absolute raw and feral need of it.

With one final pinch, I shoved Dylan back down onto the pillow, fucking into him with so much force we ended up halfway across the room before I came back into my body. My fingers pressed so hard into the swell of his hips I could make out the feel of his skin against the places behind my fingernails, my cock buried so deep inside of him I never wanted it to see the light of day again.

On the ground, spread out like a starfish, Dylan's hips jerked as he shot what had to be his final load across my imported Persian rug before letting out one more whimper that toed the line between pleasure and pain a little closer to the edge than I normally liked to go.

"Sssh," I whispered, shifting our bodies and rolling Dylan onto his side. He whimpered as I brushed his hair back from his face, wiping the sweat and the tears away as I lay down behind him on my side and wrapped him up in my arms. "I've got you. I'm here, Dylan. You're safe."

"Safe," he whispered, barely more than a breath of air out of his mouth.

I licked my lips, swallowing down a tidal wave of emotions as Dylan sought out my hand. All he could manage was to hook his finger over my pinky before he lost consciousness entirely. His breathing settled into a slow and even cadence letting me know he'd fallen into what I hoped would be the deepest sleep of his life. I kept him in my arms anyway, getting comfortable on the floor behind him.

What I realized, in that hazy afterglow, that I'd not paid attention to before was that I needed it too. I needed the quiet opportunities to sit in the love that had blossomed and bloomed in the earlier moments. I needed to appreciate the way it was Dylan's trust and his belief in my love for him...my *need* for him...that gave us the peace we now found ourselves in. Closing my eyes, I kissed his neck on the place I'd bruised him earlier in the shape of my teeth, I told him I loved him, and then I let it be.

Sleep came as quick for me as it had for Dylan, and when I woke up later, I was disoriented and sore, completely unaware of the time. Dylan wasn't beside me, so I rolled onto my back and stretched out my legs. My thighs were tight from the short time I'd had him on my lap, my palm still sensitive from how hard I'd spanked him. Blinking the sleep out of my eyes, I pushed into a sitting position, expecting Dylan to be close but finding the bedroom empty.

Very empty.

He'd stripped the sheets off the bed and the pillowcase he'd made a mess of earlier in the day as well. The bed was remade with a fresh set of sheets, my duvet spread out almost as evenly as I liked it. If I didn't know better, I'd have thought Dylan was trying to erase evidence of what we'd done together, but the cum stains in my rug were...

Not there.

With a huff of quiet laughter, I rubbed my hand across the place I knew he'd leaked all over to find it soaking wet and smelling of lemons.

He'd cleaned up.

I imagined him on his hands and knees while I slept, scrubbing at the tight pile with a rag, his cock hard and wet again between his legs. I would liked to have sucked him off like that, let him make a mess of my throat while he cleaned up the mess he'd made of my one-of-a-kind rug.

Climbing to my feet, my own well-used cock twitching back to life at the thought of Dylan's obedience and servitude, I checked the bathroom and then headed downstairs. The light coming in from the front windows convinced me it was nearly dinner time, and I found Dylan in the kitchen with a spatula in hand and a glare on his face.

"Surprised to see you conscious," I said by way of a greeting.

His head snapped up, not surprised, but angry. Shooting daggers at me, he threw the spatula on the counter and held up my cast iron fry pan, a sticky and globby mess dripping toward the handle.

"I'm never going to get this right," he said, dropping the pan back down on the burner with a loud crash.

He braced himself against the counter, head hanging low between his shoulders. He still favored his weight onto the right one, but I wasn't going to lecture him about taking it easy on the left. He was almost finished with physical therapy and well on the road to recovery. His arm wasn't the issue, though, for once. It was the fact the sex we'd just had on my bedroom floor had been as transformative for him as it had been for me.

But whereas I'd woken up ready to dedicate the rest of my breaths to his happiness, he'd woken up and thought he'd be able to fry an egg in my cast iron pan.

It was maybe...the same thing, I thought.

"Dylan."

"Help me," he said quietly, sucking in a breath that raised his shoulder to his ears. He stepped back from the counter and scrubbed a hand down his face. Turning to face me, his expression was so earnest, so bare. I wouldn't say he looked defeated because that wouldn't have been further from the truth. His shoulders were squared, his eyes clear. He was defiant in his courageousness, unafraid—finally—of asking for what he needed.

I knew I'd heard him right, but I wanted him to ask again. I wanted to make sure he was as ready for the future as I found myself.

"Hmn?" I asked, raising a brow.

"Will you help me with the egg?" He gestured toward the pan.

Crooking a finger, I beckoned him away from the stove. He shuffled toward me, jaw working back and forth as he closed the space between us. I opened my arms for him and he walked right into my chest, knocking his forehead against the front of my shoulder with a frustrated huff. I wrapped my arms around him and kissed the top of his ear, the side of his head. He still smelled like sex, like sweat, like salt.

"All I've ever wanted was for you to ask." I raked my fingers through the short hairs at the back of his neck, smiling gently as he shivered against me. "Wanted you to know that I'd help you."

I led him back to the stove and handed him the pan. Without being told, he scraped the ruined egg into the trash. Even though he couldn't see me, I smiled at the back of his head, the tense lines across his shoulders. Dylan returned to the stove and set the pan on the burner, exhaling while he waited for me to help.

"Your pan is stupid," he grumbled.

"It just needs some patience," I told him.

"I'm not patient," he said.

Even though I could barely see him through the tears that had fogged up my glasses, I slid my arm around his waist and hauled him into my side. "I know you're not patient, pet. But lucky for us both, I am."

After that night, everything changed.

For the better.

For the first time in a long time, I felt comfortable in my skin, even though my skin itself was far from comfortable. Bruises shaped like Alex's fingers decorated my ass and the back of my thighs, aching every time I sat down or lay on my back and I'd spent a fair amount of time on my back since that day. On my back, my side, my front...there was no position, no room, no way Alex wasn't content to take me and claim me.

I found myself subconsciously reaching up and tracing my fingertips over the bite mark on the back of my neck. The shape of his mouth was one of my favorite memories, and I'd begun to treat the presence of it like a security blanket. Whenever I found myself unsure or uncomfortable in the following days, the tooth-shaped bruises served as a reminder I wasn't as lost as I felt. I'd dug my nails into the outline left by his canine when I asked him about going back to work, and I had my finger against it again while I shifted my weight from side to side in the entry area to The Black Door.

I'd worried that me going back to bartending was going to be the start of a fight. Alex had made it clear I didn't need to work, that I could waste away the days in his house and play music to my heart's content. If I got a show, I got a show, if not…he would be my captive audience of one. I appreciated—more than I had words for—the safety that offer allowed me, but I wanted to be back in the world again. Life with Alex was a bubble, a nice one, but a bubble nonetheless.

Venturing out for lunch with Brooks and Tate had resulted in some of the best and most emotional sex of my life, and I crossed my fingers that the more we let the outside in, the better things would get for us. And it was with that in mind that I'd proposed the idea of going back to bartending. Alex hadn't loved the idea, but he wanted me happy and work made me happy.

It was a Thursday afternoon, hours before the club was set to open, and Alex had called in another favor to see about me getting my job back there. I'd asked about going back to Tryst, only to be met with an emphatic *no*. I had opened my mouth to argue because the fight felt familiar and safe. I'd spent my entire life fighting for the things that meant the most to be, but I'd barely gotten one word out before realizing Tryst meant nothing to me at all.

The Black Door didn't mean much either, but it was a close alignment to the things in my life that did matter, now. Alex being one of them, the things he made me feel, a close second. Though, I imagined the two of them were much the same.

"Mr. Rivers." I looked up at the sound of my name, a wave of calm washing over me at the sight of the six-foot-tall and cinnamon red-haired owner of The Black Door. "Good to see you again."

I strained my ears to see if there was any hint of condescension in her tone, but all I found was sincerity and kindness.

"Just Dylan," I said, dropping my hand away from the mark on my neck.

Her mouth quirked into a sly smirk. "Just Dylan. Come on in, let's chat."

I swallowed my nerves and followed her into The Black Door. It wasn't the first time I'd seen the place empty with the lights on, but I hadn't had enough time to get used to the duality of the space. Being there at night when it was packed full of people, the air had a different weight to it. During the day, it was any other bar with glasses to clean and fruit to cut. The scent of sanitizer lingered in the air, and I fought against the way my dick stirred.

Of all the things I'd learned about myself by being with Alex, the near Pavlovian response between my legs whenever it came to cleaning up a mess was the least welcome. Popping a boner while wiping down the bar at the end of a shift was less than ideal, let alone the way it hurt and stretched when it happened in private.

The day he'd fucked me on the floor, we'd both fallen asleep, but Alex had passed out like a prince in a fairytale. He didn't even stir when I untangled myself from his arms, and when I bent beside him on my hands and knees to scrub my cum out of his carpet, the cleaner thick and potent in our nostrils...not so much as a snore or shift in position.

Me, on the other hand...

I'd gotten hard immediately, a feat considering the protest

in my balls as it happened. Alex had told me I didn't even realize I was coming half the time during that encounter, and judging by how much the new erection had hurt me, I believed him.

"Make me another one of those martinis you're so famous for," Athena said, climbing onto a bar stool and folding her arms up beneath her, resting her chin in her hand.

Everything about Athena Smith radiated sex and control, but in the least threatening way possible. There were plenty of people who were afraid of her, but she'd only ever given me scary vibes in the way an older sister would.

"I'd hardly say I'm famous for them," I said, making my way behind the bar.

"You'd hardly say a lot about yourself, I'm sure."

I didn't know what she meant, so instead of answering, I coated a frosted martini glass with vermouth, then reached for the gin. Making a good martini was simple. I didn't think there was any real trick to it, but I went through the steps in my head same as always. Same as Marigold had taught me the night she hired me at Tryst.

Maybe Tryst did mean something.

Or maybe it was just Marigold.

Sighing inwardly, I set the finished drink on a coaster and gave Athena a weak shrug of my shoulders.

"Don't look so confident, Dylan. It's off-putting."

My cheeks burned.

Athena raised the glass, sniffed it, then took a sip. After she swallowed, her tongue darted out, licking some gin from the corner of her mouth with a surprised hum.

"This has Marigold all over it," she said.

There wasn't a question or an accusation in her words. Just fact.

"She taught me."

"I remember." Athena slid the unfinished drink and the coaster toward my side of the bar. "How long has it been since you were behind a bar?"

I didn't have an immediate answer to her question. Time had blurred into a haze of physical therapy and sex, the days and nights sometimes unrecognizable from each other. I'd spent the first week after my accident so angry. Angry at Alex, at myself...and then I'd gotten angry at the nameless man who'd drugged me in the first place...Many of the days I found myself ass up in Alex's playroom had ended with a rash of tears working through all of those feelings.

Some of them made sense and some of them didn't. There was guilt and shame and misery, but running under all of it was a steady and resilient love for Alex that had continued to grow with each hour we spent together. Eventually, like a balm, the fondness I felt for Alex and the way he cared for me in return had smoothed over all the sharp edges of the other feelings and I'd started to feel whole again.

"Weeks," I said when I realized I still hadn't given her an answer. I could go back and check the calendar to see how many physical therapy appointments I'd been to, but I was fairly certain the question wasn't that important.

"And you didn't forget how."

"I'll never forget how to make a martini," I told her.

Athena tilted her head to the side, red waves washing over her shoulder and tickling down her upper arm.

"You're involved with Alex Burke now," she said, again not a question.

"Yes."

"Normally, there's a rather strict no fraternization with members rule."

This was it, the rejection I'd been waiting for. Another door that I'd managed to get open, now closing in my face. It was hard to look at it without weighing the loss against the loss I'd have incurred by being the man my father wanted me to be instead of the man I knew I was.

"Right," I said, tucking my chin toward my chest. "I understand."

"Normally," she repeated, climbing off the bar stool and smoothing down the hem of her short black shirt. "I'll get you back on the schedule, but whatever you and Mr. Burke get up to doesn't happen while you're on the clock."

The heat at the back of my neck had to be shock.

I had my job back.

Thankfully, instinct took over and I nodded at her, eyes wide. The door I was sure had closed was open again, and I found a glimmer of hope. Things with Alex were perfect and I had a job again, and a piano I could play whenever I wanted. Maybe things were going to be okay after all.

Maybe it would all be enough.

"It won't," I promised, coming out from behind the bar.

I wanted to hug her, but that wouldn't have been professional in the slightest.

"Alright then, Just Dylan," she said with a soft smile. "I'll have Grant make sure to text you an updated schedule."

"Are you serious?"

"It'll be good to have you back." Athena gestured toward the front door, summarily dismissing me.

I stumbled over my own feet, in a state of shock over how

easy it had been to get my job back. Alex was the one to get it for me in the first place and I hadn't been there long at all before getting hurt.

"Is this because of Alex?" I asked, righting myself and double-checking to make sure my shoelaces were tied.

"Is what because of him?" Athena arched a finely drawn-on eyebrow toward her lush red waves.

"That you're giving me another chance."

She studied me carefully, taking a measured breath like she was trying to buy herself time while deciding how she wanted to answer me. I was just about to tell her never mind when she spoke, "You know, my best friend wouldn't be married to the love of his life if he hadn't gotten a second chance, so maybe it's just me paying it forward."

Of all the answers she could have given me, that was the last I'd expected.

"Oh," I said, a little dumbfounded.

"Or maybe it's just because I have a soft spot for silly men who don't know which way is up."

"Either way, I'm not complaining," I assured her.

"I didn't think you were, Just Dylan." Athena smiled and tilted her head toward the door. "Keep an eye out for a schedule from Grant, alright?"

"I will. Thank you again."

She didn't bother with a closing, just offered me a nod before turning and striding back toward the hallway that held the door to her office.

With my heart slamming around my chest like it was trying to break out, I practically ran onto the sidewalk, bending over and bracing my hands against my knees once the door closed behind me. I was dizzy with excitement and the promise of what this meant, and I was anxious to call Tate and tell him, but more than that...

My phone vibrated before I could even pull it out of my pocket to dial, and Alex's name flashed across the screen.

"Hey," I greeted, still out of breath.

"How did it go?"

"You obviously know or you wouldn't be calling me five seconds after I got my job back."

Alex chuckled. "Congratulations are in order then."

"It's just a couple days," I said.

"I know."

"Of course you do." I straightened up and tipped my head back, finding a cloud shaped like a cat floating across the sky. "Thank you for this."

"I didn't do anything."

"You let me go back to work," I said.

"It's still your choice."

My heart immediately settled, the pinpricks of nerves that had stabbed themselves against my palms retracting and going still.

"And I choose you still," I told him. "Every time, Alex."

He hummed happily, smile loud in his voice. "Come home, pet. Let's celebrate."

DYLAN HAD BEEN BACK AT WORK FOR THREE WEEKS BEFORE everything went to shit.

He'd been working weekends for the most part, which was fine with me. I knew my friends had shown up the night before because, in addition to him murmuring about how much money they'd tipped him out at the end of the night, I'd already ignored their text about coming out in favor of staying home with a book. Being at The Black Door while Dylan worked was not my idea of a good time since keeping my hands off of him made me absolutely miserable.

So it had been three Saturdays in a row I'd gone to bed alone and woken just before sunrise with his warm naked body pressed against mine. Last night, I'd reached around the front of his chest, slid my hand down between his legs, and jerked off while pressing lazy kisses against the nape of his neck. I'd stayed up too late to ride him the way we both wanted, but we had all the hours in the day on Sunday for that.

I'd not expected to wake a handful of hours later alone, Dylan's side of the bed noticeably cold. I checked my hand, finding flakes of dry cum hidden in the bends of my knuckles, so I knew the hand job hadn't been a fever dream, but Dylan was nowhere to be found. Climbing out of bed, I padded downstairs to find Dylan at the piano, cell phone in hand and the most miserable look I'd ever seen on his face.

And that was saying something considering I was certain we'd met at both of our lowest points.

"You look like you've seen a ghost," I said, leaning against the door frame and regarding him with the weariness of a predator who'd spent a lifetime hunting and just wanted a rest. Things had been so good. They'd been perfect, but the tight stretch of his shoulders—even the injured one—led me to believe his mindset was far from where he'd been after coming apart in my arms hours before.

To my comment, Dylan snorted, a dismissive noise in the back of his throat before setting his phone face down on the top of the piano. He didn't need to look at me head-on for me to see the bags under his eyes, the frown lines around the edges of his mouth.

"Do you want to listen to me play?" he asked, fingers dancing softly over the keys and repeating a melody I was sure I'd heard somewhere before.

"I want you to tell me what's wrong."

"Is that an order?" He licked his lips, throwing me a sidelong glance before depressing the lowest bass note on the piano.

"If it needs to be."

Dylan sighed, letting go of the key before wiggling his

fingers and launching into the intro of a song that sounded like the most depressing serenade I'd ever heard. I hesitated in the doorway, debating the merits of closing the space between us or staying where I was. Dylan looked like he wanted to run, and even though I was confident I had the fortitude to catch him, I hoped it didn't come to that again. Deciding against sitting, I leaned my weight on the door frame while Dylan played the song, listening to the rough sound of his labored breathing after the last note sounded.

"Did something happen at work?" I finally asked.

Of course I'd worried about Dylan going back to bartending. We'd met at a bar and any rules Tryst had about fucking patrons hadn't mattered because he'd ended up at my house the first night. I knew Athena ran a tighter ship and I also knew she'd detailed her expectations to him because she'd sternly given me the same set of guidelines before she'd even agreed to interview him the second time. It wasn't that I worried Dylan was going to cheat on me—the thought had honestly never crossed my mind—but I imagined there had to be some kind of trauma lying dormant related to being behind the bar again. Dylan's shoulder was still stiff in the mornings or if he didn't move it often enough to keep the muscle working, and the last thing I wanted was for him to be reminded of that horrible night when he'd landed in the hospital.

Dylan didn't need to work, but I respected that he wanted to. That respect would end up in the dumpster if it compromised the foundation of our relationship, though. I should have made that clear when we'd talked about it the first time.

"No," he said, shaking his head, "nothing like that. Besides, even if it had, your little crew of trophy doms were there and so was Tate."

Dylan stopped abruptly like he'd swallowed down the rest of his sentence.

"Did you want to go there with me?" I asked, resting my head on the door frame. "We can go if you're not working."

Dylan flashed a quick smile down at the piano keys, but it vanished as fast as he had from our bed the night before.

"I'd like that," he said, "but that's not the problem."

"Green, Dylan?"

He answered with a rough nod and a whisper.

I strode toward him, collaring my hand around his throat and lifting him off the piano bench in one smooth motion. He grabbed my wrist, eyes wide, and then his back was on the bed, my knee shoved between his spread legs, and our mouths less than two inches apart.

"Tell me what's gotten into you," I said, nipping at the corner of his lower lip. "Tell me why my favorite pet was not in bed and ready to get fucked when I woke up this morning. Tell me why he was in here sulking at his piano instead of coming on my cock."

Dylan blinked slowly, letting his lashes flutter and close. He exhaled, sinking down into the mattress, going pliant beneath me. I shoved my knee higher between his legs, making contact with his balls and pushing until he gasped.

"My dad," he rasped, throat bobbing against my palm. "My dad called me last night."

My first instinct was to let go of Dylan's throat, help him into a seated position, and ask him to tell me more, but down to the marrow of my bones, I knew that was the wrong course of action. That might have been right for someone other than him, other than me...but that wasn't what Dylan needed and it sure as shit wasn't what he asked for. I tightened my fingers around his throat and dragged my lips up toward his ear.

"Who cares?" I asked, absolutely serious. "You have me now. My home, my good will, my fucking money."

My name.

I didn't say the last part out loud, and Dylan arched his head back, gasping when I bit his earlobe hard enough to leave a mark. The bruises on the back of his neck from where I'd bit him weeks before were finally faded into nothing, and every day I found myself fighting against the primal urge to mark him again...and again, and again, and again. I wanted to mark him permanently, make sure everyone knew who was responsible for him.

It sure as shit wasn't Russell Lang.

Not anymore.

"The hospital sent a statement to his house," Dylan said softly.

I released the pressure on his throat so he could speak, but pushed harder between his legs with my knee to compensate for the loss. Dylan groaned, spreading his legs wider.

"Go on."

"It was paid."

"I know," I told him. "I paid it the day you were discharged."

"Why?"

"Because I wanted to. Because I can."

Dylan hummed, letting out a breath that sounded like a restrained cry. He opened his eyes, lashes ghosting across my cheek and I moved so I was more over him, so I could see him...kiss him.

"I'll pay you back," he whispered.

"No, you won't."

"It'll take a while."

"Your money is no good here," I told him, tracing the shape of his lower lip with my tongue.

"I'll pay you with sex then," he teased, flinching as the words left his mouth. It wasn't too soon, though. The history of how we came to be wasn't something I was ashamed of, and I didn't want him to feel that way either.

"You can't afford my rates," I assured him, shifting my weight so I was over him fully, one hand on either side of his head. My glasses hung low on my ears, but I wanted to see his expression so I could be sure he understood the truth of what I was going to say next. "You know if I had my way, you wouldn't work, Dylan. You would stay here like you deserve, my fucking spoiled and pampered pet."

He moaned, the sound vibrating through me and making my cock almost instantly hard.

"I'd love nothing more than for you to allow me to take care of you the way I want to, but I respect that autonomy matters to you."

"Why not both?" he asked, smiling against my lips.

"You have both," I said, "at least, as much of the first as I can manage while you insist on making drinks for men who will never be as lucky as I am."

Dylan's cheeks flushed a bright red and he licked his lips, pupils dilating as he stared up at me.

"Is it...are you going to get mad about it? Later on?"

I shook my head quickly, needing him to know just how serious I was with my promise to him. How much I meant everything I'd said up to that point and everything I would tell him after.

"I love you," I whispered, kissing his temple, his hairline, his ear. "I know I don't tell you often, maybe I say it less than you deserve to hear it, but I love you and I'm going to love you for the rest of my life. I'm going to take care of you for as much and as long as you'll let me. If you really want to pay me back for the hospital, you can."

Beneath me Dylan whimpered, and then laughed. "I don't."

"Will you let me buy you a new guitar?"

"Yes," he whispered.

"Will you let me enroll you in cooking classes?" I teased next, kissing the shell of his ear.

"Why don't you just buy normal pans?"

"Deal."

Shifting my weight, I gave one last burst of pressure to Dylan's cock and balls, then rocked back onto my heels. Spread out on the bed, he looked far less distraught then when I'd found him at the piano, and it was impossible to pretend that didn't give me a violent rush of pride and possession. Licking my lips, I adjusted my glasses back onto my face before letting my hands fall softly against Dylan's thighs.

"What do you want to do about your dad?" I asked, mouth pulled into a half-frown. "What did he say to you?"

"I didn't answer. He left a voicemail. It was just mean."

"What did he say?" I asked again.

"He wanted to know I'd gotten the money." Dylan swallowed, jaw tight. "He asked if I'd finally given up on music and gotten a real job."

"Music is a real job."

"If it was real, I wouldn't need to bartend."

"You don't need to bartend," I reminded him. "You want to."

"I..." He snapped his mouth closed and shut up. Dylan's eyes went wide for a second, and the flush on his cheeks from earlier spread down toward his throat and chest.

I arched a brow. "You?"

"I don't want to bartend so much as I want to contribute."

"The things you give me here count far more than any amount of money you could ever bring in," I said. "Even if you worked for your father or for Kale or Ford or anyone...I have more than enough money from my investments to last the both of us the rest of our lives. The last thing I need is more money. What I need is more *you*."

"Alex, I—"

"If working makes you whole, then I support it, but I don't want you to think for one second that the only way you can contribute to this relationship is financially."

"My dad—"

"Is a piece of shit," I interrupted. "Brooks and Ford have done deals with him in the past and your dad is not reputable by even the furthest stretch of the word. I'm glad you don't work for him. I'm glad you're not like him."

"Alex."

I swallowed the rest of my commentary. "Dylan."

"I've never been in a relationship with someone who doesn't want something from me."

"I want plenty from you," I assured him. "I want everything."

He rolled his eyes, giving his hips a wiggle, but all it did was draw my attention down between his legs to the bulge that hadn't quite settled since I'd sat up.

"You know what I mean."

"Yeah," he conceded, reaching up and curling his fingers around my waist and pulling me back down on top of him, brushing his lips across mine with a sense of finality. "I think I finally do."

Alex bought a brand new set of pots and pans, and while I sat at the island and watched him take each piece out of the box, I blocked my parents' phone number. I hadn't gone into detail with Alex about what the message from my dad had said, but that didn't mean I hadn't thought about it almost every day since he'd left it. In fact, I'd thought about a lot of things since I'd gotten that voicemail, the most prevalent of which being if I really wanted to keep working or not.

I struggled sometimes to reconcile the differences between the way my dad controlled my access to money against the way Alex shared it so freely with me. I wasn't going to wake up all of a sudden one day and suddenly unlearn a lifetime of conditioning around money and the expectations that came with it, but Alex was right when he said he was a patient man. He was far more patient and understanding than I would ever be.

After pulling the small fry pan out of the box, he stopped and pulled his cell phone out of his pocket, adjusting his glasses and squinting at whatever had shown up on his screen.

"Everything okay?" I asked when his easy smile began to tilt down into a frown.

"It's fine." He dropped his phone onto the counter and set to tearing down the now empty box. "Just the delivery on your guitar is delayed."

"You ordered one?"

"Of course."

"How did you know what kind I wanted?" I asked, head cocked to the side in amusement.

In reality, it didn't matter what kind I wanted. A guitar was a guitar and being cleared to play again was enough. I would have managed it on a box with rubber bands if that was all Alex had gotten for me.

Flattening the box, he folded it in half, pressing it against his chest and turning to face me. "You told me once. I couldn't remember the model number, so I asked Brooks to ask Tate."

"Tate doesn't know a thing about instruments."

"But he had pictures of the one you had before and it wasn't terribly hard to figure out it was a Martin D45."

I dragged my tongue across the front of my teeth trying to make sense of the casual way he'd said that to me. The work he'd done to get me what I needed without bothering me with the details of it. It was more than anyone else had ever done for me before and more than anyone would probably ever do again.

"I love you," I said softly, deciding in that moment I was going to call Athena and thank her for the opportunity to return, but let her know bartending just wasn't for me anymore.

"I know." Alex came around the island and kissed the top of my head. "I'm going to go throw this out."

Alone in the kitchen, I swiped open my messages with Tate.

You schemer.

TATE

Did your present come?

It's late, but he told me about it.

I hope he got the right one.

He did

Of course he did.

He loves you.

I know.

Has he talked to you about the farm?

Not yet.

We should go again, but it's hard with you working the weekends.

I debated the merits of typing everything out to Tate, but didn't think my fingers had the stamina to get through it, so I called him instead. He answered on the first ring.

"It wasn't a surprise or anything," Tate said instead of hello.

"I didn't think it was." I laughed. "But I've been working weekends so that's probably why he hasn't brought it up."

"Is work a sore subject?"

"Not at all, but...I'm thinking I'm going to quit."

Tate made an amused sound on the other end of the call. "I can't say I'm surprised."

"Why not?"

"You've never *wanted* to work," he said, and I could picture the roll of his eyes. "You worked so you could play music and now you can just play music."

"I mean, not really."

"You're cleared, aren't you?"

"Yeah."

"So it's a new development," he said. "It makes sense to me that you quit your job so you can focus on music."

I scrubbed a hand down my face with a sigh.

"It's a lot of work sometimes to remind myself that his love isn't conditional," I said. "It's what I'm used to."

"Hey! My love isn't conditional," Tate raised his voice at me in jest, and I missed my best friend so much.

"I know," I told him, blinking back a wave of unwanted tears. "You were the first."

"That's hardly..." He trailed off, both of us realizing I was right.

I cleared my throat. "Anyway. I'll bring up the farm. But won't Boston care if we keep inviting ourselves to his house?"

"My understanding of the situation is no."

On the other end of the house, the front door closed and I slid off the barstool. "I'll let you know what he says."

"Let's get together soon," Tate said. "Without them. Just like old times, right?"

The tears I'd managed to hold back finally escaped, freely making their way down my cheeks and my jaw.

"Yeah," I choked out, hoping he couldn't hear the wetness in my voice. "Just like old times."

"Brooks is calling," Tate said, happiness woven through his tone. "I'll talk to you soon, Dylan."

"Yeah, bye."

I barely managed to disconnect the call before letting out a sob strong enough to send me to my knees in the middle of the kitchen. The slap of Alex's footfalls raced down the hall and he was there—like always—wrapping his arms around me and holding me up before my knees hit the floor.

"What's wrong?" he asked frantically, pushing my hair out of my face and scanning my face for any sign of injury. He dragged his hands up my arms, going softer on the left side when he reached my shoulder. "Did you hurt yourself?"

"No, I just..."

Another sob ripped out of me, and I grabbed Alex's shirt in my fist, holding onto him for dear life. I shook my head, gasping a breath and pressing myself tighter against him. He rocked back onto his heels and took us both the rest of the way down to the ground. Bearing the brunt of both our weights, Alex managed to cradle me on his lap, stroking his fingers down the center of my back until I was able to calm myself.

Quieting down, I flexed my fingers, letting go of the sweaty mess my hand had made of the front of his shirt. He kept his hands moving over me, the soft and steady pace up and down the length of my back until my cries died down into sniffles.

"Are you hurt?" he asked me again, quieter but no less urgent.

I shook my head.

"I've been thinking about a lot lately, and I just got off the phone with Tate, and he told me that you loved me."

Alex chuckled, kissing the top of my head. "I didn't think that was news."

"It's not, even if I still...that doesn't matter. He said we should get together like old times, just me and him."

Alex's hand faltered, then resumed its track up and down the knobs of my spine.

"Did you not want to?"

"No, I do." Another wet cry tumbled out of my mouth and, embarrassingly, I wiped my snotty nose on his shirt. "It was just so nice to think about things being the way they were before."

Beneath me, Alex tensed, but didn't say a word.

"The way they were before," I said quickly, "but better because I have you now."

"Better than before," he said, tightening his arms around me.

"I want to quit my job," I told him.

"Okay."

That was it.

That was the extent of the conversation. I didn't need to tell him anything else, didn't need to explain myself or justify it. My brain gave me a flashback of the conversation I'd had with my parents when I wanted to pursue music, the argument, the bartering, and with Alex there was none of that. Being with him was easy as breathing and just as necessary for my survival.

I wiggled my right arm until Alex relaxed his hold on me enough for me to lean back. Swiping the tears off my face, I gave a valiant sniffle. "Tate said something about going to the farm."

Alex chuckled, tracing his fingers across my cheeks to wipe the rest of the drying tears away. "I take it you're done with the first part of the conversation?"

"Was there more to it?"

He gave me a quick smile, eyes sparkling. "No. I'm just still getting used to this version of you."

"What version?"

"The one who isn't scared to ask for what he wants. What he deserves."

I swallowed thickly, pinching my nose in hopes it would stifle the running. I was still getting used to that version of me too. My own unfamiliarity with myself was part of what had inspired the outburst in the first place because even though Tate was correct that it would be like old times, it would also never be like old times again.

And I was glad for that.

"And what do I deserve?" I prompted, blinking slowly.

"Whatever you want," Alex rasped, pulling his lower lip into his mouth to worry it with his tongue. "So, you want to go to the farm?"

"Tate said we'd been invited."

"It's an open door," he said.

"I missed it last time."

"So did I." Alex's mouth twisted into half a smile. "But maybe that's because I was meant to be there with you."

"I should have gone."

He shook his head, pressing his finger over my lips. "Don't start that. You can go this time and all the other times."

"Okay." I kissed the pad of his finger, and he bent it at the knuckle, pushing it in past my teeth.

I opened for him, some sort of conditioning kicking in because my dick immediately twitched to attention. The response must not have been lost on him because Alex added a second finger and a third, depressing my tongue as he stretched his way toward the back of my throat. Reflex had me pulling away when the first gag retched up from my throat, but he moved quicker than me. With his other hand cradled around the back of my head, Alex pushed his fingers toward my throat, sliding deeper when I gagged the second time.

"Right here," he said, catching my stare and holding it. My jaw ached, spread wide to accommodate the stretch of his hand between my teeth. "Right here is where my cock goes next time you suck it. Are we clear?"

"Yes, Sir," I said, the words garbled around the intrusion in my mouth.

Alex leaned in close, kissing the top of his fingers and my upper lip, sliding his tongue around his knuckles and over my teeth. I wanted him to kiss me more fully, wanted access to his mouth, and the way he made out with me even with his hand in the way was enough to have me fighting against his hold on my head in every direction I could manage to move.

"I love when you call me Sir," he whispered into my mouth, giving his fingers one last push down my throat before releasing his hold and taking both of his hands away.

I gasped and sputtered, coughing and throwing up spit all over the kitchen floor as I tried to catch my breath. Alex stood, bringing me eye level with his thick erection, but instead of taking off his pants, he reached behind him and pulled his shirt over his head. Tossing the tear-stained and crumpled garment onto the floor, he stepped away, palming his cock just out of reach.

"You made a mess on the floor again, Dylan," he said quietly, shoving his hand into his pants and stroking his cock. "You know where the cleaning supplies are. Clean up after yourself and then come find me."

CHAPTER 40
ALEX

I WENT INTO THE PLAYROOM AND WAITED FOR DYLAN TO CLEAN UP after himself. He went to the bedroom first, footfalls thumping soft against the landing when he reversed course and headed for the playroom. Dylan was naked when he appeared in the doorway, flushed from the tips of his ears to the middle of his chest. His long erection jutted out from between his legs, proud and wet.

"You're making assumptions," I said, pulling down the fly of my pants and taking my cock out for him to see.

"Am I?"

I arched a brow. "Getting bold?"

"Getting smart," he countered, taking a step into the room. "I understand you better than before."

Rubbing my lips together, I swallowed down a lump of unexpected emotion. "And what is it that you think you know, Dylan?"

He took another step toward me, then another, stopping inches away from me.

"I know that you give me everything I need."

"I've hurt you plenty in this room," I reminded him. "I've bruised your ass nearly black and made you cry so hard you lost the ability to speak."

My cock twitched at the memory, and I gave my length a slow overhand stroke from root to tip.

"I needed that," he whispered, "every time."

"And what do you need now?"

"You."

"You have me," I said.

Dylan's lips lifted into a small smile, the pink tip of his tongue barely visible between the sharp edges of his teeth.

"I want you to fuck me like you're paying me for it." He pressed the side of his thumb into the slit of his dick, eyes rolling back as a full-body shiver rushed over him.

Without thinking, I surged forward and grabbed him by the wrist. I had his arm twisted up and his back against the wall so fast, he didn't even have time to whimper. I leaned in close, dragging my nose up the burning hot slope of his neck.

"No touching my toys without permission," I warned, nipping his earlobe.

Dylan shivered against me. "Yes, Sir."

It was so rare for him to call me Sir, every time it happened was like opening the best kind of present on Christmas morning. I'd never been one of the kinds of men who demanded it of partners. I didn't want the honorific if it felt disingenuous, and so often I found the whole yes sir, no sir game to be entirely too performative for my tastes, but with Dylan...

He meant it down to the marrow of his bones.

"What's your safe word?" I asked.

"Juilliard."

"What's your color?"

"I'm so fucking gr—"

Before he could finish, I crashed our mouths together, fucking my tongue past his teeth so I could swallow his consent into the most depraved part of me. Tightening my grip on his wrist, I notched my knee between his legs and gave him another rough shove against the wall, hard enough to push the breath out of his lungs so he needed the air from my mouth to breathe. Against my hip, Dylan's dick spasmed and leaked, already so close to spilling over.

With our mouths still sealed together, deepening the kiss with every swipe of my tongue against his, I reached down and took his cock in hand, stroking him with short and rough twists of my wrist until he thrashed against the wall, against my chest.

"It hurts," he whined. "So tight."

I hummed, releasing not just his cock, but my hold on his wrist. Stepping back, I scrubbed a hand down my face to steady myself. The sight of him leaning away from the wall to chase after me was as much of an aphrodisiac as the desperate little sound that fell out of his mouth when he realized the kiss had ended.

"Why did you stop?" he asked, panting, hand still twisted up the wall even though I no longer held him there.

"You complained."

"It hurt."

I gestured toward his violently red erection. "That looks like it hurts too."

"It does."

"Which is worse?" I asked, licking my hand and making a fist around my own dick.

He thrust his hips away from the wall. "This."

"Good." I nodded. "Get on your knees and thread your fingers together at the back of your head."

Dylan's shoulders sagged on the exhale, but his knees hit the floor without an audible protest. He lifted his arms and wove his fingers together, strands of his hair sticking out from between his knuckles.

"How's your shoulder?" I asked, stepping closer to him.

"Hurts less than my dick."

"I bet a lot of things hurt less than your dick," I said, tracing the slick tip of my cock across his lips. "But your jaw isn't going to be on that list for long. Now open."

Staring up at me through the dark fan of his lashes, Dylan opened his mouth and stuck out his tongue, groaning when I slapped my dick against it. I eased an inch in, making sure his teeth didn't scrape my shaft as I made my way inside. I fucked him like that for a minute with his mouth wide open and spit running down his chin, then I stepped into him, pushing the thickest part of my cock past his teeth. To stop him from running, I covered his tangled fingers with my hand, holding him steady as I pushed the rest of the way into his mouth.

Dylan gagged around my thickness, the muscles of his throat convulsing around the head of my cock. Gritting through the waves of pleasure his mouth gave me, I waited for his gagging to settle down, then I pumped my hips forward, getting another half inch into him.

"You're such a good listener, pet," I praised him, pushing him forward until his nose was buried in the trimmed hairs at the base of my dick. His breath puffed hot and urgent against me, and I groaned, a pulse of precum spurting straight into the back of his mouth.

He choked as the small breaths through his nose quickly

became not enough to sustain his breathing in the way his brain preferred.

"This is where I always want to be, Dylan. The deepest and darkest parts of you. I want to be under your skin, in your bones."

He blinked hard, tears leaking from the corners of both eyes, racing down his cheeks and mixing with the spit on his chin.

"Make me come," I told him next, letting my hands fall to my sides. "Make me come so I can make you scream."

Dylan's nostrils flared and he tried to close his lips around my cock, pulling back enough to bob up and down my thick length. His mouth was a mess, jaw stretched as far open as it had ever been before. Saliva flying and tears flowing, Dylan curled both of his hands around my thighs. He didn't have to tell me it was to stop him from touching himself—I knew it wasn't for balance.

Closing my eyes, I dropped my head back and moaned, giving myself over to the heat of his mouth, the presence of his body. The man on his knees in front of me was the man of my dreams, of that I had no doubt. He'd somehow been built just for me, to scare me, to test me...to love me.

And for me to love in return.

"I'm coming," I warned, pulling out enough so I could watch cum shoot out of my cock and paint his tongue a creamy white. It was hard to keep my eyes open, heat igniting my spine and setting my legs on fire, but the sight of my cum on his tongue, the tears and spit on his face, the sated happiness of being used clear on his face, it was all worth the struggle.

Before he could swallow, I pulled out of his mouth and

pinched his cheeks together, puckering his face like a fish. Dylan panted, body swaying, hands still held behind his head. I knocked them down to his sides, noticing the slightest twitch in the corner of his left eye when his shoulder fell back to its normal positioning. He was out of therapy and well on the road to recovery, but it was clear he still needed a little special handling.

"Spit it out," I told him, smirking at the disgruntled expression that flashed across his eyes.

"Where?" he asked, the word garbled.

"Onto the floor."

Dylan made a sound of protest, and I gripped his face tighter, yanking him away from the wall. He fell forward, catching himself on his hands before landing flat on the ground. Cum trickled out of his mouth, and I let go of him so he could spit the rest of it into a puddle beneath him.

"Was that so hard?" I asked.

"It's a waste," he complained.

"You'll thank me before you're finished," I warned, fisting his hair and pulling him forward a few feet. Dylan yelped, my hand too tight in his hair, and then I shoved him flat onto the floor, his cock caught between his stomach and the pool of my cum he'd left on the floor.

I shoved my pants down to my ankles and stepped out of them, kicking them out of the way as I searched the room for a bottle of lube. My cock was empty but still hard, and Dylan's ass was still bruised from the last time we'd played, a dangerous combination for him...not me.

I found the lube by the spanking bench, and I put more on my shaft than he deserved before sinking to my knees behind him and spreading his ass open with one hand.

"Make this easier for me," I told him, and he reached back, pulling his ass apart and showing me his hole. "Green?"

He tested the stretch on his shoulder before answering, "Green."

"The only part of you that you can move without permission is your left arm, do you understand me?"

"Yes, Sir."

Smoothing my hand down the slope of his arched back, I pushed my cock against his hole. I wasn't going to go in without prep, even though the thought of it excited me.

"You're perfect for me," I told him softly, teasing my finger around his rim, pressing the tip inside.

"Sir."

I pressed in up to my last knuckle, not delaying in adding a second finger and a third. The need to get my cock inside of him was out of my control, and watching Dylan fuck a puddle of my cum on the floor while I fucked his ass with my fingers wasn't helping the situation at all. He moaned and lifted his hips, chasing more of my hand and then more of my spend, humping the air when I pulled my fingers free of his hole.

When I pressed my cock into him, he shouted out in relief, the cry turning into a sob as I sank into him fully. With my fingers spread around his hips, I yanked him back the rest of the way onto my shaft, grunting low in my throat when his muscles flexed around me. It was over quick after that. I fucked him hard and fast, pressing him into the floor so his cock dragged through the mess from my first orgasm, pounding him harder when he screamed through his own release.

I'd have to get the floor refinished by the time I was done with him.

I was out of breath by the time my second orgasm found me, Dylan already reduced to nothing but tears and cum and bones beneath me. His legs were splayed wide like a frog, and I hoisted him into the air, fucking him down into the floor. The bow of his back was a work of art, and I came so hard in him, I imagined it shot straight into his guts.

My cock thickened and pulsed as I poured myself out inside of him, and Dylan sobbed, thanking me over and over again. The aftershocks of my orgasm still rippled through me when I grabbed his thigh and spun him onto his back. I thrust into him two more times, falling forward overtop of him and sinking my teeth into his neck like a wild animal claiming a mate.

He found his strength after that, wrapping his arms and legs around me, neck arched as if to give me better access to the sensitive skin I was so fascinated with bruising. Biting, I twisted my teeth then licked the bruises and divots left by my mouth. Dylan's fingers scrabbled against my back, hole tightening around my shaft as a burst of heat leaked out of his cock and smeared my stomach.

"I love you so fucking much," I whispered, licking his ear, his temple, the tears from beneath his eyelashes.

"I love you." His words were watery, but clear. "Oh, fuck. I love you. I love this. Thank you. Thank you, thank *you*."

I loved Dylan Rivers.

I wanted to marry him.

And there was no way I would ever allow him to be part of the first failure of my life.

Swallowing down the promise to myself, I rubbed my cheek against his, then I gently slanted our mouths together and kissed him until we were both hard again, ready for more.

IT TOOK A MONTH AND A HALF FOR US TO FIND A DATE TO GO TO THE farm that worked for everyone. In the meantime, life went on. I quit The Black Door, my guitar finally showed up, I'd played two shows, and things were starting to get back on track. Alex and I had settled into a routine that involved eggs for breakfast every day, and I'd only ended up in the corner with one held between my nose and the wall on one occasion.

It had been my own fault—my fears and my ingrained beliefs getting the better of me one night and I'd been particularly unfair to Alex during an argument. I couldn't even remember what had set me off, but I remembered the miserable embarrassment of finding myself in the corner again, naked, with that egg smashed against the tip of my nose. The only difference from before being I knew Alex loved me and I knew how to cook the egg at the end. He hadn't eaten it; instead he'd chosen to hold my stare as he slid the over medium masterpiece right into the trashcan, then he'd taken me on the floor of the kitchen until all of my frustration over the whole thing was nothing more than a whisper of a memory.

In the days leading up to our trip to Boston and Ford's farm, Alex had been cagier than normal, and those doubts and worries had fought hard to take hold of me all over again. It shouldn't have been a big deal to go. It wasn't the first time I'd met his friends. In fact, after quitting The Black Door, I'd joined them there for a night out. If it was awkward for me to watch Tate and Brooks, I couldn't imagine what it was like for Kale to find out his brother was involved with Ford, but at the end of the day, we were all adults.

Grabbing my suitcase and my guitar, I found Alex in the kitchen, frowning down at the crossword he'd been fighting with for the past two days. He didn't hear me walk in, only looking up when I dropped my bag and carefully propped my guitar against the wall.

"You're staring at that newspaper like it insulted you."

Alex clicked his pen closed and dropped it on top of it. "Tárrega teardrop," he said.

I smirked, huffing out a laugh. "Lágrima."

"What?"

"Lágrima," I repeated. "It's...pretty famous."

Alex clicked his pen open and looked down at the crossword, counting out the letters before filling in the answer.

"What is it?" he asked.

"A short and sad little love song," I said. "Tárrega is pretty famous for it."

"Do you know it?"

"Of course."

I'd learned it my junior year of high school and while it was far from the hardest song I'd ever played, it wasn't easy either. I appreciated it was a whole piece in a two minute window, and I'd always liked the way the second part hurt my heart to play, so it had been committed to memory for years.

"Play it."

"We're already running late," I reminded him.

Alex stood from his spot at the island with a tired sigh. "The farm isn't going anywhere. Now do what you're told, Dylan, or you'll be making eggs for everyone tomorrow morning."

Something that should have tasted like humiliation rolled over me, but it was too tangled with pleasure and release to make me feel as uncomfortable as the idea should have. With a half-hard cock, I took my guitar from the case and situated myself on the bar stool Alex had just vacated, checking the tuning before launching into the surprisingly complex series of notes of "Lágrima."

When I finished, Alex scratched the side of his nose just beneath the pad of his glasses, then patted his pocket and nodded.

"Thank you," he said, swallowing hard. "Pack it up, then. The car is here."

Alex was giving me whiplash, but I chalked it up to his nerves about bringing me around his ex-boyfriend for the first time. Beamer—as the rest of their friends called him—had been a last minute addition to the weekend, invited by Brooks. Judging by the wariness that had washed across Alex's face when Brooks gave him the good news, it wasn't necessarily a welcome change to the weekend. I wasn't worried about my place in Alex's life, but I was worried that Beamer being around would remind Alex of the argument we'd had back before we were even anything relevant to each other.

"Yes, Sir," I said softly, latching my guitar back into the case and taking it to the door.

Alex rolled his eyes at me, and I knew he was particular about my usage of the word, though I did sometimes use it to let him know the dominant parts of him were leaking into uncharted territory for me. I wasn't against the choices and the decisions Alex wanted to make for me—for us—outside of the bedroom, but it was the inconsistency of the actions that always got me. I wanted him in or out, not half.

Never halves.

I'd decided to talk to him about it on the drive upstate, but as soon as the car doors closed, Alex rolled up the privacy screen and was on me. Mouth slanted against mine, hot and wet, he speared his tongue into my mouth so aggressively I choked. But after the gagging, I melted beneath him, clutching at the front of his shirt as he softened and settled into something easier to maintain.

We made out like teenagers for almost twenty minutes, my dick leaking a solid wet patch against the front of my jeans by the time he decided we were finished. Panting, I sucked in desperate breath after breath, grabbing his thigh to steady myself as he eased himself back into his seat.

"What was that about?" I asked, after blood returned to my brain.

Between my legs, my cock was hard, trapped between my leg and the inseam of my jeans.

"I didn't think I needed a reason." He adjusted his glasses, then his own erection.

"You don't."

I traced the tip of my tongue across the underside of my top teeth, letting out a breath and turning my attention toward the window. It wasn't long before the buildings of the city gave way to green, and Alex blurted out the absolute last thing I ever expected him to say.

"I want to marry you."

There was no way I'd heard him correctly.

Slowly, I rotated my entire body away from the door. Our knees knocked together and my hand was still splayed open across the top of his thigh from when we'd left his house.

"What did you say?"

He reached into his pocket and pulled out a small black box, holding it on the flat of his palm. "I want to marry you."

"Why?" I asked, which in hindsight was a stupid thing to say, but it was also the first thing that popped into my head.

Licking his lips, he flipped open the lid of the box, a simple platinum faceted band nestled in a cushion of black velvet.

"Because I want to," he said with a casual shrug, but the smile on his face was quick to turn serious. "Because I love you. Because I want to make sure you never want for anything again—"

"Besides you."

His lip twitched. "Besides me."

"Why else?"

Alex pulled the ring out of the box, holding it up between us, his fingertips barely touching the metal.

"Because I like the way you cook eggs."

I hummed, nodding and swallowing and trying not to cry all in the same breath.

"Those sound like pretty good reasons," I said softly.

Instead of giving him my finger, I held out my hand, and he carefully set the ring down in the center of my palm. It was heavier than I expected, the facet cut of the band shiny even in the tinted darkness of the back of the car.

"They're all I've got," he said, snapping the box closed. "You don't care about my house or my money."

We both laughed at that, and I handed the ring back to him.

"No, I don't," I agreed, turning my palm down and spreading my fingers. "All I want is you."

Alex's glasses slipped down his nose as he glanced at my hand before looking back up at my face. He moved slightly, holding the ring near the tip of my finger the same way he teased my asshole with his cock.

"Green, Dylan?"

I pulled my lips together between my teeth and nodded quickly.

"Very fucking green."

Dylan hadn't let go of my hand since I put the ring on his finger, tugging me toward his side of the car every few minutes to examine the band. Every time, he'd smile at the ring, then at me, and then at the ring again before letting our hands fall to my lap. When we reached the farm, I had to let him go so he could get his bags, and the ring on Dylan's left hand was the first thing Tate saw when we walked in through the door.

"Shut up!" Tate screamed, bypassing a normal hello or how are you doing.

Dylan grinned at him, dropping his bag and guitar in time to catch Tate in his arms. The two of them stumbled back into the wall, laughing, and then Tate yanked Dylan's hand between them to look at the ring.

"I can't believe you didn't tell me," he said.

"It literally just happened on the drive here."

"Tell me everything," Tate demanded, hauling Dylan through the house and toward the back patio.

Brooks took his place, giving me a proud—if not unsur-prised—smile.

"I didn't think you had it in you," he said.

"Neither did I, but he just…"

"Yeah." Brooks cut me off so I didn't need to explain. "I know."

I grabbed Dylan's guitar and pushed it out of the walkway, giving his suitcase a kick toward mine for good measure. I didn't want to assume what guest rooms Ford would put us in, and I hadn't seen him or Boston yet. The house smelled like roasting chicken and vegetables, and my stomach let out a low rumble.

"Where is everyone?" I asked, realizing even though there was food on in the kitchen, the living room was much emptier than the last time I was here.

"They're all out back drinking whiskey and watching the sunset," Brooks said. "Which means they all know you're about to be a married man."

Rubbing my hands together nervously, I swallowed down any lingering trepidation and followed Brooks toward the back door. I wasn't sure why the thought of my friends knowing I wanted to marry Dylan was so daunting. They would all find out sooner or later, but I hadn't planned on being ambushed about the whole thing on arrival. Honestly, I wasn't even sure if or when I was going to give him the ring in the first place. I'd brought it to be safe, but the box had already burned a hole in my pocket before we were even halfway out of the city.

There'd been no point in waiting.

Whatever time I decided to ask him would be the perfect time.

And it had been.

On the back porch, my arrival was met with a raucous cheer and Ford was there first, pressing a tumbler of whiskey into my hand.

"Congratulations," he whispered into my ear, wrapping his arms around me before passing me off to Boston, who then handed me to Kale.

"Marriage?" Kale asked, one judgmental brow raised into his hairline. Beside him, Christian rolled his eyes and knocked into Kale's shoulder.

"Don't be rude."

"I can handle him at his worst," I promised Christian, then I turned to Kale and confirmed, "Marriage."

"He's a forever thing then?"

"Very much forever."

The doubt on his face filtered into a soft kind of acceptance, and Kale clinked our glasses together.

"I'm happy for you," he said.

"Truly?"

He finished off his whiskey before giving the glass to Christian and asking for a refill, leaving the two of us alone. Brooks had wandered off with Ford, and I'd yet to see Car and his husband, but I did notice my own fiancé was noticeably missing from the fray.

"I just want you to have all the things you want in life," Kale said, frowning even as his head nodded. "I want all of you to have everything."

"We have everything we need," I assured him, "including you."

"Do you mean I have everything I need or I'm everything you need?"

Kale's eyes sparkled, and I took a hearty drink of the very expensive whiskey in my glass.

"You're the last thing I want," I clarified.

"And that's why you have me."

I yanked Kale into a hug, clapping him on the back while trying to ensure I didn't spill any of my drink onto our shoes. When I pulled back, he smiled at a fixed point over my shoulder, and I followed his stare to find Christian standing with Boston and Tate, engaged in an animated conversation about something we'd never know.

"And that's why you have him," I said.

"So I can go without a drink all night?" he asked with a laugh, stepping away from me to chase after his boyfriend and his whiskey.

I was still yet to find Car and Dalton Fox, though I wondered if they'd even arrived yet. Maybe news of my attendance over the weekend was enough to keep them both in California, even though Car and I had long since cleared the air. We'd spoken once or twice since he'd called me out for being in love with Dylan, but adult friendships with a country between you weren't the same as when houses had been just down the block.

Ford stepped up beside me, staring out toward the rolling hills that made up the property line of their farm.

"This is nice," he said softly, the ice shifting in his glass as it melted.

"Very."

We stood together in silence, and I inhaled deeply, enjoying the smell of grass and dirt and home that blew through the breeze over the porch.

"The future Mr. Burke is on the other side of the porch

with Beamer and Dalton, I think," Ford finally said, and I nodded at the inevitability of it. "Be nice."

"I am nice."

"You're broody," he corrected.

"I'm nice," I repeated, clanking my glass against his before weaving my way past the other group of men. From around the corner, I heard Dylan's voice, though I couldn't make out the words, and I was so focused on making sure my feet carried me to him, I didn't even see Dalton coming around the corner. We bumped into each other with a muttered curse.

I smoothed my hand down the front of my shirt, looking at the man Car loved beyond all sense of rhyme and reason. I didn't think the two of us could have been more different and that, I reasoned, was probably the point.

"Your fiancé is quite sociable," Dalton said.

"He has his moments."

Dalton worried the corner of his lip with his tongue like he was still deciding which way our conversation was going to go.

"Looking forward to the weekend with you, Burke," he said.

I cleared my throat. "Same."

Without another word or any kind of agreement, we both stepped off. Dalton toward the house and me toward the man I loved and the man I used to think I loved. They were standing close, deep in a conversation that I could only piece together when I was close enough for them to both realize I'd arrived.

"I didn't mean to interrupt," I said by way of apology.

Dylan reached out for me, waggling his fingers until I was

close enough to take his hand in mine. I kissed the ring on his finger, then the side of his head.

"You're not interrupting," Car said. "I was just telling Dylan here how happy I am for the two of you."

My heart slammed against my chest, not because there was any sense of loss or jealousy there, but because for the first time in forever, I was just so happy.

"Thank you," I told him. "That means a lot."

"And I was just telling Beamer here how I'm sure California must be lovely all year round," Dylan said, tightening his hold on my hand.

Like the emotion in my chest, there wasn't any jealousy in Dylan's comment or the way he held my hand. It was pride and ownership, it was staking a claim in front of the people who held the most important places in my life.

"I imagine it is," I agreed. "Maybe we can come visit sometime."

"I think that would be nice," Car agreed, smiling at me softly. His hair was the color of wheat, sun-kissed and more golden after a year on the West Coast. He looked healthy. He looked happy. "In the meantime, keep loving him just like that, Dylan. Love him the way he deserves."

Before either of us could say anything to that, Car reached up and ruffled my hair, laughing before setting off around the corner to join the rest of our friends on the rocking chairs near the door. Alone on the side of the house, Dylan walked right into my arms, rubbing his cheek back and forth across my chest with a content and quiet hum that vibrated my sternum on every pass.

"Are you marking your territory?" I teased, kissing the top of his head. "If so, I don't hate it."

"I think the ring is enough of a mark," he said, tilting his head up to gaze at me. *He* looked happy. *He* looked healthy. He looked mine.

"The ring is just the beginning, pet. I'm a creative man and we have the rest of our lives."

Dylan shivered, lifting onto his toes and pressing a kiss against the corner of my mouth, sliding his tongue past my lips and deepening the connection, taking what he wanted from me without any fear or rebuke or retribution.

"That doesn't sound like near enough time," he whispered against my lower lip. "But I love you, and I believe in you."

After that, he bit me.

Hard.

Smiling all the while, I collared my hand around his throat and slammed him against the side of the house hard enough for the breath to leave his lungs in one rushed breath. Dylan huffed, dropping his head against the wall and pumping his hips toward me, not caring at all that my closest friends and their significant others could probably hear us if they listened close enough.

"You love me," I repeated, flexing my hand around his throat. "You believe in me."

Dylan nodded, moaning. The vibration in his throat traveled through my palm and down my arm, right to my now insistently hard cock.

"I hope you keep telling yourself that, pet, because guest room walls or not, I'm going to fuck you later like none of that matters."

His nostrils flared, and he gasped for breath, the constriction of his throat making it easier to press him against the wall, to rob him of the one thing he needed almost as much as me.

"Promise," he rasped, cheeks dark red and eyes half closed.

I was ready to let him go, to save him for later, when Tate shouted from the other end of the porch, "The swing is great for sex!"

Laughter from my friends rang out, echoing through the quickly approaching night, and I smiled, even though Dylan was the only person to see it.

Even though he struggled for breath, Dylan managed a laugh, and I crashed our mouths together, sucking the rest of the air out of his lungs before sliding my tongue past his lips. He tried to kiss me back, even though it was hard, and so I let the tiniest exhale out into his mouth, giving him enough air to swirl his tongue against mine without passing out entirely.

"Either commit to the bit or come inside for dinner," Kale said, voice closer than Tate's had been. I didn't need to look up to know he was at the corner of the house, half on the wrap-around side of the porch. "The swing will be here all night, but the chicken won't be."

He rapped his knuckles against the wall, footsteps fading as he rejoined our friends. The noise died down as they made their way inside, and only after the porch had quieted down, leaving me with the perfect melody of Dylan's labored breath-ing, did I loosen my hold on his neck.

Dylan sucked in some air, reaching up and placing his fingers against his throat, lashes fluttering as he stroked down its length and over the top of his chest. Licking his lips, he pressed into the arch where his neck bent into his shoulder.

"Did you leave a mark?" he whispered, tracing over one spot in particular.

Reaching up, I brushed his hand away to find a pink depression in the shape of my fingers blooming beneath his skin.

"Barely."

Dylan touched the spot again, then lifted his palm to my mouth, giving me the inside of his ring finger to kiss once more.

"You'll have to try harder later," he said, taking his hand away from my mouth and joining our fingers together.

I gave our joined hands a sharp tug toward the bed swing on the far side of the porch. Dylan was a storm and I was helpless to fight after learning very early on I could only tame him by never trying to.

"I can try harder now."

"They're going to start dinner without us," Dylan said.

"I don't care."

"I'm hungry," he said.

I reached down and palmed his thickening cock. "So am I."

"You heard Kale," he teased, still breathless. The bruise on his neck was darkening, overriding any other hands that had ever marked him there before and we both knew it.

"Commit to the bit or come inside," I repeated.

"Come inside," Dylan said, "and then later you can…"

He trailed off, raising his eyebrows suggestively and laughing at me, fully back in his body after our rough little interlude. With a reluctant sigh, I reached down and adjusted myself.

"And then later I can fill you with so much cum you drown. Is that what you were about to say?" I tilted my head to the side and smiled at him sincerely.

Dylan's face paled and he swallowed, but nodded and ever so softly said to me again, as I hoped he would over and over for the rest of our lives...

"Green."

ALSO BY KATE HAWTHORNE

Trophy Doms Social Club

Humbled

Edged

Praised

Bound

Shared

Trophy Doms New York

All In

Tied Down

Cried Out

Roughed Up

Giving Consent

Worth the Risk

Worth the Wait

Worth the Fight

Worth the Chance

All in Good Time

Necessary Space

Necessary Time

Duality

Dual Destruction

Dual Surrender

Dual Defiance

Two Truths and a Lie

A Real Good Lie

A Cold Hard Truth

A Matter of Fact

Room for Love

Reckless

Heartless

Faultless

Fearless

Limitless

A Very Messy Motel Brothers Wedding

Relentless

Secrets in Edgewood

A Taste of Sin

The Cost of Desire

A Love Made Whole

Secrets in Edgewood: The Complete Series

The Lonely Hearts Stories

His Kind of Love

The Colors Between Us

Love Comes After

Until You Say Otherwise

STANDALONES

Rebound

One for the Road

Daybreak - Vino & Veritas

Unfettered

Dreams

A Thousand Lifetimes

COLLABORATIONS

With E.M. Denning

Irreplaceable

Future Fake Husband

Future Gay Boyfriend

Future Ex Enemy

With J.R. Gray

May the Best Man Win

ABOUT KATE HAWTHORNE

Kate Hawthorne is an author of character-driven LGBT romance, known for crafting emotionally intense stories with high heat and a kinky twist. Creating worlds where passion and angst collide, Kate's books bring you complex protagonists in fearless pursuit of self-exploration and happy —if not sometimes unconventional—endings for everyone.

Visit her website
http://www.katehawthornebooks.com

Sign up for Kate's newsletter
http://www.katehawthornebooks.com/extra

facebook.com/authorkatehawthorne
x.com/katewriteswords
instagram.com/kate.hawthorne
patreon.com/katehawthorne

www.ingramcontent.com/pod-product-compliance
Lightning Source LLC
Chambersburg PA
CBHW061335310726
48974CB00001B/61